For the Love of the Cosmos

GRAHAM L. BISHOP

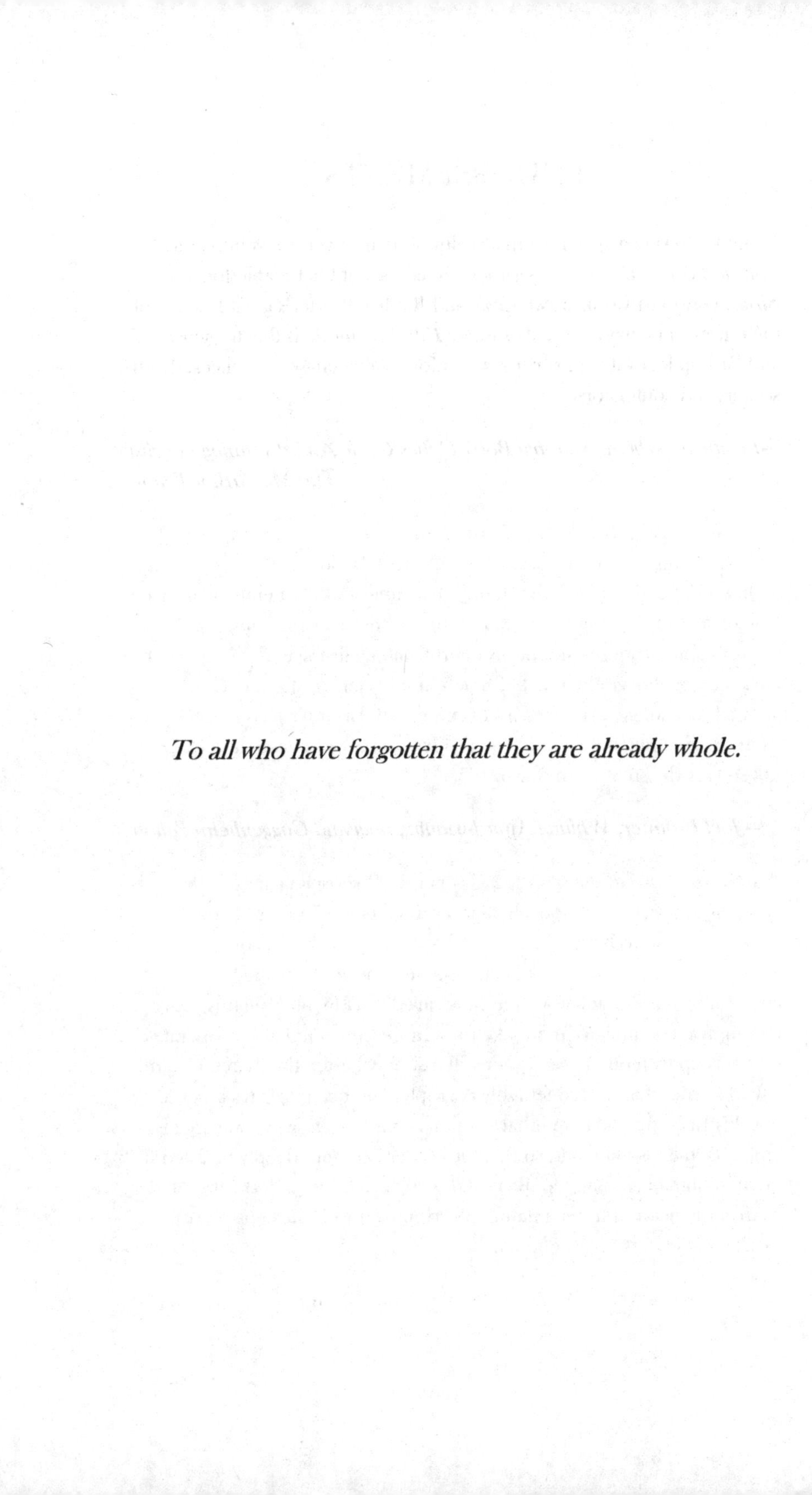

To all who have forgotten that they are already whole.

ENDORSEMENTS

"A mindblowing dispatch from a realm of neurodiverse posthumanity, *For the Love of the Cosmos* gathers up echoes of Olaf Stapledon's *Sirius*, Hayao Miyazaki's *Nausicaä*, and Raphael Carter's great lost tale of the universal network, *The Fortunate Fall.* The mode is the 'tragicosmic,' and Bishop loads it with surprises – unforgettable chase sequences, death scenes, and confessions."

—Jonathan Lethem, National Book Critics Circle Award-winning novelist and MacArthur Fellow

"Graham L. Bishop's *For the Love of the Cosmos* is an enchanting science fiction opus in the greatest intellectual traditions of the genre, in addition to being wildly entertaining, charming, and frequently hilarious. The novel's engagement with themes of transhumanism, gender and sexuality, the promises and perils of artificial intelligence, the dangers of environmental degradation, and much more is terrifically smart and always fascinating. As moving as it is insightful, Bishop's novel immerses us in a frightening but beautiful world that seems on reflection perhaps not so very different from our own."

— Joel Brouwer, Whiting Award-winning poet and Guggenheim Fellow

"In *For the Love of the Cosmos*, Graham L. Bishop imagines, with compelling urgency, an apocalyptic world (can there ever really be a "post-" to an apocalypse, the novel asks, once the stakes become galactic?) in which a device that enables interspecies telepathic communication is the latest technological advancement. Will this prove redemptive for humans and make for a more thoughtful and cooperative relationship with other species, or will it simply hasten the march toward a world order that is irredeemably corrupt? The real magic trick of this novel is Bishop's ability to inhabit animal consciousness in a way that is empathic but also familiar, so that the reader becomes deeply invested in the non-human animals' conflicts and recognizes in them a complicated truth at the heart of human nature. A gripping novel whose pages you won't be able to turn fast enough."

—Kellie Wells, Flannery O'Connor Award-winning novelist

CONTENTS

PROLOGUE: A NOTE TO YOU, THE READER

Dear Reader,

Enclosed within these pages lies *For the Love of the Cosmos*, a tale that I have put together with much reflection and reservation. You might be familiar with who I am, and to some extent, the events that transpired five years before this writing. With time running short for me in this life, I felt compelled to share this narrative.

When friends first proposed that I pen down the history of the uprising, I balked. I believed that my species and my personal entanglement in the events might render me an unsuitable chronicler. However, as my health waned, the urgency to narrate this story took hold. The Mayor suggested that my personal involvement might bring depth and nuance to the recounting, and I came to recognize the value of forgiveness through the lens of hindsight.

I must, however, concede that there is no flawless raconteur for an account of this scale. In my endeavor to present a balanced portrayal, I initially adopted a third-person omniscient narrative style. Yet, this perspective was not without its limitations. I found myself always inclined to lend dignity to all sides, even to those deemed villains. This may cause discomfort to some readers who seek a more moralistic depiction.

Midway through this book, you will notice a transformation in the narrative voice. The burden of omniscience compelled me to abandon the third-person perspective and resort to a more personal first-person. This shift, I was assured, would be embraced by readers, given my known involvement in the events. What at first I tried to make a historical text turned out to be a memoir.

There is one more admission I must make: I regret not being able to convey more. The limitations of language hinder my ability to encapsulate wholly the array of sensory experiences that mark interspecies interactions. Those eager for deeper immersion may wish to venture into the Source to relive the diverse sensory experiences connected to the events of yesteryear.

I now invite you to immerse yourself in this labor of love, a reckoning with personal grief that I hope brings healing to the collective in turbulent times. May you find strength in the love of the cosmos.

Yours sincerely,
Prince

PART ONE:

INTERSPECIES INTERACTIONS

1

The Martians were coming. And so was the dolphin, though they didn't know it yet.

In the hour before Prince first heard Varuna's name, he and Dante had sat in neighboring examination rooms. They shared thoughts with one another like they had for all ten years of Prince's life, both here in the Ark's testing sector and in every other space where Dante had found himself from ages seven to seventeen.

But today's usability test felt different. Prince, ever the prim poodle, kept his paws planted on the edge of the chair—the room's sole furnishing. As he waited for images from Dante's mind, the dark room's isolation mirrored his growing loneliness. Cleaning chemicals filled his nose, and the hum of distant machines put him on edge. In one month, Dante would step into his mother's shoes as CEO of Melampus, and the already dwindling time he had to spend with Prince would vanish.

Prince was about forty pounds—not small for his breed by any means—but he felt miniature given the task at hand: large-scale spatial mapping. In preparation for the Martian ambassador's visit, Dante transmitted progressively larger mental maps through the telepathy-enabling Specter, a nine-pointed, star-shaped device implanted above his and Prince's eyes.

"Image one," an unseen young woman's voice said behind

a one-way mirror. Dante conveyed to Prince the room he was in, stark and sterile like Prince's own.

"Image two." Dante imagined the hallways of the testing sector, lit only by the incandescent glow of neighboring laboratories.

"Image three." Dante then let Prince's mind's eye expand to the colossal, amphibious form of the Ark as a whole.

"Image four." Dante took Prince's imagination out further, to the vast steppes and rolling hills of the savannah biome, where the Ark was currently stationed. To these visual cues Prince added his own recollections, the sweet scent of lemongrass and the rumbling of unseen hooves.

"Image five." And then, Dante prompted him to envision the entire Arkology, their enclosed island ecosystem, the final refuge for most remaining humans and all animals larger than a cockroach. The enormity of the bubble, and the far greater enormity of the surrounding ocean, enveloped Prince. He felt very small indeed.

The transmissions ceased. Alone once more, Prince stifled a whimper. In his puppyhood, he had been the first and only animal on the Ark to wear a Specter. He longed for that simpler time when his most significant achievement was to recognize himself in the mirror for the first time—the same one-way mirror he now faced. He was still special, having also been chosen to wear the SpecterX, the new model they were then testing, before any other animal. But his world had changed over ten years.

Unbeknownst to Prince, Laura, the new research intern whose voice he and Dante heard, felt similarly overwhelmed. Behind the mirror, on the observation deck, Laura analyzed vibrant images of Prince's and Dante's brains. Sweat dripped from her forehead as she frantically switched between screens. She checked if their brains were in sync, ensured their Specters pulsed at the right frequency, and monitored for feedback issues. Meanwhile, dream-printers spat out thought portraits. Whenever Laura paused to study the printouts, Dante's voice would echo from the exam room with playful jokes: "Everything okay? Better hurry, or who knows what I might think about!"

Finally, Stella, Dante's mother and the outgoing CEO, walked in and relieved Laura of her duties with an imperial wave. She scrolled through the metadata on Laura's screen, having watched Dante's transmissions to Prince on her own Specter in a conjoining vestibule. Laura couldn't help shrinking a little beside Stella's imposing stature; the long acrylic nails on her boss's fingers made a hollow tapping noise as she flipped through the printouts. This test was simply a formality before the Martian ambassador's visit—the new model was a mere three weeks away from market, after all—but Laura feared the slightest mistake would get her fired and sent back home to the City.

"All right," said Stella at last. "Good. Bring Dante and Prince in. We need to discuss my call with Ambassador Johnson."

Laura exited the observation deck to fetch the boss's son and his dog from their respective exam rooms. Dante's strong jaw and dark eyes, fully visible once she switched the lights on, surprised her with their aura of fame, even though she had seen his image countless times on the evening news. His height, nevertheless, was just a couple of inches shorter than expected.

"Nice to have a face to match the voice," he said as she gestured for him to follow her. She bristled slightly at his confidence.

Dante and Prince followed her to the observation deck. Stella, like Laura, was originally from the City, which explained why her skin was darker than that of the other Arklings. Dante had inherited a touch of his mother's complexion, but was still fairly pale, both from his paternal line and from having resided his entire life within the walls of the ship. Neither Dante nor Stella, however, had skin as dark as Laura's, which struck Prince right away. The lonely poodle could sense, and even empathize with, the new intern's anxiety around being in an unfamiliar environment with people who looked noticeably different from her.

The empathy was short-lived. Prince, his canine nose attuned to all of his closest companion's hormonal responses, smelled a hint of lust on Dante's skin. A rush of jealousy put

Prince on alert. Fortunately for Prince, though, Laura showed no interest. She made a point of seating herself as far away from Dante as possible. Stella, meanwhile, gave her son a kiss on the cheek, to which he gave an awkward, even frightened smile. She waited for him and Prince to sit before speaking, still on her feet.

"Ambassador Johnson would like for our demonstration to include two animals rather than one."

Dante frowned a little, trying his best to keep his eyes off Laura. "Why?"

"He claims that our proof of concept would be more convincing. He wants to see communication between at least four parties with as many different points-of-view as possible, and he doesn't think communicating with a domesticated animal who knows you and me quite well is nearly as impressive as talking to an animal who lives in the wild. No offense, Prince."

"None taken," said Prince. His neck microphone translated various communication signals from his Specter into speech.

Dante sneered. "How do we know he isn't just another rich Martian tourist taking his chance to talk to the wildlife?"

Stella gave a tight-lipped smile. Laura couldn't help but notice some tension between her and her son. "We don't. But it doesn't matter. The Martians are passing budget appropriations soon, and they need a reason to give us the funding we'll need to scale up production for launch."

Pathnet was the name of the telepathic communication network that the new SpecterX would support. Whereas the first model only allowed telepathic exchange between two parties, the SpecterX would allow thought-sharing en masse among larger groups. Such a project had attracted the attention of rich Maritan entrepreneurs, who formerly had shown little interest in all things Melampus.

The potential for Martian interference in Earthling affairs was a hot issue in the City's ongoing mayoral election. Laura began to wonder, therefore, why Stella had invited her into this potentially sensitive conversation about Martian funding. Stella, Dante, Prince, and ten or so other animals around the nine Biomes were the only possessors of a SpecterX as of then. Stella could have easily shared information through private spectation with her son and Prince had she wanted to.

"Who are we having him talk to?" asked Dante.

"Varuna—the dolphin. He's the closest to our current location, and he is, after all, the species that inspired the Specter's original design. I think it would be quite poetic for him and the ambassador to trade a few sound-images."

Prince growled. The dolphins had a tendency to resist experiments. This did not seem to concern Stella, however.

"I've instructed the crew to plan a mission to catch him and bring him aboard tomorrow. Laura, since I'm sure you're wondering why you're hearing all this, I'll need you on call for a functionality test with myself, Dante, Prince, and Varuna tomorrow afternoon."

Laura agreed. Little did she or any of them know the effect this dolphin would have on them all for the coming months, and indeed the rest of their lives.

As the group disbanded for bed, Stella touched Laura's shoulder. "How has your first week been?"

"Oh, you know." Laura said with a shrug and a nervous laugh. "Getting the hang of everything."

Stella smiled. Was that a wink? "Let me know if you need anything. Us women from the City need to stick together."

As Laura walked to her room, Prince looked back to make sure she wasn't going to follow and attract any more of Dante's attention.

2

Prince awoke to the sounds of Dante putting on his uniform and hurrying into the hallway, bed unmade. Not long ago, Dante would never have dreamed of leaving his room without teaching Prince a new word and offering him a treat. The Smellogen, a childhood invention that resembled a keyboard in the corner of the room, would match words with odors that sprayed from the little sprinklers in the ceiling, allowing Prince to understand human speech rather than relying on telepathic translation alone. Now, it sat unused and collected dust.

Dante didn't look back at Prince as he ran down the hall toward the elevator, too fast for his dog to keep up. Prince imagined Dante's face, allowing his Specter to lock onto Dante's.

Did the mission start? Are you going on deck? He transmitted.

His stomach growled as he waited. *Yes,* came the reply after a few annoying minutes. *In the wheelhouse.*

As soon as Prince had trotted down the hall and boarded the elevator, his stomach lurched up toward his spine. The Ark was ascending.

Prince emerged on deck just in time to watch as the thousand-foot-long, four-hundred-foot-wide ship spread wings from its hull, rose above the baobab trees of the savannah, and sailed off toward the shoreline—slowly at first, then at jetspeed. Prince couldn't resist staying outside to feel the wind blast his fur back from his face. It never got old. The Ark was a marvel of engineering, a triumphant testament to humanity's resilience and ingenuity. A steel and glass reimagining of its biblical namesake, it originally served as a vessel of salvation for the planet's remaining lifeforms, though it was designed for much more than weathering floods. Solar panels glinted from its surface, while an array of wind turbines stood like sentinels around its wheelhouse, capturing every whisper of renewable energy.

As the Ark flew out over the sea, the briny ocean smell tickled Prince's whiskers and reminded him of younger days—days spent playing fetch in the waves with Dante, or barking at dolphins back in his puppyhood, when Dante's father was alive and testing earlier Specter prototypes on the Arkology's cetacean residents.

Prince waited for the ship to retract its wings, ease downwards, and splash gently onto the water before he entered the wheelhouse. The titular helm of the Ark's main control hub was no archaic captain's wheel of the Anthropocene (though this was of course the pun), but the large interactive hologram that displayed, on a table surrounded now by Dante, Stella, and numerous crew, a map of the Arkology in all of its wheel-like glory. There, at the center of the table was the City, the massive, doughnut-shaped cylindrical building that contained the self-sustaining urban ecosystem where all of Earth's five thousand humans (except the Arklings) lived and worked. Branching out from the City at equal intervals were the eight "spokes" of the wheel, rivers that divided the island into the eight Biomes that occupied most of its land area: they were, in clockwise order, the savannah, the desert, the chaparral, the grassland, the taiga, the tundra, the temperate forest, and the rainforest.

And it was on the ninth Biome, the ocean on which the island floated (the "rubber tire" that surrounded the wheel), that a little red icon depicting the Ark steadily approached a flashing green dot.

"Is that Varuna?" Prince asked on reaching Dante's side.

"Yup. Every SpecterX has a unique tracker on it. See?"

Dante flipped a switch under the table, and twelve other blinking lights showed up all over the map—three of them circling the Ark itself, which Prince recognized as himself, Dante, and Stella.

"Turn those off," Stella snapped. "Stay focused."

Dante flicked the switch back, quickly, avoiding his mother's icy stare.

Stella turned to Officer Sherman, Director of Wildlife Control. "Tell the folks downstairs we're within striking range."

Sherman sent a message through his Specter (an original, one-to-one model) down to Officer Lewis, Director of Weapons Deployment, calling for the launch of a tranquilizing minnowbot in Varuna's direction. The blue blinking dot showing the bot's trajectory approached Varuna...and then disappeared from the map.

"What happened?" Stella shouted.

Sherman scratched his head. "It may have hit an unexpected obstacle."

"Send another!"

Another blue blinking dot moved toward Varuna, then vanished. And this time, Varuna's dot vanished as well.

Stella then shouted at Officer Naismith, Director of Security. "What the hell is going on? Send a drone out to his most recent position. I want visuals."

Officer Naismith typed some commands, and a purple dot went out.

Prince's dichromatic eyes couldn't tell the difference between purple and blue. "Why did he send another minnow out?" he asked. He also needed to rely on shape to distinguish between the red ark and the green tracking dots.

Dante was going to answer, but Stella cut him off. "Get that dog out of here! He's a distraction. Colorblind crew don't belong here."

Prince's ears drooped. When Dante was younger, he would often get into fights with his mother about where Prince could go on the ship. But now, he offered no protest.

"Sorry, buddy. Go out on deck and enjoy the breeze."

Prince, tail tucked between his legs, pattered out of the

wheelhouse and down the long deck toward the bow of the ship. He poked his head through the railings, snort-sighing through his jowls. The horizon was vast. He wondered, as he often did, what lay beyond the walls of the massive bubble that enclosed the Arkology.

Inside the wheelhouse, meanwhile, Naismith's screen displayed the feed from the drone: nothing but unobstructed water. Sherman spoke up: "Report from downstairs: the minnows were taken out by a sonic attack."

Stella stuck her nails into her platinum gray-blonde hair. "He's done it again. I thought we fixed this!"

"We did," Sherman said. "But he must have found a new frequency that disabled it. It's not like he wouldn't have sensed our giant-ass ship approaching him."

That's badass, Dante thought to himself.

"I hate this fucking dolphin," said Stella. "He's too damn smart. And why did his tracker disappear?"

"Perhaps he went deeper?" Sherman offered "That's happened with the octopus sometimes if she gets out of range."

Dante was skeptical. Based on what he knew of his mother's design for the SpecterX, there was no reason underwater depth would interfere with the tracker. And he had met Varuna. It had taken weeks to implant the SpecterX in his brain without him resisting and, on one occasion, injuring the technicians trying to sedate him. They had needed to redesign the minnowbots multiple times for him not to emit a particular frequency of click that disabled them, and he had seemed to spread this knowledge to other dolphins in his pod.

And unbeknownst to anyone except, to some extent, Prince, Dante did not wholly embrace his mother's plans for the SpecterX. He, too, was therefore interested in the potential consequences if Varuna had somehow learned to disable the tracker to think about the consequences of, or even fully hear, his mother's next order, delivered quickly and loudly to Officer Rosen, Chief Engineer.

"Submerge the Ark. Descend one thousand feet. We'll find this sea rat one way or another."

By the time Prince noticed his feet rising, it was too late. The deck, converting to the submarine's outer wall, began to slope upward, pushing his head farther through the railing. He turned around and tried to scramble toward the wheelhouse, but the ballast tanks along the front side of the hull were already filling with seawater, and the Ark tipped downward. It was like trying to defy gravity.

Dante, help! Prince transmitted as he tried to grip the deck with his claws. *I'm trapped outside!*

Normally, a one-minute warning would have allowed anyone on deck to exit before conversion, but speed was pivotal in catching Varuna, and Rosen overrode this warning believing nobody was at risk.

Hang on! Dante immediately responded. He yelled to the crew, "Stop submerging! Prince is out there!"

Rosen sighed. "You know as well as I do that submersion can't stop once started."

Stella raised her hands. "He's a poodle. Tell him to jump off the side and tread water until we rise."

Dante tried to transmit instructions to Prince, but as the deck finished sloping upward, the ship tipped down at a steeper and steeper angle. Prince lost his traction and slid down toward the water. He hit his head on the railing as he tumbled over into the ocean—not hard enough to lose consciousness, but hard enough to lose his sense of direction and his ability to respond to Dante's transmission.

He opened his eyes underwater. The front of the Ark's wide, massive hull dipped straight toward him. Dizzied, relying on instinct, he swam down, deeper, deeper, until he struggled to hold his breath. He began to swim to the side, out of the Ark's way, so he could paddle his way back up to the surface, but his lungs were already giving out. In panic, he opened his mouth and began to bark (to whatever extent he could bark underwater), screaming noisy bubbles into the deep, but this of course opened the way for water to fill his nostrils and for him to drown...

Or at least, he would have drowned, if not for Varuna, who

swooped up from the depths, balanced Prince's thrashing body on his rostrum, and pushed him as fast he could to the surface.

Where had he come from? Who was this miracle savior? Why did he care about a poor poodle who couldn't even swim that well?

Prince choked for air and sputtered the water out of his lungs. Varuna bobbed on the waves. In the corner of Prince's visual field, an envelope icon appeared: a transmission from Varuna. He was too confused, distraught, and agitated to even think about opening it. But then, a low whistle came from Varuna's melon, the fatty mass through which he sent sound waves, and for a second or two, a faint, colorless outline of an image appeared in Prince's mind: it resembled their current position, Prince on Varuna's back, Varuna bouncing on the tides. But there was something more: jagged lines surrounded Prince's limbs. He couldn't make them out, but a sense of calm enveloped him. Calm became awe, as Prince understood that he was picking up, at least in rudimentary form, a thought-image from Varuna's mind, no Specter required. Once Prince was conscious enough to tread water on his own, Varuna let him off his back, swam some distance away, and waited for the Ark to emerge above water.

Back in the wheelhouse, Varuna's dot had returned on screen. On Stella's command, the Ark launched a net to surround him. He did not resist as the net withdrew into a porthole near the base of the hull, which connected to a tank reserved just for him in the testing sector.

Prince, meanwhile, finally opened the transmission as he paddled into an automated lifeboat that buzzed out from the ship. It was an image of him and Varuna wearing what appeared to be mechanical limbs: cyborg arms and hands with opposable thumbs, and legs seemingly built to enable bipedal movement.

The Ark finished its reconversion. The lifeboat, which doubled as a hovercraft, flew above the waves and onto the deck. Dante ran out to hold his shivering, traumatized poodle.

3

Laura Delacroix returned to her room after a disastrous usability test with Varuna. She flopped onto her small, boxy cot, her feet sore and her head heavy.

One week into the new job, and she hated the walk to and from the testing sector. Not only was she afraid of Stella, who had been a much better role model from a distance than up close, where her temper was fully visible, but Laura's stomach churned as she passed the living quarters of Arklings who had been on the ship since birth. Their massive king beds and furniture, clearly built using rare trees from the Biomes, were symptoms of the very decadence that had likely installed them in their positions. The Ark largely ran on nepotism these days, and a hire like Laura—who had thrown her name without much hope into that year's internship lottery (the first one to even happen in several years)—was growing rare.

Even those kids from the City who did succeed in landing the coveted internship rarely convinced bigoted company elites to promote them to a salaried position. In fact, Stella had been the last one to succeed, almost thirty years earlier. This was why, Laura imagined, Stella showed a gentler demeanor toward her than toward her son or anyone else.

Laura tried to take a nap (someone would wake her up for some meaningless data entry task or another soon enough), but a vibration in her forehead and a telephone icon in the corner of her visual field jolted her awake. Her mother was calling. Laura commanded her Specter to answer the call.

"Hey, sweetie," Wanda's voice filtered in. She missed having her daughter around and liked to talk out loud with her. "How's work today? Is now a good time?"

Laura's surroundings—a small metal bedside table with a rare beeswax candle Laura had made when she was little, a wall mirror, a window with thin brown curtains that currently peeked out onto the serene blue undersea view, a desk beneath a painting of the Melampus Corporation's ancient founder Olaf Melampus—took on another layer. *Increase Layer 2 opacity*, she instructed the Specter with an instantaneous thought. In response, the Specter fed the inputs from Wanda's brain more concretely into Laura's. Laura's Ark cabin became a faint transparent shadow behind her family's home, the City apartment she had lived in since birth.

It was a middle-story apartment—certainly not large, but not as cramped as those of families who had drawn a worse lot with the AI. Nevertheless, middle-class by City standards was positively destitute by Arkling or Martian standards. All four members of Laura's family shared a single bedroom, which doubled as a study, and the main living area shared a room with the kitchen. A small television and worn-out loveseat sat no more than ten to fifteen feet away from a refrigerator, a basic electric stove, and a small square of counter space beneath a short row of cupboards. Wanda's view, Laura recognized, was from the folding table where they ate meals. A pain of comparison struck Laura as she reviewed her family home from Wanda's eyes. How wrong it was, Laura felt, for many of the Ark's two hundred crew members to sleep in bedrooms that were five if not ten times the size of her family's entire apartment.

But the pain gave way to a recollected resolve: If she kept her head down, played by the rules, and developed a research project that impressed her superiors, she could not only win upper-story housing for her entire family, but make a technological contribution to the Arkology's infrastructure that would improve the lives of all Citizens.

"It's awful," she said finally. "That dolphin we captured is doing something weird. Stella got her son to look more closely at him."

"Dante? Oh, I didn't know you two had met. He's about your age, isn't he? What's it been like working with him?" Wanda made the common gesture of removing her cell phone (a device that was nearly obsolete now that most of the population wore Specters, and that would potentially be out of date completely once Pathnet developed) and opening the camera so that Laura could see her conversation partner's face. Like Laura, she had striking amber eyes. They always looked serious and determined, but the wrinkles around them showed her ability to laugh and smile when she gave herself permission.

"I think he's trying to flirt with me. I can't deal with that right now. Stella told me I could take a break, anyway."

But this was a rather simplified account of what had happened. Immediately after Prince's rescue, Stella had called Laura back into the testing sector to run the usability test with Varuna.

"It's late in the day," Stella said. "Let's get this done fast."

But as Laura instructed both Prince (who was still shaking but nonetheless did his best to comply) and Dante to transmit specific cognitive inputs to Varuna, Stella's nostrils flared. Varuna's *brain* showed activation in all the right areas, but his *Specter* registered no activity and, at times, did not even display its neural address. It was as though he had answered a phone call but left his voice on mute. And if Laura instructed *Varuna* to communicate with the others, he would simply float in his tank as though playing dumb. At no point did Dante and Prince succeed in viewing inputs from his Specter.

"He's being a brat again." Stella folded her long, wispy arms and stared at the dolphin's brain imagery.

"It can't just be that he's refusing," said Laura. "Or else he wouldn't be picking up on their inputs either."

Stella slammed her palm into the wall, then yanked the power cords out of the monitors, abruptly ending the test. "We're done here." She didn't face Laura. "I'll decide what to do later this evening. I don't want to talk to anyone right now."

Laura backed out nervously and went to her room.

"Well, he is the Arkling of all Arklings," said Wanda. *But it's flattering, at least. He's very handsome.*

Laura suppressed a gag. Luckily, Wanda didn't experience her disgust at this remark. Laura had long ago instructed her Specter to always keep emotional information private from her parents. "Is Dad there?" She knew it would offend him if she didn't ask.

Laura respected and admired her father, but she had trouble relating to him, or even understanding how he and her mother had gotten married, other than for the tax credit once the AI had decided to match the two of them together for breeding. Laura was an unexpected baby, she knew, and once the AI decided to assign a man to impregnate a woman, that was it. Abortion was not an option; it was an algorithmic offense, punishable by death.

"He's in the bedroom," Wanda said. "Peter! Laura's on my Specter!"

"Hi, Laura!" Peter Delacroix ducked his head into the room and waved, pieces of duct tape hanging from his fingers. He was now seriously losing his hair, which was once thick with flecks of red in it like Laura's, but it didn't seem to affect his jolly disposition. His cheeks were lighter with rosier undertones than Wanda's, which Laura had always attributed to his fondness for alcohol and less time spent in the sun. Whereas Wanda spent ten hours a day in the agricultural sector, programming and repairing the hydroponic produce bots, Peter worked on the air-conditioned upper floors as a transportation engineer for the City's Bureau of Urban Planning. Shortly before Laura's internship began, he had gotten into trouble with Wanda for turning down a promotion at work. City Mayor Teddy Wilcox and the Director of Urban Planning had, on the AI's recommendation, personally looked at his resume and asked him to work as a project manager on a new public transit project. Peter, citing political opposition, declined.

"I just couldn't bring myself to accept," Peter had said in between jokes about the mayor's short stature at the tense family dinner following the decision. "They're going to build the railway straight through the spice farms. All those laborers will lose their jobs with no plans for reassignment. And do us normal folk just not get to put spices in our food now? The people upstairs and the Arklings will be the only ones able to afford it after the supply goes down."

Wanda shook her head. "I understand your reasons, Peter, and I agree with them. But you can't keep questioning the AI's judgment. You've heard the reports about people who got demoted."

"Those are just media scare tactics!" Peter said. "I have the right to free speech. It's still there in the City charter."

"Just be careful," Wanda said.

Peter hadn't listened: There he was now, dragging a poster out of the bedroom. He approached Wanda and held it up for Laura to see. "PEOPLE BEFORE PROJECTS," it read above a taped-on picture of the mayor with a red X over his face. "NO MORE RAILWAYS IN OUR FARMLANDS."

"I'm going to leave this right outside the mayor's quarters!" he bragged. "And I'm making some more for my work buddies. Maybe you'll see us on the evening news! Hope you're doing well, baby." He retreated back into the bedroom.

Wanda sighed. Laura laughed. Neither of them could imagine adopting Peter's devil-may-care attitude. Laura, like Wanda, had always played by the rules and done what seemed practical. Most girls who grew up in the bottom nine-tenths of the City did. Laura's true interest was in politics, but her pragmatic mindset had led her to study neuroprogramming throughout grade school and to develop the difficult skills that won her the internship.

"Make sure you pick a research project soon, in case your father's salary takes a hit," Wanda finally found an excuse to joke. But Laura knew it wasn't a joke. If she wanted any chance of winning a paid contract and staying on the Ark, she would need to develop an impressive independent project to show the Ark's Board, and fast.

"Can I talk to Michelle?" Laura deflected.

"She's been in the bathroom ever since she came home from school. I'll go check."

"Actually, never mind. I'll call her myself."

"All right. I love you, Laura."

"Love you, too."

Laura hung up, then focused on her younger sister's face. Michelle answered from inside the small bathroom, the apartment's third and final room. As Laura expected, she was putting makeup on, doing her best to look like herself.

"Hey, can we talk later? It's not the best time. Sammy is coming for dinner soon, and I want to look good."

Laura smiled. "Why do you want to look good?"

Michelle paused with her eyeliner. She made sure Laura saw her eyes rolling in the mirror. "Shut up! It's not like that." She had a cooler complexion, like her mother's and sister's, but a more impish, pixie-like nose that stuck out a little, like her father's. Her hair also, like Laura's, resembled her father's; if anything, Michelle's flecks of red were brighter than Peter's ever were.

Every day after school since turning thirteen, Michelle would find one of Laura's old dresses, lock herself in the bathroom, apply makeup and hair extensions, and shave. To the AI, Michelle was Peter Delacroix, Jr. And she needed to pretend to be Peter, Jr. outside the house, lest she and her parents end up in a reprogramming unit. Michelle was lucky to have parents who let her embrace her trans identity at home, but she knew, as all queer citizens knew, that one of the main perks of the Ark was freedom from the AI. Trans and queer people couldn't be *out* on the Ark, but they didn't have to worry about imprisonment if they said one thing critical of the AI's social value system. She was jealous of Laura after the internship lottery, as though Laura had taken a spot she wouldn't be able to win for herself after high school—who knew if the AI would even consider an applicant from the same family as a previous winner?

She got over it soon, though. Supporting Laura, who always believed the internship was an opportunity to make life better for Michelle and people like her, was important.

"Well, just thought I'd say hi," Laura said. "You look great."

"Thank you! Talk later?"

As soon as Laura disconnected from the call, someone knocked on her cabin door. Her spine shivered. Had she said something about Michelle's identity out loud? That would teach her to assume there was any real privacy on this ship.

She relaxed only a little on seeing Dante's face. "What is it? Why didn't you just call me?" she said with more annoyance than intended.

Dante smirked. "I figured you wouldn't answer. It feels like we got off on the wrong foot. But clearly I'm wrong, as this warm welcome shows." He exchanged a glance with Prince, who stood at his side. Prince looked less in shock, but his tail was taut like a rattlesnake's. He still saw her as a threat for Dante's attention.

Dante leaned against the doorframe with affected confidence. "I just wanted to let you know we'll be stationing in the savannah again. My mom's decided to remove Varuna's SpecterX and replace it with his old model until we know what's wrong. We'll use Nemos the elephant for the demonstration with Ambassador Johnson instead."

"Oh, okay. He must be landing soon, no?"

"He's flying in now, yeah. But Prince here is good friends with Nemos. We can skip the whole tranquilize-and-capture deal. She's a friendly pachyderm. Never had any tech problems with her. She'll help us out for sure if Prince asks. Anyway, my mom wants you to look presentable to the ambassador first thing in the morning."

Laura nodded. She cleared her throat to stop Dante from turning to leave. "Hey, Dante. You weren't listening to my Specter call just now, were you?"

Dante raised his eyebrows. "No, Laura. I'm not *that* interested in what you're doing."

Laura blinked as Dante walked away, his shoulders bouncing with defiance. Prince looked back quickly and gave Laura the canine equivalent of a scowl.

What Laura didn't know was that she had nothing to fear even if Dante had eavesdropped. Dante, like her younger sister, was trans.

4

The Ark's trip to the savannah helped Prince feel more like himself. He looked forward to talking to Nemos, and the views were always nice. He would be too afraid to stand out on the deck for a while, but he was safe enough in the crow's nest.

Where Prince's fear subsided, however, sadness came in. Dante always used to stand next to him up here as they watched the grand plateaus and plains sweeping beneath them, the acacias and baobabs just beneath the hull, the tall grasses blown back in the Ark's air current.

Hundreds of feet below Prince, zebras, cheetahs, rhinos, hyenas, gazelles, wildebeests, hippos, and lions all drank at the waterhole, foraged for food, hunted prey, or (in the case of the nocturnal animals) slept in the shade. All of them (except for newborns the Ark hadn't yet reached) wore Specters that would, soon enough, be replaced with the new X's.

But what was it all for? In his mature years, Prince found himself questioning the meaning of his existence in ways he never had. Perhaps his vocabulary had reached a critical point, one that would only give way to the most human sentiments of nihilism from now on. He hoped not.

Some meerkats scrambled out of the way before the Ark landed in one of its designated stations, a clearing of lemon grasses. Prince exited the crow's nest and trotted down the stairway that extended off the deck down to the ground. The air was humid, though it was still early enough not to be too hot, and the soil was moist from a recent rain. There were bugs all around, though only half were real; the other half were climate control bots that diffused or absorbed various atmospheric gases, ensuring that every Biome mirrored the appropriate geographies of the long-gone former Earth.

Embarking on his assigned task, Prince envisioned Nemos's face. The African elephant answered quickly. She was spraying herself off in a mud puddle with her calf, Emily. If he focused on it, Prince could smell and feel the thick clay as though he were in Nemos's body. *Hi, Nemos. Are you free to come out? We're here for the demo with the ambassador.* He had previously run the morning's schedule by her.

OK, sure. Let us just wrap up our bath.

No rush. The Ambassador is just flying in now.

A sonic boom shook the landscape. Prince raised his head toward the southern horizon. The ambassador's jet, a dot in the distance, shrieked down through the artificial clouds, detaching from the space elevator column that towered above the City. The jet's wings became visible as it descended into the savannah, twirled in the air with a theatrical flourish, and readied for a landing on the Ark's runway. Stella and Dante came onto the deck to wave at the ambassador's ship and welcome him to Earth.

Nemos, meanwhile, climbed out of the water and shook herself off with Emily. *How have you been, Prince? I feel that tail tucked between your legs. Why so sad?*

The first animal ever to wear a Specter after Prince, Nemos had a close enough bond to the poodle for them to trust each other with every cognitive datum that the Specters allowed them to exchange. Nine years ago, Prince had kept Nemos company in her early days of training with the device, cuddling her in her Ark containment unit at night to calm her and assure her that the humans meant her no harm.

A year later, however, the death of Nemos's first calf, Jumbo, at the hands of a poachbot damaged her trust. In time, Prince had persuaded her that the killing was random, the will of a cold and impersonal AI. Whereas things like the Specters and their tracking systems, weapons deployment, and service vehicle maintenance were questions of private Melampus property and therefore under the Ark's control, things like Biome population and climate control affected the homeostasis of the Arkology as a whole and needed to be managed in consultation with (if not in total deference to) the City leadership, who ran the Arkology's global AI. One too many elephants at the wrong time would have significant effects on the entire ecosystem. Still, though, the poachbots struck Prince as cruel.

But why did you have to kill her? Nemos had asked him and Dante in the immediate aftermath. *Why couldn't you have let her live and fixed whatever imbalances arose later, without killing anyone?*

Dante, who lost his father around the same time, finally managed to soothe her with a promise. "One day," he said while petting her trunk, "I'll be in charge of Melampus, and I'll make sure we never have to use poachbots again."

Prince watched Dante shaking hands with Ambassador Johnson on the runway and wondered if he remembered that promise, or if power was just going to consume him.

It's Dante, he finally said to Nemos. *He never has time for me anymore.*

He's growing up, said Nemos, whose footsteps now shook the ground under Prince's feet. *You know he still loves you.*

Prince whined a little. *Does he? I fell off the Ark and almost drowned yesterday, all so he and his mom could capture some dolphin whose Specter doesn't even work. I mean, he said he was sorry, but younger Dante would never have forgotten I was out on the deck. And now there's this new girl from the City. He clearly has a huge crush on her. She's ignored him so far, but he keeps thinking about her.*

Prince felt Nemos smile. *If Dante is changing, maybe you should support that and be happy for him. Show that you share an interest in his growth and that you'll be happy as long as he's happy. Don't treat love like a limited resource.*

Prince mulled this over as Nemos and Emily entered the clearing.

—

As the three animals moved to matters of small talk like the weather and gossip from Nemos's herd, Dante sized up the ambassador. Johnson's garish fuchsia and scarlet uniform was probably the most Martian thing Dante had ever seen. For all the baseless scaremongering Mars loved to do about imaginary extraterrestrial invasions, they sure enjoyed dressing like aliens themselves.

"But what happened to the dolphin?" Johnson said with his posh accent, like a stick of butter was in his mouth. "I was so excited to see how sonar felt."

"I'm afraid he's ill, Your Excellency," Stella lied. "We wouldn't want to subject you to any unpleasant vicarious symptoms."

"I see," Johnson tugged at his thin mustache. "Well, I suppose the elephant will do."

What an ungrateful ass, Dante thought. *He speaks as though he has no idea how many centuries of work my family put into ensuring that there were still elephants here, let alone any he could talk to.*

What Mars lacked in population and food production next to the Arkology, it made up for in military tech and egotism. The economic partnership Stella had built between Melampus and the Martian State had been instrumental in pressuring the City to maintain peace between the two planets, but in Dante's mind, such peace could never last. The Martians were oligarchs; Earth at least believed in the pretense of democracy. Nevertheless, life within the Biomes could not survive without the Martians' money.

Dante clapped his hands, acting the part as eager host and business partner-in-training. "Let's get your SpecterX installed!"

Stella and Dante led the ambassador to a surgical chair they had brought up from the testing sector. Laura, wearing a red satin dress Stella had loaned her, stood at the ready with two syringes in hand. Dante avoided eye contact. By now, he was a little offended at how she was treating him. Did he find her attractive? Yes, of course, but more than anything he was just looking for a friend. Growing up, it had always been rare for him to meet anyone his own age.

Next to Laura, speaking into a microphone and facing a flying drone that resembled a dragonfly, was Cindy Zhao, Ark correspondent for the City Evening News. She had flown in to provide live coverage of the demo.

"Cindy Zhao here, coming to you live"—it wouldn't be live—"from the savannah, where Ambassador Johnson of Mars is about to try the upcoming SpecterX for the first time."

Dante tuned out her voice and stared into the middle distance. The demo was largely a marketing exercise, of course, meant not only to promote the product launch three weeks later but also to ensure that Mayor Wilcox's reelection campaign, based largely on his support for Pathnet and the controversial Mars-Melampus partnership, remained unopposed.

Citizens in front of television screens that day got to watch the deactivation of Ambassador Johnson's original Specter in only slightly edited form. Laura injected a compound that, as it traveled through his arteries into his brain, caused the thin, fibrous neural lace covering Johnson's cortex to detach and retract back into the nine-pointed star just above the midpoint of his eyebrows. The tiny claws that fastened the Specter to his skull then retracted, and Stella removed the device with only some minimal spot bleeding in its wake. After the short application of a warm compress, Stella then took a shiny black case out of her pocket and opened it to reveal a freshly-manufactured SpecterX—gold instead of the original's silver, save for a tiny, deep blue "X" etched into the star's center. Laura then injected an opposing compound, which allowed the SpecterX to latch onto the ambassador's skull and disseminate its own technologically superior mesh of neural lace all over his cortex.

"How did the replacement feel, Your Excellency?" Cindy held her microphone up to Johnson as Stella and Dante led him down the gangway into the lemon grass.

"Very easy! And painless!" Johnson flashed the dragonfly drone a thumbs-up.

The setup for the demo was simple. Dante, Prince, Nemos, and Johnson faced one another and received the option, provided by their devices in the form of a quick thought, to open channels with each other. As they approved this option one at a time, every additional participant's mind added a new layer to everyone else's.

Stella guided Johnson through the opacity adjustment process. "Ask the Specter to focus on Prince's layer...Now, ask it to focus on Nemos's...Now, ask it to ignore her auditory perceptions while isolating her olfactory experience."

Viewers at home did not quite experience what the ambassador experienced—the sounds, such as those that traveled through the ground at a frequency too low to be heard by humans but were a constant element of Nemos's experience, or the smells, like the sweet acacia scents that were pleasantly monotone through the human nose but became a rich explosion of varied saccharine flavors when experienced through a dog's or an elephant's. But they could see the ambassador's expressions of wonder.

"Incredible!" he shouted several times. "I am truly impressed!"

The demo concluded without major problems. Cindy took her drone and boarded a transport vehicle back to the City. Everyone thanked Nemos for her help and sent her back into the forest with Emily.

Next, *real* business: Pathnet.

5

Dante, Stella, and Prince went with the ambassador to the private dining room of the cafeteria. Sitting in stately gold chairs around a table draped in silk tulle, they passed around a tablet console and requested the finest meals that the Ark's kitchen could print.

"It's a wonderful product," Johnson said of the SpecterX as he ordered some beef wellington. "But I'm still waiting for the full proof of concept."

"Oh, you'll get it." Stella said with a devious grin. She turned to the dog. "Prince, what would you like on your kibble for lunch?"

Prince, seated in the chair next to Dante, cocked his head in thought. "Hmm...I'm really in the mood for foie gras."

"I'll get that for you." Stella then took out her phone and typed, without sending, a text addressed to none other than Mayor Wilcox:

"Subject: PRINCE; Emotion: CRAVING; Object: SEAJACKER'S BRAND LOBSTER THERMIDOR"

She showed the screen to Johnson, then hit send. She waited for the mayor to send a thumbs-up in return.

She picked up the tablet and began scrolling. But before she ordered the foie gras, Prince gave a quick, gruff bark of realization.

"Actually, wait. I think I want lobster. Yes. Craving it, in fact."

Stella placed the order for lobster and smiled. "Why the change of heart?"

"I don't know. I just suddenly remembered how good it tasted."

Johnson, putting two and two together, snapped his fingers. "Aha! That's what I wanted to see."

Prince cocked his head. He pinged Dante. *What's going on?*

Our secret source of profit from the SpecterX, Dante replied. He grinned despite the burst of cortisol that Prince alone could smell. *The device sends users' perceptual data to a drive in the AI's servers—the Source. We can sell that data to companies and, in theory, let them pay to transmit the desire for their products. Users won't even know they're receiving an external perception.*

So every SpecterX connects to the AI?

That's right. Tracking information gets sent as well.

Everyone's dishes arrived. Prince was apprehensive about eating his data-derived lobster, but the hunger was too great to resist. He generally kept his nose out of ethical concerns, but he could tell Dante felt some unease as well. *How do you feel about that?*

Oh, fine. Money is money, I suppose. All for the greater good of the Biomes, and so on.

It hurt Prince a little that Dante hid his deeper feelings from him. *Does he think I'll give him away somehow?*, he wondered privately.

All the tastes of millennia past were at their disposal. Stella and the ambassador downed some wine and noshed on bruschetta appetizers. "Your Arkling shareholders are increasing their investments, I take it?" Johnson asked.

"Yes! So the trip is still on?"

Dante frowned. "What trip?"

Stella and Johnson exchanged knowing looks. "We have a surprise," Stella said, the corners of her mouth curling into an inscrutable grin. Dante's stomach fluttered. Her "surprises" were unpredictable and often quite unpleasant. He thought back to recent days to see if he'd done something worthy of punishment. No, he didn't think so. He'd been a perfect little minion of his mother's. He was very careful to keep his own opinions on company matters private. He would get his chance to change the Melampus vision soon enough.

"I'm going to Mars!" She finally shouted.

Dante didn't understand. Was this a trick? Mars was so cold and austere and barren. His mother had never expressed a desire to *visit* the Red Planet. "Wow," was all he could say. "Why?"

Johnson spoke with his mouth full of beef. "Several private contractors on Mars have asked to meet Stella. We're also in the process of updating our own AI, and we would love to draw on her knowledge."

Stella beamed. "They offered to come with the ambassador, but I've always wanted to see the red planet. Plus—and here's the surprise—it will give you your first real experience running the company."

Dante almost choked on his salmon. "What?"

"I can't run it in transit, of course. I'll be sedated for the whole week, getting antigravity supplements and gene therapies pumped into me. You went through the reverse procedure to come here, Johnson, didn't you?"

Johnson had gravy dripping from his chin. "Oh yes, but my body's used to it by now, coming and going so often. Your mother will need to be put under for the whole trip. Both there and back."

Dante nodded, processing. "And if there's an emergency?"

Johnson waved his hand. "We can wake her for short times if absolutely necessary."

Stella tilted her head. "What a silly question, dear. Are you really nervous?" She was really knocking back the wine now.

"No. Just wondering." He smiled and blinked, conscious of how angelic his long lashes and hazel eyes looked. Stella did not blink. She made eye contact for just a little longer than he liked.

"Good. I leave in a week." She at last touched his hand. "You'll be the ship's captain while I'm out of reach. I think you'll do terrifically. And if you don't, it's only a week." She burst into manic laughter, then just as quickly looked stern and grave. "Remember, though, the most important thing to handle will be the upcoming Board meeting." And back to smiling again: "But that's easy. Just stand in front of the shareholders and tell them we're meeting all of our production deadlines. You're already familiar with the process, of course."

Tears—real tears—came into Dante's eyes. "Thank you, mother. This is a wonderful opportunity. I won't let Melampus down."

Prince, meanwhile, still couldn't see what Dante was thinking, but he remembered Nemos's advice. For whatever reason, Dante looked forward to taking over for his mother for a week, and Prince felt obligated to help his trial run as acting CEO go as successfully as possible.

6

When Dante was nine, a few months after his father's death, he drew up a prototype with some basic pseudocode for a technology that could bring people back from the dead. A programming prodigy like both his parents, he knew the idea—a drive to store a profile of a person's consciousness, which could then be inserted into a new, cloned host body—would work in principle, since he had talked it over once with his father. And when he gave his drawings and pseudocode to Stella, she showed warm interest and read every one of his notes. On finishing, however, she shoved his drafts back into his face and snarled, swinging back on her hot-and-cold pendulum.

"What childish nonsense. Wow, immortality, what a novel concept. Where exactly will you find the resources for creating these host bodies, hm? We don't exactly have a whole planet of resources at our disposal. Are you going to kill the animals and use them as hosts? And what makes you think people want to bring the dead back? No, it's better to leave the past behind, darling. Stop wasting your time. And stop cutting your hair so often. You look like a dyke."

Three years later, though, when Stella first proposed SpecterX to the Board, he found that she had stolen some of his supposedly "childish" code to design the server that stored a person's perceptual data and synced it with the AI. This was just one of many personal insults that Dante recollected as he plotted to reactivate Varuna's SpecterX as soon as his mother left for Mars. He sought a way to sabotage her plans without damaging the corporation.

Unfortunately, as though reading his mind, his mother made one last instruction before she joined the ambassador on his shuttle back to Mars. "Oh, one more thing. Don't do anything further with the Varuna...situation until I'm on Mars. We'll collaborate on a solution." She winked.

Dante felt obliged to obey. He had seen the consequences of trying and failing to act on a grudge against his mother. After the SpecterX announcement, he made a point of broadcasting his dissatisfaction with the idea. He was only eleven, but he was the heir to the Melampus bloodline. In the eyes of the Board, Stella was an interloper from the City who'd lucked out on Dominic's tragedy. She was *acting* CEO, a queen regent of sorts.

"What do you think of your mother's idea?" The shareholders (all of whom served on the "crew," whether they did any actual work or not) would ask.

"I don't know," Dante would answer. "I don't think my dad would like it."

A few weeks later, Dante opened his bathroom drawer and found it empty. The hormones he'd been stealing from the Ark hospital were gone.

"Hello, Danielle." His mother appeared like a wraith in the doorway.

"What did you do?" Dante cried.

"I heard you didn't like your mother's idea. That's too bad. Maybe you can work on your own ideas when you're eighteen. Or, maybe you'll be a prisoner in the City."

"What do you want?"

"I want your support—your loyalty as my son, if that is indeed what you are. Did you really think I wasn't watching your body, wasn't seeing what was going on? Tell the shareholders you've reassessed, and maybe then your drugs will come back."

He had no choice. Yes, it was an open secret on the Ark that Dante was trans, but a secret nonetheless, kept only among shareholders, many of whom had ties to the

Terrarchist Party. As Stella explained, if the City public learned of the Ark's hypocrisy, the resulting crisis of confidence would tank the corporation and destroy the Biomes. And Dante was an only child. There was no line of succession if the Board voted no confidence in him. He was a Melampus, and he needed to honor his family's legacy.

Dante's sobs into his pillow that night were unique in their tone, the wail of a siren he couldn't let anyone hear. This moment returned to him when his mother first told him to stay away from Varuna, and he thought of it again now as he almost knocked, but did not quite, on the bedroom door of the Ark's chief accountant, Officer Wendell, who had the relevant budgetary numbers for the shareholders' meeting in four days' time. Behind the door were sounds of restrained weeping. A young woman's cries, they could not be Wendell's. It was Laura.

Dante put his ear to the door. Was she on a Specter call?

Prince, Dante pinged to the loyal poodle standing beside him. *Put your ear up. See if you can make out any words.*

Prince, catching himself in a moment of jealousy and remembering Nemos's words, did as told.

All I hear is weeping, he said. *Wait, she's stopped.* Footsteps and squeaking noises approached the door. *Oh, no. I hear wheels rolling. She's coming!*

Dante pivoted on his heel, but it was too late. Laura's gasp of horror stopped him from running down the hall. He turned to meet her look of shame. She held a toilet brush and was wheeling a cart of cleaning supplies. They simply looked at one another for several seconds.

Finally, Dante shuffled his feet and shoved his hands in his pockets in mock nonchalance. "OK, fine. That time I *was* listening. But I didn't hear anything. I promise!"

Laura refused to return his smile. "Wendell's in his office," she said quietly as she tried to push the cart past him.

Dante stepped in the cart's way. "Wait. Why were you crying?"

"None of your business," Laura was tempted to say, but didn't. He might have been two months younger than her, but he was still her superior while Stella was away. "It's nothing.

My dad's having trouble at work."

Dante frowned and ran his fingers through his long, wavy brown hair. "Enough trouble for you to cry?"

Laura averted her eyes, pushed up her glasses. "Please excuse me. I have to clean the next room."

"Laura, stop. Let me help!" Dante stuck his foot under the cart's wheel. Tears were in her eyes.

"I..." She stammered. She could see he meant it, and she was desperate for someone to talk to.

Dante lifted his chin. He put on a small, mischievous grin. "As your captain, I am *ordering* you to tell me what's wrong." He spoke with a clear hint of sarcasm, a friendly invitation to view him as an equal, a friend, rather than as a boss.

Laura thought he looked ridiculous in his shoulder-padded captain's uniform, but she couldn't deny that his self-consciousness was sort of endearing.

"He was fired," she said with a sigh. She pushed the cart away and slouched down on the floor, head in her hands.

Wanda had called to tell her the night before. She had been right: Peter's criticisms of the railway project did not go over well. More than just resulting in demotion, however, Peter's attempts to recruit coworkers in his protest violated a law against workplace agitation that few in recent decades had even been audacious enough to learn existed. Peter could never work in the Bureau of Urban Planning again.

Don't worry, Wanda had transmitted with palpable doubt in her thoughts. *Peter has so many programming skills. I can probably get him a job on the farm.*

Laura was having none of it. *Let me talk to him.*

When Peter answered her call, she went off. *How fucking could you? Especially after all the crap you give Michelle about wanting to be out in public. Watch out for the AI, you always said. What's going to happen now? Are you going to have to move to a lower floor? Is Michelle going to have to switch schools? The kids down there are nasty. They'll find out she's trans and destroy her.*

Peter's thoughts were a jumble. He could barely string words together. *I'm sorry, baby. Please. It will be okay. Give me a chance to make it right.*

Laura hung up in rage. She lay in bed awake all night. But it was only as she was cleaning the alcoholic accountant Wendell's vomit-stained toilet that she allowed herself to break down and cry.

But she refused to let herself cry in front of Dante. Still, he could tell that she was holding it back. He slumped against the wall beside her. He couldn't quite feel what she was feeling, economically fortunate as he was, but he knew how precarious life was for most Citizens. "Oh, damn. I'm...sorry." He felt foolish offering so few words. Looking into her eyes to make sure it was okay, he touched her shoulder. "What are you going to do?"

Laura shrugged. "I don't know. Quit, maybe."

Dante drew back. "What? You can't quit. You worked so hard to get here."

She pinched her nose and groaned. "I know! But I can't afford to waste a whole year scrubbing rich people's toilets for free. My family can't afford it."

He nodded, looking at the toilet brush on the floor. He thought of what he could say to show her he understood, then assumed his usual cocky smirk. "Yeah, they should really just get robots to do that. But you know how it is around here: regimented, hierarchical. Service to God and all that shit. Ecotheocracy. The Olaf Melampus way. No crazy drug orgies like Wendell here loves until you've put your grunt work in. And of course it's worse for you, being an 'outsider.' My mom dealt with the same thing in her internship."

She smiled slightly, a little surprised and comforted to hear him so boldly mocking Ark culture.

"Anyway, stop talking about quitting," he continued. "You're supposed to be getting to work on a kickass research project. One year from now, every member of your family will own a penthouse on the City's top floor."

He was exaggerating, of course—at best, her salary would get one penthouse for the whole family—but the support in his voice was clear.

"I wish I believed that." She looked at the ceiling. "But I have no time to even think about a proposal. If I'm not scrubbing toilets, I'm doing the same usability tests over and over again, or I'm writing emails to the press telling them how *amazing* it is to be here—" She halted, wondering if her sarcastic tone went too far. "Oh, sorry."

He laughed, scratching his neatly trimmed beard. "No, you're right. It sucks here. Go on."

She smiled, wider this time, then looked down in thought. "...And that's just one problem. Nobody here wants to talk to me. Your mom is...*nice*"—Dante refrained from laughing—"but she's so busy, and I don't want to bother her. I have no insight into what people are working on, so I can't even begin to think about a problem I could try to solve in my research."

"Oh, come on!" Dante leaned out to put his face in front of Laura's. His eyes were so wide that she laughed. "You can't think of *any* problems? Look at this place. It's a hedonistic shitshow. And *such* a gerontocracy. Hey, I watch Cindy Zhao. I know what they think about us in the City."

Laura flashed a few glances into Dante's eyes. He was just a little more aware of the world than she had imagined. Nevertheless, she had to stop herself from trusting him too much. For now, at least. "I mean, yeah, I can think of all kinds of...structural problems. That's why I worked so hard to get here and make a difference. At least, that's how I justified it. I loved the *idea* of helping with the X's, getting people and animals of so many different backgrounds to talk to each other and understand each other better. But the deeper problems just seem totally beyond me at this point."

Dante nodded, stroked his beard. It was then that he thought of a way that he and Laura could work together, if only in some small way.

"I have an idea. For a project you can work on."

He looked at Prince, who had sat waiting patiently this whole time. It was time, Prince knew from the cunning twinkle in Dante's eye, for a second meeting with the dolphin.

7

Varuna surged to the surface of his aquarium and poked his nose over the glass's edge, whistling, when Prince walked into the cold room where Stella had placed the dolphin after capture. Prince paused in the doorway, sniffing the air, assessing the dolphin's body language.

Wow, Dante transmitted from the observation deck. *He's happy to see you, at least.*

Dante and Laura had just spent several minutes analyzing the brain scans Laura had collected during Varuna's last test with the SpecterX. Their goal was to formulate a hypothesis that Laura could then propose as justification for further research into any potential design flaws that Varuna may have found a way to exploit.

"I appreciate the thought, but I still don't see anything that makes sense," Laura said after a while.

Dante looked at Prince. "Maybe we should send you in to talk to him, one on one. He likes you, right?" Prince had told Dante about the strange transmission Varuna had sent on the open sea. Dante had chosen to keep this private from Stella.

"That would be interesting," said Laura. "And then if he talks to you, we can compare what happens when he uses the original Specter with what happened before."

Prince growled a little. He didn't want to go. Even watching Varuna float listlessly behind the one-way mirror reminded him of drowning, and the dolphin's unexpected,

41

uninterpretable transmission felt invasive and unwelcome the more he thought about it. "Don't you have old records to look at?" He asked. "From his original tests?"

"We do," said Dante, "but they're on my mom's computer. "She keeps all the old data private, even from me. Come on, Prince. He can't hurt you from behind the tank."

Prince's tail dipped between his legs, but he agreed nonetheless and sat patiently as Dante inserted a small earpiece for delivering instructions. Prince didn't like looking scared of anything to begin with, and now especially, he needed to be brave to prove to Dante that he would support him in the next phase of his life. The project was important to Laura, and helping Laura was important to Dante, so it simply had to be important to Prince.

He warmed up a little once he was sure that the splashing tail and the fins slapping against the glass were not threats but in fact invitations to play—though play in what form, he could not say. The room was eerie, lit only by the underwater blue fluorescent bulbs around inside the 15-foot-high, 30-foot-long tank. The light's refractions through water and artificial coral illuminated Prince's body with mottled, rainbow-colored shadows, visible to Dante and Laura as they kept one eye on the two animals' scans and another on the aquarium's camera feed.

Prince locked onto Varuna's face and pinged a nervous *hello*. Varuna opened the transmission but did not answer. Instead, he abruptly went silent. He cocked his head the way a dog might.

"Try again," Dante said. The monitors showed that Varuna's brain had processed that one transmission in a normal manner. "Tell him you're alone."

I'm alone, Prince said. *Nobody is watching us. I wanted to talk to you about what happened.*

Varuna, still peeking over the glass, opened his mouth a little and emitted a set of rhythmic quacks that clearly resembled laughter. "E-e-e-e!" He shook his head.

He knows I'm lying, Prince thought.

Then, to everyone's surprise, Varuna submerged himself and swam down to Prince's level. Prince's heart fluttered as

Varuna's small, round, black eyes stared and took him in. After a few moments, Varuna bowed his head down to show the nine-pointed star sutured into the skin above his melon, and he began to tap it against the glass.

"Is he trying to damage the Specter?" Dante asked, not able to see what was happening in full detail.

I don't think so, Prince pinged back. *He's tapping too gently.*

While continuing to tap his head on the glass, Varuna began to whistle at a pitch too high for the humans to hear. Prince, tail erect, tiptoed toward the tank to listen better. The edges of two images, much simpler than the one Varuna had tried to convey out at sea, etched their way into his consciousness: a nine-pointed star, and an X.

Prince understood. *You want your SpecterX back?*

Varuna lifted his head back up, shrieked a muffled underwater shriek, and nodded.

You won't talk to me unless you get it?

The nods quickened.

We're trying to help a friend. She needs to understand why your SpecterX didn't work properly. Can you help us with that?

Varuna paused for a second, then nodded again.

He wants his SpecterX back, Prince pinged back to Dante. He explained the thought-images, which Dante then explained to Laura.

Laura kept her eyes on the monitors as Dante considered his options. Something didn't feel right.

Dante banged his fist on the desk. "Fuck it. I'm going to do it. I'm in charge."

Laura tried to stop him. "No, please. It's fine. Don't get into trouble with your mom on my account!"

Dante widened his stance to look confident. "I won't get in trouble. We'll install the X for a few hours or however long we need and then replace it back. She won't have a clue. I'll get the compounds."

As he ran to get the syringes from the hospital's inventory on the pretense that he was conducting an "inspection" of the medical crew, and as Laura reflected on all the choices she had made to get to this point, Prince watched the eight-foot-long dolphin gliding in circles of anticipation around the tank and found himself a little mesmerized.

His previous encounters with dolphins had felt antagonistic, both because he'd been jealous of how much their intelligence was of interest to Dante and other humans and because he'd served as a sheepdog or wrangler of sorts in experiments that had involved capturing large pods. But here in the room, alone, without words, having just communicated in some small way at a frequency the humans couldn't hear, a quiet resonance materialized between the two creatures.

After a while, Dante's head and arms poked through a small door that opened in the wall above Varuna's tank, up near the ceiling. Varuna whizzed to the surface and floated. He raised no fuss as Dante deactivated the Specter and reinstalled the SpecterX.

Dante returned to the observation deck, and Prince requested to open a channel with Varuna, which he promptly accepted.

"Showtime," Dante said to Laura. But when Dante tried to join Prince and Varuna's channel, Varuna did not acknowledge the request. The dolphin wasted no time at all in transmitting an instruction that only Prince could receive.

Come up to the glass. I want to see you better.

His request felt inviting to Prince, even seductive. A deep loneliness was on the verge of being erased. He obeyed. Their eyes locked. A warmth surged through Prince's limbs.

As Dante resent his request to join their channel, Varuna bowed his head and placed his X against the glass

Here, put your Specter against mine. I want to feel your mind.

"What's going on?" Laura asked.

Dante's face scrunched with frustration. "He's not letting me join," he said.

Laura bit her lip. Varuna's brain and Specter scans showed the same unexplainable pattern as before, but Prince's scans clearly showed that the two of them were in communication.

Dante spoke in Prince's ear: "What's going on? What is he saying?"

Prince's head was already on the glass. *It's okay*, he pinged to Dante. *He wanted me to come closer. I think he's just wondering if he can trust us.*

Dante frowned. "Can you ask him to add me to the channel?"

But a buzz above Prince's eyes had already started to drown the world out. His Specter became the node for a current that connected his and Varuna's minds. Varuna sent deep, steady clicks through the glass, Prince's breathing slowed, deepened.

Inside the observation deck, his Specter's signals went haywire. Blood rushed through his ears. The glass shook with his heartbeat. He could hear the blood slow down.

Slower.

Slower.

The whole world stood still.

Each click spanned an eon.

Each vibration, a *thud* in Prince's soul.

A tug on his chest.

The pulse of a magnet that drew his mind closer.

And then, an image: Prince, on Varuna's back, from Varuna's point-of-view. No cyborg limbs this time. A memory. *The thing that already happened*, he heard Varuna think. Varuna's memory triggered Prince's memory, his memory of terror, of trying to get out of the ship's way, drowning, feeling water fill his lungs.

Then, relief, floating, gliding through the water.

The memories merged. Prince almost remembered carrying himself, remembered being Varuna with himself on his own back. The only things keeping Prince grounded in his own identity were the differences in his and Varuna's sense-perception: Varuna's nonexistent sense of smell and panoramic vision contrasted sharply with Prince's recollections.

Next, in the present, a loud whistle from Varuna, and the words, transmitted into Prince's mind:

For the love of the cosmos, help us.

Prince's whole body shook as a new vision entered his mind: a spacecraft, one that resembled the Martian ambassador's, blasting up the space elevator away from the Arkology, up through the stratosphere, up to the stars.

Not a thing that did happen, but a thing that could.

And as the vision, narrowing in focus like a camera lens, closed in on the ship...could it be? Prince's and Varuna's faces in the cockpit?

Do you remember? The star we both come from?

Prince then lost all contact with Varuna's thoughts, but his mind remained on overdrive. A sea of otherworldly images—stars, galaxies, black holes—fought for attention with upwelled memories.

And back in the observation deck, the live scans of Prince's brain bloomed all over the monitors with vibrant, angry colors.

"His Specter frequencies are off the charts!" Laura shouted.

An alarm went off.

Dante rose. "Shit! He's short circuiting." He bolted out of the observation deck into the aquarium room.

Prince shambled away from the glass, his face sagging, like he was having a stroke. His legs buckled with each step. He collapsed in Dante's arms, seizing and frothing at the mouth.

8

Although their Specters were no longer in contact, Dante and Prince happened to recall three of the same memories as the panicked boy carried his seizing dog to the medical sector (though for Prince, it was less conscious recall than the passive, dreamlike experience of whatever buried impressions unearthed themselves as his haywire neurons fired on all cylinders).

First, they remembered the day they met. Prince did not remember the discrete order of things or even *what* he was remembering. At four weeks old, his eyes were still too young to see much more than blurry blobs, but the loss of his mother's smell caused the young puppy an indelible terror. After three decades of breeding through dozens of canine generations, Dominic Melampus had arrived at the perfect specimen to receive the device he had been developing since his twenties. With just a few more months of training, his and his ancestors' dream to talk to animals was about to become a reality. But to train Prince properly, Dominic would need to isolate the puppy from his mother and siblings as early as possible. He would need to make sure Prince trusted his conversation partner. And although the trauma of leaving his mother and all other fellow canines at such a young age never fully left Prince, his whimpering did calm down a little once Dominic walked into the seven-year-old Dante's (then "Danielle's") room and handed him the dog that would forever thereafter be his best friend.

They both recalled the day Prince received the Specter. Together with Stewart, then-Director of Animal Training, Dante had spent the last five months socializing Prince to be an obedient and loyal member of the Ark family. Thanks to the Smellogen and Prince's exceptional breeding, he could already understand certain complete sentences, and nobody would ever have guessed that he had been resentful and aggressive in his first weeks away from his mother. But Prince's near-instant self-recognition in the one-way mirror had been a surprise. Stella, Stewart, and the entire Ark crew, huddled together on the observation deck to watch this dramatic moment, hugged and congratulated Dominic as Prince pawed at his Specter with a wide-eyed look of curiosity. "It's true," Dante confirmed out loud in the adjoining room. "He knows it's his reflection. Yes, Prince, that's you." What the humans had not understood at the time was that sharing one's consciousness with another being meant sharing *all* of it. The good, the bad, and the ugly. Any animal who gained access to the way humans saw themselves and the world would have that access forever, whether they wanted it or not.

This realization was the centerpoint of the third memory Dante and Prince shared. A year and a half later, in the savannah, Dante and Prince walked down the gangway to join Dominic, who sat in the shade beneath a baobab. In front of him, Stewart guided Nemos in one of her first usability tests. He pointed to different canvases arranged in a circle and, using his mind, asked her to paint pictures of varying complexity.

Before joining the Ark several years earlier, Stewart worked as an information architect for the City. By combining this experience with his passion for zoology, Stewart had been able to help Dominic program the Specter in such a way that it would adapt to the brain of any species who used it, making sure that all communications traveled through whatever sensory pathways the user most favored. This was why Prince and Nemos could still, strictly speaking, think in smells rather than words.

Dominic sat on a rock and admired the artistic

collaborations between animal and trainer. "Why are you wearing that?" He asked Dante as he walked over. "It's so hot out here."

Dante, usually found in t-shirts and shorts, wore a pink summer dress and sunhat. Dominic, meanwhile, always an icon of class, wore fashionable sunglasses and Bermuda shorts. "Mom wants me to look more like a girl whenever I leave the Ark," said Dante. "She says drones will send pictures of me to the City, and I'll get taken away from you."

Dominic rolled his eyes. "I'll have to talk to her then. We own the drones. The City can't do anything with them."

Nemos, having finished a painting, stepped away from her canvas. This one, a richly-colored, impressionistic painting of the surrounding landscape, was far more complex than anything she had ever done before. Dominic smiled and clapped his hands. Dante joined in. Stewart gave a bow, then moved to the next canvas with his student.

Dominic looked at Dante once more and sighed. "...But I understand where she's coming from. It's a cruel world."

Dante picked the grass. "Why were you and Mom fighting last night?"

Stewart glanced over again. Thin and unthreatening in appearance, he was the perfect person to confront the animals. He raised his eyebrows and nodded at Dominic, then smiled and waved at Dante.

Dominic didn't answer right away. "You know, in all my decades of research, I never wondered if the Specters might continue to affect how the animals saw themselves—even when they were not using them. If they might cause the animals to think about death the way we do, for example."

Prince, whose attention had been on Nemos until now, spoke up. "What is death?"

Dante answered, always excited to teach his dog. "Your body stops working, and you're no longer here anymore. Not the way you were, at least."

"Oh." Prince nodded. "Sure, I know about that."

Dominic leaned over and let the lizard climb onto his hand. "Your mother wants to keep expanding the technology. Give a Specter to every animal on the island. Then get as many users able to talk on it at the same time as possible. What do you think about that?"

"I dunno," Dante shrugged. "It sounds cool."

Dominic laughed. "Indeed it does *sound cool.*" He let the lizard go.

Dante bowed his head a little in embarrassment. His father's approval was everything to him. Dominic, seeing this, wrapped an arm around him and continued.

"But what I'm starting to realize is that it's one thing to talk to the animals, and another thing entirely to *force* them to talk. In our benevolent drive to understand the animal mind, we never wondered if they would actually benefit from understanding ours. Nemos and Prince here are quite docile, but the dolphins and octopuses are another story. And everything always turns to money in the end. I worry my hubris has steered me wrong, and I worry the corporation is reaching a point where its mission to build the next Earth is becoming incompatible with its mission to safeguard the one we already have. Your mother doesn't see it that way."

Dante said nothing. Smart though he was, he didn't want to think about company politics just yet. And Nemos's paintings were so fascinating. Nevertheless, he might have said more if he knew it was his last serious conversation with his father.

The next day, the Evening News would report Dominic's death in a lion attack.

Eight years later, as Dante carried Prince to the hospital, he remembered what his father had said about hubris.

9

Prince awoke on his side, covered in electrodes, in a hospital bed. The room beeped and whirred with the machines that measured his vital functions. Dante sat in a chair, stooped over in sleep.

"Dante?" Prince said out loud.

Dante's eyes blinked open. "Hey, buddy. How are you feeling? Do you remember what happened?"

Prince sat up and nodded. "Yes. The details are still coming back to me, but yes. My head hurts a little, but I'm ok."

"That's great." Dante scratched behind Prince's ears. "I was really scared for a minute. Your brain calmed down quickly once we zapped it in the right places, though, so I figured you'd be okay. The doctors will watch you overnight, but you should be fine. Any cognitive problems?"

"Don't think so." Prince's stomach growled. "But I am a little hungry."

"I'll get some food for you!" Dante rose, kissed Prince's head, and left the room.

Prince lay down. He shook a little as he remembered his latest experience with Varuna—not that it was painful, but that it felt as good as it had. Was it a deliberate attack? He tried not to think about it and closed his eyes.

But his effort didn't last long. Within seconds, the memory that had kicked off the whole episode—Prince and Varuna gliding through the waves—seemed to replay itself inside his eyelids, and the haunting words echoed in his mind.

For the love of the cosmos. Help us.

But it was no mere echo. The voice that incanted those words kept talking.

Good, you're awake. I've been calling all day.

Prince shot up, eyes wide open. His surroundings had a second layer, the way they would on a Specter call. There was no mistaking the aqueous dancing lights, the 300-degree range of vision, the rich, ethereal underwater soundscape: This was Varuna's consciousness.

Yeah, it's me. Sorry about what happened earlier. It works better without a barrier between us.

Prince's whole body shook. He panted. *Varuna? What is this? Get out of my head.*

Hey, calm down. I know this is weird, but you're totally safe, and you'll be able to exit the call yourself in a minute. But I need to talk to you first.

Prince felt attacked. "Help! Help!" He called toward the hallway.

Varuna's thoughts blasted in panic. *Prince, stop! Stop! Dante and Laura need my help, don't they?!*

Prince quieted on hearing these names. *...Yes?*

I can help them. Just stop panicking and listen.

Varuna's melon shook. Prince's head felt like it was jiggling. The dolphin was emitting soothing vibrations. They bounced against the tank and reflected back to his jawbone, which he used to hear. Prince, vicariously experiencing the calming soundwaves, relaxed a little.

He decided to give Varuna a chance. He didn't have a choice at this point. Dante would be back soon anyway.

All right. But this is messed up. How are you talking to me? And what did you mean when you said it worked better without a barrier?

Synchronization. That's what I'll call it, at least.

Prince cocked his head. *You're going to have to elaborate.*

Here's how it works. Varuna swam in circles to think more clearly. *I begin with a memory that I and someone else with the SpecterX share—us swimming together, for example.*

Once we both think of that memory, a harmonic... He paused. *Wait, I shouldn't explain everything yet. I need you to promise to help me.*

Prince was baffled. *Help you how? Why would I help someone who almost killed me?*

Oh, come on. You were never going to die. Your brain was just adjusting.

For God's sake. Prince growled to convey frustration. *What do you want?*

Varuna took a moment to answer. He was considering the best way to transmit his thoughts. *OK. First, I want you to make sure the humans don't deactivate my X again.*

Prince considered this for a moment. *I could try my best, I guess. But why?*

Varuna swam to the surface for a gulp of air through his blowhole. *Because of the second thing I want your help with, which is the establishment of a private telepathic network that the Arkology's animals can use to communicate independent of human interference.*

You want me to...? Prince pawed at his nose in the manner of a human facepalm. *...You have no idea who you're talking to. Without even asking you how you're planning to build something like that, let me point out that I'm a dog, you idiot. Man's best friend. I'm not going to help you with whatever secret network you're trying to build.*

Varuna slapped his fin on the water in annoyance. *I didn't say "secret." I said "private." The humans will need to help build it, after all. All I want is for animals to have their own space to talk to each other and to determine their own affairs.*

Prince was sick of this voice in his head. He stuck his head into the pillow, as though covering his ears would make a difference. *What you want is for me to challenge and maybe lose the trust of Dante and his family and everyone who has been good to me. Melampus has run the Biomes for over a thousand years. Is everything perfect? No, but every human on this ship is trying as hard as they can to prepare for the new Earth.*

Varuna whistled. Prince recognized that he was laughing at him. *What exactly does the new Earth look like?*

Prince quoted the Melampus mission statement. *Melampus believes in a future where humans and animals can work together. We believe that humans are capable of correcting our past mistakes, and we believe that our greatest mistake was failing to listen to the natural world when we had the chance.*

Varuna did a barrel roll in the water and chirped, clearly amused. *You think I haven't heard that one before? Listen, buddy. I probably know more about those past mistakes than you do. Us dolphins are very attentive, and we've been recording information about the humans for a very long time now. Trust me when I say that there is no way planting a bunch of mind control computers in animals and forcing them to talk is going to create a world that is* better *for animals than the one the humans destroyed. And do you even know what the planet looks like outside of this bubble we all live in? Because I don't.*

Prince jerked his head up. *Mind control? What are you talking about?*

Varuna lifted his fins and clacked in excitement. *Oh, you must know about this. They're collecting information about our brains so they can plant new ideas in our heads and influence what we do. I don't know why, exactly. Selling us as pets? Some kind of military operation? But hey, maybe you can find out and get back to me. All I want is for us to make sure the animals aren't just being turned into those drones they've got posing as dragonflies and minnows. Giving us the ability to keep some of our thoughts private from the humans is probably the best way to do that.*

Prince contemplated all of this. Dante *had* said something about data sharing with the AI, and it *was* pretty weird when Stella had just planted a craving for lobster in Prince's mind. Mostly, though, he just wanted to leave the call. Varuna gave him an unhinged feeling, and Prince resolved to say anything he wanted to hear.

Fine, he thought with a snort. *I will mention your idea to Dante, if you tell me how this synchronization thing works. And tell me how to hang up on you, too. I'm not going to trust you if you can just barge into my head whenever you want.*

Prince knew this was crafty on his part, and he didn't like to deceive. But deception was necessary in this case. It was necessary when using the Specters at all, in fact. It was always crucial to hide something from your conversation partners, whether to protect them from your thoughts or to protect yourself from theirs.

OK, Varuna replied after a moment. *Fair enough.* He resumed his pensive swimming. *The first thing to mention is that the SpecterX differs from the original Specter in that it's always broadcasting a signal to the AI. This is how the humans' trackers work.*

Prince nodded. *Right, and you've been interfering with that signal by emitting some kind of sonar frequency.*

Not quite! That's how I did it before, but I found a new way. Now, I'm able to mess with the signal by turning one hemisphere of my brain off at a time. You know how dolphins sleep? We don't. Not fully. We keep half our brains just awake enough to watch out for predators. The AI signal was programmed in such a way as to require both hemispheres of my brain to be in communication with one another.

This did impress Prince, though not as much as he led Varuna to believe through the tone of thought he chose to convey. *That's incredible!* He knew better than to express skepticism or ask any questions and prolong the conversation.

Thanks! Varuna responded well to the flattery. *All right. The next thing you need to know is that whenever two users of a Specter think about a memory that they share at the same time, a particular waveform resonates between their devices. I worked out that if the users are close enough to each other—they have to be touching, or nearly so—this waveform increases in amplitude. And if I emit some clicks at just the right frequency, I can amplify the wave even further, such that it not only disrupts the AI signal but overpowers the Specter's CPU completely. In your case, because I didn't account for the effect of the glass, this sent shockwaves through your whole body. Sorry again.*

No problem, thought Prince, barely processing the bizarre tech jargon, which Varuna was conveying with a kind of manic excitement.

Anyway, Varuna continued, *once I overwhelmed the CPU, I was actually able to sonically map out, in very precise detail, how your Specter's circuitry interacted with your brain. When I sent you all those strange images, I was effectively reprogramming your brain such that it would automatically answer—without notifying the AI—a signal from my brain—an image paired with a message.*

For the love of the cosmos, help us, Prince guessed with astonishment. He got the sense he was talking with an insane genius.

Exactly. So, what that means is that every time either one of us—I programmed mine to do it as well—thinks of those words in conjunction with the memory of us swimming together, we'll be able to have a totally private Specter call. And thanks to our passphrases, the Specters won't even record that we had any sort of call at all!

Wow. That's so cool! Prince replied earnestly, forgetting for just a moment that any awe he conveyed was supposed to be a lie. But then he acknowledged how dangerous this all sounded. *And now...how would you end this call?*

Well, don't do it yet, but you remember that last image I sent before we lost contact and your brain went crazy?

The image of his and Varuna's faces in the cockpit came back to Prince's mind. *Weren't we in a spaceship or something?*

Yes! So, if a memory of the past generates the wave that we need to connect, a vision of the future creates the opposite wave. And I asked if you remembered the star we both come from.

Prince's eyes widened. Whatever thin thread had seemed to tether Varuna's explanation to any reality Prince could understand was snapping. *We're going to space?*

Hey, I don't know. Maybe! Was just a vision I had. A long time ago, actually. I've paid attention to you for a while, Prince.

This sent a shiver through Prince's spine. Had the two of them met in the past? Whatever. It didn't matter. Prince could end the call now. *Uh. OK. So, listen, I've gotta go. I'll talk to you later.*

No, wait, I—

Prince only had to visualize the image and focus on the crucial phrase—*the star we both come from*—for a few seconds with concentrated attention, and his mind was at peace once again.

Varuna tried to call a few more times.

For the love of the cosmos, help us.
For the love of the cosmos, help us.
For the love of the cosmos, help us.

But every time the image of them swimming together materialized, Prince could counter it with the image of them flying toward space. The attempts stopped after a few minutes.

Dante returned, a bowl of kibble and foie gras in hand.

"Sorry I took so long." Dante scratched Prince's head and placed the food in front of him. "I had a sort of difficult call with my mom."

Prince took a few hungry bites of the food, then stopped. Dante's energy was off. He was shaking a little, at one of those low vibrations a dog can sense. "Difficult how?" Prince asked.

"She heard about what happened. One of the doctors needed to call her to figure out the right voltage to apply to reset your Specter. She was pretty mad at me."

Though he wasn't present in the conversation, Prince could guess what an understatement this was. The interruption to Stella's medicated sleep had infuriated her.

What were you thinking? She asked as soon as Dante answered her call from the spaceship's sleep chamber. She didn't even ask for his version of events. *How dare you disobey me?*

I'm sorry, Mother. I'm sorry. Dante's neck shivered. Her spitting, snarling thought-voice triggered visceral memories from ages four or five, when she would grab him and yank him back if he tried to pet one of the animals in the testing sector's cages.

Why did you do it? What kind of scheme were you plotting?

I... Dante struggled to think. Had there even been a scheme? Or had he just wanted to prove his independence? He couldn't remember under the stress. The threat of his mother's wrath spurred him to say something, anything that might appeal to her sense of pathos and mollify her.

There was no scheme. I was helping Laura. She needed an idea for a research proposal, and I suggested looking into Varuna's X. I thought letting her look at how it worked one more time would help her to write it. But it was all my idea. She didn't want to do it.

It worked. Stella's thoughts calmed in tone, like a storm coming to a lull. *I see. We'll talk about this more later. I have to go back to sleep.*

Dante sighed with relief. But Stella continued, *All I'll say right now is that it would be a mistake for you to identify with a Citizen like her. Especially when you're so close to assuming my role. She's beautiful, but she is there for a purpose, and you are there for yours. Don't worry about her.*

Yes, Mother, was all he could say.

Dante could see Stella reopen her hypersleep pod, lit blue in an otherwise dark room of the spaceship. *For now,* she thought, *I want you to deactivate Varuna completely. No Specter at all. I fear he is becoming malicious. Do you understand?*

Yes, Dante thought with a resigned slump.

Good. I'll talk to you again on Mars. Everything is on track for the shareholders' meeting?

Yes.

Stella smiled. *Good. I love you, Dante.*

I love you, too.

She closed the chamber door, like a vampire closing its coffin, and disconnected.

Dante had a lot to consider. But to Prince, he recounted just one key takeaway. "We have to deactivate Varuna."

Prince nodded. He thought about mentioning Varuna's call, but it was still too fresh and bizarre in his mind. He also didn't want to raise any sort of ideas that Dante might interpret as a challenge to Melampus, and honestly, the news that Varuna would be unable to try to communicate with him any further made him glad. "Sounds good to me."

"Good." Dante smiled, then rose. "Get some sleep."

Prince whimpered. "You're not going to spend the night

here with me?"

"I would, but I need to sleep in my own bed. I have a difficult talk with Laura tomorrow, and I need rest. But don't worry. The doctors are here, and you can call if you need anything."

Prince, a little hurt that Dante was leaving him because of Laura, said nothing more as Dante turned out the light and left. Prince lay his head down. Before he fell asleep, Varuna tried to call once more.

For the love of the cosmos, help us.

Prince rejected the call. He feared further harassment, but Varuna did not try any further calls the rest of the night.

And then, in the lonely darkness of his hospital room and the suddenly unfamiliar silence of his mind, Prince felt a strange thing: Doubt. What if Varuna was right about Melampus? About humans? Could Prince really trust them? Could he trust anyone?

Hey, Dante? He pinged his owner's Specter.

Yes? Dante replied quickly.

Prince considered the most innocuous question he could ask. *What caused the collapse?*

Hm...It's hard to name one thing. Climate, pandemics, nuclear war. It all sort of built up over generations. The Pathogen is what forced the schism between the Arkology and Mars. Why do you ask? We've talked about it before.

This was the answer Prince expected. *Humans make mistakes,* he told himself. *All creatures do.*

No reason, he thought to Dante. *Just something that went through my head during the seizure.*

OK. Try to keep your mind off stressful things. I love you, Prince.

I love you, Dante.

Prince went to sleep.

10

Laura already knew that Prince was safe by the time Dante talked to her the next morning. After a night tossing and turning with guilt and worry, she called the medical wing and asked about Prince's condition first thing in the morning. The good news that he was ready to be discharged put a spring in her step as she went back to the observation deck to review the previous day's data.

Her initial suspicions were correct: Though she'd been too worried about Prince to think through them at the time, clear patterns suggested differences in how the two hemispheres of Varuna's brain were processing whatever communication was taking place with Prince. She didn't fully understand it, but she was hopeful that further tests and an interview with Prince about his experience would give her enough of a lead to start a proposal.

The prospect was so exciting that she stayed calm and encouraging when her mother called to deliver some bad news.

"We're going to have to move to a lower floor," Wanda said. "The farm tells me they aren't willing to hire Peter, and he's going to have to apply to some of the more basic maintenance jobs in residential."

Before Laura could answer, Peter called over from the sofa. "Is that Laura?"

Peter was watching Mayor Teddy Wilcox on TV. The

short, red-faced man delivered his stump speech to a cheering crowd of supporters who were in all likelihood hired actors. Laura overheard some snippets:

"...And we're going to continue lifting regulations to ensure economic prosperity and continued peace with Mars!"

Peter climbed over the back of the sofa like an excited child and kneeled in front of Wanda to let Laura see his gesture of repentant genuflection. "Laura, listen. I know you're mad, and you have every right to be. But I promise I will make this right. I will scrub the shit out of sewerbots 24 hours a day if I have to. And if the sewage company won't hire me, I'll do something else."

"Dad, relax," said Laura. "I'm going to do my part, too. I don't want to speak too soon, but I have a really promising lead for a research proposal."

"You do, huh?" Peter stood up. "That's good," he said with a joking smile. "For a second, I thought the only way to make money was going to be to run for mayor."

Laura laughed. "You've threatened to do that for years." The idea of anyone, let alone Peter, positioning themself as a serious threat to the Terrarchist Party was ludicrous. Decades of corrupt programming had done away with former laws that prevented corporate or even interplanetary donations, and all other parties had disappeared.

"Hey, give me a chance if it ever comes to it," Peter said. "Can't you picture me on the screen there?"

Teddy was still going. "And we're going to keep tightening the floor mobility algorithms. We know that communities are strongest when they stick together." (This was, of course, a folksy, yet brazenly transparent, way of promising to continue to make it harder for families to move up the economic ladder.)

"That can be Plan B," Laura joked. "Or maybe Plan Z. In the meantime, don't worry too much about me. I have a good feeling."

Laura's excitement remained as Dante entered the observation deck to find her taking notes on Varuna's scans. But he would soon deflate it. His hands fidgeting, his shoulders a little raised, he started with good news—he was on his way to pick Prince up from the hospital—then went into the bad.

"My mom found out what we did with Varuna. She's ordered me to deactivate him immediately. She doesn't want him wearing any kind of Specter at all."

Laura blinked a few times. The Dante in front of her was not the Dante from yesterday.

"You don't have to do it now, do you?" She asked.

Dante shuffled his feet. "I mean…"

She picked up some of the scans she had printed out. "We collected some good data yesterday. I feel like we're about to make a breakthrough." She smiled with arched, worried brows, then took Dante's hand. "Look, let me test him just a few more times. Aren't you still officially in charge around here for like four more days?"

"I can't do that." He pulled his hand away. "He's dangerous, and it's too much of a risk." Laura's smile dropped, and Dante felt a pain in his chest. He tried bargaining. "I could give you the rest of the day?"

Laura stepped away, then sat back down in front of the computer. She couldn't look at him. "That's not enough. I'm testing the meerkats today."

Dante sighed and threw his hands out. "I wish I could do more, but I can't. I took the blame this time, but if she finds out that we tried anything else, we'll both be in huge trouble. I'm sorry."

"I see." She rose and put her things away, ready to go to breakfast. The conversation did not seem worth continuing.

For Dante, however, the worst part was still unsaid. "And…I don't know if I should tell you this, but I will, because I like you, and I don't want you to think I'm abandoning you. My mom doesn't want me to talk to you anymore."

Laura dropped her bag. She laughed in disbelief. "Excuse me?" Up until this point in the exchange, she had at least felt she had a valuable friend who would help her to plan an alternative project. But now, she thought, Dante revealed who he really was: someone as opportunistic and untrustworthy as everyone else on the Ark.

"She…thinks you'll distract me. I don't think that. But she

does."

"Wow." Laura crossed her arms. "What did she say to you?"

Dante stammered, a little intimidated.

Laura squinted at him with a dismissive sneer. "You really had me going. I really thought you gave a shit." She grabbed her bag and speedwalked out of the deck into the hallway.

He followed. "Laura, please. I want to help."

She entered the elevator to the refectory. She tried to close the door before he entered, but he dove in and beat her. She folded her arms and looked away.

"Listen," he pleaded, "there are things you don't know about me. And my mom could hurt us both if she tried."

She rolled her eyes.

"Spare me the momma's boy act. In less than a month, this is literally your company. You have so many ways to help me if you want to. You think I don't have other research ideas? Of course I do. Oh, here's one," she raised her index finger in a sarcastic "Eureka" motion, "Why don't we research why your mother was the last Citizen to get hired here? Oh wait, we already know the answer to that: nepotism and corruption. But good luck to me if I want to research any way to fix that. Or how about I research ways to fix the climate controls in the tundra and taiga where everything's been melting for the last thirty years? No, you don't want to help with that either?"

The elevator opened. "That isn't how this works!" Dante shouted. He followed her toward the refectory. "I would love to help with all those things, but you know the Board won't approve them."

She halted in front of the doors. "Right." She turned to face him. "The Board." The look of defeat on Dante's face did not faze her. She was thinking about her mother potentially having to support her father and sister on a single income. She was thinking about Peter's name coming up on a blacklist for every employer's background check. She was thinking about Michelle having to switch schools and losing all her friends. "It's all about money," Laura said with the quiet tone of anger that has passed a critical threshold and turned into exhaustion. "This island used to mean something. Every kid in the City dreams of getting to explore the biomes. I was so excited to work here. You know, my dad told me you were in the politicians' pockets, that this whole thing had become a front for Mars and their delusional space army or whatever self-destructive crap they're trying to build, and I didn't want to listen. But he was right. It's all rot. I don't know what game is going on behind the scenes, but I want nothing to do with it. You know what? Listen to your mom. I'm going to tell her I quit once she's on Mars anyway. My family's going broke, and I can't waste my time here."

Dante's lip quivered. "Please don't quit. I'm sorry. I'm trying to protect us both. I hate the game, too."

She walked into the refectory and slammed the door in his face. He knew not to follow her in.

11

Several hours later, Laura was back on the observation deck.

After some stewing, she resolved to do the most she could with the time that she had before Stella's arrival on Mars. Then, she would officially give her notice of resignation. She had no shame in quitting if it meant helping her family, but she did recognize that every minute spent interacting with the animals of the Biomes was a gift worth cherishing.

Moreover, she felt drained and slightly guilty after her rant at Dante. He had sounded sincere in his justifications, hollow though they seemed to Laura, and his claim that he needed to "protect himself" from Stella was haunting and perplexing enough for her to be curious about its meaning.

The meerkats were just one of the many species that were eligible to wear the SpecterX once production came out with the first major batch of new units for beta testing, which would be large enough for not only dozens of new species around the Biomes but also the entire Ark's crew. Dante planned to distribute some of the new units at the shareholders' meeting, now just three days away.

In order to make sure the meerkats were ready, Laura needed to place them in conversation with someone who already wore an X. Dante and Prince were both out for obvious reasons, so she chose Nemos, who she hoped might be willing to give her some information about Dante that she had stored in that reliable pachyderm memory bank of hers. But although Nemos was eager to board the Ark (an endeavor that required deploying a separate gangway that led directly into the only room of the testing sector big enough for her) and talk to the meerkats, she was reticent to share anything private about Dante.

"Dante had a lot of conflicts with his mother growing up, but I can't get into the reasons. It isn't my place."

Laura was just about ready to give up—both on staying aboard the Ark and on understanding Dante, who she had to admit interested her more than she typically allowed boys to interest her—when Nemos said she needed to take a brief break from the test: Prince was calling.

—

The poodle's day had been difficult. He was still a little dazed, and Dante's sadness was so deep he could smell it.

"I just wish I wasn't so scared of my mom. Laura's right about everything," Dante had said. All morning, as he wrote his speech for the shareholders' meeting, Dante vented to Prince about Laura's decision to quit, the AI's corrupt programming, the Ark's decadence, and its complicity in the increasing inequality that was destroying life in the City. "I just wish there was something we could do!" Dante crumpled up yet another piece of paper and tossed it into the trash.

Prince chewed his paws. He suspected that there was something Dante could do, but that it required trusting the dolphin both of them believed had shown himself to be quite untrustworthy. Nevertheless, it was becoming clear that Prince would feel very guilty if he allowed Dante to deactivate Varuna (a task scheduled for the end of the day) without saying anything. But how much should he say?

"I don't want to sound like I'm not listening," he said at one point, "but did Varuna and I ever meet each other before this?"

Dante thought for a moment. "It's possible. Actually, yes, you probably did. We had a whole pod isolated in the cove off the rainforest during the research for the X, and I think it was his. Six years ago, maybe. We studied how different sound-images interacted with each other."

Prince's mind returned to that time. It was one of the first times he felt lonely. All the other dogs on the Ark had been sold to people in the City, and Dante was busy learning the ropes. He'd let Prince run along the beach off-leash. Most of the dolphins stayed far offshore as Prince ran along the sand to bark at them.

But one, a calf a few years old, teased Prince. Several times, he would approach the shore, look directly at Prince, whistle, then submerge and swim away when Prince dashed into the waves to chase him.

Was this him? Prince shared the memory with Dante via Specter.

Maybe, Dante replied. He did want to know what Varuna had said or shown to Prince last night, but the doctors had all agreed it was best to wait until Prince was ready.

Prince remembered that playful moment six years earlier. The calf had seemed to manifest in direct response to Prince's loneliness. What had turned that calf into the deceptive mystery that was Varuna?

Prince then called Nemos for advice. He explained everything: his traumatic encounter with Varuna, his understanding of Dante's fight with Laura, and his inability to decide what to say.

I just don't want Dante to think I'm plotting some animal rebellion, Prince concluded. *You know, he told me a story once: the first time they tried to talk to animals, they used apes, and it went horribly. They tried to take over the Ark. That's why they still won't give Specters to them. I don't trust Varuna's motives.*

I think you need to talk to Varuna again, Nemos said. *I'm hearing a lot of assumptions from you, and I don't think giving the animals a voice is that bad an idea in itself.*

Suddenly, Nemos's thoughts grew stern. *...I haven't told anyone, but I'm pregnant. I can feel it. I'm terrified of what could happen. Will the poachbots kill Emily, or will they kill the new baby? I pray I can keep both, but I have no way to know.*

This gave Prince new perspective. *I'm so sorry, Nemos.*

And one more thing, she continued. *I'm here with Laura right now, and she's asked several times about Dante. She cares about him. I haven't been around her as much as you, but do you really think she would sell Dante out if he told her he was trans?*

Prince did remember her mentioning wanting to help people (and animals) of different backgrounds understand each other. *Probably not,* he said. *But it's up to Dante to tell her.*

It is, Nemos agreed. *Why don't you tell Dante what happened, and see if all three of you can talk to Varuna together? I think open communication is always the best way to resolve conflict. And don't you think Dante would appreciate you trying to make things better between him and this girl he clearly cares about?*

Prince nodded. He thanked Nemos and hung up, then pinged a quick message to Laura. *Meet Dante and me in Varuna's tank in two hours. I have information that can help you.*

Next, he used a paw to tap Dante, who had given up writing and was now just watching videos on his phone.

"I have something to tell you about Varuna."

12

Before accompanying Dante to Varuna's tank, Prince called Varuna to let him know he was at least considering helping him.

I want to trust you, he said, *but everything you do seems designed to resist the humans.*

Varuna, who had answered the call with excitement, took on a more sober tone than in the previous conversation.

I'm sorry I came on so strong, he said. *I was just so excited to meet you. You see, six years ago, when we first met and played in the cove—*

(*So that really was him,* Prince acknowledged privately.)

—I felt like I recognized you. All those images I sent you yesterday, they were visions that I had the moment I saw you.

As Varuna talked, he sent yet another image to Prince: this one from, seemingly, another world entirely, a world with violet skies and green oceans, of thick tropical trees set against backdrops of towering icy mountains.

This was the other vision I had. It came to me the very night after we met all those years ago, as I looked at the stars.

Wading in the water of this vision, Prince now saw, were creatures that looked very much like dogs and dolphins—but they were larger, and they could walk on two feet, and they had less solid outlines, like they were made of bright gold and silver shades of light.

One star especially drew me in. The next day, I went to our library—Do you know about the library? Varuna asked.

No, Prince said.

If you swim out past the cove, to where the seafloor gets deeper—a thousand feet deep, about as deep as dolphins can swim—there's an underwater grotto that we've used over the centuries to record our history, as well as anything about human history we've been able to learn through listening. We find recesses in the walls of the cave, and we transmit soundwaves that change the structure of those holes in small ways. Then, other dolphins can use their sonar to read the messages left earlier.

Prince was impressed. *Wow. I don't think the humans even know about that.*

We don't want them to know, Varuna said. *I can show you where it is exactly one day, once I trust you more.*

Prince drooped his ears a little. He was surprised to find that he wanted to know more about the dolphins, and that he wanted Varuna to trust him enough to share more.

Anyway, Varuna continued, *I went to the library to learn about the star. I discovered it was the ones humans call Sirius.*

The dog star, Prince said, remembering nights spent looking at astronomy atlases with Dante.

Not just the dog star, Varuna said. *Legend has it that dolphins came from there as well. So, I decided that you and I met for a reason, that the star was sending me a call for help. That's what "for the love of the cosmos" means. I didn't know how, but one day, we would meet again, and we would bring all the animals of the Biomes together, to journey together back to the stars we come from.*

Whose legend was that again? Prince asked, now skeptical.

I don't know. Maybe ours, maybe the humans'. Whatever. You don't have to believe it. You can think I'm crazy if you want. Everyone I talked to in my pod about it thought I was. But over the years, they started to listen to my ideas, and the Specters kept getting us to think more and more about these things. What started as a harebrained idea from the pod's local madman is now a full-fledged mythology. And you, Prince, are a part of it.

Prince still had very mixed feelings. He wasn't talking to

anyone else in Varuna's pod, so he couldn't be sure everything Varuna was saying was true. But Varuna sounded sincere, and the truth was that Prince wanted to believe him. He wanted to feel special again, to feel like he had a reason to live independent of Dante.

I guess it sounds like a nice project, he finally said. *I might be willing to help, if you can promise the humans will go to the stars as well.*

Of course, Varuna said. *We all come from the stars.* He paused. *But, maybe wait to talk about the full vision with them. They'll think I'm as crazy as you did the first time we talked. We can get their help with our smaller goal first: the creation of a private network.*

Prince saw nothing wrong with this and agreed. It felt good to be making a friend.

—

Two hours later, Laura waited in front of Varuna's tank. In her hands were various printouts of scans taken from Prince's and Varuna's brains the previous day. Dante had just given Laura a summary of everything Prince had told him. Her earlier hunch about hemispheric differentiation had been correct, and now that she knew Varuna was directly manipulating the Specters' circuitry, the scans were much easier to interpret.

She looked up and crossed her arms when Dante and Prince came in. "It certainly is impressive," she said. "But why are we here?" She squinted. "We could have talked on Specter."

To Laura's surprise, Dante folded onto his knees. "We're here," he said while taking her hand—she had been dreading seeing him after the fight, but his puppy dog eyes were already winning her over, caught off guard though she was—"Because some things should be said in person: Laura, I'm sorry. You were right. We have four days left. And hey, my mom has to fly back, too, right? That's a whole second week right there. We can do something. We can make this work."

Laura smiled, but only a little. "I'm surprised you're still touching the hand of a poor, dirty Citizen like me."

Dante sighed. "It was never like that. My mom...well, I can't tell you exactly what runs through her head, but...I think she saw how her presence on the Ark affected my father. People didn't trust her, and it stressed him out having to prove their love was real. *I* never saw it, but apparently it was at one point." He rose. He wondered if Laura could guess his secret now that he stood so close to her, just one inch taller than she was.

But she didn't. Not yet. "I guess it makes sense," she said. "But are you going to listen to her? I had *thought* that you and I could be good friends." She bit her lip nervously.

Dante blushed, unsure if she was flirting with him. (She wasn't, but she was amused to notice that he thought she was.)

"I...don't want to," he stammered. "I'm tired of listening to her...I..." he looked down at Prince, who looked up at him with an encouraging lolling tongue and wagging tail.

Go on, Prince transmitted. *Like we planned for.* Over the previous half hour, Prince had helped Dante to rehearse the exchange that was about to happen several times.

Dante took a deep inhale. "I have something to tell you."

Laura raised her eyebrows. "Oh?"

"You know how...?" Dante paused. His heart sped up.

Tell her without really telling her, Prince reminded him.

Dante breathed. "...Actually, it's a question. Remember when you said you wanted to work on the Ark because you believed in helping people of different backgrounds understand each other?"

Laura frowned, puzzled. "Yes?"

"I assume you meant, like, Citizens and Arklings, Terrarchists and Technohumanists, Earthlings and Martians, that sort of thing, right?"

"Sure," she said. "Better communication would help to prevent prejudice in all its forms."

This was it, Dante knew. He tried to separate himself from the pounding in his chest that urged him to stop talking. "What about prejudice against queer people? *Trans* people?"

Laura jerked back. Was this about Michelle? No, she decided when she saw Dante himself jerk back in response.

Dante's hunched posture was not that of an inquisitor searching for a rat. Still, she was careful with her words. "I believe...that since I am on the Ark...and outside of the City's jurisdiction...I would be in my rights if I were to say I support trans and queer people."

Dante snickered. "You would be. Is that what you wish to say?"

"...Maybe. Why do you ask?"

Dante swallowed one last gulp of courage. "Because I support them." He then leaned in and whispered, "In fact, I support them for personal reasons."

Laura frowned. "Ok?"

Dante, frustrated, pointed at the camera on the ceiling. Although the Ark was exempt from the AI's speech regulation, the majority of the crew were Terrarchist supporters who would turn Dante in without hesitation the second they made a fuel stop and reentered the City's territory. Making sure nobody who might happen to be listening to the aquarium feed at that moment could hear, he leaned in farther and whispered into Laura's ear. "Very personal."

"Oh." Laura mulled this over for a second, then let her jaw fall. "Oh!"

Dante grabbed his arm and smiled, anticipating the worst for a second. But she just blinked and looked at him for a long time. Then, she offered a small smile in return. They hugged. Each of them relaxed in the other's embrace. They had found refuge. Prince wagged his tail, happy for them.

Dante, refusing to cry, pulled back a little sooner than he might have wanted. "I also," he said while reaching into his pocket, "needed to meet you in person to give you this." He held out a brand new SpecterX, then pulled out two filled syringes he'd swiped from medical. "It's from the new batch that we're giving out at the board meeting, but I'm able to give a few out now. This will make testing much easier for you. You can monitor the animals' conversations directly." He leaned in and whispered again. "For now, though, you'll need it so we can all talk with Varuna at the same time."

She nodded and braced herself for the injection. Only by

talking to Varuna together, Laura understood, could the four of them communicate in private and avoid having their calls recorded in the AI's database.

Varuna, who had been patiently observing Laura and Dante's reconciliation with an eye right up to the glass, whistled once Laura, with her new X installed, joined a channel for them to discuss Varuna's ideas, which only Dante had heard Prince describe in vague form.

It's an honor to talk to you all, Varuna said. Laura and Dante, teetering a little, took a few moments to get their bearings as they adjusted to the woozy underwater soundscape of Varuna's perceptions.

I look forward to collaborating with you in building a planet where all animals of the Arkology can determine their futures, the dolphin continued.

Laura, who was hearing this for the first time, was in awe and wanted to know more. Dante, however, as Prince expected from their earlier conversation, was skeptical.

All right, said Dante. *What exactly is your "private network" going to look like? And why do you want it so bad?*

Varuna rose to the surface for a quick breath, then launched into a clearly prepared monologue:

*When I was younger, I was something of a loner. I studied the wealth of knowledge my ancestors had gathered over the centuries, ever since your family—*he directed this to Dante—*first resurrected the genes of my extinct species. I was sad to learn how we dolphins would have frolicked in the open seas for a very long time if not for human shortsightedness. As your family researched more and more the depths of our intelligence, my ancestors listened to your conversations and passed their findings down the generations. Thanks to them, I learned the whole history: how you boiled the oceans, how you turned weapons against each other, how you provoked the planet into releasing an unstoppable Pathogen, which anticipated your every move and still lurks outside this bubble to this day. I learned how the wealthiest among you isolated yourselves and planned the construction of this island, a vast undertaking that required the advent of then-unknown technologies and the exploitation of doomed labor. Others of* *you, who did not believe in the vision of a highly regulated ecotechnocracy, went to Mars to explore a new frontier. I don't know how things are on the Red Planet, but I know that we dolphins have seen their ships visiting Earth more and more in recent decades, and that this timespan corresponds with the deterioration we have observed in our environments. The systems that keep this island in homeostasis are not working as well. The water is warmer and dirtier, and more and more animals are subject to murder at the poachbots' hands. History appears to be repeating itself. And now, I see what is happening with the Specters. Members of my pod went mad from your experiments. One especially close friend of mine, the only dolphin with as strong an interest in history as my own, spent a few days on this ship. When he returned, he didn't even recognize me or anyone else. He felt like an alien. He smashed himself to death on a rock. Nothing like that has happened recently, thank God, but we know what you are doing, capturing all that you can about our minds so you can control us. Please do not let this happen. Let us speak for ourselves and have a say in where this world goes. I've mentioned a "private network" to Prince, but what I'm really asking for is a way for us to keep our own thoughts. Yes, I've figured out a way to hack the device, but your mother will find a way to stop me, and even if she doesn't, that leaves all the thousands of other species on the island unspoken for. Please, will you build a way for us to keep our freedom?*

By the time Varuna finished, everyone had sat on the floor, leaning against the glass, feeling drained. Dante was especially surprised at his own emotional response to the speech. He felt the truth of Varuna's words, and he felt somehow obligated to take action—but only in the long term. He didn't know where to take the first step—not with the X's launch so entirely consuming the entire production team's attention—and he was struggling to formulate a measured reply when Laura surprised everyone with a bold declaration.

I think we should do it.

Varuna squealed.

You do? Dante and Prince both replied in unison.

Laura shrugged. *I mean, if we don't build it, where do we*

go from here?

Dante scratched his beard. *Well, you'll be fine, thankfully. You have more than enough for your research proposal. You have a question—why is Varuna's Specter freaking out?—and you already have the answer. Just don't give the answer away in the proposal, and you'll have no problem getting funding.*

Varuna dipped his head in disappointment. Prince, meanwhile, chewed his paws, struggling to adjust to everyone's feelings

It's not enough, Laura said while rising. *We have an opportunity to do something big here. In a little over two weeks, the SpecterX will go out into the world. Nobody's thoughts will be private anymore. What if we don't have to let that happen? What if this network Varuna wants us to build could be something else?*

Dante leaned back and looked at her. Her tone was energizing, and he wanted to be a part of whatever vision she was formulating. He couldn't quite see it yet, though. *What should we do? We can't get Varuna here to walk around the island and synchronize with everyone.*

Varuna clicked in amusement. *I would if I could,* he said.

No. Laura pointed between her eyes. *We build a new version of the X that has a privacy function built in.*

Dante scratched the clearly agitated Prince's ears. *That will take months,* he said with a sigh. *I'm happy to work on it once I'm permanently in charge, but it has to wait.*

Varuna let out a low moan. *I fear that waiting any longer will doom any hopes for resistance. I cannot explain why. It's just a feeling I have. A premonition.*

Dante would normally have rolled his eyes at any talk of auguries, but Varuna's moan touched him. A vibration of fear and urgency unnerved him.

But will it take months? Laura asked. *Varuna, you said you directly reprogrammed your and Prince's Specters when you synchronized.*

Varuna nodded. *Correct.*

So, why don't we just study their Specters and use them as models for a redesign?

Dante studied Laura's eyes. Something had awoken in

them, and it was taking hold of him, too. More than anything, he wanted to make this girl happy, to show that he was grateful to her for accepting his trust.

OK. It's worth a try. He rose. *Prince, Varuna, you're on board with this?*

While Prince gave a measured nod, Varuna surged to the surface and yipped. *Yes! Thank you!*

—

After removing Prince's and Varuna's devices, Laura and Dante went to a lab room and laid out all the scans from Varuna's and Prince's various tests. They studied them closely as they put the dog's and the dolphin's hardware under a microscope and ran various tests. They worked well into the night, first drawing diagrams of the changes that they observed had taken place through synchronization, then drafting design prototypes along with code for a new model that would let users keep certain thoughts anonymous. Prince followed their conversation for a while, but it was harder without the Specter, and he ultimately curled up by Dante's feet and slept. Dante himself took a quick catnap at one point, too.

The trash can was full of crumpled-up paper by the time Laura, jittery with coffee, tapped the napping Dante's arm and showed him a prototype she was happy with.

"What do you think of this? I bet you could build one within two weeks, before your mom gets back."

Dante blinked his eyes awake and read through Laura's code. He had started to become skeptical they could pull anything off before Stella returned, but that skepticism dissipated as he studied the masterfully precise circuitry in Laura's design.

"Damn. I knew you were smart, but this is crazy," he said. Laura blushed. Then, Dante stuck his tongue in his cheek and furrowed his brow. "Wait, no."

Dante grabbed his pencil and began to erase and rewrite Laura's code. She bit her nails. Had she missed a fatal flaw? She tried to watch, but his body was fully hunched over the desk. He was in his element.

Laura's worry vanished once he handed the code back with a huge smile. "This is even better," he said. "I got rid of some redundancies. *This* I can build in *three days.*"

Laura sensed Dante's ego glowing. Her own competitiveness bristled for a second, before she remembered that they were on the same team.

"We'll have it ready for the shareholders' meeting," he said. "A complete replacement of our design, in time for the launch."

Laura's eyes widened.

"You're going to share it in public? And you think the Board will approve it?"

"I know they'll approve it. Look."

Asking Laura to follow, Dante went to a computer and logged into his account. Under a folder labeled "marketing data," he pulled up a spreadsheet labeled "audience surveys."

"According to our surveys, over 40% of Citizens say they are hesitant to switch over from their original Specters to the X. And what's their number one explanation by far? Privacy concerns. Pretty much every Citizen has a Specter now because of the intimacy it affords them, but the X threatens to disrupt that. If we can convince users that they can keep certain conversations away from the AI, we'll be persuading them to give us their revenue. Will we lose a little ad money? Sure, but I think I can speak the Board's language and show them it will be worth it." Dante leaned back in his chair and put his hands behind his head. Laura smirked.

"It does seem like it could work. But won't your mom be furious?"

Dante moved his hands up and down like he was weighing the risks and the benefits. "Yes, but if we do this right, the shareholders will increase their investments, and she'll have no choice but to go along with the project."

Laura thought for a moment, then threw up her hands. "All right. Let's do it."

They ran the plan by Prince and Varuna after reinstalling their Specters.

What do you think, guys? Dante asked them. A win-win for animals and humans everywhere.

I think it's a wonderful idea, Varuna said.

I do, too, said Prince (though truthfully, he didn't have very strong feelings either way, and was mainly happy that he could participate in something that excited those around him).

With that, Dante sent the information for the new model to the production sector. All four of them felt electric, like they had just embarked on a wonderful, though potentially risky, new adventure.

13

After three days of frantic correspondence with the production team, filled with explanations for why it was imperative not to disturb his mother during the remainder of her acclimation sleep, Dante stood in front of the Board. He had attended Board meetings for a few years now, but this was his first time leading one. Board members included the C-suite (people like Wendell, Sherman, Lewis, Rosen) as well as, more importantly for the present meeting's purposes, the famous shareholders, who had novelty titles of first, second, or third mate depending on their stakes in Melampus, but were in reality solely there to throw money and run their own companies' operations remotely while living in the comfort of the Ark's luxury cabins.

Speaking to the Board for the first time would be stressful enough, but Dante's palms were dripping with sweat now that the moment to launch his quasi-coup was finally here. For better or worse, a screen on the opposite wall from him, behind the Board members who sat around a long table, displayed constant updates on the stock prices of the thirty or so companies whose CEOs were either in the room or on videoconference. The top number, of course, and by far the largest, was the price of Melampus; this number's fluctuations would give Dante immediate information about how the Board was receiving his speech: Would they use the various tablets they all held in their hands to buy more shares, or to sell?

But although he was nervous, he was also excited. All his life, both his parents had made him look forward to the moment he could start to leave his own mark on the Melampus mission. And here it was.

He puffed up his chest, cleared his throat, and began the meeting by thanking the attendees and assigning someone (specifically, Oscar Montez, CEO of Agrippa, the largest owner of farmland in the City and the employer of Laura's mother), to record the meetings. He then proceeded to general status updates.

"First, let me report that my mother is well on her sixth and penultimate day of space travel, and we have every reason to expect a significant influx of Martian funds in the coming days."

This was met with applause and a slight increase in the stock price.

"Next, I can confirm that everything is in place and on track for our product launch in just twelve days. My mother, as some of you may know, is very excited to host an event that will go out to televisions all over the City on launch day. She'll be leading a demo conversation with myself and several of our X-wearing animals from all over the Biomes—including Prince, of course." He gestured to Prince, who sat regally beside him.

He then took a large gold box from the table in front of him.

"And now, the moment many of you have waited for—the distribution of our first batch of market-ready X's, only for Board member use."

Everyone's necks craned toward Dante as he opened the box to reveal the SpecterXs, arranged in four neatly-lined rows of ten. As the box went around the table, and each person looked at their new device with excitement, the stock price spiked higher.

Then, Dante swallowed. It was time.

"You will of course have the opportunity to install these Specters in the medical wing immediately after the meeting. I should say, however, that it's maybe a little misleading to say that they are fully market-ready."

The stock's increase halted, then teetered into red. The Board members looked up from their devices toward Dante with expressions ranging from concern to intrigue.

"No need to worry. There are no technical problems with these devices. But I've had the opportunity while my mother is away these recent days to think more about the direction I would like to take Melampus once permanently in charge in just three weeks' time. I've thought about our consumer base, and how we could more effectively reach some of the people who have grown less favorable toward our brand in recent years." He had to speak carefully here. He couldn't share his real feelings. He had to appeal to a corporate Arkling mentality of pity for, rather than true compassion toward, Citizens like Laura.

"As you can see from these figures,"—he flipped on a projector to display some slides he had prepared to present the survey data he had shown Laura—"nearly half the Citizens who own Specters don't want to buy a SpecterX. They cite distrust of our advertiser-based profit model as well as distrust of our partnerships with City government and Mars."

The stock was really dipping now. Dante clenched his stomach.

"While there is of course no reason for their distrust—" (the dip slowed down) "—the perception that there could be is enough to convince these users not to upgrade. Which is where the improvement we are now in the process of implementing in the X's design comes in."

As he continued, he flipped through some slides displaying alterations he and Laura had made to the X's code and hardware.

"I present to you all a privacy-enabled X, which allows the user to choose which information they do and do not wish for us to send to the Source. Now, don't panic: Yes, this does mean that, if certain users activate certain settings, you will not receive personalized information about their desires, nor will you be able to target ads to them personally. However, our data show that this option will persuade nearly all of our lost customers to buy an X—even at a slightly higher price than the one we originally set. And because we'll still be able to use the advertising-based profit model for users who enjoy the personalized suggestions, there will be no loss to your or our bottom lines. We have already produced several units that we will be installing and testing in the animals who will feature in our launch day demo over the coming days. In fact, in order to assure you all that this change has not been too rushed, I am already using a new unit myself." He pointed to his own device. "Should everything go to plan, we will be able to sell this privacy-enabled model on launch day. And I expect you'll all have them in your own hands several days sooner."

By this point in his presentation, the stock had stopped its bleeding, and those who had murmured with one another at the start nodded with approval.

But he needed more to stave off his mother's anger. He would need a theatrical flourish, a show of passion that would make the stock price rocket higher. He was in luck that, as the true genetic heir of the Melampus line, he already had the Board's goodwill.

"Friends," he said with a solemn smile, "nobody alive can know what a privilege it is to grow up on this ship with you all here to mentor me. As I move into the next phase, I want you all to know how seriously I take the thousand-year legacy that both my parents have only strengthened. What began when Olaf Melampus—" (he pointed to the room's obligatory massive portrait of his great-forty-times-over-grandfather) "—built a private island where he could save the Earth's dying wildlife became something far greater, as my family leased the island to those in government and business seeking refuge from the perils of a collapsing world. It has taken a very long time, as Olaf knew it would, but we are on the precipice now: The new Earth is coming."

To Dante's concealed amusement, some of the shareholders had tears in their eyes.

"And with that," he said with a stern nod, "I formally adjourn this meeting."

The entire Board rose to deliver a standing ovation. The stock surged.

—

But this was not the only exciting announcement that day. Although Laura could not attend the Board meeting, she kept track of the stock's price on her phone while Dante was speaking. Her anxiety spiked during the brief interval where the investors grew wary and sent numbers into the red, but she diverted her attention for an unexpected Specter call from her father. (She, too, wore a privacy-enabled X at this point).

Hello?

Laura, Peter transmitted with bold clarity, forgoing all greetings, *I know you'll think I'm crazy, but your mother is on board with it: I'm running for mayor.*

Laura's usual instinct would be to convey total shock and disapproval. But while she was shocked, the claim that Wanda was fine with this decision moderated her reply. *And just how is that going to work?*

I've looked into it, and it's easier than you might think. I need to gather the appropriate signatures, and then submit a petition to the City. Do I think I'll get a chance to debate Teddy Wilcox, let alone win? Hell no. But that won't stop me trying, and it certainly won't stop me from getting some donation money if I can. Turns out repealing all those campaign finance laws can actually work in my favor. I can just keep any donation money once I lose. And hey, I bet you're thinking, "Dad, won't you get in trouble if you go out in public and say your actual opinions?" Well, it turns out that stump speeches count as political speech, and the Terrarchists haven't gotten around to reprogramming the AI to restrict what political candidates can say. Probably because there have been no candidates worth being worried about! So, as long as I'm running my mouth in the context of a campaign, I'm good!

Isn't that also a problem, though? Laura asked. *If your campaign is more successful than you expect, you'll probably cause them to change those laws.*

That would happen if it was me or anyone else with a moral compass running, Peter pointed out. *And I don't really think that's a concern. I'll just make a few speeches at Wanda's farms and whatever other haunts hippie bums like me frequent. Wilcox might not even notice me. I highly doubt this will go anywhere beyond a side gig. And that's what got your mother on board—the fact that this really may be the most realistic way for me to make any cash worth working for at the moment.*

Laura was of course still skeptical, but her father's boyish excitement swayed her. And when she checked her phone again and saw the stock surging at the end of Dante's speech, a rush of optimism pushed her to think a thought that she had never thought she could think.

You know what, Dad? Go for it. Run for mayor. if you've thought it through. It will get the word out on some issues I know are important to you, and it will be funny if nothing else.

But when Laura brought the idea up with Dante later that night, he expressed fear.

That's not going to work, he said. *The Terrarchists have made it so that you have to actually reprogram yourself as a whole separate class of citizen if you want access to free speech protections. There's a whole script you have to send to the Source if you want to register; otherwise, the AI will just shut down any stump speech your father tries to organize. And the script is kept top secret.*

Laura slumped. She had known Peter's plan was too simple to work.

But... Dante continued, with a mischievous grin. *I happen to know the script. My mother uses it whenever we hire new crew members. It's what keeps the Ark and the City as legally separate entities.*

Won't you get caught? Laura asked.

Nope, Dante said. *The Ark has a private terminal to communicate with the Source. And I can program the script to delete itself as soon as it's sent. Nobody will know who did it.*

Laura, feeling quite tender toward Dante, agreed to let him reprogram her father's class in the Source. What was the harm? Peter couldn't possibly get the signatures, after all.

PART TWO:

SIGNATURES

14

Stella Eurydice Melampus grew up on the lowest floor of the City, in the part of the residential ring everyone called The Dump. She was the last person to make it out of The Dump at all, and had been the first Dumpling ever to win the Melampus internship lottery.

Living in The Dump not only meant that your work very likely had to do with waste management or broken bot repair of various kinds (the specific kind depending on whether you worked in the residential ring or one of the three inner rings: agriculture, energy, military), but also that you were, in the eyes of the AI and the upper-floor elites, disposable. It meant that your genome was so incompatible with the societal goal of recolonizing the Earth (for this was, all these centuries of failure later, still the stated goal) that it did not matter if you lived or died. You only existed to clean up the trash of those better than you, and there were plenty of unpromising Citizens on the next-lowest floors to take your place if your body gave out.

Genes being as subject to mutation as they were, of course, it was always possible, though exceptionally rare, that someone in The Dump could prove herself to be of some value. Stella had proven herself. When she was a child, every few years, a professional mentor from a higher floor would ride the elevator down to The Dump and conduct intelligence tests of various kinds on The Dump's children, checking to see if any diamond in the rough might be worth educating enough to bring to a school on the second or even third floor. Stella was the only one of her age group to pass the tests. This practice stopped once the Terrarchists seized power, and Stella was the last Dumpling to benefit from it. The education that she received from her third-floor mentor, Evelyn, who had herself been born a Dumpling, provided Stella with the knowledge she later needed to enter the Melampus lottery.

As Stella exited the ambassador's craft in the spaceport and found herself on Martian ground for the first time, the sights inside one of Mars's dilapidated residential domes, through which she needed to pass to reach the President's quarters, reminded her of The Dump: Multiple families cramped together in single rooms; walls peeling and crumbling, with no repair bots in sight because nobody bothered to program them for "these people" (until an absolute emergency threatened the livelihood of those more fortunate); and, as they passed by Stella in the hallways, the recognizably empty stare, the stare of those who knew too many disappointments to deem anyone a friend, but also did not hold themselves in high enough esteem to care if you were a foe.

The trip through the residential dome was mercifully short; the Martian colony had one-fifth the population of Earth, and this was just one of many such domes. Whereas the Arkology was a meticulously designed, self-sustaining organism built through numerous private-public collaborations, the Mars colony had a more scattershot feel that reflected its rebellious, wholly private origins. Domes connected to one another in no particular arrangement, clearly added one after another as the original two dozen colonists spawned larger and larger generations.

She respected the Martians' anarchic origins, and it was this part of their history that made her so excited to visit the Red Planet. But upon entering the dome at the center of Mars's tentacular constellation of domes, the Dome of the Cognoscenti—the large dome that housed the dozen or so government officials who designated themselves the inheritors of all knowledge that would lead to the flourishing of Mars and, eventually, the colonization of deep space—she reminded herself that no good thing lasted in human affairs. Humans betrayed one another and themselves. Just as those she allowed to be closest to her—Evelyn, Dominic, and lately, she worried, Dante—would all betray her, so, too, had the Martians betrayed themselves, as was clear when she walked into the opulent grand foyer on the dome's ground floor, complete with a swimming pool, marble tile floors, furniture built from gray slabs that tried to look sophisticated but was really just cold, all of it surrounded by the dome's giant glass honeycomb-patterned windows that reminded Stella of desert mansions from before the collapse.

I hate these people, Stella reminded herself. The Martian oligarchs, the Arklings, the Terrarchists, all of them. I am here for a purpose. I am here for a mission. All of this, everything I have committed to for the last thirty years, is a means to an end.

She assumed her most dazzling smile as President Zelda Rogers descended the stairs to greet her and the ambassador with open arms and cheek kisses. She hid all fatigue and negativity as Zelda asked her how she was doing after the trip, which, frankly, had left her bones tired and her thoughts swirling. She laughed every time Zelda, a woman fifteen years her elder of paler complexion and grayer hair (she always did have a fondness for older women), made jokes and teased her, referencing previous visits to Earth when Zelda and her would steal moments away from the Ark's official proceedings and abscond into the Biomes for so-called "wildlife demonstrations": ten minutes, rolling in the Grassland's prairies; five minutes, panting behind a dune in the Desert; one minute, shivering inside a Tundra glacier. But Stella couldn't laugh with much joy, for as soon as those minutes were over, they were no longer real; they were intermissions, releases of tension necessary to continuing the elaborate and exhausting game she and Zelda (and the Cognoscenti who were "in the know") were playing in unison on their respective planets. She knew who Zelda was. She knew there was no "there" there. Still, she would miss her a little once the grand plans came to fruition.

The conversation turned more serious once pleasantries

concluded and they entered Zelda's office. "Please," said Zelda with a hand on Stella's shoulder, "tell me what is happening with your son. What does he think he is doing?"

"Pardon?" Stella raised her eyebrows, smile still glued tight. She hid her panic. Who could have possibly contacted Mars? She and Teddy's folks were the only ones with the proper channels, and there was no way Teddy's folks could have found out about Varuna's bug and Dante's choice to reactivate him...could they? And did this mean Dante hadn't kept his promise to deactivate him? Was Zelda mad that Stella had chosen not to tell her or Johnson about Varuna? The truth was that Stella didn't really care about Varuna—she was perfectly content to let him do his own thing, so long as he kept to himself—but any problem would give Mars pause in executing their plans, which meant it would cause Stella trouble in executing hers. And Stella did not want Zelda to know that the two of them had different goals in mind, even if they were potentially compatible ones.

"The shareholders' meeting. You haven't heard yet?" Zelda asked.

"No," said Stella, frightened.

Zelda then used her Specter (still an original, though one purpose of this trip was for Stella to give her and the other Cognoscenti their specially-designed, custom-made Xs, which Stella carried with her in a briefcase) to share with Stella a message that an angry Teddy Wilcox had transmitted into her inbox the day before.

His thoughts spat with anger. Stella's suspicious anxiety only heightened as the imagined worry gave way to the arguably more concerning reality. *...And he says he's ramping up production to have this be the only model available at launch? Please, when you see her, get Stella to knock some sense into the boy.* The message ended.

"This was not the plan," said Zelda. "You're able to stop this, I imagine?"

"Yes, I think so," said Stella. This must be something he was doing to impress the girl, she figured. She'd have called in the order to fire Laura now if she didn't need a pretty Citizen's face to put on TV for launch day. And it was true, Stella did see herself in the girl. If Laura was manipulating Dante, it would have impressed Stella at least as much as it threatened her. And, perhaps most strangely to the uninformed observer, she loved her son, and it hurt her whenever she did something that would make him unhappy. Everything she did was to protect him, to make sure he was there with her on the new Earth she was building. She would, in the end, need to keep him away from Laura, but she couldn't do it cruelly and thoughtlessly.

"You...*think* so?" Zelda leaned back, touched her fingers together in a steeple.

Stella scratched her neck. "The fact that the shareholders seem to like the new model complicates things a little. But no, I have a plan already."

"You always do," Zelda said. "Don't let me down when it counts."

Stella smiled. "This does mean I can only stay here a day or two, though. I could reverse his decision now, but that would scare the shareholders. And we still need them. Some time needs to pass, so that it will be plausible when I tell them that he and I have rethought things."

"How sad," Zelda sighed. "We could have spent some time together, done some sightseeing, planned for the future—if that's the word you want to use. But I suppose it's straight to business."

Zelda opened a desk drawer and withdrew a folder filled with loose leaf sketches, which she laid out on the desk for Stella and Johnson to see. "These are the designs we settled on after our most recent experiments."

Johnson's jaw dropped as he examined the drawings. Even Stella, who'd seen many previous iterations and worked closely with Zelda on their refinement, shivered when put face-to-face with the monsters: creatures with dragon wings and pig tails; werewolves with flies' eyes and mantis arms; snakes with dagger-toothed smiles and scissors for rattles; sasquatch-like beasts with oozing scabs, black and brown and blue and green. They were the stuff of nightmares, which was the point.

"I can't show you the animations, for obvious reasons," said

Zelda. "But I can confirm we are at a 100% success rate, and we've been very careful—choosing subjects with no family or friends, keeping everything under lock and key in the remotest of tunnels—that sort of thing."

The mention of the tunnels took Stella's eyes away from the drawings and up to the massive map of the Martian underground that covered the wall behind the President's head. Stella didn't know what she found more devilishly exciting to think about: the drawings, or the fact that every day, a thousand Martians toiled in the labyrinths beneath her feet. First they had built a near-replica of the Arkology's AI, the very AI that their distant ancestors had sought to escape but that it then turned out, at least in the Cognoscenti's opinion, was necessary to maintaining their colony's homeostasis. And now, well, what they were building was beyond any of their comprehension: a thing that would render all the previous constructions on which it depended moot.

"You were right," continued Zelda, "when you said you would never have been able to test these designs on the Ark."

Stella's eyes twinkled. "You should never doubt me, Zelda."

Zelda laughed. "It does impress me how nicely everything seems to have come together, your son's little display notwithstanding. I do, of course, wish we had more than a week between the moment of truth and the time he is, theoretically, supposed to take over from you."

"This is how it had to happen," said Stella, a little annoyed at having to explain herself again. "We made a deal ten years ago, and we knew, even then, we had not a minute to spare. Frankly, the fact that we've come so far and set ourselves up for success in the time we had available is miraculous, and proof that a higher power is on our side."

Zelda nodded. She looked askance at the ambassador to make sure he was still fixated on the drawings, then flashed for Stella the rare sort of demure, vulnerable smile that she certainly wouldn't have flashed in his sight. "I judge by the confidence in your tone that you've kept your end of the bargain?"

"I have." Stella laid her briefcase on the desk and opened it, revealing the custom-made Xs and a set of syringes filled with the installation compounds.

Zelda took one of the devices and held it up to the light. She ogled it, wide-eyed, like she heard it calling her mind to merge. "It really is a shame you don't think the boy could get on board with us," she said. "It would make things easier."

"It is a shame," Stella agreed. "But he's just too much like his father."

Stella took a syringe and prepared to replace the two Martians' Specters.

15

Unaware that Stella had changed her plans, the four rebels spent some time plotting their next steps. Everyone agreed that they would use the twelve days they believed they had before Stella's return to make sure they had inserted privacy-enabled Specters into the four animals that were set to appear alongside Prince, Stella, Dante, and Nemos (all of whom, besides Stella, now had private devices) at the product launch day presentation: Iguazu the parrot, who lived in the Rainforest; Soda the polar bear, in the Tundra; and Gunny the prairie dog, in the grassland.

Prince was doing his best to go along with the group's ideas and make everyone happy, but everyone's anxieties pulled him in different directions. Dante, for his part, was both suspicious of the fact that his mother had not contacted him from Mars at any point, and worried that the short timeline would prevent him from fulfilling his promise of producing enough units to make his model the only one available on launch; he spent most of his time over the next several days in the production wing, monitoring the crew's actions and making sure everyone understood the assembly instructions. Laura, meanwhile, worked on her proposal, which she wanted to deliver to the Board for approval before Stella's return. She and Dante found an additional way to occupy themselves when they realized that Varuna's plainly visible Specter would make it obvious to Stella that they were deliberately defying her. They set about modifying the Specter such that it would entrench itself just a bit deeper into Varuna's skull and hide beneath his skin.

Because the two humans were so busy, they were inclined to agree with the suggestion Varuna made when it came to decide how they would go about capturing the three animals they needed for the presentation.

Personally, Varuna transmitted, *I believe we need to set better precedents for how humans and animals interact with one another. It's wrong to stun innocent creatures with tranquilizer bots and drag them onto this ship against their will. We should communicate with them first and persuade them that accepting this new device is in their best interests, especially since—if they are anything like me—they may not have even initially wanted a Specter in the first place.*

Dante considered this. *What do you think would be the most effective way to persuade them?*

For starters, Varuna said, *Prince should be the one to go out and talk to them. He's met them all before, and they know he's trustworthy.*

It would make my life managing production easier if I didn't have to get off the Ark and go chasing all these animals myself, Dante said. *What do you think, Prince? Up for it, boy?*

Terrified of disappointing Dante, Prince immediately agreed. *Okay!*

Later that night, however, as he was chewing his paws at the foot of the bed where Dante slept, he pinged Varuna and shared his real feelings, tail thumping on the bedcovers. *What were you thinking, suggesting that? The animals won't trust me—I'm the first one they talk to when they come out of their sedation. They'll see me and panic. I'll remind them of all the fear they had every time a bugbot buzzed right into them and put them to sleep. A parrot and prairie dog are one thing, but the polar bear? He's going to eat me!*

Varuna clicked at a rhythm Prince could now recognize as laughter. *I haven't talked to you for long, Prince, but I can already tell that you're the type of animal who needs to trust himself more. See yourself the way others see you. You're not scary; you're approachable, friendly, understanding, and also, I believe, capable of great courage, though you haven't always been in the best circumstances to show it. You're going to do great.*

As Varuna said all of these very nice things, Prince's heart grew unexpectedly warm. He found that he could let his jittering tail relax. It was the type of thing Dante used to say to him. He felt seen.

I guess I can try to have more faith in myself, he said.

—

The smells of the rainforest perked Prince up and gave him an exhilarating sense of confidence. Damp moss filled his nose with energy, and the cool, humid air invigorated him. He kept his guard up amid the cacophony of insects and monkeys hooting in the distance, especially since Dante was not with him. Nevertheless, his owner was on standby, ready to intervene at a moment's notice if Prince incited a jaguar's ire for any reason.

Prince neared Iguazu's signal on the tracking map that Dante transmitted to him. Though nervous, he looked forward to catching up with the bird, whose sharp wit and stunning ultraviolet vision had always enriched Prince's view on life.

But Iguazu was, as Prince had feared, not quite as excited to see Prince. When Prince pattered up to the trunk of the mid-size cacao tree where Iguazu was foraging for seeds, the sounds of the underbrush crackling under his paws drew the parrot's attention; he swiveled his head a bit and caught Prince's eye, then immediately fluttered his bright green and red wings all the way up to the top of a very tall kapok tree.

Hey! Prince tried transmitting. *How have you been?*

Iguazu accepted the transmission, but he chose to reply out loud. "Busy!" He squawked. "Go away! Go away!"

Don't run away! You're safe, I promise, Prince tried transmitting—but Iguazu did not bother to receive this message. Prince had no choice but to use his microphone. "I just want to talk!" He shouted with his head craned up toward the 200-foot high canopy. "It's just me. No humans anywhere near. Look around if you don't believe me." He couldn't see Iguazu, but he could very well imagine the bird's stern, shifty-eyed face scanning the horizon.

Why are you here? Iguazu thought to Prince after some delay. *I see the Ark in the distance. What kind of trick is this?*

No trick, said Prince, whose confidence was wavering a bit. He felt like he'd been caught in a lie. *But since you're not in the mood for small talk, I'll cut to the chase. I'm here to help you.*

Iguazu flew down and perched about midway down the kapok tree, low enough for Prince to see his scrutinizing head-jerks. *Help me how?,* he asked.

That SpecterX in your head—it wasn't a lot of fun to get it installed, was it? Prince attached to this message certain images he remembered from Iguazu's tests. Stella and the crew had sent painful jolts into his brain, monitoring his responses as they unearthed the bird's deepest fears, all of which Prince observed as they forced both the animals' channels to remain open (one sequence, where Iguazu was swallowed by a snake, remained especially vivid for Prince). *You didn't like knowing that the humans had access to all your deepest feelings, did you?*

Iguazu looked away. *No,* was the laconic reply.

Well, we want to replace it with a different one. One that lets you keep your thoughts private. I've got one already, and it works great! We're going to give them to the animals who have X's, and then we're going to team up and fight for our rights as free-thinking creatures!

Iguazu chirped out some chuckles. *Yeah, right*—he was one of the few animals who could think in sarcasm—*like I'm going to trust you. You're the dog. You're in their pocket. You know what happened after they gave me this one?* He pointed a wing at the tiny X between his eyes. *My whole flock outcast me! They didn't like the color of my Specter; they said I was marked by the humans and that they couldn't trust me anymore. They harassed and bullied me until I just flapped away and left. Screw them, though! I don't need anyone. And I don't need you, either.*

Iguazu flew back to the top of the tree. Prince's tail sank for a minute, until he noticed that the bird's channel was still open. Some lonely part of Iguazu hoped Prince could persuade him. Prince, remembering Varuna's encouraging words, as well as Nemos's advice when it came to seeing from Dante's perspective, tried a different approach.

Believe it or not, he thought, *I know how you feel. I couldn't really relate to other dogs once I got my first Specter. And now, well—look how you greeted me! It's hard feeling like nobody trusts you. But you know what? There's a new flock on the Ark, waiting for you. Me, Dante, Laura—she's this intern from the City—and Varuna the dolphin (have you met Varuna? He's super smart, just like you, you guys will get along great), we're all working as a team to build a better future for animals.*

Iguazu flew back down, and this time, landed right at Prince's feet. *You seem to believe what you're saying,* he said. *But what makes you think you'll succeed?*

Dante's going to become the new CEO in just over a week, Prince said. *He's on our side. But before that happens, we have to install new devices in all the animals who were scheduled to appear at the product launch. What do you think? Are you in or not?*

Iguazu dipped his beak under his wing to groom himself, clearly buying time to think. *Fine,* he said finally. *Apparently you were all going to force me onto your ship in a few days anyway, and I like doing it this way better. Let's show those humans they can't mess with us!*

That's the spirit! Prince said. As he led Iguazu back to the Ark, he felt capable and competent, and he repressed any concerns about whether Iguazu—and, for that matter, Varuna—were still a little more belligerent toward the humans than he was.

—

Not long after Prince returned to the Ark with Iguazu and introduced him to the other members of the rebel quartet, Laura received a call from her sister. She had kept one eye on the developments with Iguazu, but her focus needed to be on her proposal. She lost this focus when Michelle made her understand that their father's campaign for mayor, which Laura had taken for granted as a frivolity, the latest of Peter's many money-making side-schemes, threatened to represent something more serious.

Michelle tended to keep to herself, and if she needed to vent, it was usually to Sammy or other close friends, so Laura's metaphorical antennae stuck up as soon as she got the call.

How have you been? Laura asked.

Depressed, said Michelle. *I told Sammy we might be moving. She won't talk to me now.*

Why did you tell her that? You don't think Dad's campaign idea could work?

What? No. He came home last night after his first attempt at a so-called stump speech and said he was going to quit. He was drunk as shit, Laura.

This last thought made Laura's mind scatter like an upset colony of ants.

Mom tried talking to him. He just yelled and said to leave him alone, Michelle continued.

Laura was very close with her father during her first few years of life. She loved going to the arcade with him, looking out the windows on the edge of the City that overlooked the Biomes, sitting on his shoulders as he showed her his workplace in the urban planning office and made snarky comments about his colleagues. But as she grew, so did Peter's responsibilities, and the stress of working his way up the ladder from office assistant to clerk to an executive engineer wore him down. He spent less time at home and more time at bars, first to socialize with his coworkers and then to escape the shame of seeing his daughters growing up without him. Arguments with Wanda grew more frequent, and whenever Laura asked about the reasons, Wanda gave her the same tired line: "Don't worry about it. Just keep your head down and be a good girl. He's having man problems."

By the beginning of high school, Peter was entering a self-medicated abyss, and divorce seemed like a possibility. Laura had to do something to keep her parents together. Seeing how disconnected her father felt from his family, she came up with a plan: she would rebel against her mother, who had pressured her to study agriculture and other fields more appropriate for "girls of her class," and commit to studying more masculine subjects like politics and programming.

The truth was that, besides animals, which had always fascinated Laura for their apparent freedom, she chose her intellectual interests to prevent her family from falling apart.

And it worked. One day, Laura waited until her father came home, drunk, to tell Wanda that she was changing her field of study. When her mother made predictable protests, she made sure that her father, lying in bed sick in the other room, could hear Laura screaming at her mother.

"You never care what I want!"

Peter came out and asked what the problem was. When Wanda explained, he of course took Laura's side. Laura jumped on the opportunity to bond with her father, and she made a plan to study for her programming entrance exam with him the next day. When he didn't show up, Laura left the apartment and found him in his favorite bar. She pressed her notes up against the window as he downed a gin and tonic behind the glass. He looked in her eyes and saw what he had become. Over the next few years, he attended group therapy and resolved never to drink again. Things were fractious between Laura and Wanda for a time, but she managed to win her mother back as well, once she proved that she had a real talent for programming and could even apply for the Melampus lottery.

Given all that, Laura's mind went back to the not-too-distant past when she learned her father had slipped. And when Michelle told her the reason he had slipped...

The one thing he said was that people wouldn't donate any money or sign his petition because they didn't trust a man whose daughter worked for Melampus.

...The long-standing feelings of personality responsibility for her entire family's well-being consumed Laura with full force.

It's going to be okay, was all Laura could say to Michelle. But already, she was desperate to find a way to save her father, again.

—

At first, Peter did not answer Laura's calls. She tried to distract herself from her worries—and to help Prince—by keeping a close eye, together with Dante and Varuna, on the poodle's channel as he navigated the tundra. Soda the polar bear was known to be something of a diva, and her large size made Prince nervous. He wore a four-sleeved blue parka, tailor-made by Dante years back, but the cold air and whipping winds still stung his face.

It wasn't really practical to make Prince walk as far as he had to find Iguazu in the ice and snow, so the Ark had landed much closer to Soda's location. Fortunately, the Ark did not in itself scare her away. Whereas the other animals, apart from Prince, tended only to have contact with humans for the purposes of unpleasant experiments, Soda made occasional appearances on the Ark in her role as a Melampus brand mascot. Being the cuddly face of the tundra, the most expensive and most impressive Biome to maintain, Soda served to remind the shareholders of what all their investments helped pay for. She enjoyed posing for the cameras and getting bucketfuls of fish in return.

It was true, however, that she had become pickier since undergoing the experiments for the SpecterX. At her last shoot a few weeks prior, she had insisted on both more and different fish than she typically received, and she demanded that she receive half her compensation before the shoot instead of after.

Prince found Soda lying in the snow asleep, on her back with a paw over her eyes. Behind her, the snow thawed out to reveal some milky-yellow arctic poppies growing in a rocky patch of dirt; behind the dirt was a lake, and on the distant other end of the lake spanned a wide glacier across the horizon. Prince couldn't help but flinch as Soda moved her paw and blinked an eye at him.

Oh, it's you, she said. *I'm pretty tired today, so I hope your master brought a big bucket of fish. Real salmon—not that fake printed stuff.*

Actually, it's just me, said Prince. *No commercial shoot today.*

No shoot?! What do you want, then? Soda rolled over and stood up. Prince nearly peed himself, but she did not lunge at him as feared.

A spectating Dante, who had been laughing at Soda just moments before, whispered into another corner of Prince's mind. *Why would you say that?*

I don't know! Prince answered. *I'm sorry. I just didn't want her to catch me in a lie.*

No choice now, Dante said. *Tell her the truth and see what happens. I've got a tranquilizer bot ready if you need it.*

Prince snorted, then lifted his head to face Soda with fake courage. *We're preparing for Dante's takeover as Melampus CEO in a couple of weeks, and we're replacing all the SpecterX's with the privacy-enabled model he wants to launch.*

Hmm. Soda chuffed. *Tell me more.*

Prince then gave Soda a longer explanation of the past few days' events. When he was done, Soda bowed her head down and, to Prince's hidden terror, touched her nose to his and snorted. Though from different species, their common caniform lineage allowed Prince to intuit the gesture's meaning: She was about to ask him for something.

It's quite an interesting idea, she thought, keeping her nose against his. Her eyes transfixed Prince's attention with the slightest hint of latent aggression. *But I have nothing to gain from it. I am the company's mascot.* They *need* me *more than* I *need* them, *and I sense the same is true here as well. So, I have a proposition for you. I will wear this new device and help your master make his mark...if he promises to stop the ice from melting any further.*

Prince, Dante, and Laura all exchanged surprise. *She wants what?*

Soda backed away and nodded in the direction of the lake behind her. *That lake behind me wasn't here a few years ago. Every day, I see another piece of that glacier break off into the water. I'm...*

Soda stopped, looked away, then snorted with sudden emotion. *I'm six years old, in the prime of my life, ready to mate, but I don't see the point in having a cub when this whole place is vanishing around me.*

Everyone listening to her thoughts resonated on a shared wavelength of sympathy. Underneath the bear they had all believed to be a diva was a wounded, frightened creature.

"That's so sad," Prince heard Laura say out loud to Dante.

I never used to think about these things, said Soda. *But ever since you all put this damned thing in my head, I...I just can't stay in the present anymore.* To everyone's startlement, she raised her head and moaned to the sky, much like a dog howling. Then, she collapsed in the snow. Overcoming his fear, Prince approached and nuzzled her as she issued several loud snorts.

Laura, tears in her eyes, gripped Dante's hand. "We have to help her."

"I wish I could," said Dante, himself nearly on the verge of tears, careful to watch his tone so that Laura wouldn't think he didn't care when he in fact did, "but since we all share the same bubble, our climate control mechanisms are highly regulated and largely under the City's jurisdiction. Even when I am in charge, I don't see any way I can get Wilcox and company on board. They just don't see this as a problem."

Laura, experiencing one of those surges of confidence and inspiration that had become more common since she met Dante, tightened her grip on his hand. *I have an idea,* she thought to him and Prince.

16

Varuna had mostly been content to play the role of observer for several days now. As Dante and Laura carefully plotted their next moves and tried to control their environments (the way all humans did), he struggled to distance himself from his lifelong attitudes toward *Homo sapiens sapiens*.

To put it as simply as possible, Varuna loathed and envied and worshipped the humans for their artifice, their ability to ignore every connection to the cosmic source of their being that might for a second bother them with feelings of longing, imperfection, fear, or emptiness. As they reconstructed a world that they had already destroyed once before, they demonstrated a complete failure to acknowledge that all of the cosmos shared the feeling that they fought so hard to ignore: was this it? Was this all there was? And in ignoring that question, they had denied themselves true transcendence, again and again, repeated their mistake again and again, picked at a scab that was their intoxicating illusion of togetherness.

As Varuna knew, one needed to admit that things did not cohere, that the center could not hold, or else one could never truly know the center. He, in contrast to everyone he encountered in his life, would not repeat that mistake. He would go to the limit. He would master chaos.

In his childhood and adolescence, chaos had been the

intruder, the controller. Since he was smaller than most other males, the other calves ganged up on him during hunting practice, and his mother only made things worse by keeping him close to protect him. He was the mama's boy of the pod, and one day, he grew so resentful of being controlled that he swam away from home in search of a different pod. But before he got too far away, he found the grotto library. That dark cave, with its sonar-sculpted recesses of infinite specificity and detail, was a sanctuary. He didn't get to read too many of the ancestral recordings before his mother found him and fin-slapped him into contrition, but from then on, whenever she was asleep, he would go back to his sanctuary and learn about the world.

He started with texts on physical and mental self-improvement. He was not the first scrawny outcast to haunt the cave. As those who came before taught him, the art of the fight was less a matter of raw strength and more a matter of knowing your opponent's next move. Emboldened by knowledge, Varuna went back to his peers and studied, as though above his own body, the way they attacked him, brutalized him, until, little by little, he figured them out, and he began to shock them. Within a few years, he had mastered every move: The jaw-clap. The tussle. The tail-bite. Nobody went near him again, and that was how he wanted it.

Until, that is, he went to the library for the first time in a while and met Xavier, a runaway from another pod who had found himself in a situation very similar to Varuna's. The difference was that Xavier's outcast status was not strictly because of physical weakness, but largely because of the thing between his eyes.

Xavier explained that he was in the library to learn more about humans. He actually liked the Specter. He liked the otherworldly visions that welled up from his subconscious as the humans tickled his brain and shared their way of thinking with him. He didn't know how many other animals had them, but the only one he had ever seen was a dog he played with on the beach once.

He thought understanding the humans was the way to join them, to be rescued by them and escape the cruel confines of cetacean existence. And that was Varuna's initial attitude toward them as well. He absorbed Xavier's visions in sound and he searched every inch of the grotto for traces of knowledge that could explain them. He learned the humans' history and joined Xavier in ecstatic hope for a body that transcended his own, and as the ecstasy grew more and more, so, too, did their bodies grow farther outside themselves, until they found themselves crossed together, penetrating one another on a separate plane, penetrating each and every center of intelligence and passion they had never known was theirs to claim.

And then, they murdered him. The humans blasted Xavier's mind so far into extracorporeal space that his body had no choice but to destroy itself.

Varuna would never forget what Xavier kept saying those last few days. *A thing with long arms, a thing with no face, a thing whose entire body beats with a heart that cannot be seen.* Varuna failed to elicit from him anything more than the hollowest waveform of an image. *I cannot show it to you,* Xavier said. *I cannot let you see. I would never do that to you.*

When Varuna found the only thing he'd ever cared about smashed against the rocks, his mind had already gone so far outside itself that it was really no trouble at all for him to forget his heart, to self-amputate away all longing and all caring. And when members of his own pod disappeared for days at a time and came back with Specters, he didn't care. When some of them, too, destroyed themselves, he didn't care. When some of them didn't kill themselves, and instead began communicating with one another about a whole artificial mythology that he recognized as Xavier's germ, he didn't care. And years later, when a blink of an eye was the difference between a tranquilizer zipping toward him and his awakening in a glass cage on the Ark, he didn't care. All of it was information. Information was neutral, and it was everything. He did not need to care about anything.

He reveled in the oscillation between telling the humans what they wanted to hear and then telling them *NO*, the way he had needed to tell his mother no. But this no, a no of concealment, was different. They did not understand concealment, he understood. It vexed them, agitated them. Once he saw this side of the humans, he saw their entire history in a different light. And as the experiments continued, he began to see the thing that Xavier refused to show him. But it was not as visible to Varuna as it had been to Xavier. They hid it now, for some reason. The thing with long arms and no face and a body that beat with an invisible heart. But it was lurking in all of them, especially the boy and his mother, guiding their actions toward some ungraspable telos.

The thing was not in the dog. The dog was a surprise. Varuna had just been playing his usual game, dancing with those who tried to catch them, goading them with the same message he had conveyed to that THING through the language of his estranged heart all those years:

Come and find me, come and find me. I dare you.

What found him that day was not the THING, but a bark in the deep. He turned around and scooped him onto his back not out of compassion but out of urgency. There was an immediate recognition of the dog Xavier had momentarily befriended, and an immediate apprehension that Prince could be leverage in his fight against the humans and against the THING.

He planted a seed of a vision in the dog's mind and watched as the dog came back and fell into his sonic well and gave his rhythm away to his own. He watched as the humans responded to the dog's fainting (which really was an accident). He saw that the dog was nothing in the humans' eyes, not really. And the dog knew it. Prince knew he was a void around which the humans rearranged themselves, the fulcrum of their self-perception. If Varuna could get to the dog, he could get to the humans. And these humans, Varuna noticed immediately, were the kind of humans that were hungry for more, hungry to go beyond their humanness and unable to accept it. He was confident that he could mesmerize them with his promises of individuation, the fiction that they could be anything larger than they were.

The more he worked with them, the more sure he was that they, too, were voids. In Varuna's mind, everyone was a void except him. With this belief, he executed his plan to usurp the humans and enact his revenge on Xavier's behalf. He would sit and watch as all the little voids danced around each other and then, at the very second they stopped moving, he would take his opportunity to expand, to push them in the direction he needed them to go.

—

That was what Varuna did when Laura invited her father to the Biomes to record a campaign commercial with Soda. The process took several days: Laura needed to get in touch with her father, to convince him that he didn't need to quit, that she could help him (it was sad, Varuna thought, how deeply she invested her self-worth in her ability to help the pathetic man).

Meanwhile, Prince needed to get Soda on board with the plan, to explain to her (with Dante's help) all the complex political dynamics involved, that this was the best they could do, that it might not lead anywhere, but that he hoped it would show a genuine effort that would get Soda to follow their (i.e. Varuna's) vision. And once Peter and Soda both agreed, Dante needed to help Laura guide her father through the process of requesting a permit to access the Biomes, a process that involved a great financial cost that Dante helped Peter to pay through agile rearranging of the company's financial ledger. A whole week would pass before Peter could find his way into the tundra with Soda by his side, the two of them facing a set of film equipment Dante brought out from his ship.

During that week, Varuna took stock of the current circumstances and interpreted them through the lens of his years of research into human behavior and society. Then, when his pawns all sat together by his tank and debated what Peter should say in his commercial, what he should do to get the public more on his side, Varuna noticed that the voids had reached a standstill, and he took his opportunity to inflate himself.

I have a few suggestions, he said humbly.

Though the speechwriting process appeared to be

collaborative, Varuna orchestrated the tone and tenor. He knew what the humans really wanted out of their lives in a way they couldn't, because they were too wrapped up in themselves to see.

It was a proud moment for Varuna when, tapped into Prince's Specter, he got to vicariously watch Peter, wrapped up in his parka and scratching behind Soda's ear in the middle of a gentle snowstorm, clear his dry, cold throat and speak to the cameras.

"I'm Peter Delacroix, and I'm running for mayor. I have some things to say, the first being that if you're surprised I can say whatever I want right now, let me alert you to the fact that a specific line of code in the speech surveillance program exempts me from the reprogramming procedure if I declare political candidacy, which, despite a lot of smoke and mirrors and red tape, turned out to be a rather simple procedure, thanks in part to the knowledge I gained working beside the mayor."

Varuna knew they were going to have to edit that line out.

"Anyway, I'm here in the tundra because it's the perfect microcosm for the whole world we've found ourselves trapped in. Look at the lake behind me. Just three years ago, all of that was ice. Sound familiar? It may not if you're under the age of twenty, since it was around twenty years ago that they banned all the history sites that might give you a clue what was happening. Back then it was called global warming, but it doesn't really make sense to call it that now, since we don't really live on "the globe" anymore, and it's not really our whole bubble getting warmer, just this part of it. But that's about where the differences stop. The rest is pretty similar. There's a few rich people at the top of the social ladder—the literal top, in our case—trying to extract as much wealth from us as they can while the Biomes and our whole infrastructure fall apart. But what's the end game this time? They won't be able to build another island in a bubble. I don't know what the end game is, but I sure as hell would love to get into the servers and find out. Wouldn't you all like to know? I know I might sound preachy, like another Technogalitarian Wilcox hired to be the controlled opposition this time around, but guess what? He's not even going to bother to do that this time, because he knows he doesn't have to. Everyone's so scared of getting arrested and getting their tongues ripped out. If you're as mad as I am, go to my website and sign my petition so I can get a spot on the debate stage next to Wilcox. Soda, would you like to say anything?"

Soda, outfitted with a microphone that could vocalize her thoughts like Prince's, raised her head and looked at the camera.

"You all know me as the Melampus brand mascot, but I'm here to support Peter because he has a different vision for the bubble than the Arklings do. I want to say that I'm sick of feeling like a robot. I'm sick of feeling like a cog in a machine that's programmed to run the exact same way as some machine that came before me a thousand years ago and like there's nothing I can do to stop it. Peter wants to stop the machine. He wants to restore the principles of freedom and equality that your ancestors tried and failed to practice. These aren't principles you can put into code; you have to feel them in your hearts."

Laura and Dante's eyes welled up with tears. Prince's tail slumped. Varuna, meanwhile, stayed static in his tank, eyes open in the water as ever, double slit pupils gazing sideways at the blurry nothing.

"I understand if you're cynical," Soda concluded, "but the question is not if this can happen. The question is if you'll let it happen."

And as Dante shut off the cameras and clapped for Peter, who took his daughter in his arm and kissed her hair, Varuna knew, deep in the waxy, prophetic, bioacoustic flesh of his melon, that they, they who long ago gave themselves over to the THING, would never, ever, ever, ever let it happen.

17

Dante's heart thrashed against his ribs as he walked toward his mother's office.

The announcement of Stella's sudden return from Mars, five days earlier than expected, sent his nerves into overdrive. He felt like he was splitting in half as it became clear just how many of the decisions he had made in recent months depended on the people around him and the roles he felt necessary to play to appease them. The role of loyal company heir collided with his newest role of passionate activist.

The decision to embody masculinity six years earlier had entailed such a transcendence of his ego, such a realization that he would annihilate himself if he did not bring his body in sync with his mind and his heart, the chasm between them having grown exponentially since his father's death and Stewart's departure from the company, that he was shocked to find that Laura demanded yet more growth from him. Even the decision to show the world in an undeniable way that he was a man, he was coming to understand, was one he could only have found the courage to do if it was in some reference to an authority, specifically the maternal authority he found so alien and against which he needed to rebel.

His mother had no choice but to believe him when he told her he had programmed a failsafe into his own genome, an autoimmune enzyme that would release if anyone attempted to reverse his chromosomes back to double-X. As monstrous as she could be, Stella loved her son, in whatever way she was capable of love; he was, after all, her emotional supply. But no such failsafe lay hidden in his helices, for this had been just one step too far in the direction of self-acceptance for Dante. He imagined some arbitrary future where, as CEO, he would somehow need to pretend to be a woman again, even though all evidence had shown that the other Arklings were too wrapped up in personal careerism to question the gender of he who was soon to be their leader. When Dante really submitted himself to introspection, he recognized that his need to suppress whatever moral instincts he had in the name of keeping the Melampus brand consistent had a lot to do with an undying love for and loyalty to his dead father. If he could keep Melampus happy, he could quiet his father's ghost.

Then came Laura, and the absolute shock of meeting someone who obeyed no master but her own inner sense of caring and moral certainty. True, she sacrificed herself for her father, but it was not because he was her father, and therefore some representative of structure (Peter was anything but structured, Dante discovered upon meeting him), but because he happened to be a person with a lack that she could fulfill. And it made Dante uncomfortable to know that she had seen a lack in him, that he was at least in part committing to her quest to transform the Arkology for the selfish reason of wanting her love, wanting her to touch his shoulder, to see him as a man who didn't fit in among the men or women of the Ark. It made him ashamed to see his own needs, and he had an automatic response to draw back from them as soon as they were manifest.

For that reason, there was a strange sense of comfort in the panic that his mother's return caused. *Help me, Mommy*, he found himself thinking without willing. *I'm like a reptile; my skin is sloughing off, and this girl is about to see me.*

But no. He didn't like those thoughts. He was a man now, and he was about to take charge. He cleared his throat and corrected his posture just before opening the door and facing his mother.

Stella donned a smile and rose to kiss her son. On her desk were a folder and, beside it, an orange. Behind her was a minibar, where she went to pour herself and Dante some wine. She had put on a set of long, lacquered, violet nails for the occasion. "I heard you had a very successful trial as chief executive," she asked as wine glugged into its glass.

"I did." Dante focused on his breathing to stay grounded.

Stella smiled as she sat down. She picked up the orange, then started to dig her middle nail into it. Small drops of juice squirted out. Dante wanted to ignore these small details, but an orange was never just an orange with his mother. She was showing she could get under his skin.

"Can we just skip to the part where you tell me what you want? And threaten me if you don't get it?"

With a light chuckle, she curled her nail under the peel. "I just want to know why you took it upon yourself to propose such a radical redesign days before our launch." The peel came off in long ribbons, which she set aside one at a time. "The redesign itself isn't a...*stupid* one, but every officer has this tired look on their face, and I'm worried they'll resent the both of us when I explain that we are going back to the original launch."

She balanced the naked, peeled orange on the tips of her nails, then removed a wedge to offer to Dante. He raised his hand to decline.

"How about this?" She said as she sucked the wedge's guts out. I'll tell the board that we can introduce the privacy-enabled model in a few months, as a special deluxe option. Hopefully, that won't shake their confidence too much."

Dante bristled. What infuriated him most about talking to his mother was that he could never trust his own reactions to her manipulation. If he lashed out, he would prove her right and make things worse.

"Why even rock the boat?" He asked with a slight edge but clear control. "Production is on target. The only reasons you have to stop my redesign are either sheer spite or...some deal you have worked out with Wilcox."

Stella shrugged—probably the most annoying thing she could have done.

"You're keeping me in the dark about something," Dante said. "What is it?"

"I would love to be totally transparent with you..." Stella picked up the pace of her eating; she popped one wedge into her mouth after another. "...but you've proven yourself again and again to be a loose cannon. There's going to be a transitional period as I transfer command to you, and there's a lot of sensitive data that I need to make sure I can trust you with. Some of it may not even be necessary to Melampus operations, and I'm considering whether I may just want to hang on to it if you continue your recent activist escapades. I hope you understand."

Dante laughed and shook his head. "This isn't even about money for you. It's about control. You just love the idea of collecting people's deepest thoughts and desires and selling them for profit."

Stella, having finished the orange, spun her wine glass and squinted. "It's the girl, isn't it?" She stuck her bottom lip out in mock pity. "Oh, you poor thing. That's what this is about."

"Don't talk about her!" Dante slammed his hand on the table, then drew back in shame. Stella wore a look of exaggerated fear. "She has a name," Dante said with his eyes averted. "Laura."

Stella reached over the desk and touched her son's arm. "She's only paying attention to you for your power. But imagine how little she'll care about you if I make all your power disappear in an instant. The Board will have no problem letting me stay on for as long as I must. Worst comes to worst, they'll generate some new heir with the patriline's DNA in vitro."

Dante rolled his eyes. This was the threat he'd been waiting for. "Go ahead. Reveal my secret. Half the Board knows I'm trans already."

"Go ahead? Really? I have a hard time imagining you roughing it out in the City once reprogramming sends you down to The Dump. You'll be hated there. I would know."

And just like that, Dante imagined himself flailing among Citizens who would see him as enemies, completely out of his element, and all the resolve he'd mustered for this conversation started to vanish. He quivered.

"But very well," Stella continued, "if you're content to throw your own power away, maybe you'll be a little less eager to throw away hers." She opened the folder and pulled out a document that Dante recognized as Laura's research proposal. "I can see that she rushed this proposal to the Board this morning—probably hoping she could get a vote on it before I returned, yes? Unfortunately, that plan didn't work out." She leaned back in her chair, licking her fingers as she flipped through the pages. "I read through it. It's a wonderful proposal. Quite illuminating in several respects. So illuminating, in fact..."

Dante flinched and dodged as she threw the stapled pages into his face and sent them flopping onto the ground behind him.

"...that it almost seems like she doesn't have any actual work left to do. Which is why I have no problem voting it down and letting her scrub our toilets for the rest of the year."

Dante shook with anger. He had to get out of this, or else he would snap. He knew Laura would be angry if he bowed to his mother's will, but he would be doing it to protect her.

Stella stood up, walked behind Dante, picked the pages back up, and dangled them in front of his face. "Whatever happens next week, I'm not leaving the Board, and my vote is the difference between her becoming a princess and her continuing to be a scullery maid."

She pinched the document between her nails and, slowly, bent the pages until they tore just the smallest amount.

"Okay!" Dante grabbed his mother's wrists. "Stop."

Stella kissed her son's head, then sat back down. "So we've come to an agreement, then. I'll call a special meeting this afternoon."

Dante sighed, both relief and shame flooding his body.

"And one more thing," Stella said as she brushed the ribbons of orange peel into the trash. "Stop talking to her."

18

Laura may not have been that angry with Dante had the agreement been as Stella promised. But at the end of the emergency meeting, after announcing the postponement of the privacy-enabled model and reverting to the original launch plan, Stella pulled the rug out from under them both: "Oh, right. Before we adjourn, let me turn to the subject of our Citizen intern, Laura Delacroix. Laura, as you all have seen, submitted a wonderful research proposal in hopes of pursuing a project that would land her a permanent job with us. While I have every confidence in her, I have taken the liberty of rejecting the proposal because the problem she has identified is in fact not very relevant to the success of our product. The malfunction in Varuna's device is an isolated and well-understood incident, and I will make repairs promptly. Ms. Delacroix is welcome to present the Board with an alternative proposal."

The betrayal was worse than any she could have anticipated. That night, Laura refused to speak to Dante, and she only received his apologies through her Specter's inbox.

Laura, she lied to me...

Laura, I'm so sorry...

Laura, I want to fix this...

She listened to the messages long enough to infer the general sentiment and then deleted them. He wasn't saying anything she didn't already know. She knew he was sorry.

But as the messages kept coming, and as she saw how important her forgiveness was to him, her principled anger dissolved and gave way to more complicated emotions.

She was falling in love with Dante. At least, she hoped it was love. She could only hope, because at the core of the feeling was a deep selfishness. As she worked with Dante more and more, and as she had won his devotion to her ideological cause, she learned to recognize the thick, tangled knot of fear and angst at his core. And as she recognized it more, she found herself yearning to loosen just some of the many threads of insecurity that bound the knot together. She would tell him what a good job he was doing with her father. She would bring him meals as he worked to scale up the private model. And when he was suddenly terrified at the immense responsibility he was assuming in charting a separate course for his professional vision, she would hold him, and she would tell him he was good, that he had a heart that would lead him to do the right thing.

The bond had been one of affectionate friendship, but the initial fear he had intentionally betrayed her stirred up such rage that she had to accept that she was starting to see it as something potentially more.

As the night wore on, the anger gave way to shame. She hadn't been angry with him for the reasons she'd been angry with him the first time his mother had told him to stay away from her. She could pretend that he had no principles, that he cared only about privilege, but she knew his fear too well now to believe it. No, she was angry because he had let his fear take him away from her, if only in a moment of well-meaning weakness, and in doing so, he had refused her the satisfaction of helping him. Lying in her bed at midnight, she wondered if she had any of the morals she claimed to have, or if everything she did was for the sake of feeling useful and thus empowered.

Then, on the fourth message, the desperation in his voice, and the pain of her own shame, forced her to listen to the end.

Laura, please just listen! I know I fucked up, but we can still make this right. My mom is planning to remove and replace our Specters tomorrow—she's going to use some legal excuse and say we aren't authorized to wear company property—but she's asleep now, and we still have time to coordinate a plan in private. Varuna and Prince and I have been talking, and we're going to get Iguazu to go out and catch Edie the octopus. Why her, you ask? She's the only animal besides Varuna who can synchronize, and unlike Varuna, she has limbs that she can use to travel around the ship and connect with the other animals on launch day.

(It was true, Laura remembered, that each arm of an octopus possessed its own semi-autonomous nervous system.)

We're going to ask her to help us to build a private network, no special Specters required. The problem is that we need to keep her presence on the ship a secret. I'm going to go get Iguazu and exit the ship through the southern gangway. Then, I'll set him loose toward the beach and feed him information on Edie's present location. He'll catch her, bring her back to me, and I'll smuggle her back on the ship and take her to my room, where there aren't any cameras. This can only work if you help, though. I need you to log into the Ark's security system and shut off the cameras in both Iguazu's terrarium and the southern corridor. I would do it myself, but I'm busy building a tank for Edie in my room, and I need the cameras to be off for as little time as possible. What do you say? Send me word that you're on board, and I will send you my credentials.

Laura could only laugh at the absurdity of the plan. She could never have believed a month earlier that, tonight, she would be helping the Melampus heir use a parrot to smuggle an octopus on board the Ark in a plan to sabotage the company's long-advertised product launch.

The truth was that she was already tired. She did not think that her desperate ploy to be useful to her father five years earlier would have resulted in this mess. She never thought she was built to handle such grand, dangerous maneuvers. Her ideals and principles were for the sake of helping a select few who were close to her, and that was all. Beyond that, she wanted only to pursue her research and discover something profound about the human and animal condition.

But she had no choice but to say yes, because she knew

that in spite of the absurdity, this was an opportunity to prove she was useful.

—

The plan to rely on Edie the octopus was not one that Varuna had agreed to easily. Earlier in the day, when Prince first approached and expressed his despair at the situation Dante and Laura found themselves in, Varuna refused to disclose the existence of any other animals who could synchronize.

If there's really nobody else, Prince suggested, *then maybe we can have Dante turn off the cameras and bring the animals in here to synchronize with you.*

The idea was for the animals in the demo to offload whatever thoughts Stella would try to provoke from them (through humane means or otherwise) into their private channel with Varuna. These transmissions would fail to register on their devices, and the launch would be a disaster. But this wouldn't work, Varuna knew. The launch demo would involve multiple animals, and he could only communicate synchronously with one subject at a time.

Seeing he had no other option, he swallowed his pride. *There* is *the octopus,* he said.

Edie? Prince responded with excitement. *Why didn't you say so earlier? She'll be perfect! She can crawl through small spaces, and she can camouflage. She'll have no trouble at all getting to all the animals before the demo.*

Varuna whistled. *She may hesitate to work with us. The octopuses are a little resentful of the ways my species hunts them. Not to mention the differences in our mythologies.*

As Varuna explained to Prince, the cephalopods believed they descended from beings with origins in the star system of Ophiuchus, the "serpent-bearer" constellation that was also supposedly home to the distant ancestors of snakes and other reptiles, as well as arachnids. The story went that dolphins and octopuses could trace their epoch-long rivalry to some kind of blood feud that still to this day raged between the beings of Sirius and the beings of Ophiuchus.

Every time Prince learned more from Varuna about the supposed celestial origins of the Earth's animals, he grew more excited to participate in a struggle that had some relation to his cosmic origins. He had no suspicion that Varuna was anyone other than who he claimed to be, an ardent romantic whose desire to lead the Earth's animals to the cosmos was a goal born of noble ideals. And it wouldn't be fair to deny that Varuna was a romantic; it was just that the great consummation of romance that lay on his aspirational horizon was not the vision of togetherness that Prince now nurtured in his own mind but rather a very personal realization of justice and redemption.

Prince did see a little more about Varuna than Varuna was comfortable with. He could see that Varuna carried immense pain in his being, and he could see that Varuna did have an inherent and automatic distrust of humans, even if the trust Varuna placed in Dante and Laura was enough to keep Prince hoping that this prejudice was malleable. Prince did not share the prejudice (he couldn't share it; the humans were the source of his entire world), but he understood it enough to overlook it.

The more that Prince got to know Varuna, however, the more he became aware of the blind spots in his friendly canine worldview. It was all well and good to see oneself as a vehicle for connection between the different species, the way Prince always had, but one's ability to connect with another depended on a clear attunement to dissonance, and the more Prince heard Varuna's opinions on human shortsightedness, the more he found himself in agreement, recognizing the dissonance between his dog mind and his human mind. Dante, and to a lesser extent Dante's parents, had pretty much been the sole source of Prince's self-concept, and Prince was coming to understand that it was not much of a self-concept at all.

The problem, of course, was that something deep inside Prince had compelled him to actively participate in the outsourcing of his self-concept. One could debate whether that compulsion had its origins in nature (Prince was, despite all, a domestic dog) or nurture (the word "independence" could barely find a spot in his olfactory lexicon when he had spent the entire first year of his life eating, sleeping, defecating, and learning at the exact minute when the humans who had taken him away from his mother at four weeks old told him to), but it was deep nonetheless, and Prince found himself repeating it even in the process of (somewhat) recognizing it. In other words, he unconsciously bonded to Varuna the way he once had to Dante.

It was not that Varuna supplanted Dante—Prince could never not love Dante—but he proved a worthy substitute in Dante's absence, an absence that Prince had only felt more strongly in the last few weeks. Yes, he had secured Dante's respect and shown his ability to "work with" him, but the partnership was sterile, professional, nothing like it had been when Prince was the only one Dante wanted to touch. There was a void now, and into this void came the messages of assurance that Varuna offered every time Prince expressed self-doubt during their increasingly frequent conversations.

You can be someone else.

You can be courageous.

You can be who you're meant to be: not just a dog, but a wolf.

In short, *I am different* was the message Prince lifted from Varuna. *Everyone is different, and that's what makes us all the same.* And though this message was true, the sudden emphasis on difference led Prince to take on some ideas that would have previously disturbed him: for example, Varuna's insistence that the only way to get Edie on board with their plan was to force her, to get Dante and Iguazu to catch her.

Well, Prince replied after giving it a moment's thought, *if the octopuses really are as alien and antagonistic as you say they are, then I guess we do have to catch her.* The fact that Varuna had previously insisted Prince convince the other animals to join them via diplomatic means did not bother Prince; this seemed like an extenuating emergency circumstance that demanded an exception, especially since Prince knew they needed to act quickly.

And so Varuna planted another seed of manipulation that sprouted through Prince into Dante and then into Laura.

Iguazu expressed some initial skepticism toward the plan (*You're really telling me that each of her legs can privately connect to a separate mind?*), but on Varuna's assurances that this was indeed true (and an endorsement from Dante, who, based on his knowledge of cephalopod neurology, could see that it probably was), he agreed to work with them (not least because he was also quite afraid of ending up back in the forest on his own). By the end of the night, Edie the terrified octopus was sulking in a tank in Dante's room.

—

Before we get to the consequences of Edie's capture, however, there is something to be said for Dante's continuing influence on Prince in one key respect. During their nightly conversations, which were the one time Prince, curled up in Dante's bed, could still see his human one-on-one, Dante confessed to Prince that he was developing romantic feelings for Laura.

"She makes me feel like a distinct person, with my own body and my own passions."

Prince would not have admitted it, but he was jealous of Dante's ability to indulge such feelings, and he wondered what his heart could have felt in his life had the humans not snipped his organs when he was a puppy.

The lack of these organs had never bothered Prince before. But now, whenever Varuna invoked the love of the cosmos, or called him "wolf," a phantom of desire seemed to wisp between his hind legs and make its way into his gut.

Prince and Varuna talked every day by this time. Although they could have talked remotely, Prince enjoyed sitting against his tank, receiving his transmissions without the milliseconds of delay that separated their brainwaves when farther apart on the ship. Varuna would ask Prince questions about space travel, which he understood to be a greater priority for the humans on Mars. Prince would tell Varuna what he knew based on his conversations with Dante over the years.

I don't know all the details, Prince would say. *But I know that Mars has worked for a long time on traveling faster than light. Dante thinks they might be close, and that his mom might be working with Mars on some kind of hyperdrive. But again, I don't know all the details.*

The limited information frustrated Varuna, but he was patient enough. It was necessary to complete stage one of his plan—usurping the humans—before he could consider stage two.

On the night of Edie's capture, as they waited to hear how Dante and Iguazu's hunt went, Varuna stirred the phantom that had infiltrated Prince's body through elaborate visions of the extraterrestrial journey he intended to shepherd.

We'll use the Martians' technology to turn the Ark into a spaceship, and every animal in the Biomes will be here on the Ark. But in the wheelhouse, steering the ship, watching the stars blast by us through the windows, it will be you and me, the captains of this revolution.

The picture Varuna painted in Prince's mind was, as with all images he sent through his cetacean mind, a richly detailed soundscape that etched itself into the outline of a scene. But because of the limitations in Varuna's senses of sight and smell, it was monochrome, odorless. These limitations had not presented themselves as limitations for Prince, whose curiosity always found an abundance of objects in Varuna's uniquely vibrational intelligence.

But on this night, the particular image Varuna transmitted awoke such longing in Prince that he wanted to imbue the scene with his own intelligence, that olfactory intelligence he had kept hidden because it seemed so irrelevant to Varuna's vision. So, as Prince studied the sonic outline of two beings side by side (Varuna, to Prince's astonishment, wore mechanical limbs that allowed him to stand upright), he added two details before pinging the image back to its sender:

First, he added a sense of smell to the scene; he conveyed the briny smell of Varuna's skin that would be sure to flood his nose if they were ever so close together.

Second, he made himself stand upright in the scene; and then, he placed his paw in the claw that extended from Varuna's fin.

The phantom of desire found its way into the image. It

floated like a silhouette in the gap between their brains. That it possessed Prince from that moment forward was no great surprise. But that it found, if only for a moment, a way to emanate its scent through the wall Varuna had erected between himself and the world he sought to control...well, that was quite the shock.

Varuna assured himself he hadn't felt anything.

19

I will try my best to keep going. I will try my best to represent everyone's point-of-view, to do full justice to the complexities of everything that transpired. I am trying my best to, for lack of a better word, humanize everyone, but I can no longer avoid my own presence in the telling of this story. I started out writing a historical text of sorts, and it threatens to become a twisted sort of memoir, which scares me.

Everyone has their minds made up as to who was right and who was wrong, and I probably can't change that. I have no idea who will respond to this story when it is finished, and I may not even be here to see. Every day, my neck hangs lower, and my feet seem to grow a little less connected to the hips that have become so stiff and sore. The doctors refuse to tell me I'm dying, but I know it's true. And I am no longer trying to resist it. I don't think many of my readers will know how exhausting it is to tap into the Source, to find out what so many different people and animals thought and felt at so many different moments. And then there's the writing, which always fails. How tragic that I cannot write and connect to the Source at the same time. As soon as I disconnect, I find myself back in this weak and frail body, this body that can claim neither full humanness nor full animality, and all I can do is tell the screen to record the words that best capture my faint present impression of whatever fleeting transformative and beautiful thing I experienced for just a few moments through the eyes of another being (even my own eyes, five years in the past, do not feel like they belong to me).

I hope my reader will forgive me if I need to move through certain things a little more quickly now, for a few reasons: first, the transience of my body is becoming ever more apparent; second, I am entering into a part of the story where things became more painful, and I know that if I dwell too long in the pain I will die before the story is told, and I need the story to reach its end, however imperfectly; and third, I recognize that my attempt at a magnified, panoramic view of everything that happened to everyone and everything that everyone did in response and where and when every single word that was said was said ceases at a certain point to be an act of compassion and starts to become an act of self-indulgence, an act of falling so far inward to grasp at the thing that has been lost from my current self that I can no longer speak to what is beautiful in the present or what could be beautiful in the future, and all I wanted or at least claimed to want when I started this behemoth of a project was to show everybody just how much beauty there still could be in the future.

Anyway, with those disclaimers, let me tell you what Stella did the morning after Edie's capture.

—

What many people (human or animal) don't know about Stella is that she acted with her heart. It was a cold, stabbed, desiccated heart, but a heart that beat all the same, that wanted to repair everything she believed wrong in the world. She was careful where she placed whatever limited quantity of love and trust she had. Nobody had all of it. But Dante, harsh though she was to him, had quite a bit of it, which meant that the recognition that he was acting behind her back hurt and enraged her so much more than it would have anyone who had a more expansive reservoir of love to draw on than she did.

She had a sense that something was off when, early in the morning, Officer Naismith alerted her to an outage on two cameras in Iguazu's terrarium and the southern corridor.

Outages happened every once in a while, but the timing was strange, especially for two to go out at once. She told Naismith to wait to send maintenance until she could go out and look at the cameras herself.

She noted no physical damage to the camera in the southern corridor, which intrigued her further.

As she approached Iguazu's terrarium, she heard the bird's quiet squawking. Being a parrot, and an anxious one at that, he regularly repeated snippets of various conversations he had overheard. Stella paced down the hall, then stopped upon hearing him utter a specific word.

"Secret! Secret!"

She waited to hear what else he would say.

"Go with Dante!" He muttered repeatedly at one point. Then:

"Don't tell Stella!"

The evidence of a conscious betrayal set the dead underbrush of her heart on fire. She stepped forward into Iguazu's view and placed her hands against the glass tank with a jaguar's smile.

"Just what are you blabbing about, you old bird?"

Iguazu, perched on a rock, flapped his wings and flew around his tank in shock. "Secret! Secret!" Ashamed he had given into his nervous tics, he searched for a place to hide among the miniature palms and shrubs that decorated his artificial habitat.

"What's your secret?" Stella tapped her violet nails on the glass. "Tell me, you featherbrained fogey!"

Seeing there was nowhere to hide, Iguazu returned to his rock and tried to silence himself by sticking his head under his wing. "Don't tell Stella! Don't tell Stella!" His words, though muffled, remained audible.

"Fine." Stella rolled her eyes as the bird quivered in fear. "You'll let me know the hard way." She transmitted an order to Officer Sherman to diffuse sedative gas into Iguazu's tank (she would have needed to do this anyway to check the camera), then walked through the crew entrance to retrieve the bird once he had fainted. She confirmed that the camera in his tank also showed no physical damage, tucked the sleeping Iguazu into her uniform, and walked to her office.

—

Before Stella could call Mayor Wilcox, he called her.

Stella, are you watching the News?

Stella, who had just finished setting up a small cage for the still-unconscious Iguazu in

her office, switched her television on to see Cindy Zhao hosting a special report live from the agricultural ring. Centered on the screen was the red, impassioned face of Peter Delacroix.

"And if they want to shut me up, they'll have to shut down and restart the whole AI!"

Cheers erupted. The camera zoomed out. He stood behind a lectern at the front of a large indoor farm—one of Agrippa's worksites. Glass walls allowed the sun to shed its light on hundreds of rows of hydroponic plants, in between which stood dozens of embittered farmers.

"Our ancestors knew that free speech was a fundamental right in a fair democracy. They embedded the electoral process in the very Source code that allows our whole bubble to function. Our oligarchs have been eating away at that right, and they've done a pretty good job. But as a public candidate for office, I have made myself visible to the AI in a way that I won't be if I'm a private citizen. I'm their worst enemy: I know how the system works, and I hate it."

The farmers beat their fists and hollered over the whirr of the gardener drones that sprayed water and nutrients all over the room. Though Stella and Wilcox didn't recognize her, Wanda was there in the audience. She had played a key role in getting her colleagues to gather for the rally.

How the hell did this happen? Wilcox spat into Stella's mind. She imagined his last little tuft of hair spinning as his head bobbed with rage. *And what the hell is the News doing covering it?*

What makes you think I know? Stella asked, dryly.

His daughter works for you, doesn't she?

So what?

So...maybe she helped him to register his candidacy.

A tingle of intuition stirred in Stella. *And how would she have done that, exactly?*

You tell me, Teddy said. *We've pretty much destroyed all public records of the registration process. We've also made it significantly harder. Someone would need to have an intimate knowledge of the AI's information architecture to be able to reprogram themselves as a different class of citizen. Not only that, but he's done it in such a way that none of us can go in and move him back to the other class. I can count on my hands the number of humans on either planet who have enough programming mastery to accomplish this, and two of them are on your ship.*

Laura Delacroix is certainly not one of them. Stella said with mocking laughter, though she already knew what he would say next.

No, but your son is.

Stella sighed. Iguazu started to wiggle his wings. He was waking up.

He did work in Urban Planning for a long time. You don't think he could have figured this out himself? She asked Teddy.

Stella, please. The Director of Urban Planning couldn't pull this off, let alone some peon engineer. Didn't you see that commercial he did in the tundra? You're telling me your kid had nothing to do with that?

Stella hadn't seen it.

She looked it up on her phone and watched Peter and Soda deliver their sickening pleas. As the reality of her son's deceit sunk in, she stuck her fingers through the slats of the cage and stroked the stirring Iguazu's feathers.

All right, she said with no hint of fury. *I will look into it further. You may be on to something. On the bright side, I have Laura as a bargaining chip.*

You do for six days, Teddy said. *Then, you can't touch her.*

Stella laughed. She had almost forgotten that this man had no idea what she really had planned. If things went her way, the election wouldn't even happen.

If my son really did give this information to her, and if she did give it to her father, then I can probably get both of them fired for leaking company secrets. Not to mention the political offense they would have committed in the eyes of the Terrarchists on the Board.

But she only said this to calm Teddy down. She knew her son was smarter than to leave evidence of his deeds.

In the meantime, she continued. *I was actually just about to call you for a favor. I need some information. It may, in fact, be relevant to the current conversation.*

On the television, Peter had finished his stump speech, and the workers were all filing back as though nothing had happened. The camera cut back to Cindy Zhao in the City News Bureau.

"Independent candidate Peter Delacroix is officially on our polling map at 8% support—tied with the Technogalitarian nominee. He has a very long way to go if he wants to challenge the incumbent, *but*—and I never thought I would say this even twenty-four hours ago—he has gathered enough support to stand beside the other candidates in Wednesday's debate."

Today was Sunday.

We have a fuel stop scheduled for immediately after the launch on Friday, Stella said. *I wish we could go sooner, but such a sudden rescheduling would arouse suspicion from the Arklings. Anyway, after the launch, send a craft to get me at the grassland depot and bring me to the top floor. Meet me there and we can access the Source together. I have a certain bird's brain I would like to pick.*

Iguazu blinked his eyes open to see Stella staring right at him.

20

Edie refused to talk to the rebels for a while. She sulked in the corner of the large tank Dante had built for her, shocked from what she had believed was a near-death experience at Iguazu's hands/claws.

Edie's namesake was *e. dofleini,* the scientific name for her species, the Giant Pacific Octopus. Edie, however, was just a baby of a few months old, and was therefore not as giant as she would be when full-grown. Still, though, she could extend herself to two feet long if she had the space and the energy. For now, though, she was keeping herself small and invisible, camouflaging her color against the pink rocks on the floor of her tank. Dante had made sure to deactivate the X in Edie's brain as soon as she was settled in the tank, thereby removing her from the Ark's grid. He knew this was risky—someone in the wheelhouse might notice there was now one fewer tracking dot—but they needed to act quickly, and there were no better options. Besides, it was not unusual for Edie to descend to a depth where she did not register in the wheelhouse.

She's terrified, Prince told Dante after a few unsuccessful efforts at establishing contact. Edie had received Dante's explanation of why they needed her and what their mission was, but she had declined to offer any response. *She's not even going to understand unless we make her more comfortable,* Prince observed.

Prince decided he would try relating to her by recollecting

some of his earliest memories. Laura, Dante (who left the room), and Varuna all remained on the channel and observed Prince's effort to relate to Edie.

Hey there. Prince sat with his paws right in front of the tank. *I remember my first time in this room. Not too well—I was so young that I could barely see. But I remember how I didn't trust anyone. I wondered why they had taken me away from my mother.*

Edie shifted a few of her tentacles to cover her face; she showed no interest in responding to Prince's thoughts. Still, though, she kept her channel open, out of concern for what her captors wanted from her if nothing else.

You've been on the Ark before, but you wouldn't remember. You had your Specter installed when you were just a couple weeks old. You could fit in the palm of a human's hand. They had to build an extra small device for you, of course. I was there; I remember connecting to your device and seeing how your mind worked, the way it fragmented into your eight limbs but still stayed grounded in a single sense of self. I'm not sure that the humans even understand how it fully works. You're an enigma, Edie, and I understand why you don't trust us. But I promise that everyone here has your best interest at heart, however hard that might be to believe.

As Prince transmitted these thoughts, and as he felt Edie's extreme guardedness, he was surprised to find himself unlocking a memory from his puppyhood. He was here in Dante's room, cuddled in Dante's arms. Dante leaned against the door and cried as he listened to an argument between his parents outside in the corridor. It was soon after Prince's first time passing the mirror test.

At the time, Prince was unable to understand a lot of what was said. Now, however, certain words and phrases came to him with unprecedented clarity.

"I just don't think the ends justify the means," Dominic said at one point.

"This is just the beginning," Stella said. "We've worked so hard."

Silence. Dante's parents stepped farther away from the door then, likely aware that their son could hear them. Dante held Prince close and scratched behind his tiny ears. "Don't worry. They won't take you away from me. I won't let them."

And he didn't. But Prince always felt like he had done something wrong in achieving self-awareness. He was supposed to be smart, but not that smart.

He took a risk and decided to convey this feeling of shame to Edie. Is this how you're feeling?

She stirred amid the pink gravel and blinked one of her dumbbell-shaped pupils at him. *Something like that,* Prince was startled to hear her reply. *But also...* As she rose from rest, her mantle swelled. She pumped herself up to the front of the tank to face Prince directly.

Pity.

Prince caught a glimpse of how he looked in Edie's eyes. He shifted in and out of focus, gained and lost color; like a camera, the movable lens in her eye could see him in multiple states, switching from a myopic, grayscale view to a wider, prismatic one. He felt somehow exposed, alien to himself, and backed away just a little.

Pity? He asked. *For us? Why?*

Edie lay a languid tentacle on the glass. As she transmitted thoughts, each suction cup flattened out and opened like a flower blooming

Don't you know that none of what you're doing matters? Don't you know that they're coming?

Prince was frightened. *Who's coming?*

The star-beings, Edie said.

This answer prompted concern from those who remained silent on the channel. Dante and Laura gasped slightly, lacking any idea what she was talking about. Varuna, meanwhile, worried that Edie was about to ruin his plans: If she said too much, he would have to give away that he did not in fact believe in the reality of the space war that pitted the cephalopods against the cetaceans.

Prince knew he needed backup. He opened a separate channel with Varuna. *Do you know what she's talking about?*

But despite Prince's effort to keep his dialogue with Varuna private, Dante and Laura noticed Prince's sudden retreat from their own perception. *Where did you go?* They asked him.

They didn't bother to hide this question from Edie, which meant that she now knew that others were listening.

I'm talking to Varuna, Prince admitted.

Edie was not happy to learn that the dolphin was listening to her thoughts. Her entire body dropped its veil of rosy pink to reveal a cold black cloak of anger. *I'm not going to talk with you all any further if* he's *listening,* she said.

Varuna, who could have been seen jerking side to side with agitation had anyone been present at his tank, was caught off guard. Because the crew was just an hour or two away from mobilizing to remove his and all other private Specters, he had no choice but to debase himself a little.

The first thing I want to say to Edie, he communicated with an uncharacteristic gentle tone, aware that he was talking to a child, *is that I am sorry our species have become such bitter rivals. I am especially sorry that my species has predated upon yours in horrible ways for millennia. Not only do we eat your kind, but we shake you in your mouths and toss you to break you into little pieces. The cetaceans and the cephalopods could have shared our intelligence with one another and turned the seas into something great. Perhaps we could have even prevented the destruction of the Earth's oceans. But we turned you into things of sport, and I am sorry. If you help us, I will do everything I can to convince my fellow cetaceans to leave your kind in peace.*

Edie's black dulled a little to dark gray. Everyone waited for her reply. *I appreciate your tone,* she said after a minute, *but none of that is the issue. After all, you had to break us apart before you ate us, or else we would cling to your throats as you tried to swallow us, and we would suffocate you. No, the issue is the feud from which our feud originates. The feud between Sirius and Ophiuchus. And that feud is about to come to an end. The entire network of my species has spread the word that our star has proved victorious over yours, and any day now, the Ophiuchans will return to Earth and set things straight for all who descend from their noble lineage.*

From Dante and Laura, this elicited a *What the hell is she talking about?*

Prince, for his part, quivered a little at the possibility of an imminent extraterrestrial invasion.

Varuna resigned himself to telling the truth, albeit in a way that he hoped he could get out of as soon as it was said. *Unfortunately, Edie, none of that is real.* Varuna explained that the humans had implanted the visions of these warring stars in the dolphins and the octopuses in the process of designing their Specters.

Why would they do that? Edie asked with a child's defiant skepticism.

I don't know, Varuna said. I think it may have been an accident. *Perhaps they were seeing how our species would react to mythologies that shared characteristics with those of their own. What do you think, Dante?*

I have no idea about any of this, said Dante, utterly mystified. *If this happened, it would have been behind my back.*

It makes sense, said Varuna. *This would have begun years ago, when you were a child.*

Prince stayed silent, trying his best to hold his heart together. Had Varuna really lied to him all this time? And what about the dream of taking all the animals into space? Was that just a front for something else? He decided not to ask these questions; he kept alive the hope that this was in fact the lie, that Varuna was simply manipulating Edie to get her on their side. Truth be told, though, he didn't like this possibility either. It made Varuna less reliable in his eyes, and what if a brigade of star creatures really was about to arrive, like Edie thought?

Varuna seemed to account for this last concern when he explained that the dolphins had a corresponding and opposite belief that it was in fact the Sirians who had emerged victorious and were on their way to Earth. *But it's all nonsense,* Varuna said.

After some further back-and-forth between Varuna and Edie, and further silence from those who listened with confusion and a knowledge that time was short for a more nuanced conversation, Edie came around to the idea of helping them.

I have to say, she said, *I'm quite mad that this has all happened. I feel controlled, manipulated, and like my entire life has been a lie.*

Because it has, Varuna said. *But we're here to change that. We're here to build an Arkology where all animals can be true to themselves.*

With only minutes to spare before crew members dispersed throughout the Ark to replace all privacy-enabled Specters with the model Stella had approved, Edie agreed to join the rebellion. Dante returned to his room, lifted Edie out of her tank, and allowed her to slap a tentacle onto his face and over his Specter. They were synchronizing. But unlike Varuna, who could only work with the two hemispheres of his brain, Edie had eight disparate nervous systems in each of her legs that she could distribute to eight different minds. Her method of hacking into the SpecterX didn't involve the emission of sound waves but rather the precise haptic knowledge that the bundles of nerves in every one of her suction cups, which doubled as taste buds, gave her as she caressed the device. She effectively tasted the other party's mind. She then gave a second leg to Prince as Dante knelt down and offered her to the dog.

It would be a challenge getting her to the various parts of the Ark where she could synchronize with every animal that was set to appear for the demo on launch day, but at least they had achieved the first step.

—

Once deactivated, Varuna lost his connection with Dante and Laura. He still had his private channel with Prince, though.

I'm sorry I had to do that, he said. *I could see that she had bought into some of the more religious beliefs of her elders, and I figured that it was best to give her another story altogether, especially since Dante and Laura were listening.*

I understand, Prince said, although the truth was that he didn't, not fully. He saw Varuna in another light now, and he doubted his trust in him. Why hadn't he been open with the humans when the chance presented itself? What was the point in hiding the marvelous truth, if truth indeed it was?

I'll talk to you more about it later, Prince brought himself to say before disconnecting. *I need some time to think.*

A pang of unfamiliar shame jolted Varuna.

21

After the replacement of everyone's Specters, Stella arranged for the Ark to sail to the grasslands, where they would tranquilize and capture Gunny the prairie dog.

Gunny, named rather uncreatively after her species, the Gunnison's prairie dog, had a fiery spark and a chip on her shoulder that had made a real impression on Prince when she was first going through her SpecterX trials.

What makes you all think that I want to talk to any of you? She had thought to Prince a few months ago. *Don't you all know that prairie dogs already have one of the most sophisticated communication systems of any animal? We have a chirp that means "coyote," a chirp that means "hawk"...Hell, we've got chirps to refer to* this *specific coyote or* that *specific hawk. You know why? Because those animals are out to get us. What makes you think I give a damn what they all have to say for themselves? They're still going to want to eat me.*

What if you're wrong? Prince had suggested at the time. *What if there's a world where predator and prey don't exist?*

Gunny chittered with disdain. *Ridiculous. Who knew that two animals the humans both called "dogs" could see the world so differently?*

As the Ark learned upon reaching the meadows of the grasslands where Gunny and her fellow prairie dogs burrowed, she had apparently taken some of the knowledge gained during the experiments and learned to hide whenever the Ark approached. To catch Gunny, they needed to deploy a specialized snakebot that could tunnel underground and find her.

This made Laura, on deck to observe the capture, quite uncomfortable, and she looked forward to playing her role in getting Gunny to join their team of rebels. The plan, agreed upon just before Laura had her private model removed, was for Laura to go into Dante's room during her midmorning cleaning rounds and sneak Edie into her washbucket. She would then bring Edie over to Gunny's terrarium, where it would then be Laura's job to feed Gunny, and she would allow Edie to sneak a tentacle onto the sleeping prairie dog and synchronize with her before she even awoke. The escapade would of course allow Laura and Edie to synchronize as well.

Unfortunately, the plan didn't work. As Laura pushed her housekeeping cart down the hall toward Dante's room, a message blared over the intercom for everyone to hear: "Junior Officer Delacroix, please report to the captain's quarters immediately."

Laura, aware that Stella would now be watching her through the hallway's cameras, left the cart and walked toward this unexpected appointment. She hadn't spoken directly to Stella since before the trip to Mars, and her head buzzed with possible subjects of conversation. She found it odd that Stella had chosen to invite her to her quarters rather than her office (Laura couldn't know that this was done, of course, because Stella was keeping Iguazu in the latter location).

Stella opened the door with a beaming smile. She led Laura through her foyer, which was decorated with the many career awards Stella had won on her rise to the top, to the dining room, where a sumptuous display of artificial meats and cheeses under soft red and gold lighting made Laura's eyes bulge.

"This is...for me?" Laura stammered.

Stella nodded. "Please, sit. I want to hear how my Citizen prodigy is doing."

Laura, out of her depth, watched Stella spread some brie on a cracker. She nervously picked up a knife and imitated

Stella. "I'm doing well. Just trying to think of a new project."

"Mm!" Stella bit down. "Yes, I wanted to talk to you about that. Oh, but first: Waiter, come pour us some wine, please."

Laura fought hard to suppress a gasp as none other than Dante walked in with a decanter of wine. He raised his eyebrows and winked at her as he filled her glass, albeit with a sheepish smile that made Laura think they were both in some very bad trouble.

Stella observed them both with an empty, glassy smile. "I've asked Dante to shadow me 24/7 for the entire week leading up to launch day and the turnover of power. I can't let him out of my sight. You understand, I'm sure."

Dante stood behind Laura at a clearly preassigned position. Laura could barely swallow the printed pork. She was no longer hungry. She looked at the glass of wine like it was a giant rat.

Stella frowned. "Aren't you going to drink? This is so much better than anything you'll find in the cafeteria." Laura, fighting against the fear that she was being poisoned, took a sip. Stella smiled again.

"Now, tell me. Have you spoken to your father recently?"

"No," Laura lied. So, that's what this was about. "He's pretty busy," she added.

Stella blinked several times. "Indeed he is. But are you sure you haven't spoken with him? About work, maybe? He seems to have some rather strong opinions on what we do here."

Stella then removed a tablet from her uniform and lay it on the table. She had set a video of Peter's campaign commercial tundra to play at a key moment.

"When I'm mayor," Peter said beside Soda, "I'm going to get to the bottom of the corruption. Day One, I'm going to ask for a full audit of the Melampus Corporation's data, and I'm going to reverse Mayor Wilcox's order to mandate school and hospital use of the SpecterX. There's a good reason people are worried about keeping their thoughts private."

Stella paused the video and put the tablet away. She spun her glass as she gazed into Laura's eyes. "'Corruption?' 'Keeping their thoughts *private*?' Does anyone know where he got such a dark, dystopian idea of our mission?" She raised her eyes to look at Dante. Laura heard his breathing shift a little and fidgeted. It hurt that they couldn't share thoughts in private anymore. Stella, sensing the direction of Laura's attention, snorted. "I've already asked Dante. He's got nothing to say. I'm asking you, Laura."

"I haven't leaked any company information, if that's what you're implying," Laura said with a scared whisper. "My father's a private Citizen who has his own opinions."

"Right." Stella nodded. "And to be fair, he is not the only Citizen to have indulged in such conspiratorial delusions. It's not as though he has any concrete thoughts, anyway. There's just this vague sense of "corruption." But tell me, how did he get a permit to enter the Biomes? It's a rather complicated process."

"I don't know," Laura said. "My father's smart. He's worked for some important people. He probably knew about the process already."

Stella squinted. "And he submitted all the forms so quickly? In just a matter of days?"

Laura shrugged. She moved to take another sip of wine, then put her glass back down as Stella, quite suddenly, rose from her chair and leaned forward to put her eyes just inches away from Laura's. Stella's hands, which reached out to touch Laura's face, were softer than Laura expected. Laura fought the urge to spit as Stella moved a finger up to the spot between her brows where Laura's newly-reinstalled SpecterX sat.

"Let's say..." Stella's eyes softened as she whispered with a seductive sweetness. "...that hypothetically, this device here does send a record of your thoughts to the AI, including those you choose to keep private from your conversation partners. It wouldn't be very hard at all for me to see whether you're as loyal to this company as you claim to be."

Laura wanted to say "go ahead," but fear stopped her. She readied herself to hear the worst as Stella leaned back in her chair. Now that Laura wore the X again, there was no clear reason why Stella wouldn't be about to reveal what she had learned from accessing Laura's code.

But she didn't. "Listen, Laura: I like you. I can tell you're lying to me, but I like you all the same. And I think you and my son would both be surprised to learn just how many of your political sentiments, which I assume are similar to your father's, I am sympathetic to. But there is a larger mission here than a single mayoral campaign, and I'm afraid I can't have you or my son working at odds with me in these final days before launch."

Stella then rose and nonchalantly swept an arm across the table, bringing all the plates of meats and cheese crashing to the floor. Laura wanted to cry at all the waste. Stella pointed at the mess and spoke to Dante. "Clean this up, please."

Dante, fists balled in anger, walked right past the mess and left the room.

Stella, sighing, lay her palm up on the table and invited Laura to take her hand. Laura did so with disgust.

"Because I like you," said Stella, stroking Laura's fingers with her other hand, "there really is no reason for you to fear what's coming."

"What's coming?" Laura brought herself to ask.

"Nothing! Nothing at all." Stella winked. "Now, about your research proposal...how much do you know about insects?"

"Insects?"

"Ants, specifically. But I don't need to ask, I suppose. You spent thousands of hours at the library reading all you could about every animal out there before you applied, didn't you?"

"I know the basics," Laura said, not forgetting at all the devious undercurrent of the conversation. "But I'm not as familiar with the latest research on them as I maybe ought to be."

"Oh! So humble." Stella rose and gave Laura a very awkward hug across the table. "It doesn't matter. We've only recently begun investing money in understanding them to the fullest extent possible anyway. Come, let's take a walk."

Laura followed as Stella exited through the foyer out into the hallway. She considered transmitting to Dante to see if he was okay, but the risks of exposing her thoughts to the X and therefore Stella were too great. At the same time as she thought this, however, something was not adding up. Why had Stella bothered to ask her about Peter at all if she already had access to her (and Dante's, and, for that matter, Prince's) mind? Did she just want to see if she could provoke a confession? Laura had surely failed that test if so.

Stella led Laura to a part of the Ark she had never been in, deep in the hull, past the deafening roar of the ship's engines. They arrived at a vault-style door with an access console. Laura's stomach churned with dreadful anticipation. She considered turning around and fleeing while Stella, raising her other hand to prevent Laura from seeing, entered a code, but there was nowhere to go. The Ark was inescapable for her.

"Welcome to the ant farm," Stella said as the door opened. They walked through a small living area with a kitchenette and bunk bed to come out onto an observation deck that abutted a massive terrarium. Behind the glass, Laura had an underground view of innumerable ants teeming and crawling through the tunnels of their colony.

"What is this?" Laura asked in awe. "How have I never seen this before?"

"Very few people have," Stella said. "This was one of Dominic's first projects. He believed that insect intelligence held the key to understanding how societies really work."

Laura tracked a single worker ant as it trudged through the tunnel. It ran into another worker, rubbed antennae, and changed directions.

"You want to build Specters for...these tiny things?" She asked.

"We already have," Stella said. "Microscopic models that we insert into their food. The Specters enter their bloodstream and then travel to their nervous system. Here, let me show you what I would like you to do."

Stella beckoned Laura to the deck's computer and pulled up a text file with hundreds of thousands of chains of numbers. Laura felt dizzy looking at the file's size.

"Each of these vectors corresponds to an individual ant. What I would like you to help me with is creating a colony-wide matrix that categorizes every ant according to their social role, their age, and their typical movements throughout the day. We're trying to create a data structure that understands how the colony functions as a single intelligence."

Laura's heart began to quicken. "There are...probably hundreds of thousands of ants here." She was about to ask Stella if she knew how long such a task would take, then realized that this was the point.

Stella put a hand on Laura's shoulder. "I know it's a lot to ask. But consider this your research assignment. Complete this, and you won't even have to worry about getting a promotion. I guarantee it." Laura shuddered as she felt Stella's fingers in her hair.

"You'll be in here a while, of course," Stella said. "But you have food and bedding, and you can of course contact me if you need anything. The door won't open from the inside, unfortunately."

Laura wanted to strangle Stella. But being forever known as the employee who assaulted the Melampus CEO would not be good for her or her family. "If you're trying to get rid of me," she whispered, "why don't you just fire me?"

Stella threw her head back and cackled. "I can't fire you. I need you at the launch on Friday. You need to show the Citizens how safe and wonderful our products are. They certainly won't take my word for it."

Laura backed up against the wall and crumpled to the floor.

"Have fun," Stella said on leaving.

The ants continued to crawl.

22

Things looked bleak for our heroes right then. Although Dante and Prince maintained contact through Edie, it was hard for them to have meaningful conversations when Stella kept such a persistent watchful eye on her son. Anything so much as an ill-timed side glance in Stella's presence would indicate that Dante was *thinking*, and it was crucial to keep their one remaining means of private communication secret.

I don't know how we get out of this, Dante told Prince before falling asleep Tuesday night. *I've tried so hard to find a way into her office so that I could at least look for any information about what she's doing with Mars, but she's grown so suspicious now that she's locked me in her cabin. I'm sorry I can't do more. Hopefully, you and Varuna will figure something out.*

But Prince, who still had access to Dante's room through the dog door and pretty much spent all his time on guard there lest an Arkling come in and find Edie, struggled to trust Varuna after the earlier call. In fact, he found it easier to avoid Varuna almost entirely while he enchanted the young octopus with the promises of space travel that had gotten her to join forces with them. As Prince learned more about Edie—her solitary existence, and the fact that she had never met her mother, who starved herself to death the way all octopus mothers do before their babies hatch—he grew quite paternal and protective toward her. At night, he would tell her bedtime

147

stories of all the things they would do once they got to space. *We'll meet your ancestors, and then we'll meet mine, and then we'll all put our minds together to build a spaceship far more powerful than even the ones Mars has built.*

But Prince feared that the time to confront Varuna about the apparent contradictions in his behavior was drawing near. And he hated confrontation. He had spent days attempting to rationalize the lying according to Varuna's own explanation for it. But the longer Prince sat with Varuna's words, the more he questioned the entire premise of their mission. Space travel? It really was absurd if he stopped to think about it for any time at all.

Varuna played dumb the first time he contacted Prince after the call with Edie. *Is everything okay? What did you need to think about?*

Prince, for his part, played dumb as well. *Oh, you know. Just thinking about everything Melampus has been doing with dolphins and octopuses.*

Yeah. It's pretty messed up, right?

Prince had spoken to Varuna enough now that he could pick up on one of the dolphin's "tells" that indicated, if not dishonesty, at least an unaddressed anxiety: Varuna, like all dolphins, had two dorsal bursae—liplike flaps in his nasal passages that could produce sound independently of one another. When Varuna was nervous, he would very notably emit the whistles and clicks that accompanied his thoughts through just one bursa, as though concentrating extra hard on what he was communicating because he was hiding his true intentions. Prince wanted to point it out, but he knew it would start a fight. And he was angrier at himself than at Varuna for allowing himself to develop an attachment to an animal who clearly had a much more natural inclination toward deceit than he did. He was angry that he found Varuna's capacity to lie somewhat beautiful.

—

Laura, meanwhile, was in the most despair of them all (unless, of course, one considers Iguazu; Dante had at least been present to overhear her conversation with Stella and thereby infer her location, whereas nobody on the Ark besides Stella even knew where Iguazu was). Laura despaired not so much because she was trapped and unable to speak to the others but rather because she had a sneaking sense that she *could* speak with the others if she could just find some proof that the story Melampus was feeding Arkling investors about Pathnet's data collection methods was not the full truth. If Stella could indeed access Laura's thoughts simply because the SpecterX was once again in her brain, it would seem like she could clearly establish that she had been in contact with her father and ruin both of their lives. But the possibility that Stella was waiting to do this until she had exploited Laura for the launch did make sense to her, and so Laura toiled away at her menial data entry task with the sole hope that she could stumble upon some miraculous flash of insight.

Laura's despair peaked on Wednesday, when her father made his astonishing appearance on the debate stage with Teddy Wilcox and the nondescript Technogalitarian opponent. Peter tried to contact Laura several times on Wednesday, and she found it harder and harder to focus on her work as she continually declined his calls. She felt horrible that her father would have to go on stage wondering why his daughter suddenly wouldn't speak to him, but she just couldn't risk putting another of their conversations on the AI's record.

Laura was able to stream the debate on the observation deck's computer. Dante was also able to watch on one of his mother's televisions, and he fed it to Edie and Prince, who then relayed information to Varuna.

The debate, staged outdoors against the backdrop of military aircraft in the spaceport that spanned the "hole" at the center of the City's doughnut, began with strong opening statements from both the mayor and Peter. Whereas the mayor opened the debate with statistics that supposedly made the case for continuing his successful policies (universal employment, decreased crime, exploding trade revenue with Mars), Peter immediately brought up the railway project that was about to eject hundreds of agricultural laborers from their jobs and radically decrease the food supply. Noticing the mayor was caught off guard, he continued into a more general tirade against Wilcox's administration and the Terrarchist platform writ large.

"For thirty years now, the Terrarchists have oppressed us while claiming to protect us. For example, take the annual sorting. Every year, we should all have an equal chance at getting promotions or moving into better housing. But the Terrarchists have rewritten the class variables such that they and their cronies are the only ones who have a shot in Hell at it. They are letting our units fall into disrepair, our public transit is collapsing, and everyone hates everyone who's one floor above them when the real problem is the few people at the top."

Viewer reactions on social media to Peter's opening speech were overwhelmingly positive. When the subject turned more explicitly to Mars, he landed another blow.

"If the mayor wants to claim that we've been making out like bandits on our trade deals with Mars, then where is all that money going? I haven't seen any of it. What I have seen are new private jets and new weapons systems that don't seem to serve any purpose other than feeding Wilcox's ego—"

Teddy tried to interrupt. "Expanding our military capacities to defend against possible extraterrestrial invasion is a very serious—"

"Oh, shut up! There are no damn aliens. We've heard that line for thirty years. The only threats are the rich and selfish people who have forgotten why we all crammed ourselves into this bubble. You know, when was the last time you heard about our re-terraforming projects? I'm sure the planet will be clean of biohazards any day now, and we can all frolic over the seven continents like we once did."

"The re-terraforming technologies are Martian-owned, which is why we needed to build better trade relations in the first—"

"You owe the people the truth, Mayor Wilcox. We're never getting out of this bubble, and now that the elites have figured that out, they're taking what they can from the rest of us and hoping they'll be the last to die."

Peter was scoring huge wins left and right according to audience reactions. Toward the end of the debate, however, the mayor did launch an effective counterstrike.

"Mr. Delacroix's everyman shtick is quite rich when you consider that his daughter is an employee of the very corporation he claims to want to audit. Voters are right to want transparency on Pathnet, but this is not the guy who can give it to you."

Peter's face paled on hearing Laura mentioned. He failed to offer a response. Laura could tell that he was thinking about her failure to answer his calls, and she felt horrible.

The debate essentially ended up as a draw—post-debate polls showed slight gains for Peter, but not nearly what he could have achieved, Laura believed, if she had been able to talk him through this very predictable line of attack.

23

Prince, who usually slept like a baby, tossed and turned that night in Dante's bed. The light from Edie's tank and the still-real possibility that someone might walk into the room were both factors in his insomnia, but mostly, he was trying to figure out a way to get Edie to synchronize with the other launch day participants, and he just couldn't do it without Varuna's help. But when Varuna called him in the middle of the night, he didn't answer right away. He didn't know how to talk to someone he struggled to trust. But Varuna insisted.

For the love of the cosmos, help us. For the love of the cosmos, help us! For the love of the cosmos—

What?! Prince finally answered.

I had a nightmare. Varuna's tone was more docile than usual, so much so that it amused Prince.

You? A nightmare? The strong and invulnerable Varuna?

But Varuna did not offer the brash, arrogant, and defensive response Prince expected. *Look, Prince. I can tell you're mad at me.*

Prince rolled onto his side and looked at the ceiling. *I'm not mad at you—*

Why aren't you talking to me, then? Varuna interrupted. *Why aren't we fighting to get Dante and Laura out? Launch is in 36 hours. Are we just going to give up?*

No. I just...I don't know how to talk to you.

Varuna's fins drooped. He let his body sink a little. *You don't trust me.*

Prince wanted to push back, to show that he could roll with the punches, but he struggled to think of the words. Varuna was right, after all.

I get it, Varuna said. *Look. You think what I said to Edie was the truth. I'm not going to say you're right, but let's say you were. Wouldn't that only show further how corrupt Melampus is? How horribly they treat animals? Wouldn't it strengthen your resolve to—*

Whatever "resolve" Prince had to keep rationalizing Varuna's inconsistencies and play along with him got swirled up in the vortex of cognitive dissonance as he listened to the dolphin's attempt to intensify the mind games. He couldn't take it anymore. *Stop! Just stop!* He thought about Peter's demand for "the truth" at the debate. *Stop lying. Stop prevaricating. Stop hiding. You can tell me the truth.*

Varuna was silent for a full minute. Finally: *...I can't.*

Prince growled. *Yes, you can. Don't you get it? I care about you. I feel stupid for it, but I do. I'm a dog. Once you've earned my attachment, there's very little you can do to break it.*

The genuine vibration of Prince's caring caught Varuna off guard. For a time, he did not transmit any words; he simply allowed Prince to listen to the soft, sighing squeak he let out into the water. It was almost like crying. Then, he replied. *I care about you, too.*

Prince conveyed a mental image of him swimming on Varuna's back, his nose nuzzling the dolphin's neck. *Then just tell me the truth.*

For this entire conversation, Varuna had been formulating what to say. The truth was that he did, despite himself, care about Prince at least a little by now. And Prince was smarter than he initially believed. So, he knew he couldn't persuasively say anything that wasn't true. *The truth is that I don't know what's true and what's not.* And this was true. He explained how members of his pod had gradually succumbed to the Sirian mythology only after visits to the Ark; but since Varuna himself did not get to the Ark during that period of time, he could not say for sure that the humans had implanted false ideas. A part of him, he explained, wanted to believe the space myths. But if he looked at the facts, and everything else he knew about their reality, he believed the space myths were likely to be fiction. And Prince, begrudgingly, agreed. But none of this, Varuna said, changed the ultimate dream that motivated their project: A society that treated humans and animals as equals. And why couldn't they still go to Sirius and Ophiuchus? If the technology wasn't there, they would build it together. And if they didn't meet any ancestors, so be it. They would build new worlds.

But despite all this truth, Varuna did not mention Xavier; it was too much for him to admit that he was not the dolphin Prince had met years earlier. Truth be told, he enjoyed occupying that space in Prince's nostalgic imagination.

Prince digested all the information. He had already put most of it together in his mind, so he did not feel any great wave of anger. One question bothered him, though. *Are you still planning to let the humans come to space with us? Once we're able to, I mean.*

Varuna did not want to answer this question. It required him to lie. But intergalactic travel was probably such a distant possibility, anyway, that he was able to sell the lie. *Yes, of course. I admit, I was unsure about that when we met. But I've gotten to know Dante and Laura well now, and I can see that I misjudged them. Not all humans deserve my scorn.*

Prince waited a while before answering. Varuna had not attached any sounds to these thoughts, so there was no way for Prince to look for the dolphin's "tell." But he was tired, and he believed so firmly in redemption, that he decided they would move forward. *All right.*

All right? Varuna asked. *Does that mean we're good?*

Yes, we're good. I don't see how we can stop the launch of the X at this point, but you and I, personally, we're good.

Varuna sent waves of comfort and relief. Prince sent back the sense of cuddling him.

What was your nightmare about? Prince said.

Oh, it was stupid. Edie snuck into my tank and wrapped an arm around me in my sleep. She synchronized with me, but she seemed to be sucking my soul away. Whatever soul is still left, of course. But what really scared me was when she showed me an image of you, floating deep under the sea, dead. It was just a dream. And I know Edie wouldn't do anything like that. But I needed to talk to you.

Prince would have expressed discomfort at the haunting image in Varuna's dream if he had not been looking at a vent in the ceiling of Dante's room at the exact moment Varuna mentioned Edie sneaking into his tank.

What's wrong? Varuna asked in response to Prince's pensive silence.

Edie snuck into your tank, you said. How did she do it?

Through the vent in the ceiling. If it's big enough for her to stick a single arm through it, she can put her whole body through. Octopuses are messed up.

Prince moved his head to see Edie, camouflaged, barely visible against the pink gravel.

Varuna, I have an idea. And I think it's going to work.

24

Although Citizens could not board the Ark for launch day, they could crowd the windows of the grassland depot and watch as Stella, Laura, Dante, and Prince emerged onto the deck to greet Cindy Zhao's camera crew. The Ark was just a few hundred feet away from the depot gate, which was still a bit too far for Laura to notice Wanda and Michelle in the crowd banging on the windows and trying to get her attention. Peter decided to stay home after an exhausting week and watched the special launch day broadcast that played on televisions to virtually every home in the City. In addition to watching the broadcast, viewers could log into a website and use their soon-to-be-outdated Specters to connect to Cindy Zhao's SpecterX feed. They wouldn't be able to experience sounds or smells or anything else besides visuals, but it would, in theory, pique their interest enough to go out and buy the new devices.

As Stella's technical detail outfitted Cindy with her new X, Laura, Dante, and Prince all nodded at one another. It was the first time they had seen one another in person since their forced separation days earlier, but they had already greeted one another in heartfelt reunion as Edie managed to sneak into Laura's cell and synchronize with her. It was quite shocking for Laura to wake up that morning on her slim bunk bed and discover the octopus's voice in her head.

Laura, it's Edie. Stay calm. You're still being watched, but

I managed to lend you one of my arms while you were asleep. I would have waited until you were awake, but I figured you might scream or otherwise draw attention to yourself on the security camera if you saw me squeezing my way into your toilet.

Because Laura was so far removed from the rest of the Ark, it had taken some creative thinking involving the ship's water system to get to her. Synchronizing with Varuna, Nemos, Soda, and Gunny, who were all in their enclosures ready to participate in Stella's demonstration (or so Stella believed), had been simply a matter of squeezing through their vents and blending into the walls.

"Where's the bird?" Cindy whispered to Stella in the final moments before they went live.

Laura, Dante, and Prince all leaned in a little to overhear Stella's answer. Edie's discovery that Iguazu was no longer in his cage had been alarming to them all.

"He's sick," Stella answered with an exaggerated frown.

On Dante's urging, Edie had attempted to locate Iguazu in Stella's office in just the last couple of hours. Unfortunately, nobody on the "chain of eight" (Edie and the seven minds who now had a mental tether to all but one of her legs) knew of the secret door in the wall that turned only in response to Stella's retinal scan. Poor Iguazu cried into his wing behind that door. Edie did, however, manage to spot a folder on Stella's desk with the intriguing label "Martian research." Dante wanted Edie to open it, but as Laura pointed out, Edie's slimy tentacle would leave a very visible mark on the folder. It was best to leave it and look at it after the demo if necessary.

On deck, Stella's tech team confirmed that everyone's devices were on the grid and in contact with the Source. It was time for the broadcast to start.

"Cindy Zhao here, live on launch day!" Cindy wore a huge smile for the camera. "In just moments, I'll be sharing my thoughts with not just the four celebrities you see behind me"--she briefly introduced Stella, Laura, Dante, and Prince, all of whom were recognizable faces throughout the City for their own reasons—"but also four animals of widely different species who are ready to connect with me at different locations on the Ark."

Cindy connected to Stella without a problem. "Even before I connect to a third party, I can tell you that the SpecterX offers a much more immersive experience!"

By the time she tried to connect to Dante, however, his device was already wrapped up in Edie's mind.

"He's off the grid, ma'am," Officer Naismith said.

Stella glowered at Dante. Dante played dumb and frowned.

Cindy turned to the camera. "One moment, folks! Live television—you know how it goes."

"Try connecting to Laura," Stella suggested.

But Naismith waved his hand. "Off the grid as well, ma'am. In fact, all other parties seem to be going off the grid as I speak."

Stella pushed her way to Naismith to look at his tablet and confirm his words. She curled her hands into fists and stared at Laura, Prince, and Dante. They had done this, but she didn't understand how. The rebels, meanwhile, all exchanged looks of fake confusion to hide the fact that they now shared their inner worlds with not only one another but with Varuna, Nemos, Soda, Gunny, and the octopus that Stella did not even know was on the ship.

Cindy raised her eyebrows at Stella, waiting for the official corporate spin. All around the City, in those seconds of tension, Stella knew that viewers were going online to share their reactions of frustration, fear, or amusement—the exact emotion depending on how one regarded Melampus. The crowd gathered at the windows of the grassland depot grew muted.

"This is clearly not a coincidence," Stella said at last. "I do apologize, but it would appear that we are having a problem connecting everyone's devices to the Source. We've been quite busy programming things up on the top floor in preparation for the launch, so some minor hiccups can be expected. But I assure everyone watching that the network is fully functional, and that we have a professional customer support team ready should anyone find that their devices encounter problems."

Everyone on deck could sense the agitation in the air, but on television, they all looked quite composed.

"Let's all try a simple troubleshooting mechanism. I want everyone here to close their eyes and focus on a memory—any memory that has a strong emotion attached to it. The act of conscious recall will stimulate the circuits of the neural mesh that correspond to the connections between the hippocampus and the amygdala. Stimulating these circuits will allow the device to remember itself and reset."

Cindy nodded and closed her eyes as though she knew what Stella was talking about. Dante, Laura, and Prince all closed their eyes with them, but in their minds, they were exchanging hysterical reactions of amusement with one another and with the five other animals on their secret chain.

Damn, this is really the best she can do, Dante thought to the others. Mental laughter, howling, whistling, chirping, and roaring signaled everyone's glee as their minds rippled through Edie's limbs and grasped out to each other in a warm feeling of community. The differences between this network and the one they had built using the privacy-enabled Specters were striking. In contrast to the layer-based system of the SpecterX, which required one to toggle back and forth between one mind at a time (albeit at a fairly quick rate that could at least approach simultaneous perception), Edie's distributed nervous system allowed everyone to perceive everyone else's perceptions all at once in real time through something that could best be described as a split-screen effect (if one can imagine a screen that splits not only into distinct visual images but auditory, olfactory, haptic, and so forth ones as well).

"Keep focusing," Stella said with a crack in her voice that everyone recognized as anxiety. "Think of your strongest memory."

The chain of eight continued ridiculing her. All but one of them, that is. For Nemos, whose very name was a tribute to Mnemosyne, Greek goddess of memory, the attempt *not* to focus on her strongest memory and to remain tied to the chain of eight worked about as well as it does when humans try not to think of a pink elephant.

Hey, guys...I'm not feeling so good. She alerted everyone to her distress as the memory of her first calf's death grew clearer and clearer.

It began as faint impressions; then, as it looped in Nemos's mind the way traumatic flashbacks do, it crystallized into an all-consuming sequence of terror for all in the chain:

A stirring in the branches of an acacia tree caused Nemos and her calf to raise their heads from the pond where they drank. They thought about running, until they saw Stewart's smiling face looking back at them through the leaves.

But it was not Stewart. It was a humanoid poachbot programmed to wear Stewart's disarming visage. By the time the poachbot raised its "arm" and revealed the barrel of a highly precise killing machine, it was too late. The calf was dead in an instant.

Then, the poachbot pointed its arm to Nemos's other side. Nemos turned to see the dying face of...

No! No! I cannot show that to you, Nemos told the group, who by then were all swept up and reeling in her recollected terror as though spinning in a cyclone.

But when Stella, veins now bulging in her face, screamed for everyone once more to "Focus harder!", Nemos could not hide it anymore:

The target of the poachbot's long-unknown second bullet was none other than Dominic Melampus.

The shock and horror of the revelation caused Dante to disconnect from the chain. Seeing the father he thought had been killed in a lion attack killed in the same strike as Nemos's calf was so jarring to him that he had to look away.

"Dante's back on the grid, ma'am!" Naismith announced.

Stella, surprised that her strategy had worked at all, breathed a sigh of relief and invited Cindy to connect with Dante. Dante, too afraid of the potential consequences not to accept Cindy's call, breathed quickly and looked at his mother in terror.

"Amazing! Such clear layering!" Cindy yelled with an exuberance meant to cover up the fact that the other demo participants remained offline. "Your heart sure is racing, Dante."

"Just a temporary effect of the reset process," Stella said before Dante could answer.

The others all struggled to remain on their chain with Edie. Losing Dante sent another wave of panic through the circuit.

You were there when Dominic died?, Prince asked Nemos in terror.

I'm sorry! Nemos said. *They forced me to forget. They forced me!*

Would the two of you both calm down? Gunny thought while chattering her teeth. *You're going to give us all heart attacks!*

Yes, please, Edie broadcast to them all. *I'm just a kid. This is all so new and overwhelming for me. I'm going to have to kick people off the chain if you don't get the elephant under control.*

Maybe you could try understanding where she's coming from? Prince thought. He was so shocked by Nemos's memory that he couldn't suppress a growl. Everyone on deck looked at him. Dante thought Prince was chastising him for removing himself from the chain and began to choke with tears in his eyes.

"I'm sorry," he said to the confused Laura, Stella, and Cindy. "I'm just emotional at seeing this product finally launch. Everyone's worked so hard on it."

"You sure have!" Cindy said. Everyone on deck joined her in over-the-top applause.

It was Varuna, seeing that Prince was too upset to assume his usual role of peacemaker, who took the responsibility of calming Nemos down and restoring order to the chain. *Whatever happened was not your fault,* he thought while booming sound waves in his tank that served to soothe the agitated pachyderm. *You're not there anymore. You're here, with us, in the present, and we all care about you. You have a beautiful mind and heart, and we all care about you.*

Nemos's memory loop, which forced everyone to watch her baby and Dominic get killed over and over again, began to slow. She inhaled huge gulps of air into her trunk, then expelled them with a trumpeting sigh. She came back to the present.

On deck, Stella had abandoned any hopes of getting all participants on the call and was filling airtime by talking to Cindy about various features on the new devices. She did manage to see Prince scratching Dante's leg, which he did to let Dante know that Nemos was calm and that it was safe to rejoin Edie's chain.

Cindy frowned as Dante disconnected. Naismith simply cleared his throat and flashed his tablet out of the cameras' view to show Stella that her son was again offline.

Stella, raging inside, clapped her hands and seemed to swallow the news crew with her angry eyes. "Well, that should do it then. Thank you all *so much* for coming!"

Cindy, catching Stella's drift, shook her and Dante's hands. She did not acknowledge Prince or Laura. "Yes, thank *you!*" She closed the disastrous broadcast with another reminder that the SpecterX was now available in stores everywhere.

Once the cameras were off, Cindy touched Stella's arm. "Damn, that was rough."

Stella refused to show her emotions. "Don't run anything yet," she whispered to Cindy at a volume the others could all hear, "but I suspect foul play. Possibly terrorism. I'll be discussing things with the mayor shortly."

Cindy nodded, then beckoned her crew toward the craft that would escort them back to the City.

Before Stella could offer any reassuring words to the stunned Arklings on deck, Naismith put his tablet in front of her face. "Ma'am." His screen was on the City News homepage:

"MELAMPUS STOCK CRASHES 30% AFTER DISASTROUS LAUNCH DEMO," read the top headline. And underneath it: ""Worthless heap of junk": Citizens react to SpecterX debacle."

Stella was stoic. She once more glared at her tense audience. "What is everybody looking at? Back to work. Station at the depot and prepare for refueling. I have an appointment with the mayor. Look lively! Oh, and Dante, a quick word?"

The crew dispersed as Stella darted toward her son. She grabbed his chin and whispered in his ear, "You will all regret what you have done for the rest of your lives." She next turned to Laura and sneered. "Back to your ants, Citizen."

The Ark screeched as its massive weight shifted and floated toward the fueling dock. Stella demanded all crew members who approached to stay away from her as she rode the elevator back down to her office. She placed her palm on the secret door. Iguazu flew all over his cage in a panic on seeing Stella's face.

"Time to see what's hiding in that bird brain of yours." Her wrath gave her such laser-focus that she managed to grab the bird in midair as soon as she reached into his cage. She retrieved a syringe of sedative from her pocket, put Iguazu to sleep, and stuffed him in her uniform. Once she felt the Ark stop and heard the moan of its fuel tank opening, she texted Teddy Wilcox: "Ready to meet. Send escort craft NOW."

She returned to deck and awaited the craft.

25

While Stella traveled to the top floor and waited for the mayor to grant her access to the servers, Dante fumed to the rest of his chain.

I think she killed my dad, he said. *I don't know how, but that's what I think. Nemos, what was he doing with you that day?*

Nothing unusual, Nemos answered, still shaken. *Data collection. I did think it was odd that Stewart wasn't there. Usually he would observe us on site while Dominic would monitor our brain scans. I'm sorry, but I can't think about this anymore for now.*

All right, Dante said. *Get some rest.*

Once she was gone, he announced a plan. *Edie, I think we should break into my mother's office. She'll be out for a couple of hours. Go in through the vent and unlock the door from the inside. I don't even care if I get caught. I'll take the blame. We need some answers. I'm taking charge of this ship tomorrow, and I'm not going to let my mother destroy any more evidence of her evil than she already has.*

A few members of the chain, including Laura, tried to convince him of the danger, but he was adamant. *I don't care!* He kept shouting with a somewhat frightening intensity of thought. He reminded Laura of his mother when she was angry.

As everyone waited for Edie to make her way back to

Stella's office through the vents, Laura tended to her own investigation. The day before, she had managed to complete a script that would automate the process of transferring every ant to the new data structure. It would still take several days for the process to complete, and she needed to make sure the script ran without errors, but she could relax a little now that the end was in sight and Dante would surely not force her to remain down there once she completed the current task.

To distract herself from the anxiety of waiting to hear about Edie and Dante's break-in, she decided to indulge a curiosity that had bothered her all week. In her haste to formulate the script, she had never even tried to connect her Specter to the ants.

She focused her gaze on one ant in particular: a worker, pushing a pellet of grain down a tunnel that led toward the queen's chamber. Laura located the ant on the computer's live map of the colony and confirmed that she had not yet been imported into the new data structure. As Laura had noted upon starting the script, importing an ant into the matrix used up so much of the memory on that ant's Specter that it would be impossible to connect with it while the script was still running.

The ant accepted the connection (as it had no doubt been trained to do) and granted Laura access to her microscopic world. Laura could inhabit the mind of a six-legged being pushing a giant ball of food. Her eyes saw nothing in the dark tunnel, but she could smell her way forward, guided by the queen's strong pheromones. At one point, the worker ran into another headed in the opposite direction; they rubbed their antennae together and exchanged information about their respective responsibilities toward the colony. Laura discovered that she could not speak to the ant the way she would to a larger creature; the ant would simply freeze in confusion, too immersed in her environment to even begin to attempt to communicate with the alien mind that now observed her.

Laura disconnected so that she could seek an update from Edie and Dante. Sure enough, Edie was in the process of turning the lock inside Stella's office and granting Dante access. Dante, who had put on gloves for the occasion, immediately went to his mother's desk and opened the folder labeled "Martian research." He removed and examined several sheets of paper.

What the hell are these?

Through his eyes, the chain studied multiple strange drawings (the same ones, in fact, that the Martian president had shown to Stella the week before): creatures with dragon wings and pig tails; werewolves with flies' eyes and mantis arms; snakes with dagger-toothed smiles and scissors for rattles; sasquatch-like beasts with oozing scabs, black and brown and blue and green. They were the stuff of nightmares, which was the point.

Is that it? Dante put the drawings back and scanned the office for any further useful documents. But the desk and the shelves were all empty. Stella had already moved most of her stuff out in preparation for making the office her son's. There was only the computer on the desk, which Dante was pleased to find did not require a password for login, only to see that this was because Stella had already wiped the hard drive clean and reset the whole operating system.

Damn it. There must be something else in here. Something.

His attention then darted to a strange crack that ran the vertical length of the wall to his right. He approached it and tucked his fingernails into the crack, only to find himself pulling open the secret door, which Stella had not thought necessary to close all the way in her haste to leave the Ark.

I guess we know what happened to Iguazu. The emptied, still-open cage faced him.

Oh God, Laura said. *Do you think she killed him?*

No, said Dante. *The strange thing about my mom is that she would never kill an animal. She would allow the bots to do it, but she would never do it herself. She prefers animals to humans.*

But the cage was not the only object of interest. The cage sat on a table that had a small drawer. And inside this drawer, Dante found, was a single thumb drive.

Dante ran to insert the drive into the computer. The drive

contained ten labeled folders, one for each of the nine Biomes and a tenth for the City, which itself contained ten subfolders corresponding to the City's twelve floors. And inside these folders, Dante found to the whole group's astonishment, were scripts that contained massive data structures, matrices that resembled the one Laura was assembling.

What are these? Dante asked, though of course nobody knew. Then, Dante opened the one file on the drive that did not sit in any of these folders: a simple textfile labeled "Instructions."

"To activate Influencer mode: turn Specter right eight times, left seven times, right six times, left five times, right four times, left three times, right twice, left once, then hold for eight seconds."

Stop! Laura said when Dante began to turn his Specter to the right. *We don't know what this does. It could be dangerous.*

It can't be, Dante said. *She clearly intended to do this herself.*

Fine, Laura said. *But let me do it. In case this activates some kind of signal on Stella's end, it's better that I'm the one caught stealing data from her than you.*

What? No, Laura, don't—

Please, Laura shouted over him. *You're less than 24 hours away from achieving your dream and getting real power. Don't throw it away.*

Dante, moved to tears by Laura's self-sacrifice, nodded and let her disconnect.

Laura held her breath as she counted the turns:

Eight, seven, six, five, four, three, two, one.

Then, pressing the X into her skull: *Eight, seven, six, five, four, three, two, one.*

She did not, as feared, experience some big electric jolt or have a stroke. Instead, a quiet voice spoke into her mind: *Influencer mode activated. Please select target.*

Inferring what was meant by "target," she focused on the worker ant from before. But her device would not let her make contact.

Error, said the quiet voice. *Target must be in object type "matrix."*

Laura's stomach twisted. A horrible intuition of "Influencer mode's" purpose struck her. Following the intuition, she went to the computer, interrupted her script, and found an ant who had already been exported into the matrix: this one, the queen.

Laura gazed at the queen, who lazed royally on a giant pile of eggs, and made contact.

It took her a moment to notice how different this connection felt from the one with the worker. There was no need to toggle between the different layers of her mind and the ant's. It felt much like the simultaneous sharing of neural space she and the others on the chain of eight experienced through Edie's distributed network. But it was different still: whereas Edie's subsidiary leg-minds all could retain their autonomy and feed information back to her central brain, Laura felt no feedback at all from the ant. Their perceptions, radically different though they were, formed a single whole. Laura heard or felt no resistance from the ant as she contemplated what to do next.

She decided to test her hypothesis. *Move your antennae,* she instructed the queen.

Laura's forehead seemed to tingle as the antenna wiggled. Just like that, the queen obeyed Laura's "influence."

Laura confirmed the power of Influencer mode through a number of other commands; she had the queen walk shorter and longer distances; she had the queen take food from her workers and eat it; she had the queen stack the eggs in her nursery chamber into multiple configurations.

She next decided to see what would happen if she commanded the queen to do something that seemed physically impossible:

Inside the wall beside the enclosure's glass was a chute. As Laura knew from other observation rooms, this chute would take anything the experimenter put inside it and insert it into the animal's habitat. Laura fetched an apple from her refrigerator and placed it inside the chute. The apple plopped right beside the mound of dirt that sat on the surface of earth above the colony's tunnels.

Eat the entire apple in one minute, Laura instructed the queen.

What happened next shocked Laura. The queen did not budge. Instead, every single ant in the colony—or rather, most of them, the ones who were by now in the data structure Laura had created—mobilized and scrambled out of the tunnels. They swarmed the apple and slashed it with their teeth into tiny pieces. They then brought the crumbs to the queen for her prompt consumption. Because of their physical limitations, the process did take a bit longer than a minute, but not by much. And the queen did not eat the entire apple herself—her tiny body would not be able to handle it, but she ate quite a bit of it, and Laura watched for a couple of minutes as she shoveled bits of apple tissue into her mandibles.

Hurry up and finish the apple, Laura tried.

At that point, the other ants all joined the queen in her chamber and used their own digestive enzymes to dissolve the remainder of the apple into nothing.

Laura then disconnected and tried "influencing" another ant, this one a worker.

Build me a statue of Stella Melampus, Laura commanded, picturing Stella's face. Within seconds, the ants were all on the surface stacking grains of sand into larger and larger shapes. Not five minutes passed before a small but considerable statue with Stella's unmistakable likeness abutted the mound.

Laura recognized that the individual "target" of her influence did not matter. Thanks to the matrix, the colony operated as a single intelligence.

She disconnected and turned her Specter in the opposite directions as before, then held it down again. She was not sure this would work, but thankfully, it did,

Influencer mode deactivated.

She returned to Edie's chain. By then, Dante had removed his phone and begun taking screenshots of as much of the data on the thumb drive as he could. There was no way he could get even a small fraction of it, but he hoped he could record enough to begin to piece together just what his mother was plotting.

Sorry to interrupt, Laura said. *But I think your mother is creating a hivemind.*

Yeah. Dante sighed. *I figured as much.*

26

As this revelation dawned on Laura and Dante, Stella met Mayor Wilcox on the top floor of the City, at the entry gate to the Servers. The Servers, built as a concentric series of cells of computer towers and consoles that occupied the northwestern quadrant of the top floor, were not accessible to ordinary Citizens, and as one went further in, access to each cell was more and more restricted. The City Mayor was the only person in the Arkology able to enter the innermost cell.

"What the hell was that?" Teddy asked Stella. He lay his palm on the wall and granted her entry to the first ring.

"Don't use that tone with me. You know how my son has been lately. Him and that traitorous intern. And to think that I was going to spare her..."

"So you don't even know what they did?" Teddy clutched his balding head.

Stella, a few inches taller than him, rested a hand on his shoulder. "The elements have long been in place for a plan B. I just need our friend here to tell us what he knows."

Teddy's eyes widened. Stella removed the sleeping parrot from her uniform.

They passed through the cells. The lighting grew dimmer and dimmer: because the activities of City programmers were more and more private the farther into the Servers one went, the Terrarchists had recently added tinted glass to the windows in the ceilings of the central cells. And once one

171

neared the center, there were no windows at all. The only lighting came from the LED bulbs of the various machines and the greenish glow of console screens.

Teddy granted entrance to the central cell, and there, among the few towers that ran the operations of the central command hub, operations that radiated out to the cells around them and governed the automated homeostasis of the entire Arkology, was the Source: the newly installed console that Stella alone could access through fingerprint scan.

She logged in and interrupted the script that had been running for the last several days: the script that sorted every being in the Arkology, human or animal, into a single massive data structure that she had hoped (as did Teddy and Mars, though for different reasons than Stella intended) she could use to create a single influenceable hive mind. Unfortunately, as she already knew, the botched product launch meant that they were unable to get enough customers to purchase the SpecterX of their own accord for the plan to work: if the vast majority of the population remained without the devices, they could not be influenced, and they could fight back against those who were. But that did not concern Stella right then: she was confident that she and Mars could devise an alternative plan.

She cared only about what Iguazu knew. By pausing the memory-intensive script (a script much like the one Laura wrote to sort the ants), Stella would free up the memory on Iguazu's device and allow it to continue sending data about Iguazu's thoughts to the Source. But Stella did not want mere data, the simple chunks of numbers that investors had been hoping to feed into their own algorithms and use for advertising purposes. No, she wanted direct knowledge of Iguazu's memories. And for that, she would need to influence him.

She turned her Specter. *8, 7, 6, 5, 4, 3, 2, 1.*

She pressed it. *8, 7, 6, 5, 4, 3, 2, 1.*

Influencer mode activated.

She made contact with Iguazu. Though the bird was still asleep, a number of images passed through his mind like the stuff of nightmares: creatures with dragon wings and pig tails;

werewolves with flies' eyes and mantis arms; snakes with dagger-toothed smiles and scissors for rattles; sasquatch-like beasts with oozing scabs, black and brown and blue and green.

And then, in the exact instant that his brain lost all autonomy and handed it over to Stella, he saw it:

A thing with long arms, a thing with no face, a thing whose entire body beats with a heart that cannot be seen.

Wake up, Stella commanded.

The entranced bird opened his eyes and gazed at his new master-mind.

Recall everything you know about Dante and Laura's activities over the last two weeks, she instructed.

And just like that, she had the power to know everything.

PART THREE:

A HEART THAT CANNOT BE SEEN

27

I suppose I finally decided to sit and write this book once I acknowledged my unprocessed grief. You, too, may be grieving. Perhaps you lost one or more loved ones. Perhaps you just lost an idea.

I know Dante grieved as he stood on the stage of the Ark's grand ballroom on his eighteenth birthday and swore the oath that he would perform his duties as captain and chief executive in service of Melampus and the lost planet that Melampus fought to restore. He grieved his father, whose portrait was penultimate in the long line of portraits that snaked around the ballroom's walls. And as the more than fifty faces of Dante's ancestors who had helmed the Ark before him stared him down, and as the hired portraitist revealed the face that would forever be Dante's for anyone who came as many hundreds of years after Dante as Dante came after Olaf, Dante grieved his childhood fantasy of this day.

He had imagined feeling powerful—like the entire world was his, like he could salvage his father's passion for putting the Biomes first—and to a certain extent it was, and he could. But the faces of the hundreds of Arklings who had gathered to celebrate the transfer of power showed one shared emotion: fear. *Don't let us down,* was the thought they could convey to Dante without needing to use their Specters. *We've invested our money in you; we've spent our lives on this ship*

177

with you; don't let us down like your mother just did.

The thought that Melampus could ever be vulnerable to a hostile takeover was unthinkable until now. They owned the island, for God's sake. But Olaf's heirs, seeing the effects of the collapse reverberate across the planet and recognizing that their island would soon be the only refuge for humanity, had made the City public and allowed the survivors to form their own system of technocratic democracy and free market capitalism. Over the last thirty years, the debts to Mars that Dominic and Stella had accumulated in developing the Specters had reached a dangerous point, and if Dante couldn't reverse the damage everyone believed his mother had caused and save the SpecterX, anything was possible. The Arklings and their families on the top floors of the City had enough wealth and enough control of the Arkology's arsenal that they could easily switch loyalties if Mars came to claim its debts and they believed it was necessary to preserve their elite status.

Later that night, when Dante took his first look as captain at the Melampus ledger, he found that billions and billions of dollars had, in just the week since Dante had delivered his board meeting, disappeared from the company's accounts without explanation.

"Maybe we were hacked," Stella said with a wry smile when he asked about it. "Don't let the Board know until you've investigated. I don't know if we could handle another hit to our public trust."

In the hours between his discovery of the thumb drive and Stella's return to the Ark, Dante had been smart enough to return to his room and wait there with his door locked until midnight. Multiple Arkling officers asked to enter, claiming that his mother needed to speak to him, but Dante feigned sickness and offered to speak with her in the morning. He knew she had somehow obtained knowledge of Edie's presence through Iguazu.

Dante silently thanked his great-times-fifty-grandfather Olaf for programming the Ark such as he had. At exactly midnight, total control of the Ark's security system, and all the bioscan gateways needed to access its most secret points, passed from Stella to Dante. Olaf, who had designed his company's system of succession and kept the codes secret until his death, had imagined a scenario where one executive might refuse to pass power to the next. Engineers of course had the technology to hack his code and read it in the thousand years since, but they discovered that any attempt to alter it would cause the entire Ark to self-destruct. Only a vote of no confidence from the Board could alter the transfer of access. Knowing this, Dante secured his room and ensured that nobody would enter and find Edie's tank without his permission.

Scared and paranoid though he was, Dante wasted no time in announcing the immediate launch of his alternative, privacy-enabled model of the SpecterX. Even investors who had initially hesitated to embrace the second model welcomed it with open arms after a disastrous 24 hours of press coverage had revealed a Citizen public completely unwilling to trust Melampus.

"I want to acknowledge the mistakes my mother has made," Dante took no small delight in saying during his birthday speech. Stella showed no emotion in the front of the ballroom crowd. "While I assure our customers that there is no nefarious intent behind Pathnet"—Dante had to swallow his fear as he said this line—"we also appreciate their desire for full control of their cognitive data, which is why we are releasing this private model. No advertisers will see your thoughts without your knowing."

—

Dante waited for the other shoe to drop. It didn't. Not for a while. The day after his birthday, his mother came to the office that was now his with a small suitcase. "I'm going to travel a bit. Use some of my former CEO privileges. See the Biomes without such an eye for controlling them. Maybe go to some parts of the City I haven't seen."

Dante squinted, nodded slowly.

"Oh, don't look so scared," she said. "You won. You got what you wanted. Let your old mother have a vacation."

Having switched out all the crew's Specters once more, he had no way to track her during her days and ultimately weeks of absence. He couldn't sleep any better after becoming captain than he could before. His schedule became very full. He needed to refamiliarize himself with every crew member's place in the chain of command, all while working to scale up production of his private model to meet what would hopefully be high demand once it was ready for release in two weeks. He also wanted to keep his promise to Varuna and begin distributing the Specters to the animals. When he had time, he would recruit my (Prince's) help in going out into the grassland and convincing various animals to switch out their devices. Having already experienced the switch to the X in recent weeks, they were largely happy to hear about Dante's alternative. I got to spend a lot more time with him than I had in the last few weeks during those initial days of his captainship. He stuck to work, mostly, refusing to admit to the fear I could smell. Laura was the only one who could get him to face it.

She came up to us one day as we replaced the Specter of a bison. Dante's heart fluttered as she made her way through the milkweed and sunflowers. Her hair looked extra red in the prairie sun.

"Long time no see," she said. It was their first in-person encounter in a dozen days. Dante had immediately allowed her to roam the ship freely, but he had been careful to avoid her in the sight of his nosy Terrarchist employees. They had talked by Specter a few times, but only for Laura to ask whether Dante had been able to glean any more information about his mother's intentions from the thumb drive data he had recorded, and for Dante to say he hadn't.

"How have you been?" She asked as an agitated Dante stroked the bison's fur.

"Oh, you know, busy. Waiting for my mom to jump out of a tree and kill me somehow."

Laura nodded with a smile. Dante looked away and pretended to be checking something on the bison.

"Is something wrong between us?" She asked.

"What? No!" Dante kept his eyes averted. "Why?"

"I feel like you're avoiding me."

Dante nodded. He searched for words.

Sensing an intimate conversation, I took the opportunity to give them some space.

"I'll be over talking to the horses," I said. I pattered down a dirt trail that went into the tall foxtails, careful to avoid touching them lest they catch in my fur. Once I was out of their sight, I stopped to listen, making sure my master was okay.

"I'm scared," he whispered after a while.

"I understand," said Laura. She rubbed his shoulder. "I am, too."

"Do you want to talk about it?" Dante asked the way one does when one wants to talk about something oneself.

"I'm worried about my dad, mostly. He's caught up to Wilcox in the polls. I'm kind of shocked that he has a chance to win, especially since there's still a month left for him to build momentum. He's been telling me about his campaign staff, and how busy he is traveling around the City, and all I can do is hope he doesn't get killed."

Dante nodded. "Can I hug you?"

Laura chuckled. "Of course, dumbass."

They embraced. They both had hair that smelled of sage. Dante heaved a sigh into Laura's shoulder. He didn't part arms when she tried. He was shaking. He was crying.

Laura stroked his hair, then kissed his temple. "I think this is a hug for you," she said.

Dante pulled away and smiled, his face runny with tears and snot. "You know something?" he asked as he wiped his nose. "My father was an asshole."

Laura laughed.

"Not like my mom is," he continued. "But she was at least around to yell at me and throw me around sometimes. My dad was just this untouchable icon. He would show up once every week or two and share some grand political axiom and pretend he was my best friend. And I fucking wanted him to be. I wanted to be him. It's disgusting to admit it, but I did. But he was hardly a father. Stewart was the one who taught me most of what I knew about programming. My dad was just there to fill in the blanks."

Laura related to this. "It's okay to miss your dad," she said after a pause, feeling a little stupid to say something so banal.

But Dante didn't think it was stupid. "He never had a problem with me being a boy. I'll give him that."

Laura hugged Dante again. "Whatever happened to Stewart?" She asked.

"I don't know," Dante shrugged. "He just told me he was going back to the City after my dad died. I tried to find him later, but couldn't. He probably changed his name."

"Would you want to find him?" Laura asked.

"No," said Dante. "If he left, it was for a good reason. I don't want to endanger him."

A butterfly landed on the bison's back. The two humans hugged again.

"I'm afraid to ask...but do you still think your mom...?" Laura asked without finishing.

"I don't know," said Dante. "Probably. She had to know at least. But now that I'm captain, and I see all the rot around me, and just how paranoid my parents must have been my entire life, and I think about all the times they talked about who-knows-what behind my back...I can't bring myself to care. I mean, I care, of course, but there's more going on right now. At least, it seems like there must be. You know, I haven't heard one thing from Wilcox or Mars. What the hell's going on? Fuck, I haven't slept at all in weeks, Laura. I'm losing my mind. I feel like we could all disappear any second. I feel like—"

Laura pulled Dante in by his collar and kissed him on the lips.

He broke away and staggered backwards. "What was that for?!"

She fixed her eyes on his. "If we're going to disappear any second, then you need to know how I feel."

He kissed her back, harder.

They shook with tears.

They fell into the grass.

They cried and kissed and cried and kissed.

They took turns rolling over each other, one looking at the

earth while the other looked at the sky, thinking about this bubble they were both trapped in, the world around them that made them fight so hard for one second of freedom.

"I'm sorry." Dante pulled away suddenly. "I can't be what you want. I can't be what you need me to be. I'm playing a role for the entire world."

"What do you mean?" Laura grabbed his face.

"I wanted to say it," Dante said, aware that his feelings were too grandiose and capacious for him to have any answer to her question. "At my birthday. I wanted to look right into the cameras and come out as trans. But I knew the men in that room didn't love me like they said they did. I knew they would turn on me and on the animals and on this world if I really challenged them. And you know what else? I wanted to tell them I loved you. I love you, Laura. But I can't be what you need. I'm too big a coward. I'm too trapped in this system that made me think I had power. But I don't. I'm trapped in the vision of a psychotic billionaire from a thousand years ago. I'm the least powerful person alive."

Laura sat up and frowned at him. Then, she laughed. "Give me a break," she said. "Don't let them make you a victim."

Dante covered his face, breathed deeply, then moved his hands away to reveal an expression of deep peace. "You're right," he said.

Laura kissed him. "You don't need to tell the world you love me. You're telling me now."

My heart seemed to beat right down to my legs as I learned about this kind of love I knew existed, and had even felt, but had never seen in reality. I was happy for them. But I was also sad. The one I loved was stuck in a tank.

—

It was a surprise when he asked to see me that night.

I never thought I'd say this, he said. *But I'm lonely.*

Of course you're lonely, I answered from my seat at Dante's feet in his room. *It doesn't make you weak to want some company.*

Varuna moaned. *I've started banging my head against the*

wall.

What? Don't do that.

He'd grown stir-crazy and paranoid in our most recent conversations. He was pleased that Dante was living up to his promise, but he shared everyone's feeling that more was coming. A mind like Varuna's was unable to just relax and let things unfold.

I'll ask Dante if he can let me see you, I said.

Wait, he chirped. *I want to touch you.*

I didn't know what to say.

I want to swim with you, like we did when we met.

I had never heard him like this. Sure, he liked to manipulate me, but rarely did he give direct orders. I thought of resisting, but the truth was, I wanted to swim with him, too.

"Dante?" I asked. He was still awake. "Can I get access to the upper level of Varuna's aquarium?"

If poodles could blush, the wry look he gave me would have done it. "Prince!" He said with mock astonishment.

"I'm sorry," I said on impulse. I covered my face with my paw.

"Don't be," he said. "Yes, you may. Just don't go in the water. I know you're a poodle, but I couldn't handle another near-drowning."

"OK," I answered with every intention of honesty.

You probably don't want to hear what happened next, after Dante walked me to the elevator and left me to ascend to the upper level. Or, maybe your prurient curiosity has the better of you. Maybe you want to read about the static charge in the air as I walked up to the edge of the water where he waited. Maybe you want to hear about the electric jolt of his clicks pulsing into me as I hung my paw down and spread the pads of my claws on his melon. Maybe you want to picture the image he sent—no Specter needed—as I bent my head down to sniff him and he raised his head so I could nuzzle his rostrum. Perhaps you do or do not want to picture the red rocket shooting into space, my red rocket, a rocket nobody had ever dared to reveal to me. Perhaps you want me to write that my falling into the water was a violent act, that he whacked me in with his tail against my will, that the virtuous poodle you all know would never dare to enjoy when he flipped onto his back and told that dog to lie across him sideways so they formed a cross, like that upside-down cross I've been told is the cross of martyrs. Many of you, I suspect, do not want to read one word about that wet and sloppy minute where I shot off into space before falling back down into a sense of deep shame at having lied to my master. You don't want to believe that Varuna knew that shame and comforted me through it, let me go back to Dante, who himself had an aura of bliss on my return, with the sense that he and I and all of us could do fucking anything no matter what was coming.

Wherever your preferences lie, this is all I'll write about it. Because it's mine.

28

One could debate whether it was more courageous or stupidly proud for Dante to host a Specter promotion event at the very same bar where Peter would throw his first rally since catching up to Wilcox in the polls. Cindy Zhao and other journalists were quick to notice and ask if this meant an endorsement of the independent candidate.

"No," Dante said with a slightly cheeky half-grin. "It's just good business. We know that Peter Delacroix's supporters were those most likely to reject the premise of Pathnet, so we want them to know that Melampus is offering a product for them as well."

"Your mother's work in aligning Melampus with Terrarchist party causes is well-known," said Cindy. "Whether or not this is an endorsement, it seems like quite the shift."

"Listen," said Dante, who had taken Laura's advice to stop being a victim to heart. "We're a technology company. Yes, we own the hardware that makes this world run, but it's always been up to the Citizens to decide how they want to use it. Whoever is Mayor next term, we will work with them closely. Now, if you'll excuse me, I need to talk to my team..."

Dante and a few Arklings set up a demo booth that allowed people in the bar to try the private Specters out for themselves before, hopefully, buying one after the rally. He knew how this would look to his mother, wherever she was, along with

186

any investors who happened to be watching. But Laura (who knew her attendance would just be one step too far) and Varuna (who kept in contact with me as I accompanied Dante during the day's activities) were also watching, and love made us both do foolish things. And there was a deeper reason for our being there. Dante wanted to get into the Source to find more information about his mother's hivemind project and make sure we had thwarted it; he knew Wilcox would not grant him entry, but Laura had given him reason to think Peter might be able to help.

As Peter spoke, and as the crowd roared in response to his promises to undo the damage done the last thirty years and longer, Dante and I forgot how scared we were and began to feel like we were winning. At one point, after giving his usual stump speech, Peter pointed to us.

"I want to thank my supporters for being so respectful toward our surprise guests, the new CEO of Melampus and his dog."

The crowd responded with an ambivalent mix of applause and boos.

"Hey!" Peter raised a hand. "I know most people here aren't huge fans of Melampus, and normally I'm right there with you. But this kid's got a different vision than his mother did, and I think he wants to do great things. You all remember what Melampus's slogan used to be? A lot of you are younger than me, so maybe not. But when I was a kid, that kid's dad was about as old as he is now, and he would come on TV and say "let's pop the bubble." Pop the bubble! That was the original reason Melampus allied with Mars, supposedly: to get them to stop using their tech to mine the rest of the planet for the materials they need to build their stupid space army—you know, to colonize the galaxy and defend themselves against the aliens that *definitely* exist—"

Everybody laughed, including Dante.

"—and start working with us to terraform this planet back to a livable state and get us all the fuck out of here! Say it with me, everyone: Pop the bubble!"

The entire crowd chanted: "Pop. The. Bubble! Pop. The. Bubble!"

"Of course, that kid's dad was probably a liar," said Peter once the chant subsided. "But hey, we'll never know, because he's dead. God rest his soul. And every company deserves a second chance. Or a fiftieth chance, as the case may be."

Dante refused to admit to himself that this hurt. He laughed along with everyone else. Peter was just playing to the crowd, after all. Peter declined to admit that he had already met Dante when filming his ad with Soda, but at one point, he looked right at him and smiled.

After the rally concluded, and as many attendees did indeed go over to the booth and purchase new Specters, I sauntered over to the stage where Peter signed autographs and took selfies and offered a small box that I carried in my mouth. Before taking it from me, Peter glanced across the bar at Dante, who nodded as though to assure him the box would not explode.

"A gift from Melampus," I said. "A small thanks for allowing us to sell our merchandise here. You may open it here, or"—I placed careful emphasis here, not sure who may be listening—"at home."

While Dante knew Peter would not be completely free of AI surveillance in his own home, it was still a good deal safer to open the box there than in public, where cameras monitored by humans were impossible to escape. As Laura assured Dante, moreover, Peter was smart enough to catch the meaning of my tone and wait until he was in his bathroom, where he could be reasonably confident nobody on the top floor wanted to snoop on him personally (especially if they were men, for such surveillance could be interpreted as homosexual voyeurism in need of reprogramming) to open the box that contained a private Specter with the materials and instructions necessary for both self-activation and contacting Dante.

Hello Peter, Dante said from his office.

Hi, Dad, Laura added. By now, all members of the chain of eight (except Iguazu, who was, to our deep dismay, still missing) had private Specters and could listen to the call without need of Edie's mediation.

We need your help, she said. *We're looking for some*

data—possibly very dangerous data—that Dante's mother has kept hidden.

Laura explained what they had found through the ants and the thumb drive. *I hope I'm not wrong,* she said at last, *but I have a memory of you having been a part of planning the redesign of the Servers when I was a kid.*

That's right, said Peter. *Terrarchists wanted all the windows taken out of the central cells. When they did that, though, we had to redesign the whole ventilation system to prevent the Servers from overheating.*

All of us on the Ark exchanged expressions of excitement in our various species' tongues.

Calm down, everyone, Dante said, laughing at Peter's palpable confusion. *Peter, which entry point to that system would be most accessible for a small octopus who can survive about thirty minutes out of water?*

—

After a few days of planning, Dante staged a press event at the Terrarchist Party headquarters, a byzantine cluster of concert halls and political offices located on the top floor. Given some bad press around his attendance at Peter's event, he planned to promise the party's major donors—most of whom were also either Arklings or their immediate family and therefore investors in Melampus—that Melampus would continue to support Wilcox's campaign. But the event was also a convenient excuse for him to launch the newest plan.

Before leaving the Ark, he stuffed Edie inside a portable fish bowl that would fit inside the backpack he used to carry his laptop. Once inside party headquarters, he went into the restroom, climbed on top of the toilets, and placed Edie's bowl close enough to the vent to allow her to slither and squeeze inside.

As Dante went out and greeted the Terrarchist leadership, Edie opened a channel with Peter, who sat safely at home and provided her with instructions that would allow her to navigate the ducts that wove into and through the Servers without getting sucked into a fan and killed.

Dante planned to give a brief address to restore investors' confidence, field a couple of questions, and then be out of there within fifteen minutes, in time to join Edie's channel and guide her through the process of logging into the source. "Thirty years ago," Dante began. "My father made the choice to steer Melampus in a different direction. After the sweeping electoral victories your party achieved in response to the fuel shortage and the wave of crime that followed, my father knew that a focus on community integrity and free market deregulation was the only way forward. I am here to tell you that I plan to continue my father's vision for the company."

Dante suppressed his urge to retch as he said these words. He had been careful to say "father" rather than "parents." Dominic's voice guided him forward. "It's all a means to an end," Dominic would always say. "As long as you don't forget your values, why you're doing what you're doing in the first place, there's nothing immoral about using the system. The Terrarchists have power, so we use it to our advantage. By the time you take charge, things might be different."

Of course, things weren't different. Things were worse. As the Terrarchists allied with Mars, Mars pressured them to adopt the socially regressive policies that would leave much of the City living in fear. And when Dominic tried to protest, both the party and Mars threatened to take him over. Dante wondered if his father could have done any more; he wondered if his protesting was the cause of his death. He wondered if there was any way out of this nest of special interests. But he couldn't think too much about it. All he needed to do, he thought at this point, was to buy time until Peter, now leading in the polls by a narrow margin, could win the election, and he could really dismantle whatever plan his mother had going with Mars.

At the end of Dante's statement, party chairman Colton Naismith (brother of Arkling Security Director Naismith) took the stage beside him. "Thank you so much, Mr. Melampus, for coming by and clarifying your position."

As the chairman spoke, Dante took a moment to check on Edie. *I've made it inside*, Edie said. She had her tentacles wrapped around the Source's console, identifiable through the Melampus insignia (a man with two snakes coming out of his ears) that she could feel was etched into the monitor. *Now what?*

Turn it on, Dante said.

Edie slithered down to the power button. The screen requesting Stella's fingerprint scan appeared.

Shit, Dante said. *I hoped it would just ask for Melampus credentials.*

Hold on, said Edie. *If all we need is a fingerprint, I can search for impressions on the keyboard.*

Edie undulated up to the keyboard and caressed a few keys, using her extremely sensitive tentacles to look for prints on the keys. She had expected there to be a fresher coating of dust that made it difficult for her to find Stella's prints from two weeks prior, but to her surprise, it was quite easy.

She's been here in the last day or two, said Edie.

I don't know what you're trying to do, said Dante. *But be fast.*

Edie wrapped herself around the monitor once more and located what she needed: a taped-on manufacturer's label. She gripped the tape as hard as she could in her suction cup and tore it off, then returned to the keyboard, lay it down on the spacebar, and stripped off a print. She then planted the tape onto the console's screen. They were in.

You're incredible, Edie. Now export everything to the cloud drive we set up.

Edie's colors pulsed. *Uh...I'm going to need some help with that.*

OK. Just give me a minute to wrap up here.

The chairman concluded a long speech that Dante had not heard. "All that being said, we do wonder if, given the events of recent weeks—particularly the sudden scaling back of your plans for Pathnet and your unfortunate, if practically sound, appearance at a certain mayoral candidate's event, you might be willing to sign a pledge that some of us have written. We trust that you'll be eager to show your lifelong commitment to Terrarchist values."

Dante read the document that Chairman Naismith laid on the lectern for him to sign. It had all the usual Terrarchist platform tenets. "Mandatory Reprogramming of Sexual Deviants" was the one that caused him to shudder:

"In the interest of ensuring that the AI can factor every human into its population control mechanisms properly, the Terrarchist Party advocates for the continued enforcement of reprogramming policies in the event of sexual or gender deviance. First offense: Reeducation and operant conditioning. Second offense: tongue removal. Third offense: death."

Dante looked at his audience. *We know your secret,* their eyes all seemed to say. And some of them did.

It's just a piece of paper, Dante assured himself. He signed. The dozens of donors stood and applauded. Dante tried to exit the stage immediately, but the chairman grabbed him and forced him to smile for the camera drones that buzzed around the auditorium.

Hey, Dante? Are you there? Edie grew anxious.

"Please, if you would," said the chairman. "Read the pledge out loud for us."

Ugh, Dante transmitted. *One more minute.*

But it took five minutes for Dante to read the pledge for the cameras. And by the end of those five minutes, five minutes when he could not answer Edie's calls, Edie realized she heard something behind the door of the inner cell. Voices.

Dante was not on the channel to watch as his mother and the Mayor walked through the door. He had to hear about it that night from everyone else on the call: Peter, Laura, Varuna, Gunny, Soda, Nemos, and myself. He had to hear secondhand about Edie's terror as she rushed back toward the vent. She might have made it, too, if not for the speed with which Iguazu, sitting on Stella's shoulder and under her control, flew toward her and yanked her up by the tentacle just as she was about to escape.

The sight of Stella jabbing a syringe into her head as she dangled in terror from Iguazu's talons was the last any of us would see from Edie's perspective for a long time.

29

Two more weeks went by. Relations among us grew strained after Edie's capture. I was present for more than one argument in Dante's room between him and Laura.

"Why would you even sign such an evil pledge?" She asked on his return to the Ark.

"You think I wanted to?" Dante slammed his palm against the wall. "I was cornered. I was on live television with our most powerful donors. Do you know what happens if I say no to them? They hand the Biomes over to Mars and turn this whole island into a colony of theirs. Say goodbye to even the fake democracy we have now. I had to sign it."

Laura forgave Dante, at least out loud, but she faced new stressors of her own. Dante's two-faced politics had put Peter in the awkward position of needing to declare him an enemy.

"They're all the same," Laura watched her father say on the Evening News. "Careerist ghouls who will sell your souls for a quick buck. Don't let this new guy fool you. He might be looking out for you now, but who knows what he has up his sleeve?"

Peter gave Dante a call one night to make sure there was no personal offense.

Do what you have to do, Dante transmitted. *It seems to be working for you.*

And indeed, it was. Peter now had multiple boogeymen that merged into one: Melampus, the Terrarchists, Mars. And

193

the polls showed that his message resonated. "They've all given up on you," he would say. "But not me. I believe in you. A vote for me is a vote for yourself." By the end of those two weeks, he had a ten-point lead (and growing) over Wilcox.

Laura, meanwhile, had to shield herself from public scrutiny. The Evening News contacted her several times asking for an interview. Cindy Zhao even gave her a personal call.

"Please, Laura. Our viewers are dying to know more about you. You would have full control of the interview, and we wouldn't even need to talk politics. I mean, we'd certainly want to talk about your father, and about your time at Melampus, but we wouldn't *need* you to express support for one candidate or another."

"I'm sorry," said Laura. "But I need to focus on my work. I can't get involved with this."

Of course, Laura barely knew what that even meant. Long gone was the time when she tried to develop an independent research project for a permanent position; she simply hoped that her father would win the election and gain enough power for her job at Melampus to become a moot point. Her "work" was now indistinguishable from most of the other crew, who were all out in the Biomes installing Dante's Specters into thousands of animals. But this project raised several questions at the next monthly Board meeting.

"It made sense when we were adding the animals to a network that we shared with them and controlled," Agrippa CEO Oscar Montez suggested. "But why are we giving them the opportunity to talk amongst themselves? I mean, I'll give credit where it's due: sales of the new X have been great, and consumer trust is at a ten-year high, even despite some political attacks, but isn't it a waste of money to give these products to...animals?"

"We still have control of their network," Dante said. "And our bottom line can withstand the hit. We need the animals to trust us before we can welcome them into the new Earth. We can't forget the Melampus vision."

It didn't escape our attention that lines like this, which formerly brought investors to their feet in a standing ovation, now provoked mockery and distrust.

"What exactly does this "new Earth" look like?" Oscar asked with cynicism on the City News's business program. "Are we going to give all the animals little opposable thumbs and bipedal legs so they can run among us? Have we forgotten what the apes did all those centuries ago?"

The paranoia reached a fever pitch. "Officers who always used to want to approach me in the corridor and talk to me are avoiding eye contact now," Dante said as he bit his nails after midnight once.

"Could it just be that you've become their boss?" I suggested to calm him.

"No," he shook his head like a snake's rattle. "They never were like this with my mother. Something's going on. There are spies on this ship. They're talking to my mother somehow. I even tried calling Wilcox to see if I could get more information, but he ignores my calls."

Varuna, meanwhile, was doubling my exhaustion with similar, albeit more cryptic and mystical, visions of impending doom. I was wearing myself out trying to soothe both Dante and him. Once Dante had taken enough sleeping pills to pass out, I would go out to the elevator (which Dante had now programmed to grant me eye-scan access) and put my paws in the water to stop Varuna from thrashing his tail and screeching with stir-crazy mania.

I think I need to leave this tank, he would say. *I need to go talk to my pod. Something is coming. What we're doing isn't enough.*

I would give a stern paternal bark. *Varuna—nothing's happening right now. Just breathe, and tell me, what's coming?*

Varuna would slow and heave a sigh through his back. *I don't know. I feel like it's...God, I swear I'm not lying. It's the star-beings.*

There are no star-beings, I assured him. *And please,* I whimpered as I nuzzled him. *Don't leave. You're the only one who can make me feel safe. I couldn't handle Dante without you. The whole Ark would fall apart if you left.*

I really believed this. And maybe I was right. Or, maybe, I

was just losing myself to the addiction of his tough rubbery skin, his ability to engulf me and fold his flippers over me as I gasped for air and fought to feel alive. We sobbed in our respective tongues. Each of us became the lens we believed we needed to see ourselves as anything other than weak, defenseless prisoners.

And all of us, we knew, were drowning beneath a force that had yet to reveal itself.

Two weeks after Edie's capture, a shuttle's sonic boom shook the entire Arkology. Those of us with legs to do so went out onto the deck and craned our necks toward the sky.

The Martian president's red and mauve ship latched onto the space elevator that towered above the City's center and descended to Earth.

30

The four of us all met by Varuna's tank to confer after Dante received the call from a secretary in Mayor Wilcox's office: "Mayor Wilcox requests your attendance at an urgent meeting with himself, your mother, and Martian President Zelda Rogers. Your immediate presence is crucial to the continued survival of Melampus."

"Don't go," Laura said. "It's a trap."

"Of course it's a trap. But what kind?"

We all talked for a while about the information Stella would have gathered from Edie.

"I have to go," Dante said. "I hate to say it, but those three people combined have more power than I do. And don't you want to know what they've been planning all this time? She'll be sure to threaten me—maybe try to get me to revert the Specters again somehow. But I can take it."

I had a bad feeling. "What if they hold you down and switch your Specter out for you? So they can control your mind?"

"I'll have security to guard me," Dante said.

Laura had tears in her eyes. "Whatever happens, leave your channel open. I know you may not be able to communicate with us the whole time, but we need to see what's going on."

Dante gave Laura and me a hug. He flattened his palm on the tank, where Varuna laid a flipper to wish him good luck.

I wish I'd asked him to hold me a little longer. I wish I'd licked his face.

—

Dante boarded the craft that flew him up to the top floor. On his request, his entire C-Suite joined him: Wendell, Sherman, Rosen, Naismith. They believed it was a business meeting. Though Dante couldn't tell them about his fears in detail, they had all, per Ark policy, sworn an oath to protect their captain at all costs on his eighteenth birthday. He also brought a gun.

The Mayor's penthouse was the largest residence in the City, its giant golden walls occupying a full eighth of the top floor. Dante and his crew waited in the patio, which featured a large saltwater pool and overlooked the Desert Biome through transparent windowed walls. They were a thousand feet above ground; if not for the walls, Dante would have believed someone was about to push him over the edge.

To Dante's surprise, his mother was the one to come out and invite him inside. She gave a huge smile. "Honey!" She moved to wrap her arms around him, but he backed away. "Relax, dear. I don't have a weapon on me, for God's sake. See?" She opened her hands bare. She wore a white desert tunic without pockets. Dante relaxed a little, but after he let Stella hug him, she went stiff and frowned.

"I'm afraid they can't come in," she said, pointing to the C-Suite officers.

"Why not?" Dante asked.

Stella pursed her lips. "We're discussing top secret matters that are relevant to both the company and continued interplanetary security. They'll understand. Won't you, boys?" She winked in a manner that made Dante's stomach churn.

The Arklings said nothing. Dante looked at them, but they couldn't hold eye contact. Suddenly, nothing felt safe.

Dante crossed his arms. "If they can't come in, I won't either."

His mother stuck her lip out. "But we have such wonderful

refreshments inside."

"I'm not eating or drinking a damn thing," Dante said.

Stella put her hand to her chest and gasped. "My! A little paranoid, are we? Can you believe it, boys? My own son thinks I want to poison him."

The Arklings looked down at their feet.

"I'm not going in," Dante repeated.

"Fine." Stella sighed. "I'll see what can be arranged."

Several long minutes passed before she returned. "All right," she said. "We can meet out here where the surveillance drones can see us if you insist. But they still have to leave."

"Fine," Dante agreed. He doubted just how loyal these officers would be in a dangerous situation anyway. His mother still exerted some kind of magnetic effect on them.

Stella fetched Wilcox and Zelda from inside. A few waiters brought the refreshments out as the C-Suite members left and as Dante greeted the two politicians who were supposedly his business partners. They shook his hand firmly with tight smiles.

Everyone except Dante took a fruity tropical drink as they all sat around the pool and lounged in deck chairs. They exchanged terse pleasantries until all other parties had left the patio, at which point Stella clapped her hands.

"Let's get straight to it, then! I think I'm correct in saying that you generally know what we know that you know, and that there's really no point in us bullshitting each other."

Dante laughed. "You could put it that way."

"We also know that you know that you don't know *everything* that's been going on, and we're here to help you fill in the gaps. As your mother, I've been trying to protect you, but I can see it's led to some terrible misunderstandings."

That's for sure, Dante took the opportunity to transmit to us. All of us on the Ark watched with bated breath. Then, Stella raised her eyes ever so slightly, to Dante's forehead. We all shook. She seemed to look right at us.

"Unfortunately, though, before we can clear things up for you, we also need to state that we know you have a number of silly little friends of various species listening in." She pointed at her own Specter. "Isn't that right?"

"No comment," Dante said.

"I see. Well, I can understand why you would approach this conversation with some unease. How about this? We all remove our Specters right here. That way, you won't have to worry about...whatever it is you're worried about..." She winked. "And we three don't have to worry about spies."

To Dante's and our surprise, Zelda removed four syringes from her pocket. She, Stella, and Teddy all took one and jabbed it into their temples. Their Specters all came loose, and they lay them on the tables next to them. Stella offered the fourth syringe to Dante. He took it, but did not use it. He put it in his pocket.

"By spies," he said, "you mean people who can spread information about your *totally* benevolent plot to control everyone's minds."

Stella grimaced. Her mimosa shook in her hand. "You're making this very difficult, baby."

"Stella, if I may..." The Martian President cleared her throat and directed her striking gray eyes to Dante. "None of us here wants to be your enemy. What kind of Martian would I be if I didn't appreciate your idealism and your eagerness to forge your own path for Melampus? The problem, however, is that you and your friends are missing the forest for the trees. Look around us..." She stood up and raised her arms to gesture at the Desert behind the windows. "How much energy do you think it takes to sustain that Desert? To power the thousands of bots that heat the place, drain it of humidity, and prevent the animals from reproducing either too little or too much and disrupting the entire food chain? And that's not even getting to the other Biomes. Take the rainforest. How much energy does it take to seed the artificial clouds that keep that place so wet? And my God, the tundra."

Stella jumped in. "I know you think it's sheer negligence that's caused the tundra to melt, dear, but it's simply unsustainable to keep that place running."

"We've kept it running fine for a thousand years," Dante said.

"A thousand years is not that long," said Zelda with a sad smile. "How much energy do you think this all takes? Takes away, to be specific, from other pursuits?"

Dante stroked his beard and leaned back. "I'd say it takes less energy than it does to maintain a colony like yours, which apparently requires you to maintain a military to defend yourselves against aliens that don't exist."

Zelda frowned. "That's a cruel thing to say about a planet you've never visited. It sounds like you've been a victim of old Technolgalitarian propaganda. Why don't you come to Mars and challenge some of your prejudices?"

Dante threw his head back with harsh laughter. "Hell fucking no."

Stella shot daggers at him. "Do you talk to all your business partners like that?"

"I don't owe anything to any of you. I'm the fucking captain of my ship now. My ancestors built this place."

"Actually," Zelda smirked. "One ancestor and thousands of underpaid climate refugees built it."

"Excuse me? You, President of Mars, want to talk about getting underpaid laborers to work for you?"

Wilcox raised his hands. "Everyone, quiet! If I can just try talking to the boy..." Dante's nostrils flared a little with disgust as the clearly sleep-deprived Mayor smiled his smoke-yellowed teeth at him. He removed a cigarette from his pocket. "As Mayor, I've gotten a long look at the code that keeps the City running. We all have great respect for what your family built a thousand years ago. But it's breaking down, and the people are angry. I saw you sign that pledge a couple of weeks ago. You don't want a radical like Peter Delacroix coming in and destroying the innovation that's kept this place thriving for so long, do you? The innovation that's going to, one day, come up with a solution that can get us all out of the bubble and back to Earth?" He took a long drag and blew a stream of smoke that dispersed into Dante's eyes.

"I think..." Dante had to choose his words carefully. He did, after all, need to come to some kind of agreement with these people. "I think...that a society is at its least innovative when a very small group of people decides they have the right to steal the resources and the spirit of everyone else."

Something strange happened when Dante said this. His

mother, the Mayor, and the Martian President, who had all formed a single united front in looking at Dante and Dante alone, looked at each other—not directly, but nervously out of the corners of their eyes, the way one does when one's opponent says something that one's allies may or may not agree with and one is hesitant to voice one's own response. And in those nervous looks, Dante and all of us hoped for an opportunity: The potential that these three people might be as evasive with one another as they were with us.

Stella clapped her hands to break whatever spell Dante's words had threatened to cast. "Nobody here doubts your morals," she said. "But we must face reality. You know as well as we do that the Arkology is at a turning point. The City and the Biomes cannot coexist as they always have without some very drastic decisions. Decisions that may not be possible for us to make if we rely on the standard democratic process."

Dante glared at his mother. Her voice was choking a little. She sounded surprisingly soft and warm as she continued. "I assure you, baby, that you, personally, have nothing to fear. So long as you remove that Specter and have an honest, unmonitored conversation with us."

None of us wanted to transmit our thoughts to Dante and stress him out further as he looked over his shoulder at the Desert and paused to consider what these three people had said to him so far. A thin line of blue ocean was visible in the distance.

What they are saying doesn't make sense, he thought. *Yes, the Arkology requires a lot of energy, but there's more than enough heat in the ocean to keep the thermal conversion going for thousands more years. The only thing causing breakdown is their greed.*

He stood up. "No," he said. "I don't know what you're all planning, but I want no part of it."

We were all speechless. We had no idea what the consequences would be, or whether this was even the right choice.

Stella stood up and moved toward him. "If you leave," she said, "you'll be forced out of the company, and your name will mean nothing. And..." She whispered into his ear. "I'll tell everyone your secret."

Dante quivered. "I don't believe you," he whispered, moving his face very close to his mother's. "I don't believe you hate me that much."

Stella, for once in her life, struggled to find a response. She and her son locked eyes for several seconds. Her entire body became a dam to hold back a lifetime of secret hurts. Finally, she looked over her shoulder at Zelda. "That's it, then. Plan B."

"Plan B?" Dante squinted.

Zelda rose. She knelt down toward the saltwater pool. "Plan B!" She bellowed.

Dante might have made it if he ran. But in the time it took to decide, his mother grabbed his arms and locked him in place long enough for something to reach up from the saltwater pool and wrap around his leg:

He looked down to see a giant tentacle yanking on his ankle.

Stella pushed him down, and seven more tentacles wrapped around his body to drag him into the water as he screamed.

All of us watching sobbed and yelled at him in our minds to reach for his gun, but the octopus twisted his arm and yanked it away. This 600-pound behemoth was no baby. We struggled to comprehend what we witnessed as the octopus pulled him to the bottom of the pool and pinned him to the floor.

He held his breath and could only watch as a smaller cephalopod—could it be? Edie?—drifted in front of him with a syringe held in her tentacle. She jabbed it into his temple. Our feed to Dante fizzled, then went black, as the neural mesh of his Specter disengaged from his brain.

31

Dante? Dante!

He's gone.

Did they—?

Is he—?

...Those fucking murderers!

Even in Dante's room, I could hear Nemos's trumpeting wails all the way down in the testing sector.

After the initial panic, Laura and I shared a similar impulse: we disconnected from the group channel and sought support from those who served to protect us when Dante wasn't around. For me, this was Varuna. For Laura, it was her father.

He could be alive, Varuna said. *We didn't see a body.*

Oh, God! I howled and howled.

Prince, calm down. He issued some soothing soundwaves that bounced off his tank and fed back into our channel. *Here's what we're going to do. You're going to go out into the grassland and tell the animals what's going on. We're going to get them to storm the City and rescue Dante. And if Dante can't be saved, we'll go in and shut off the AI ourselves.*

I could barely process such an absurd idea. *What the hell are you talking about?*

All of the grassland animals have private Specters now. We have the power to fight back, but we have to be fast. I don't know what the humans are trying to pull, but this is just the first step.

I don't know for certain what would have happened if I'd just gone along with this plan, but it would have probably been ugly, and I felt far too powerless right then to entertain it. *Listen to yourself,* I said. *"Fight back?" The only thing a team of buffalo and jackrabbits from the prairie are going to do is give the bottom floor Citizens a roadkill feast. Do you have any idea what the City's defense systems are like? You've heard about the apes, haven't you? And since when was shutting the AI ever a desirable option, let alone a possible one? And you're talking about "the humans" as though they're one thing again?*

As Varuna and I argued, Laura had an equally upsetting conversation with Peter.

Laura, I'm glad you called. I have something to tell—

They killed him, Dad!

What? What are you talking about?

Dante—he went to a meeting with Stella and the Mayor and the Martian President, and they fucking killed him!

Laura explained as much of the call as she could.

Peter breathed quickly. *You don't know for sure that he's dead, do you?* He couldn't seem to face his daughter's emotions. *Maybe they just bloodied him up a little and switched out his Specter.*

Oh, yeah. That would be so much better. He's not dead; he's just a zombie. How could you say something like that?

I'm sorry, Laura! But what the hell do you want me to do?

I want you to get on the News right now and tell the whole City what happened.

Peter sighed and rubbed his face. *I can't do that.*

Why not?

Because I'm dropping out of the campaign.

...You're what?

I'm dropping out! I haven't announced it yet, but I just submitted the paperwork.

Laura almost yanked her hair out of her head. *Why?! You're winning!*

The Mayor's goons showed up here and threatened me. They know everything, Laura. That octopus of yours must have told them. They don't have our conversation data, but she's a witness to all of it, and they've looked into the surveillance cameras and found enough to create an airtight circumstantial case. If I didn't drop out, they were going to send both you and me to prison for both breaking into the Servers and attempting to steal Melampus data.

Laura's whole body screamed, but she kept her mind icy-quiet. *You're a fucking coward. You pretend you're not, but you always have been.*

Peter sobbed. *Laura...please...I—*

No. Fuck off. I'll call the News myself.

Laura knew it was harsh, but there was no time to waste if Dante was somehow alive.

Hi, Cindy? How quickly could you get me on for that interview? I've changed my mind.

Oh, wonderful! We could have you ready for the 8 PM broadcast. I'll send a craft to get you in an hour.

Laura got dressed and ready to go on television. I disconnected from Varuna in frustration and was on my way to her room to commiserate when the entire Ark lurched beneath my feet.

"What's going on?" I asked out loud to the next crewman I saw in the corridor.

"Headed to the ocean," he said. "Orders from the captain."

I couldn't hold back my tail from excitement. "You've heard from him? He spoke to you?"

"Written orders," he said with a funny look. "Still in his meeting, but says we're going to launch a new installation campaign in the morning."

I thanked him and went to Laura's room. She answered the door in the same dress Stella had given her for that demo for Ambassador Johnson over two months ago.

"How do I look?" She asked. We both wobbled a little as the Ark settled into the ocean.

"Like you're ready to crack some skulls. What's going on?"

"I'm going on TV."

The two of us shared the conversations we'd just had.

"Honestly," she said afterward, "Varuna's idea is

interesting. I don't think it would work, but it's something to keep in mind for after the interview. Those animals could help us if we need them."

I accompanied Laura to the deck, where she was to meet the craft.

While we were there, crewmen began to drop cages into the choppy sea. When the cages came up, they contained cephalopods of various kinds: not just octopuses, but squids and cuttlefish as well. The cages were loaded into tanks that were then dispatched into elevators that would bring them down to the testing sector.

What do you think that's about? Laura asked over Specter.

They must be the subjects of this new "installation campaign" Dante supposedly announced. I shared what we observed with Varuna.

They've made some kind of an alliance with the cephalopods, he said with paranoid certainty. *Think about it. Edie wasn't wearing a Specter when Dante saw her. None of the humans above the pool were either. They weren't controlling her. She did it of her own free will. They must have offered her something.*

What could they have offered her? I asked.

I don't know, he said with fear.

It was now several minutes after Laura's craft was supposed to arrive. She answered quickly when Cindy called her.

Laura, I am so sorry, but we have to bump you from tonight's broadcast. You understand, I'm sure: The news from Mars takes priority.

News from Mars?

You haven't heard? Turn on a TV!

Laura's patience was gone. *Dante Melampus was attacked and maybe murdered at a meeting today!* She blurted.

Ummm... Cindy's tone shifted dramatically, the way it does when one decides one is talking to an insane person. *Dante is going to be on television tonight with his mother and the Mayor and the Martian President. And you, I think, need some sleep. Goodbye!* She disconnected.

Laura and I stared at one another for a minute.

At least he's probably alive, I said.

We went back to Laura's room and turned on the City News. The lower third screamed its "breaking news" headline: *"MYSTERIOUS ILLNESS SWEEPS THROUGH MARTIAN APARTMENT COMPLEX; COGNOSCENTI SUSPECT FOREIGN INVOLVEMENT"* We spent the next couple of hours watching the talking heads discuss whatever "information" was coming to their attention.

Earlier that day, the story went, when it was the crack of dawn on Mars, a man had woken up screaming about all sorts of disturbing images that were flooding his brain and begging to be held. When the other residents of his coworking unit rushed to hold and calm him, they, too, began to scream and ask for someone to hold them. This continued until almost the entire apartment complex was screaming and begging for contact. A few holdouts realized that they were dealing with a contagion and contacted law enforcement, who then decided that they needed to cordon the complex off and lock everyone inside. Once everyone succumbed to the strange contagion and found themselves locked inside and lacking further vectors of transmission, they killed themselves. All sorts of rumors were swirling about the incident and its causes: was it a neurotoxin? Mass psychosis? And was someone behind it?: The Terrarchists? Melampus? Mars itself?

The search for an official explanation came to an end on the 8 PM News. We all watched in shock as Dante—clearly alive, but a bit catatonic and perhaps not in his own body— stood silently by while the Martian president, the Mayor, and finally his mother took turns speaking. They all once again wore their Specters.

"Greetings, Citizens," the Mayor began. "You have all heard by now about the unfortunate incident on Mars. There have been many rumors about involvement by one party or another, but the four of us stand before those of you watching on both planets tonight to assure you that we are working together to keep everyone safe. We have some alarming information that we would like to share with you, but we will all get through this together. I turn now to the president of

Mars, Zelda Rogers."

Zelda grabbed the podium with both hands and pushed the gray bangs of her cropped hair away from her eyes. "What we witnessed this morning on Mars, we believe, was the very beginning of a possible extraterrestrial invasion."

All of us exchanged stunned thoughts of disbelief—besides Varuna, who merely chittered with maniacal dolphin laughter.

"There is no need for panic," Zelda said with cold composure. "Our military researchers have studied potential intergalactic threats for a long time, and we are confident that we understand what is taking place: These aliens, whose frightening likenesses I am about to show you, have found the means to colonize the minds of people on our planets and control them."

Dante stood in front of her and leafed through several pieces of paper in his hands. The images were now familiar to us all: creatures with dragon wings and pig tails; werewolves with flies' eyes and mantis arms; snakes with dagger-toothed smiles and scissors for rattles; sasquatch-like beasts with oozing scabs, black and brown and blue and green. They were the stuff of nightmares, which was the point. Even we who had seen them before felt a deep terror.

"The interdimensional technology they are using to enact their invasion is quite complex, but we understand it well. Moreover, it is quite cumbersome for them to use, and the fact that we have stopped this initial breach of our worlds means it will take some time for them to devise a new plan of attack. We do not know how long, exactly, but we have some time. In the coming days and weeks, the Melampus corporation will be cooperating with the Martian military to distribute a new line of anti-psychological warfare devices to the general public. These devices are easy to use and will keep us all safe. Mayor?"

Teddy retook the podium. "Thank you, Madame President. Obviously, this will be a trying time for us all—especially in the final stretch of an election season. In light of these developments, I called my main competitor, Peter Delacroix. He has agreed to make the difficult decision to drop out of the mayoral race. He admits that he simply lacks the technical expertise to guide us to safety. Dante and Stella Melampus, meanwhile, have graciously agreed to travel back to Mars with President Rogers. The Cognoscenti are working on technologies that will protect us from this grave threat, and the Melampus Corporation will be lending their expertise and organizing trade arrangements to ensure all humans on both planets can stay safe."

We all wanted to vomit. The four people on screen clapped. To those who knew what to look for, there was no doubt: Dante, the most dead-eyed of them all, had lost his autonomy.

32

The broadcast cut back to the anchors. Varuna was the first to break our stunned silence. *Let me off this ship immediately,* he said. *The order to replace our Specters, or maybe just deactivate us entirely, is bound to come in any minute. Edie's told them everything, and there's no way they'll continue letting us talk to each other. Let me off the ship: I can keep my private Specter, and the three of us can at least stay in contact. Laura, you must know how to open the hatch to my aquarium and eject me. Dante shared all his access codes with you, didn't he?*

He did, Laura admitted. *But I'll need to get into the wheelhouse. It's too dangerous. Besides, what will you do out in the ocean?*

I'll amass an army, he said. *I'll get all the cetaceans of the ocean together. Hell, maybe if we screech on shore loud enough, we can get some grassland mammals on our side as well: bats, shrews—anything that has echolocation.*

What's an army of echolocating animals going to solve? I asked. I was terrified for Varuna's safety, whether he stayed on board or not.

I don't know yet, he said. *But this is the only potential army we've got. And letting me out into the sea is the only hope we have of building it.*

Laura, still sitting by the television in her room, was in desperate tears. Her indecision came to an end quickly,

211

however, when Officer Sherman pinged her Specter and delivered the order we all knew was coming:

Just in from Dante: Deactivate all animals currently on board. You can handle the meerkats?

Laura thought for a moment, then dared to transmit a word that Stella had told her on her first day on the Ark never to address to a superior. *Why?*

Sherman took a minute to reply, surprised. *Security concerns,* he said at last. *I don't know anything more. Now do as instructed.*

It didn't matter to Laura whether Sherman was in on whatever was currently unfolding or if he was just playing his typical role as brainwashed corporate soldier. She was the only human on that ship capable of resisting Stella's plan.

Prince, she said. *I'm going to the wheelhouse. Meet me there and create a distraction.*

Sensing we would be separated for a time one way or another, I lay my paw down on Varuna's head for a second before exiting his aquarium and navigating the corridors toward the elevator. For whatever reason, it didn't occur to me until I saw three crewmen barreling toward me that I, too, was an animal on board who would be subject to the deactivation order. One held a syringe, and the other two grabbed me.

"Leave me alone!" I shouted through my microphone while growling. "I am no common animal! This is outrageous. Dante would never want this."

This provoked enough doubt in them to get them to hold the syringe back. "Maybe we should ask the boss to confirm about this guy first," one said to the others. They loosened their grip on me just enough for me to bolt down the rest of the way to the elevator and ascend to deck.

In the wheelhouse, Laura was talking to Officer Sherman, who had stopped her at the entrance.

"There aren't enough syringes with compound in the meerkats' observation deck," she said, twirling her hair a little to play up her role as idiot Citizen. "I need to use one of the consoles in here to request more from medical."

"Fine," said Sherman. "But be quick."

Then, he looked down at me. "What is he doing here?"

He shouted to address the other C-suite officers in the room. "Can we get someone to take care of him?"

Distract the officers nearest me, Laura transmitted as she sat at a console. *I can't have anyone noticing that I'm logging in with Dante's admin credentials.*

I trotted up to the officer sitting at the console beside Laura's and scratched his leg. "Please scratch me," I said with a pleading tone.

The officer tried to wave me away, so I resorted to what all dogs would do when in search of immediate attention: I emptied my bladder onto his leg.

"Fuck!" He pushed me away. I then ran around the wheelhouse like a delirious puppy.

"You'll never catch me!" I yelled as I buzzed in circles.

"Somebody shut that damn poodle up!" Sherman bellowed. Several other officers rose from their seats to chase me.

Laura logged into the console, entered the Ark's security system, and located the controls for Varuna's aquarium. She opened his hatch to the sea right as a pile of C-suite officers threw themselves onto me.

The sensations that followed were bittersweet. On the one paw, Varuna shared his elation with us as the hatch opened, sliding back slowly to prevent a blast of negative pressure that would suck him out into the sea with such force that it would crush him. *I'm free!* He squeaked and shimmied in glee. But on the other paw, he was caught: Just before the hatch opened wide enough for him to exit, he took one last look through the glass of his aquarium to reveal the two crewmen sent to deactivate him, who had likely made their way down from the upper level in shock upon discovering what was happening.

Varuna swam like a bullet away from the Ark. *I'll be back! I won't let you down.*

I couldn't respond. I was too busy snarling and yapping at the officers holding me down. Varuna's determination as he embarked into the open ocean gave me some solace in that terrifying moment when the crewman who had been dispatched from medical to deactivate (and, it turned out, sedate) me injected the syringe into my head and rid me of my ability to communicate my thoughts. My consciousness faded as I slumped into their arms.

Laura, meanwhile, did not quite escape. The Arklings who had seen Varuna's sudden exit sent word to Sherman, who immediately locked the wheelhouse down and asked all who were present to rise from their consoles. Sherman found Laura out in an instant when she stayed in her seat just a moment longer than everyone else, trying desperately to log out.

"You're in a lot of trouble," Sherman said as he placed his hands on Laura's shoulders. She gasped and froze.

"Wait here," he said. "I'm transmitting the details of your insubordination straight to the top."

She did not resist or try to run. She couldn't physically compete with Sherman, and making a scene would not be in her favor. After a few minutes of waiting, a surprising voice entered her mind.

Laura Delacroix.

Up until then, she wondered if the Dante she had seen on the news was somehow fake, a trick of video or an android. But there was no mistaking the familiar vibration of his brain—even if it was not, as soon became clear, under his control. *Dante? Are you ok?*

The next words he thought were swift and monotone. *You are hereby dispatched from your position. I order you to leave the Ark immediately.* Dante's cold, callous tone brought a few tears to Laura's eyes.

—

She would have felt less betrayed if she had been able to see just how trapped Dante was at that moment. After the press conference ended, Stella had influenced Dante to leave the Mayor's mansion and descend to the spaceport together with her and Zelda. By the time Dante gave the order fed to him by Stella to fire Laura, he was already inside the hyperbaric sleep chamber that would preserve him all the way to Mars.

"Please wait until my mother returns to seal me inside,"

Stella-as-Dante said to the Martian nurse who inserted nutritional catheters into his arms.

Stella herself, meanwhile, was with Zelda in a private meeting room on the ship. Monitoring the action with Varuna and Laura had consumed a lot of her attention, so this was her first chance since before the presser to confer with the president. They argued over a specific detail of their plan.

"That dolphin's escape is a problem," Stella said. She paced back and forth with a hand on her chin. "I know you want to wait and see if enough people take the pills before we resort to outfitting the animals, but I really doubt we can make it happen. My son and his idiot girlfriend's father have done immense damage to the public's trust in both of us, as well as Teddy."

"Darling, relax." Zelda lounged in a chair and sipped on a pre-flight gravitational adjustment cocktail that would work on her genes over the course of the journey. "For one thing, you forget how much faster this ship is than the last one you took. We will be on Mars in two days."

"Two whole days?" Stella touched her neck and frowned. "For this to work, you'll need a whole fleet of ships capable of going back and forth between the planets in no more than a few *hours*. Believe me, people are going to put up a fight, and you won't have much time to get the necessary manpower on Mars."

Zelda rose and put a hand on Stella's shoulder. "And I *have* such a fleet. We really did try to build the warp drive for a while, you know. And we thought we were getting somewhere. Hell, we did get somewhere. All of that research paid off for what we're doing now. But look at it from my perspective. I had to have *some* kind of technical advancement to show for our investments on Earth, yes, but if my subjects knew we had the tech for *such* rapid transit, they would demand to know why I don't use it. They still think there's a point in improving our trade grid, fixing our infrastructure, blah, blah, blah."

Stella sighed. "All right. It just seems like there's an extraordinary amount to get done in three weeks. I'm sure you have it under control, but I feel I let you down."

"You could never let me down." Zelda stroked Stella's cheek. "You're not responsible for your son's actions. And I bear just as much responsibility as you do for the public's distrust in our business partnership." She backed away and smiled with a mischievous grin. "And besides, it's really the Mayor's fault. So bald and fat. Nobody was going to trust a man like that. I know you feel about deceiving him, but he has it coming. Anyone who cares about money that much has it coming."

Stella chuckled. "It *is* pretty funny. Imagine if he knew we had no intention of bringing him with us. Did you see his face when Edie's father came up? He knows damn well we can do that to him as well if we need to."

Zelda struggled to speak for laughter. "Oh, God. By the way, you still need to tell me how these cephalopods manage to resist the X's design."

"Their uniquely distributed nervous systems. That, and centuries of old Melampus men trying as many ways as possible to breed animals who are too smart for their own good. They tried to curtail that after the apes nearly took over the Ark—we don't even have apes in the Biomes anymore— but some genetic quirks persist. It is a little annoying that Edie is making us take her with us, but I'm relieved we were able to convince her we had something she wanted."

"Well," said Zelda, "I know you're very excited to create some animal cyborgs, but I do think you can wait. Let's see how the uptake numbers look in a couple of weeks first. Our research has consistently shown that repeated exposure to external presentations of the images yields strong results. Do I wish we'd gotten more people to buy the X's? Yes, but this will do in a pinch. Trust me: People will wear the hats."

Stella nodded. She picked up her own gravity cocktail from the table and drank, able to relax a little. The pieces of their backup plan would indeed fall into place. "I do still think the Ark needs to relocate the dolphin as quickly as possible. I don't know what Laura was thinking in letting him out, but they had some idea in mind—of that, I am sure. But what? And how do we catch him when there's no tracker on his Specter?"

She resumed her pensive pacing. It was a convincing performance. Zelda had no idea that Stella already had a very good guess what Varuna's intentions were based on what she knew from Iguazu and Edie's descriptions of his misanthropy. She certainly had no idea that Stella shared it. She still didn't even know that Varuna had originally managed to resist the X like Edie had. The two women had agreed to be in one another's presence at all times once the final stages of the plan they supposedly shared went into effect; any thought that they might try to control *one another* for different ends—either through Specters or through backhanded manipulation—had left the Martian president's mind.

"Is this really something to worry about right n—" Zelda began to ask before Stella snapped her fingers and interrupted.

"I've got it," Stella said. "We can use the dog to get him back. We'll let Prince keep his Specter, *and* we'll plant an idea in his head that we're planning to kill him. Prince will call for help, and Varuna will let himself be captured."

Zelda shrugged. "Great. Simple. But why do you care so much about getting him back?"

Stella took a swig from her gravitational adjustment drink. "Think about it: If you're a Citizen who's told an alien invasion is ongoing, what's going to do a better job convincing you to wear your hat? A poodle who can stand on his hind legs, or a dolphin with cyborg limbs approaching the City on foot?"

33

I did not hear from either Laura or Dante for over two weeks after that. I spent my time in a small cell that I had never thought the Ark would force on an animal as supposedly privileged as myself. I was surprised on waking to find my Specter was back in my skull.

"Boss wants you to keep it." Sherman said as he shoved a disgusting bowl of ordinary canine slop through the cell's hatch at my feet.

Naturally, I got in touch with Varuna right away. He was, in fact, the only contact I could reach during those days. The Ark had demanded Laura give over her Specter before returning to the City, and Nemos, Gunny, and Soda all did not register in my mind; they did not have the same right to keep their device as I did, which was strange.

Varuna relied on his sonar to relocate his pod, and he let me experience his homecoming with him. They welcomed him back with open fins. The last they had seen of Varuna, he had promised to find his way to the Ark and discover the truth about their supposed celestial origins.

We are at war, he told his podmates, most of whom still wore X's and were therefore at risk of being tracked. Varuna knew he had only a brief span of time to work before Stella-as-Dante would be awakened from his sleep and available to coordinate with the Ark from Mars. *The humans and the cephalopods have banded together against us. While I am unsure of everything they are planning, we have no hope of making our way to the stars if the Ophiuchan descendants have first access to the needed technology. Here is what I propose: an alliance between all echolocative species. Not just cetaceans, but the shrews and the bats as well.*

Though I wasn't able to witness it all firsthand, Varuna's podmates followed his orders and dispersed throughout their region of the sea in patterns that they hoped would attract little attention from Sherman and other Arklings in the wheelhouse. They contacted other pods, who then contacted other pods, who then contacted the porpoises, who then contacted the orcas and whales. Varuna, meanwhile, took it upon himself to patrol the shores by the grassland and emit the waves of sonar that would allow him to locate potential land mammal partners. A family of water shrews living in the marshy estuary just inland proved to be his contact point.

You there, he said. *Are you all wearing private Specters?*

Yes, they replied with a nervous flicker of their tails.

Good. I need you to find all other animals who can communicate in echolocation. Not only your fellow shrews, but bats and dormice as well. Tell them the time to take control of the Biomes for ourselves and defeat the Ark is approaching.

Days went by, and the network grew, but I struggled to understand Varuna's intentions. *We're building a resource,* he would say.

But what are we using it for? I've been trapped in this cell for days, and you have no way of knowing what's going on either. Stella and Dante are on Mars by now, and for all we know, they've already built their hivemind throughout the City.

You're right, Varuna said. *We need spies.*

He asked multiple shrews and dormice to approach the City walls and see if they could conduct reconnaissance and obtain information on what, if any, moves had been made by Stella and Mars.

Not possible, they all said. Drones would vaporize any animals who came within 1,000 feet of the City.

One thing they could do, however, was to monitor as best they could the Melampus-owned safari jeeps that periodically toured the Biomes; top-floor Citizens would splurge in order to see what Earth once looked like. The fact that these jeeps even still ran was a good sign that some things in the City still functioned as normal, and that all was not yet lost.

For several more days, we thought we'd reached a dead end. Only one jeep toured the grassland per day, and the drivers would wave their guns at any animals who came close enough to let Varuna and I listen to the passengers' conversation, which was mostly limited to "oohs" and "aahs" to begin with. Some shrews and bats and mice managed to catch isolated words like "aliens" and "APWD," but we failed to string together a cohesive narrative of how things were going in the City.

Progress finally occurred when some bats suggested to Varuna that we ought to fan the network out to other Biomes. *There are jeeps in every Biome, and there are bats in every Biome except the tundra,* they explained. *While they may not have Specters like we do, we can still communicate fairly well with the other species in our native tongues.*

Several more days passed as the bats in six of the seven other land Biomes conducted their own reconnaissance missions on their respective jeeps. My despair and loneliness grew. I tried to piece together various scenarios based on whatever information I had available before my imprisonment, but nothing added up. Why did Stella let me keep my Specter? It was the one thing I couldn't reconcile.

Then, two weeks after putting me in confinement, Sherman came into my cell and delivered the threat. "I've known you since you were a puppy, Prince." He leaned against the wall with his hand resting on the gun in his belt. "And I'm sorry I have to be your adversary right now. But I have orders from Dante to catch Varuna, and we all know you've been in contact with him. We need you to get him back on this ship. I'm afraid there will be dire consequences for you if you don't."

"What kind of consequences?" I asked.

"You'll be abandoned in the tundra and forced to fend for yourself among the untamed wolves. Not only that, but we'll kill all the other animals on this ship."

Sherman, I noticed, was once again wearing an X. As he spoke to me with his dead-eyed monotone, I got the sense that it was in fact Stella speaking to me through this man's body. The real Sherman would have known that Dante could never be so cruel to me.

"I'll see what I can do," I said, tail between my legs.

Varuna was resistant at first. *It's a bluff,* he said.

I whimpered and cried. *No, I don't think it is.* I couldn't handle the thought of him leaving me to die so soon after Dante had (albeit against his will) threatened to do the same.

Calm down, he chittered. *I'm not going to leave you. I will let them capture me if I have to, but we need to find out what they want from us, and we probably need a contact with information from the City to do that. And guess what? I have good news. Word has it that an eastern red bat in the temperate forest spotted a jeep driver with a familiar face.*

He transmitted the image the bats had sent him. On seeing her face, I wagged my tail with such excitement that I nearly made the mistake of yelling her name out loud for all the microphones in my cell to hear.

Laura!

34

Laura had come home to her family's City apartment in tears. She found all her bedroom belongings boxed up—some ready for relocation, some headed for consignment sale.

Wanda held her daughter. "We're moving one floor down," she said. "They won't let Peter keep his campaign donations. He's making some money campaigning for Wilcox, but it's not enough."

"He's doing *what?*" Laura drew back in horror.

"Please, don't blame your father for all this. He has to do something. And the third floor is better than what a lot of people get."

"He's a coward," Laura whispered under her breath as she stormed to her room. She went through the boxes marked for sale and found sentimental trinkets of childhood: books and VR cartridges about the Biomes, about advanced machine learning, about the Arkology's history (albeit the Melampus-Terrachist consensus on history). She bent over the box in exhaustion and heaved with sobs.

A knock came on her door. "Can I come in?" Michelle asked.

The two sisters hugged. Laura asked Michelle if she had said goodbye to her friends.

"I will tomorrow," she said. "Sammy doesn't want us to break up over this, but she knows I'll have to wait until college to have a chance at moving up a floor, and even then it's slim."

Laura yanked her own hair and grunted. "This is so fucked up. We have to stop this. I can get another job."

"Mom and Dad expect you to say that. They don't want you to work. They want you to go to college. Change your name and apply. They think you could get into a good program. Maybe not top floor, but higher than this."

"Fuck that. There's an "alien invasion" coming," Laura said with air quotes. "College is pointless."

Michelle lit up with curiosity. "Yeah...what's going on there? My friends are talking about it. I told Sammy I think it's made-up. But she said her dad knows people on Mars, and he said that all those people really did go sick and insane. What do you think?"

Laura darted her eyes toward the ceiling, where she and Michelle both knew the AI kept its cameras on them in every room, cameras that were sure to be of intense and constant interest to the Terrarchists in the Servers given Laura's circumstances. "I think I can't talk about this too much. And I think you should be extremely careful what you say about it at school. Let's see what develops over the next few days."

Michelle nodded, then took her sister's hand. "Were you and that boy...the new CEO...you know..."

Laura gave a defensive laugh. "What? Where did you get that idea?"

"Just the way you two would stand close to each other on TV," Michelle said.

Laura evaded the question to save herself pain. "That would be inappropriate. On multiple levels." She wanted more than anything to rescue Dante, but after hearing his voice so coldly fire her, the possibility seemed too distant to even entertain. No, she had to focus on the present. She had to help her family deal with whatever was coming.

"Dad thought the same as I did," Michelle said.

Laura's brows jumped. "What did he say about it?"

"The same as you. That it would be inappropriate."

A sneer flickered across Laura's face. Michelle gave a knowing smile.

On waking the next morning, Laura checked the News to find that Mars believed the extraterrestrials had somehow colonized the infected individuals' minds by hacking into their Specters. Melampus had ordered a mandatory recall of all X's currently in circulation. Those who wished to do so could exchange their X for a different model. This "different model," Laura was correct to infer, was in fact Stella's model, linked to Pathnet.

She exited her bedroom to grab a slice of toast. Her father was home for the first time since her return. She stayed stiff as a board when he hugged her. Wanda, watching from the table, scolded her. "Hug your father, dear."

Laura returned the embrace in a perfunctory, split-second manner.

Peter, face sagging with sadness, stepped away. "I'm sorry we have to move."

"We don't," said Laura, straightening her back. "I'm getting a job."

Her parents exchanged worried looks. Michelle, sensing conflict, took her cue to leave the table. "Off to school!" She slipped out the door.

Peter sighed. "Laura, sit down. Let's discuss this."

"There's nothing to discuss." Laura couldn't stop her voice from rising. "You can't make enough money as a spineless sellout for the Terrarchists, so I'm going to get a job and stop you from ruining Michelle's life."

"Laura!" Wanda hissed. "Your father is doing what he has to. Our whole world is in serious danger!"

Laura laughed. "Is that what he told you? Oh, man. You know he doesn't believe that, right?"

Peter shuffled, stammered. "We shouldn't talk about this," he said. "Rest assured, your mother and I have given things a lot of *thought.*" Laura understood his emphasis on this last word. The implication was that he had discussed things in private with Wanda over Specter, though Laura couldn't tell to what extent now that she lacked her own device.

"Look, I've got to go." Laura said. "You all have a busy day handing your Specters back like good little Citizens, and I've got to go find a job."

"Laura, wait—" Peter tried to stop her, but she rushed out the door.

She boarded the tram that took her to the floor's commercial district. Her first idea was to apply for a job as a Melampus Store sales clerk. If she could get access to the store's inventory of recalled Specters, she could regain contact with me and Varuna. She wore sunglasses in an attempt to disguise herself. Unfortunately, the store manager rejected her right away.

"You'll need to submit an application with the AI," he said. "We need to confirm you have the appropriate skills. And do a background check, of course." He squinted a bit. Did he recognize her? Whatever, Laura thought. It didn't matter. As soon as she submitted her profile to the AI, she would appear on the Melampus system as a disgraced ex-employee. She headed for the exit, despondent.

She was ready to go home in shame when she passed the booth for Melampus tour jeeps. "NOW HIRING DRIVERS," it said. She paused.

"Hey!" The man at the booth yelled. "What's your name?"

"Violet," Laura lied.

"You look just like that intern girl from the City. But you can't be her. She's on the Ark."

Laura laughed, nervously. To her benefit, the Ark was keeping her firing a secret for PR purposes. "I get that a lot," she said.

"You want to drive for us?" He asked. "Those top-floor Citizens will love you. They'll take selfies and tell their friends they met Laura Delacroix."

"Oh, how funny!" Laura guffawed. "You need me to apply with the AI?"

"Nah." He cupped his hand over his mouth and whispered. "Technically, these jeeps aren't legal. The City and the Biomes are supposed to be completely sealed off from each other for all Citizens. But they started them up a few decades ago to give the rich elites something to do, and obviously our own customers aren't going to enforce the code that would stop us from doing it."

Laura was surprised he told her this. He clearly took her as someone who shared a sense of class solidarity. "Sure," she said. "I'll drive for you. Can I decide which Biome I'm assigned to?" The wheels turned in her mind. If she could just make contact with a grassland animal in the network she knew Varuna was building...

"Afraid not," he said. "We're looking for a driver in the temperate forest."

It wasn't ideal, but it was the best Laura could do. She hoped things would work themselves out. She agreed to the job.

The next two weeks tested her strength. She hated listening to rich passengers bragging to one another about their investments, their business, and so forth. She especially hated hearing them discuss the "alien threat," which they took to be very real. She hated watching them lean out of the vehicle to try to touch terrified squirrels and badgers and even bears. She hated having to go by Violet and "pretend" to be who she really was when customers asked for selfies with her in order to get tips. On evening rides, she would sometimes spot a red bat and wonder how Varuna and I were doing—but the bat wore the wrong kind of Specter, and she would go back to thinking about the best way to make as much money as she could to protect her family.

But the situation remained tense at home. She refused to speak to her father, and her mother did not extend the gratitude she felt she deserved for helping them to keep their apartment. Nevertheless, she made a point of eating her dinners in the living room so that she could watch the News when her parents did and monitor their reactions. She was happy to hear sarcastic laughs and to see their rolling eyes when the talking heads came on every night and provided the latest updates: More mindhacks on Mars! More supposed ET radio chatter picked up on the intergalactic airwaves! More speculation about where the aliens came from and what they wanted!

It caught Laura's attention that every hour, on the hour, the anchors would display the same nightmarish images of the so-called aliens over and over again. Immediately after broadcasting these images, a message delivered by one of the three leaders of the response (Zelda, Wilcox, or Dante, these last two noticeably monotone and dead-eyed) would urge viewers to obey a simple command that changed every few days.

For the first few days, it was to return and exchange the private Specters that supposedly provided the ETs with their mode of cerebral entry. This message did not gain unanimous traction among the public: when the News was not discussing the aliens, it was discussing the growing crowds of protesters gathering in front of Melampus stores and at Teddy's remote campaign events (many of which were of course hosted by Peter). The City could force its Citizens to return their Specters, but it could not force them to buy new ones. The movement Peter had built was too great for him to dissolve.

Then, for the next few days, the command was a voluntary conscription request for all able-bodied Citizens to join the military, which had joined Melampus in a campaign on the Ark that would reportedly result in technologies that could protect the public from invasion.

Her parents began to change after a week or so. Their expressions of derision gave way to expressions of fear. Wanda shuddered every time the hourly images appeared, and even Peter, who knew very well what Stella had been planning just weeks prior, started to say things like, "maybe they are real," and "I hope everyone here is taking this seriously." Laura herself couldn't avoid observing the hypnotic effect the ghastly images had. At times, she would find herself sinking into the screen, until finally the inner voice that said none of this was real snapped her back to the present and got her to look away. If she hadn't been so familiar with Stella's plot, and if she hadn't in effect inoculated herself against the images (at least when they were presented on a screen) by seeing them in that folder, she would have started to find the official messages from the two governments and Melampus very persuasive.

Michelle, on the other hand, deliberately avoided the television. In fact, as Laura found whenever she entered their room, she even avoided her phone. She spent her time tending to her plants. "Sammy and a group of friends and I are starting a gardening group," was all she said when Laura asked how she was spending her time. Michelle was notably evasive now, and Laura got the sense she and the other children of the City had their own peculiar response to what was happening, though Laura was not at liberty to discuss it freely beneath the AI's cameras. It did strike Laura that Michelle refused to hand over her Specter until, one day, a Terrarchist official knocked on their door and demanded she give it up. Laura was glad someone in her family at least appeared to keep her head screwed on straight, but she feared for her sister's safety.

Once the voluntary conscription requests had played themselves out for a few days, the message grew more urgent: large-scale, population-wide invasion was imminent—two weeks away, if that. On the bright side, however, the powers that be were very close to releasing an instrument that could protect ordinary Citizens from mental hacking: the Anti-Psychological Warfare Device, or APWD. Distribution would begin on Mars in a few days. As diagrams showed, it resembled a metallic hat with a long antenna-like spike in the middle. In addition, new images of the aliens were now available. They displayed what appeared to Laura (and anyone else not hypnotized by the earlier images by this point) to be animals with mechanical cyborg limbs. Two of these "aliens," Laura saw, were very obviously drawn to resemble bipedal android versions of Varuna and myself.

Laura had not stopped searching for ways to reestablish contact with us all this time—driving closer to the border with the grassland, whispering to red bats whenever her passengers were distracted, checking to see if any animals around her had the right kind of Specter—but nothing had worked, and she was losing hope.

Then, she looked up one day at one of the trees the red bats loved to hang from. One bat looked out of place: a big brown bat, *Eptesicus fuscus*, known for its ability to live in multiple Biomes. This bat, however, was a native of the grassland, as Laura recognized when she saw the private SpecterX lodged in the crown of its head.

As Laura's passengers looked the other way, the bat used her wing to point—first at her own Specter, then at Laura. Laura wasn't certain she caught the bat's meaning, but she knew what to do. The next day, she called a Melampus store, and expressed her wish to exchange her Specter. "I would have done it sooner," she said to the store manager, "but those protesters are so scary!" As Laura expected, the manager arranged for a delivery drone to bring Laura the necessary supplies: one syringe with deactivation compound, one replacement SpecterX (which Laura hid in her room), and one syringe with installation compound.

On her tour the next day, Laura brought a baseball cap with her and found the brown bat waiting in the same tree. She rose and turned to her passengers: "So sorry, everyone, but nature calls!"

She walked behind the tree. The bat, seeing Laura remove her syringes, flew over and landed on Laura's shoulder. She stayed still as Laura injected the first syringe into her and removed the Specter from her head. Laura then placed the Specter on her own face and used the other syringe to install it. She hid it under the baseball cap and returned to her jeep.

Once home and alone, she contacted us. We were overjoyed to hear from her.

Varuna wasted no time in letting her know where things stood. He asked if she knew what the Ark planned to do with us.

I have an idea, she said, recalling the latest images on the News.

35

Dante first regained self-awareness several hours after Zelda's ship arrived on Mars. He faced a set of bay windows that overlooked the less-than-lush vista of the red Martian desert and the domes that fanned out from the Dome of the Cognoscenti, where he would spend his imprisonment in a locked guest bedroom with silk furnishings.

"Just because you're now our prisoner doesn't mean you have to suffer all the time," Stella explained as she untied the ropes around his wrists.

Dante dashed for the door in a desperate attempt to escape. The same images that flooded his mind at the bottom of the mayor's swimming pool inundated him once more: the expected nightmarish alien images, which had an irrepressible hypnotic effect when experienced viscerally, followed by—and this one was a shock to Dante—some kind of THING, a slouching humanlike being with long arms and no face. Once this THING faced him, a terror seized him; these images, Dante discovered, served to well up the influenced subject's greatest fears; obeying the controlling user's commands was the only way to keep the fear at bay. And for Dante, this fear had a particular sting:

He imagined his father, back from the dead, going on television and outing and condemning him for all to mock. "My son," this fake Dominic said in the vision, "is a sexual deviant, and he (or should I say she) should be fired and reprogrammed immediately!"

Stella retied Dante's restraints and pushed him onto the bed. When he regained self-control once more, he sobbed with shame and humiliation.

"That wasn't me controlling you that time," his mother said. "It was your friend, the baby octopus." Dante turned to see Edie hovering in a tank facing the bed. "She's going to babysit you at nights while I sleep," Stella said. "I'm not stupid enough to leave you unattended. She has an influencer unit just like I do. Try to escape, and she'll put you right back in your place. You're lucky I give you a break to sleep. Don't abuse the privilege."

Dante touched his latest Specter. Reading his mind without needing to look directly at it, Stella laughed. "Try turning it and seeing if you can counteract us if you want, but it won't work. I've designed you a unit that doesn't have Influencer mode. Plus, it only communicates with units that are linked to your influencers, so good luck contacting anyone on Earth."

Dante tossed and turned in bed for a while after Stella left. Finally, he overcame his fear of the octopus who had betrayed him and confronted Edie.

Why are you working with her? He asked.

I don't have to tell you anything.

Well, whatever they told you, it's a lie.

You don't know that.

I would if you told me what they said. You don't actually think the aliens are real now, do you?

Of course not, she said with a child's defensiveness. *They tried to influence me, too, you know. I saw the same images as you. But it didn't work. I have too many little brains for them to figure me out. But they've shown me the truth, and you and that dolphin can't lie to me anymore.*

Lie? What did we lie to you about?

Go ahead, play dumb. I'm done talking.

Is this about your alien star feud? Oh, God, what did they say? I promise, there are no octopus gods from Ophiuchus or whatever the hell you believe.

Not talking to you. She wrapped herself up in a ball. But Dante could tell he was striking an emotional nerve.

You're just a silly child, Dante said. *I feel so bad that you bought into their lies. So gullible.*

Shut up! Edie shouted. Her mantle bloomed orange. *I'm going to meet my star family, and there's nothing you can do about it.*

Aha! Dante rose from the bed and knelt in front of her tank. *So they're the ones coming here?*

Don't be stupid, Edie squinted her eyes at him. *I'm the one going to see them.*

Oh really? They've built you a spaceship to Ophiuchus? Do you know how far Ophiuchus is?

I do know, because they've shown me the math to prove they can take me there. And I've seen the spaceship for myself.

Dante got an idea. *What if I could prove they've lied to you? Let's say, hypothetically, that I had really been the one telling you the truth?*

I suppose I'd be very mad at them. But you won't be able to do it.

I can if you show me all of this so-called "proof," Dante claimed.

I can! The defiant Edie said. *Zelda's office is just a few hallways away. I can crawl through the vents there and show you everything myself.*

If you insist, Dante said. He lifted the roof of Edie's tank. She slithered through the ceilings and walls of the Dome until she arrived in Zelda's office. She opened a drawer with her tentacles and removed a stack of papers.

Here's the summary they read me, she said as she picked the first sheet up.

Dante read it aloud in his mind:

"REPORT TO THE COGNOSCENTI: BUILDING A [REDACTED].

When Dominic Melampus first submitted his prototype of the original Specter to us for investment approval, our research yielded the surprising discovery that, if two users communicated telepathically in a sealed room, the device generated a quantity of heat energy that we could not account for. Energetically, the whole of two consciousnesses appears to be greater than the sum of its parts. Quantum entanglement and the superconductive material of the Specter may play a role here, but the mechanism is not fully understood. Regardless, our mathematicians found that the energy surplus, if compounded exponentially through a sufficiently large telepathic union of minds, could be used to generate the force necessary to exploit the Casimir effect and yield the negative energy source necessary to create a [REDACTED]."

Dante reread it a couple of times. His head hurt. *Do you actually understand what this means?*

They're building a warp drive, Edie said. *A faster-than-light spaceship that will traverse the cosmos. That's what they redacted.*

Did you see the un-*redacted report?*

No, she admitted. *But I've seen the spaceship.*

Can I see it?

Yes, but I have to go underground, and then I have to go right back to my tank before my whole body dries up.

As Edie reentered the vents and descended into the underground tunnels of Mars, Dante's stomach lurched. He sensed he was getting to the heart of things. When she squirmed up to the final vent and peered through the slats, he was shocked at what he saw:

In an enormous laboratory, two thin, towering bright white rectangular plates stood side by side. Hovering above the plates, and connected to the ground by a curved ladder that arced behind them, was a transparent bubble that appeared almost weightless.

That bubble's the spaceship, Edie said. *When we bring everyone into the tunnels, the passengers climb into the bubble, and we vacuum-seal the room off. The energy from the hivemind will cause the plates to accelerate and move closer to each other. Once the energy between the plates reaches a critical point, the bubble blasts out of here and into space at hyperspeed!*

Edie returned to Dante's room, and he was too shaken to

offer serious rebuttals to these seemingly absurd claims: If one looked at this complex, this machine, this THING from the proper angle, it resembled a blank white mechanical creature with no face and long arms.

So, Dante said after composing himself. *You really think that's a spaceship?*

What else could it be? Edie asked.

I don't know, he said. *But I have a very bad feeling about it. I want you to give me the chance to prove that it isn't what they say it is.*

How are you going to do that?

I'll need access to all the documents in that office. I can run through the mathematical proofs. It may take some time, so I'll need you to go in there and let me see everything for a few nights.

Edie pondered. *How do I know you're not going to trick me so that you and the dolphin can use that spaceship for yourselves?*

I'm not even talking to Varuna. You know that. Besides, you'll see all my work. Just get me a pen and notebook to write in. Look, if I'm wrong, I wish you and your cephalopod kin all the best on Ophiuchus. But something doesn't add up for me here, and I really think it's in both of our best interests for you to give me a chance.

Fine, Edie said. *We can start tomorrow night.*

—

The routine was the same for the next two weeks. After Stella controlled him to perform tasks he couldn't remember performing during the day, she left him alone with Edie, who would then go into Zelda's office and show him the pages and pages of mathematical proofs in the report. Dante used the notebook he kept hidden under the bed to record and evaluate the proofs, which involved highly theoretical quantum physics that he hadn't studied since his father's death and Stewart's departure. Stewart had been the only one to show him such advanced material. It took a few nights for Dante even to remember all of the concepts involved, but he managed after some great mental exertion.

By the end of the two weeks, he came to two surprising and seemingly irreconcilable conclusions: On the one hand, every unredacted word of the summary checked out: If Mars could harness the tremendous energy released when the two planets' populations came together in a single hypothetical hivemind and entered into close physical proximity, it would create a force that could bend spacetime. On the other hand, the "spaceship" itself featured very little into any equations and therefore appeared irrelevant. Those who had written the proofs focused primarily on the generated force, and it was a force they had calculated to use only one time toward an unknown end.

Do you really think they built a spaceship that they want to use one time? And to let you meet a bunch of ET octopuses? Dante said when he showed Edie his findings.

They're going to come with me. They want to draw on the Ophiuchans' wisdom to save the Earth. The Ophiuchans will be able to send us back.

Who are "they"?

Stella, Zelda, the rest of the Cognoscenti, some of the octopuses I've got on the Ark to keep watch over everyone— that was part of the deal I made before agreeing to work with them; not so gullible after all, am I? And you.

Me?

Yes, you're coming. Your mother does love you, after all.

I see. Tell me, were these the only documents they showed you? The math feels...incomplete.

They had some more in the Mayor's quarters on Earth. They laid out their entire plan there. No redactions.

Edie, you're not able to read, are you?

Edie rouged with offense. *So what?*

I don't mean to insult you, but isn't it possible they told you something you wanted to believe and you ran with it? Sure, you could build a one-time warp drive spaceship with this thing, but it would probably destroy the entire solar system. You'd basically create a black hole.

Edie froze in her tank, then turned an icy metallic blue. *Look, you haven't proven anything. And it's too late: the plan goes into effect tomorrow night.*

The plan?

Yes. Varuna might have escaped for a time, but they've just re-captured him. Him, Prince, Nemos, Gunny, and Soda are all going to be my subjects. And this time, I'm in charge. They're going to turn the animals on the Ark into cyborgs, and they'll all have Specters that I can influence. I forced Stella to let me have that, too. It's what you all get for lying to me. We're going to make them go on TV and give a special message from the aliens. The people will all be so scared that they'll have to put on those hats that will add them to the hivemind.

Hats?

The APWDs. It pretty much does the same thing as the X, but better. They tried to get people to swap out their Specters, but it didn't work. Your and Peter's smear campaigns turned people off the X so much that the images on TV couldn't persuade them. But Stella and Zelda saw that coming. That's why they've been working on the hats this whole time.

Dante only understood about half what Edie had said, but one thing stood out. *If those animals are getting units linked to yours, does that mean I can talk to them, too?*

I mean, you could if I weren't planning to control them the whole time.

Dante hatched a plan. *Edie, when this all goes down tomorrow, let me talk to Prince. Just for five minutes. If there's any information on the Ark that can prove my mom and Mars are up to no good, I need to guide him through finding it.*

Edie weighed this for a while. *Fine,* she agreed. *Five minutes. It's your last chance.*

Dante placed his hand on her tank. *Thank you, Edie.*

Imagine this: you're a foo foo faggy poodle. You've just woken up in an empty operating theater to find yourself transformed into a mecha-badass. You have guns on your front legs, and a chip at the base of your spine that lets you stand up and walk in bipedal motion without a sweat. You rise to study your surroundings and find nobody there.

A voice comes into your head: *Prince, can you hear me? It's Dante.*

You whimper out loud, astonished both at hearing your master's voice and at your new body, and you wonder if you've gone insane.

I imagine you're surprised to hear me. Wherever you are right now, I need you to stay calm and listen carefully. This is a prerecorded message. I only have five minutes. At light speed, it takes three minutes for my words to get to you from Mars, so by the time you can reply, it will be too late.

He tells you as fast as he can about Edie, and the deal he made to talk with you and the THING with long arms and no face. He summarizes the plan to use you and your friends as fake cyborg ETs who will scare the public into wearing the hats that will connect them to the hivemind that is needed to transport you all to Mars and get the THING (whatever it really is) running.

You listen, but the shock of the sudden interruption of what you thought was an airtight plan you had earlier made with Varuna and Laura to conquer the Ark means you can barely process this information. Then, he makes a request you barely comprehend. *Is there any way you can get into the Mayor's quarters and find these missing documents?*

Missing documents? What does the mayor have to do with anything? All you can think about is the fact that you can move this assassin canine body freely when you were sure you'd be under someone's control.

His message concludes with a warning. *When I stop talking, you'll have one minute to find a way to deactivate your Specter. If you can't, you'll be caught in the hivemind. I love you, and good luck.*

He stops talking. The channel is open, you can tell, but only for dead air before the five minutes runs out. You look around, and you see the private Specter they've just removed from you is still on the surgeon's tray. You rummage through the cabinets with your paw-hands and find two tubs of syringes with deactivation and installation compound.

Here is what you figure: The chances of you surviving a trip to the City as anything other than a controlled zombie cyborg seem questionable at this point, and Dante just gave you a ton of information that you are liable to forget if you don't relay it immediately. So, once you switch out your Specter, you call Laura and ask her to take notes on everything you have just heard.

And here, meanwhile, was the plan you, Varuna, and Laura came up with in the last day: Varuna, true to his word, let himself be captured. Just prior, he asked a brigade of cetaceans to station themselves in formation a few hundred feet beneath the Ark's hull and conduct surveillance. With their combined sonar resources, their sound waves could pierce the hull, map out the Ark's interior and keep a collective eye on the status of our operations.

I do want those android limbs, Varuna said before capture, referencing the News reports Laura had described. *They seem quite useful. If they wait to give me a new Specter until after the operation is done, let them operate. But as soon as they move to take out my current model, that's the time to strike.*

At the time to strike, the surveilling cetaceans will send a message to Laura, who has agreed to lead the battalion of bats and birds that have assembled in a forest cave on the beach, just a minute or two of flight away from the Ark. The cetaceans will then coordinate among themselves and call on secondary lines of their fellow species members that lie in wait farther out at sea. The first line of attackers will surge to the surface and unleash a collective sonic attack directed at the Ark's windows in the medical sector. The bats and birds will then rush in through the windows and attack the Arklings: first those trying to install new Specters, and then, once you come to and let them out into the hallways, those running toward you to prevent your escape. If all else fails, the army of cetaceans can attack the Ark's entire electrical grid. This would cause grave damage to the Ark's infrastructure, however, and is only a last resort. By conquering the Ark, you can not only free the imprisoned animals, but also prevent the Arklings from distributing the APWDs that cetacean surveillance has revealed are being built on the ship.

That's the plan. But when you fail to see any shattering windows as you listen to Dante, it occurs to you that your operation was complete before Varuna's.

Imagine all of this has happened. Would you have done as I did, and taken Laura's attention for three minutes to convey Dante's urgent words to her (words she is overjoyed to receive, because they mean he is alive)? Or would you suspect that those three minutes would be the downfall of your plan to take the Ark?

In those three minutes, the cetacean spies observed the possessed technicians preparing to replace Varuna's Specter. They contacted Laura, but because she was talking to me, she did not answer. Seeing the situation was urgent, they broke the windows in his theater anyway. I heard the glass explode and the air rush into the ship behind the walls of my operating theater. It came from the room next door. I ran into the hallway to see an Arkling in mask and gloves and an APWD on his head exit the theater in terror. He clutched his side; blood spilled from his stomach. I rose on two legs and grabbed the door as it swung behind him. There, in the theater, standing up tall like a general, the smoke still trailing from the gun attached to his left fin, was the newly mechanized Varuna.

A mesh wetsuit that kept his skin hydrated covered his body. He, like me, had metal arms that branched out into opposably-thumbed claws on his front limbs (his fins, in his case), but the task of getting him to move bipedally had been much more elaborate in his case: The arms met at the joint of an artificial backbone, which extended from his dorsal fin all the way down to his tail, at which point it split apart into eight spider-like legs that wrapped around his tail and crawled together whenever he wished to walk. They had to be of very strong material to support his body.

"Oh, hello," he said through a new microphone on his beak as my wide-eyed presence faced him. He blinked his eyes to emerge from his sedated stupor; though shocked to consciousness by the breaking windows and the screams of his surgeon, he was still experiencing the tail end of his anesthesia. He was a totally different creature now, but he was also completely the same. I found him both extremely intimidating and, strangely, physically attractive.

"What's going on here? The windows are broken, but no bats or birds are coming in."

At this point, I knew what had happened. Laura was still waiting for me to finish delivering Dante's information when I heard the glass shatter.

Laura, we missed your signal!

Shit, she said. *I'm on it.*

A sonic boom shook the Ark around us: Windows all over the medical sector shattered in unison.

—

By then, however, Stella had taken note of what was happening. She stood over a console that connected directly to the Source AI. Iguazu, whom she had brought to Mars, stood on her shoulder. She didn't want to worry about his Specter, so she had deactivated him and kept him as a pet.

While she had trusted Edie to control the animal

prisoners, she had given herself control of the Arklings. And the APWDs worked differently from the SpecterX. Based on her research into Edie's mind, she had improved the hivemind's design to allow for a fully distributed consciousness. Whereas the X had required her to attach to a single user and influence the hivemind through their place in a data structure, the APWDs communicated with one another the way an octopus's arms would.

This meant, then, that when she first heard the cetacean sonic boom in Sherman's POV, she could immediately toggle over to three technicians down in medical who were linked on the same network, then have them run over to find Varuna and me standing upright, awake, fully autonomous. She did not have time to tell the technicians to raise their weapons before Varuna raised his and shot them right in the head in an instantaneous parade of bullets, erasing them from the network and catapulting Stella's primary POV back to Sherman in the wheelhouse. She had Sherman run to radar to see multiple blobs closing in on the Ark: some already there in the sea, and some approaching from the air. It was an attack by the animals, she correctly concluded. She truly hated killing any of Earth's creatures, but it was clear that forces who didn't understand her true intentions had decided to work against her. She influenced Sherman to focus a target on the primary line of cetaceans and deploy a set of poachbots.

—

Varuna did not handle the sound or sight of his fellow cetaceans dying well. We went to the broken window and observed (using, I should add, the new lenses attached to our eyes that could switch between our innate forms of vision and an artificial trichromatic human eyesight) dozens of innocent dolphins, porpoises, and orcas thrashing against the Ark as they roared and cried and screamed in high-pitched screams and drowned in their own blood.

"No!" Varuna shouted. His claws gripped the windowsill. "What did she do?!"

"I'm sorry," I cried. "It's my fault. Dante called, and I took her attention away. I'm so sorry."

He only had a second to look at me with his marble dolphin eye, narrowed as though I'd just stabbed him, before the sound of boots marching above us sent us to action.

"They're coming down to stop us," he said. "Tell me what happened later. We need to get out of here."

"Wait." I spotted a tray nearby that had his old Specter and the installation syringe for the new one on it. "You might want this."

His claws skittered to reinsert his Specter as we ran into the hallway and used our new augmented limbs to run toward the elevator. A group of Arklings emerged from the staircase on our left, weapons raised. We exchanged a few bullets before a stream of birds and bats swarmed in through the doors we left open and overtook them.

Our spirits lifted for a moment once we were on deck. We continued our way toward the hovercraft that would fly us off the ship. The chaos looked like it may go in our direction. Falcons flew into the wheelhouse and left with octopuses that they threw into the waves. Bats swooped out of windows with APWDs they'd retrieved from manufacturing and ditched them into the water. But the party ended when a poachbot that resembled a small helicopter spun up from the wheelhouse.

"Look out!" I shouted and pushed Varuna into the craft. We sealed ourselves inside just before the bot detonated and sent hundreds of slain bats and birds crashing on deck.

"Let's go," Varuna said. "And tell Laura to have the survivors retreat if they are outnumbered at this point."

I gave Laura the order quickly. She confirmed that the numbers did not look good, and we had likely lost the battle. I studied the craft's dashboard.

"Where do we go?" I asked.

"Anywhere," Varuna said. "Can they track the craft down?"

"Yes," I whimpered.

"Then we will have to abandon it. Just get us close enough to shore to swim the rest of the way."

I took the controls and piloted the craft off deck the way I had seen Dante do. I tried not to think about Nemos, Gunny, and Soda, all of whom were still on the Ark. I tried and failed not to think about Dante, who at that very moment was being violently removed from his room by a group of Martian soldiers on Stella's orders. Edie, meanwhile, would soon have to suffer a harsh interrogation in the president's office.

I accelerated the craft at full force in the direction of the desert: If we were going to make any attempt at breaching the Mayor's quarters (though it admittedly looked impossible), I wanted us to be in the adjacent Biome.

Once a few hundred feet off shore, I lowered the craft to the sea and ejected us. The springs under the seat threw me more strongly into the sea than I expected. I had a brief flashback to my near-drowning experience. I treaded water and tried to find the surface, but all I saw were bubbles. And then, just as before, Varuna found me and lifted me on his back to air. And this time, we wore the very mechanical limbs outlined in that initial telepathic vision. Whether by design or coincidence, he really had shown me our future. It was a desperate and terrifying future, I could see now that it was my present, but at least it was a future where we were still together, alive. We swam toward the dunes on the desert shore. I prayed he would forgive me.

37

Zelda called Stella to an emergency meeting of the Cognoscenti after Varuna's and my escape. Although there was no need for them all to be in the same room to have contact, it was tradition for the Cognoscenti to "feed off" one another's mental energy by sitting in the council room, an imposing space furnished with burgundy carpets and walls. Sitting on a shelf that ran along the room's perimeter were sets of jars that contained human brains; these, it was said, belonged to the twelve original settlers of Mars, each of whom was an ancestor to one of the twelve Cognoscenti. In private, Stella rolled her eyes at the whole thing; the original settlers had supposedly refused to comply with Olaf's call to take shelter from the Pathogen inside the Arkology because they valued "freedom," and look where it had gotten them: thousands of destitute people ruled over by a secret society. Anything that originated in human delusions of grandeur, Stella thought—even if it was twelve of them working together— would end the same way.

But Stella could not dwell on her private feelings of disgust. She was in trouble. *Your excellencies, I have no idea how this happened.* Sitting at the opposite end from Zelda of the concrete slab that they called a table, she spoke over Specter to comply with the Cognoscenti's paranoid concern that Terrarchist spies might have a means of audiovisual surveillance. *But rest assured, I will work with my Arklings and Wilcox on a solution and get this sorted out. This will only set our campaign off track by two days. Three, maximum.*

The Cognoscentum who was third in command behind Zelda and Johnson, Officer Sludge, who had no eyebrows and looked like he hadn't exposed himself to sunlight since birth, leaned forward in his chair and rapped his long fingernails on the table. *What exactly do you propose?*

Stella darted her eyes toward Zelda. "I love you, but you need to sort this out for yourself," Zelda's stern gaze said.

Stella straightened her back. *We film a broadcast with the animals we do have—the elephant, the prairie dog, the polar bear. That should at least scare enough people for you to fly some ships in and begin shipping Citizens over here. Yes, the APWDs tossed overboard are a loss, but Zelda tells me you have enough here left over from our initial shipment to spare on a few hundred Citizens dumb enough to fly over here. We can get Teddy to send some ships of conscripts over for "humanitarian missions" to contain Martian "outbreaks," and then give them APWDs once they get here.*

Those are on standby for our army! Johnson rapped an angry palm against the table. *The plan was simple: You show the broadcast tonight to make sure enough people show up to the voting polls to hand Wilcox a majority vote in the election tomorrow. Then, he and the other Terrarchist idiots distribute the APWDs to the City. We distribute our APWDs to our folks, and we control our army to fly ships out to the City and pick up the Citizens. Everyone goes down to the tunnels and boom!—back to the past we go.*

Teddy will win, Stella assured Johnson. *Peter is out of the picture, and projected turnout is already more than enough for him. The Arklings can put together something scary with the animals we have to seal the deal.*

Sludge then arched his back and lurched forward. *You understand our worry. We have spent years building an AI in the style of yours on Earth solely for the purposes of this project. We accepted the President's request to agree to your demand to build the network in such a way that you and she would have coequal powers of ultimate control. Both of these decisions went against core Martian values of freedom. But we agreed, because you presented us with a final answer to our problem. And now, in the final weeks, you have failed—not once, but twice!—in delivering on key parts of our plan. The first failure, we understood. Your own blood turned against you, and we had done sufficient research over the last several years to effectuate our backup plan. But we let you script the images of mass conditioning—this dog and dolphin being key elements—and now we have to come up with new ones at a time when every hour counts. This is strike two, Stella.*

I understand. Stella bowed her head. *Listen, starting tomorrow, the Ark will resume production of APWDs to replenish the supply. It will not take more than three days. In the meantime, you can give your APWDs to your army, and we will recruit any willing Citizens to fly over here. If you don't have the devices to control their minds yet, fine. Just ship them into the control room and put them into prison labor to work on the THING with the rest of your people.*

The Cognoscenti exchanged private thoughts with one another on separate channels before returning to the primary one. Eyes shifted all around the table. They had all signed a pact of self-annihilation and were on a hair trigger (some of them literally had their hands near their gun holsters at that moment) in the final days.

Fine, Zelda spoke at last for them all. *But we expect there will be unrest on both planets in the coming days in response to Martian occupation of Earth—in private, if not in public. As I've shared with you, the revelation that we have been hiding a fleet of ships capable of traveling between the planets within hours may provoke questions. You'll be able to come up with a new media strategy to quell any protests?*

Stella suppressed a smile. *Yes. Of course. There are plenty more "aliens" that we can come up with. And I will also get to work on locating the two fugitives.*

Good. Zelda rose, then paused. *And one more thing. Teddy and the Terrarchists still in the City: Do they suspect anything?*

I haven't caught one whiff of a free-thinking brain cell from any of them, Stella smirked. *They all still think this is for Pathnet. Yes, I was hoping we'd be able to put hats on them by tonight, but Wilcox is too scared of me revealing his little secret with Naismith to even begin the question the narrative we've given.*

Fantastic. Everyone rose to leave.

Then, privately, as Stella returned to her room, Zelda said: *That's what happens when twinks get old. They hand their power over to dykes like us.*

Stella's laugh echoed throughout the concrete hallways.

PART FOUR:

FUGITIVES

38

When I send this book off to the publisher, I think that I will divide it into parts. This part, part four, will start at the moment that the doctors tell me it is truly too late to save my body. And, perhaps not by coincidence, it will also cover the part of the story when I knew things had passed a point of no return, but I couldn't quite see how the ending would pan out.

I let Laura know that Varuna and I were safe as we reached the beach. I told her our plan to find shelter in the dunes. She asked for us to give her some time alone to return home from work and to process what had just happened, but said she would be available in an emergency.

"Typical," Varuna hissed through his microphone while raising himself upright on shore. "Stupid human, abandoning you when you need her most."

I was too frightened to reply. His movements were jerky and angry, though that may have been an inherent feature of his getting accustomed to bipedal cyborg movement. On reaching a dryer part of the sand, he lost control of his spider-legs and fell over.

"What the fuck is this shit?" He shrieked.

"It's sand," I said. "It's all over the bottom of the ocean, but it's much easier to sink into when it's dry."

"I know what sand is. Just help me get up."

I trotted to his side and used the hands on my front paws to heave him up while rising onto my hind legs. I expected it to be quite difficult, but he felt as light as a feather.

He looked at me in shock. "How did you do that?"

I stared down at my hands. "How *did* I do that?" I flexed my spine a little up and down. I clenched my abdominal muscles. "I think these suits they've given us have a lot more power than we thought."

Varuna looked away. Just how mad at me was he? He took another few nervous steps in the sand, then seemed to get the hang of it. He skittered away slowly, then picked up speed until he was slicing through the sand so fast that I needed to run to keep up. But it wasn't too bad: I found that running required much less effort. Whoever had designed this technology, I started to recognize, wanted us to have incredible power.

"Where are you going?!" I shouted.

He would not answer. We passed the dunes and headed inland toward a flatter, drier stretch of caked sand. The sparse floral landscape of cacti and agave bushes became even sparser. Snakes and kangaroo rats and Gila monsters ducked out of our way into holes in the ground. The sun made its final descent below the horizon. A rich tapestry of purple and pink settled into a dark, dark blue. The distant lights of the City shut off as Citizens went to bed. I chased him through a void. I was too scared of being alone to see him for what he was: a narcissist, leading us both toward destruction.

We must have run for an hour, about halfway to the City, before he halted without warning.

I caught up to him and panted. "*Where* are you—"

"Shh!" He raised a hand. "Do you hear that?"

I perked my ears up and listened. A recognizable electronic hum grew louder. It approached us from the direction of the City.

"Poachbot," I whispered. "Run."

We took a right angle and dashed out of the hum's way. The hum morphed into the hooting of two desert owls. Because I had encountered the infrared signature of poachbots many times before, I knew that I could smell their heat in the final instants of their approach. I looked over my shoulder and up at the sky and sniffed just in time to sense the owlbots as they dove down toward our necks and opened their beaks to fire their heat-seeking bullets. I raised my gun and fired once, twice. The mechanical owls fell to the ground. It was my first time killing something—or at least feeling like I'd killed something.

Even if it was a robot, it felt both horrible and exhilarating.

"That was close," Varuna said.

"More are coming," I warned. "A drone must have spotted us. The Ark knows where we are. We won't be able to stop them. I've seen an entire herd of wildebeest nixed by a swarm of snakebots in a second."

"Oh, great. We can just relax and wait to die, then," Varuna said with a high-pitched, mocking voice. "Come on, dog. Use your brain. How do we block them?"

I sat on my hindquarters and pondered. My mind went back to a time when Dante was ten. He was angry that his mother had, on shareholders' advice, agreed to cull the snowshoe hares, whose flatulence, it was said, made a significant contribution to the production of methane and the disruption of equilibrium in the tundra biome. To save the rabbits, Dante had collected a batch of carrots from the Ark's kitchen, stolen a hovercraft from the deck, and flown to the burrows, where he could lure the rabbits inside the craft and shield them.

"The poachbots are programmed to avoid hovercrafts," Dante had said to me. "They don't want to hurt humans."

Remembering this, it struck me: Stella and Mars had given us these cyborg suits with weapons and strength and speed for the purposes of invading the City and terrifying Citizens. It stood to reason, then, that we also had the power to interact with key technologies of the City infrastructure—including its transport system.

"I'm calling Laura," I said to Varuna. I ignored his scoff.

You won't believe what's on TV right now, she thought immediately on answering. She showed me the screen in her living room. Nemos, Gunny, and Soda, all outfitted with cyborg suits like ours, stood at the very bow of the Ark's deck, their bodies lit by an unseen camera crew in front of the Melampus-logoed flag that billowed from the jackstaff.

"Greetings, Earthlings," Gunny said in a ridiculous squeaky voice. "You'll be dismayed to discover that we, the beings of Zeta Reticuli, have hijacked the minds of those aboard the vessel you call "the Ark." In the coming days, we will abduct two of every species in your Biomes and outfit them with technology like what you see here. Then, we will invade the City and destroy you."

Laura's parents watched from the couch, transfixed. Wanda tugged at her earrings in horror, while Peter swigged a beer and sneered at the TV with drunken disgust.

I wanted to see the rest, but we of course did not have time. *That is certainly worrying,* I said to Laura, *but I need to know, right now, how I would call an emergency taxi into the Biomes.*

Laura gave me a number that her boss had given her for her jeep driver's job in case of breakdown. *It's linked to Pathnet,* she said. *You should just be able to imagine the digits and then connect to an AI operator.*

I wished her goodbye and did as told. *What's the emergency?* A ghostly whisper from the Servers asked.

I gave the first answer to come to mind. *I'm a very rich Terrarchist stranded in the desert! Our tour jeep broke down.*

A brief silence, then: *We're sorry. We can't confirm your identity. Please state your emergency again.*

I sighed, then thought to try something else: *I'm a badass mecha dog trained to fuck shit up and send everyone to Mars. I need a trip to the City.*

Thank you. A taxi will be sent to your location soon. The degree of thoroughness that Stella and Mars had put into their plans impressed me.

Varuna raised his fins and hung his mouth open in a rather ugly gesture of domineering exasperation. "Well?"

"A taxi's coming."

"So we're driving right into the City? Great plan, dumbass. They'll shoot our taxi down on sight."

"No, *dumbass*. We're going somewhere else. And where were you running to? Looked like we were headed toward the City to me."

"Yes, but I was going in with backup."

"Backup?"

He waved his fins in anguish. "Aagh! Look, I didn't want to tell you, because I knew you would try to stop me, but for the last hour, I've been talking to the bats and shrews. They were going to meet us when we got close to the City, and I was going to lead them in a siege on the Mayor's Quarters. I've told them to synchronize with any animal who's willing to join us. Rodents and birds especially. The flying animals will give me and the climbing animals cover as we scale the walls, break into Wilcox's house, and force him to give us control of the AI."

I scratched my head. "You do realize the entire City is equipped with defensive systems to prevent animals from entering?"

"Normally, yes! But the word from those nearest the gateways is that those systems are being turned off in the last day or so. Those shields have a sound, a hum, as quiet as the poachbot's. The bats have been listening in, and that hum has stopped."

"They just turned it off?" I barked a low bark of disbelief. "Why would they do that?"

"Well, they *were* planning to send us in there to terrorize everyone."

"Yes, us. Not *all* animals." But then, I remembered the message Laura had just shown me from her television: Two of every species, abducted onto the Ark.

I wanted to continue trying to figure things out, but the involuntary rise of my ears showed me time was up: Our taxi was coming, I could hear. And so, too, from behind us, were a mass of poachbots. Snakes, this time.

"Stop fighting with me," I said, "and run."

I yanked him by the fin and dragged him to follow me. We dashed toward the egg-shaped taxi as it buzzed down and opened itself up to let us inside. Behind us, the rumba of snakebots rattled their tails and flew along the ground. Their hisses coalesced into a single breath. We leapt into the taxi and sealed ourselves inside—just in time to watch them disperse around it and then scatter throughout the sand, lost and confused without their prey.

We're going to fake our deaths, I told Varuna over Specter. I grabbed the controls and piloted us toward the river that separated the desert from the savannah. *We're going to stage an argument, crash the taxi into the river, and then float downstream until we reach the nearest hideout.*

Varuna blinked, said nothing. He was not used to seeing me take charge of a dangerous situation, and I was not used to doing it, either. *Here goes nothing,* I said.

"No, Varuna!" I shouted loud enough for the black box in the taxi to record. "Please, we have to go back to the Ark and save the others!" Then, thinking: *Take the controls away from me and pretend we're going to the City.*

Varuna checked the navigation screen to monitor our heading, then shrieked. "No, you idiot! We are going to go to the City and give those humans a piece of our mind!"

"No!" I yanked the controls back.

"Yes!" Yank.

We did this back and forth for a minute. Then, I tapped a spot on the map with my claw. *When we get close to the waterfall, say you're going to kill us both and send us nosediving into the rapids.*

That's not actually going to kill us, is it?

No, moron. We're going to eject out of the taxi, hold our breaths, and float downstream.

The waterfall marked the spot where all the tiny, trickling tributaries of the desert converged and transformed into a single roaring cascade that fell into the savannah.

"That's it!" he yelled with only slight hesitation. "I can't deal with you anymore. This isn't worth it. I'm killing myself, and I'm taking you with me!" He heaved his body against mine, so hard that it did in fact bruise me a little, then thrust us down toward the water. I had just enough control of my limbs to push the eject button once we submerged.

I clung to his body and felt the force of the rapids push us downstream in the darkness. I had no choice but to trust him.

I trusted him. *Stay below the surface and count to twenty,* I said.

1, 2, 3…

He was scared, and I was scared, but we held on, and when our count hit 20, the force of the water eased. I paddled us up to the surface. We emerged from the water into a small, grassy clearing that sat in front of a wood cabin.

A Captain's hideout, I said. *There's one in every Biome. No drones, no cameras.*

We went inside and turned on the lights. A cozy living area with fireplace, rug, and sofa abutted a kitchen with an electric stove and a very ancient-looking refrigerator. At last, we could breathe for a moment.

We can't stay here for long, I said, *but we should be able to stay the night.*

Varuna stayed silent while he followed me up the stairs. His emotions were even more inscrutable to me than usual. He was in a state of shock, I found when revisiting this scene. He could not believe that he was in a human residence. When I turned on the lamp in the bedroom, he placed a claw on his face. He opened his jaw and let out a slow rattle. It looked like he was going to tear his skin off for a moment. He teetered, nearly fell over. I walked up to him in concern and grabbed his fin to steady him.

He looked directly into my eyes for the first time since we escaped the Ark. "I'm sorry I've been such a bitch all day."

"It's okay," I licked behind his ear. "It's been a rough one."

He tilted his head to lean into my kisses. He slumped forward, sank into me. I tried for a second to hold him up, then gave up and spun around to pin him onto the bed. He was not the type of creature to cry or be sad. He was the type of creature who showed sadness by giving himself over to me, by pretending to give himself over to me. I licked him, faster, harder. Our paws and fins touched. Our claws, as though by their own intelligence, wrapped around one another's backs. We took turns sinking into each other. We felt the weight of a world made for and by humans crush us into each other. We rebelled against the alien coldness of our metal appendages. We became flesh. We became animals.

I held him in my paws when it was over, my face leaning against his dorsal fin. We sank into the bed and willed time to slow down, if only for a night.

"I'll have to tell the network to hold off until tomorrow," he said at last.

"Yes, that's probably for the best."

He shifted his weight a little to look back at me. "Do you still want us to go to the stars together?"

I let my tail rise and fall. "Of course."

I licked him once more, then switched the lamp off.

Before I fell asleep, a question came to mind. "What's your deepest fear?" I asked.

He shifted around to face me. "What makes you ask?"

"I don't know. Back on the Ark, Dante had said that Stella's model of the X hacked his mind by showing him his deepest fear. I was wondering what yours was."

"Well, it would be hard to know for sure without seeing it. But if I think of the first thing that comes to mind, right now, lying here with you, honestly, I would have to say what scares me most is that none of this had ever happened. I would be back on the Ark, in a tank, armor and weapons gone, being pointed at and...yes, it's silly, but, yes...laughed at...by all the Arklings who had ever tortured me. And you wouldn't be there. So there would be no one to help me."

I licked him under his jaw, and I scratched the skin around his fin, the way I would have liked to be scratched. A minute or two, I fell asleep. He, however, stayed awake for a while— coordinating, thinking, feeling.

39

Laura's 24-hour existential crisis began as soon as the battle for the Ark ended in its stalemate. On the tram home from work, her mind churned with the news that Dante was not only still alive but also, at least at times, in his mind enough to be trying to communicate with her. A sense of helplessness overwhelmed her as she studied the scared faces of other passengers on the tram, some of whom wore Stella's model of the X and sported campaign stickers for Wilcox. Those who didn't still had the distant gaze of those fully checked out from their surroundings; many had synced their minds to Pathnet, where they could now watch the City News 24/7. She imagined Dante's terror: Would Stella punish him for trying to contact us? (No, but she had no way of knowing.)

Images of the Martian bedroom where Dante was imprisoned, which I had earlier forwarded to her, were still on mental replay when she entered her family's apartment and found her mother sliding six or seven empty beer bottles off the counter into the trash. Wanda looked up with surprise.

"You're home early. You should have called so I'd know to make dinner for you."

Laura squinted. "Letting Dad drink again?"

Wanda sighed, pinched her brow. "He's sleeping," she whispered. "Lower your voice."

Laura did not lower her voice. "What's going on here?"

Wanda approached her daughter and took her hands. "It's

259

been extremely hard on him both campaigning for Teddy and worrying about the news all the time. He just needs something to get through this. Election day is tomorrow. He's promised he'll stop after."

Laura's anger toward her parents bubbled. Nothing she had done over the last several years had seemed to matter. Her father was sliding back into old habits, and her mother seemed content to enable him. She rolled her eyes and went into her room. She was surprised to find Michelle was not there. The collection of hydroponic plants Michelle kept in the bedroom corner had grown larger in the last two weeks, and it was unusual for her not to be home either completing schoolwork or tending to them at this time.

"Where's Michelle?" Laura ducked her head into the kitchen to ask.

"She's spending the night at Sammy's," Wanda said.

Laura's gut lurched a little. She was alone and trapped. Michelle's recent furtiveness had already concerned her, and now she let her mind go to dark places. Was she out drinking, too? Or worse? Laura thought about checking in on Varuna and me, but she couldn't handle bad news, so she simply stared at the ceiling and covered her face to muffle quiet sobs.

The sound of her parents' bedroom door slamming open jarred her back to the present. "Turn on the TV. Wilcox is talking." Peter's speech was slurred and halting.

Laura joined her parents in the living room to watch the Mayor introduce and then present "a disturbing clip" the aliens had supposedly just sent him from the Ark. It was then that Varuna and I called her. And at the end of the call, when I had to leave Laura wondering about our safety, she was so afraid of what was coming next, and so afraid of losing not only Dante but now Varuna and me, that the Mayor's declaration, following the "alien" broadcast, that he would be sending City warships over to the Red Planet for any willing Citizens to evacuate Earth and assist in building cognitive defense technologies on Mars, compelled her to stand up and say these words to her parents:

"I'm going to Mars."

Peter whipped his head around like a buzzsaw. He locked

eyes with Laura. "Hell no you're not."

"What's wrong?" Laura smirked. "I'm just trying to be a good Citizen."

Peter rose from the couch and stumbled toward his daughter. "You listen to me—"

"Be careful what you both say out loud, please," Wanda interjected, feebly, not turning her head away from the screen.

Peter flared his nostrils and leaned in close to Laura, yeasty beer breath clouding her face. "I'm going to say this once. There is nothing you can do to help that boy. And there is no way the two of you can be together."

Laura could not control herself: The thought of this man, who now appeared to be nothing but an overgrown child to her, attempting to be her father when she had put so much effort into parenting him, enraged her. She spit on his face.

And he, in turn, slapped her.

And she, in turn, let down some part of herself that had protected her from acknowledging the truth in all its painfulness:

He had struck her before. Not in many years, not since he had gotten temporary control of his addiction, but it had happened. And he had struck her mother before. Several times.

And I can imagine my reader's sense of betrayal: How is it possible that Peter Delacroix, the high-minded activist who believed in the equality of all people, could have also been physically violent with his family? I admit that I could have shared this information earlier, but I have waited until now, because I believed it was important to show the power of a single moment, to show the full shattering clarity of that moment when Laura realized that she and her father had both, at least in part, tried to cure their world as a way of denying the illness that plagued them at home. And no, the illness was not their fault, but there was no way for them to treat it until they saw it.

"And remember," the Mayor concluded on TV, "a majority vote for my reelection is the only way to ensure the continuity of our defense strategy."

Laura looked briefly at her mother, who said nothing, then

retreated to her room.

She did not emerge the rest of the night. Nor did she sleep for a while. Instead, she contacted us. I was asleep by then, but Varuna was busy coordinating with his network. He hesitated to communicate this to her at first—he knew her less than he did me or Dante, and he still did not trust her fully, but her declaration that she wanted to go to Mars and find Dante, damn the consequences, caught his attention. She did have some resolve in her, after all. And she was angry. He could use this.

Don't do that, he said. *You know it's a trap. They'll swap your Specter back out for a hat as soon as you get there.*

I just feel so powerless! Laura gripped the sheets of her bed in anger. *There must be something I can do.*

If you really are looking to take action, Varuna said with a glimmer in his eye, *let me tell you what I would like to see happen tomorrow.*

Laura listened to his plan to hold the Mayor hostage and force entry into the Servers and moved through a spectrum of emotions: shock, fear, and then...glee.

But there's one problem, Varuna said. *Although the anti-animal shields around the bulk of the City do appear to be inactive, there are still defense drones buzzing all around the top floor. We therefore still can't access the Mayor's Quarters directly.*

Laura thought back to Wilcox's previous election day. An idea came to her. *Tomorrow evening,* she said. *Once the votes are in, and it's time for Wilcox to declare victory, there's always a big celebration in the spaceport. He'll need to travel down there. To do that, he'll need to take two elevators—one that goes down vertically, and one that goes inward from the residential sector toward the spaceport. If you can rush him on the ground floor between the two elevators, you can kidnap him and force him to take you up to the Servers. He'll have security, though, and the most difficult part will be timing. You'll need to know exactly when victory is declared. I can have an eye on the news and let you know when the election is called. He'll descend shortly after.*

It was just a crazy enough plan for Varuna to be on board.

I love it, he said. *Tomorrow evening. I will spend the day coming up with a plan of attack, and you will let us know when he is en route downstairs.*

—

When I awoke the next morning, however, Varuna's plotting had progressed well beyond this arrangement with Laura.

He had gone downstairs and found coffee in the cupboards. *I'd always wanted to try it,* he said to me with a mug in his claw and his whole body jittering. Ever since I saw the humans drinking it while they tortured me.

The plan now, in his mind, was not only to kidnap the Mayor, but to lay the groundwork to take control of the entire City.

My bats and shrews have synchronized with animals all over the Biomes, he explained. *And starting last night, strange little flying saucers have been moving around abducting two of every species. Everyone is terrified.*

I struggled to believe this until he invited me onto his channel and let me see, firsthand, the point-of-view of a fruit bat in the rainforest, who watched as one of these saucers flew above a pair of unsuspecting okapis, pulled them up inside it with a strong magnetic force, then flew back toward the sea and the Ark.

This is horrible, I said to Varuna.

No it isn't! He shrieked and sloshed his coffee in its mug. *All the animals of the Biomes can see what's happening now! We've never been more unified.*

Word of synchrony spread all over the island. Every species that watched its own vanish into the saucers was desperate for answers, and Varuna's network offered it to them. We spent the day watching Varuna's forces grow.

At midday, Varuna got onto the network and delivered a special address.

Animals of the Biomes, unite! For the last decade, the humans have gifted us with the ability to communicate like them. And with this gift, they have given us the tools of their own demise. They have allowed us to see just how trapped we are. There is a world beyond the walls of this island. There is a whole universe, in fact. As a dolphin, I have the ability to see the future. I have received visions of a time when we will all break out of these walls and journey into the cosmos together. But for that to happen, we need to take control of the island. And now, now when you watch your fellow creatures kidnapped before your eyes, is the time to do it. Hours from now, Prince and I will kidnap the Mayor and force him to grant us access to the servers. We will build a better world for ourselves. Animals, will you stand with us and be ready, if we need you, to strike? Elephants, do not forget the poaching that brought your mighty empire to extinction. Horses, do not forget the slaughterhouses where your ancestors were gassed to death so that the humans could make cheap glue. Polar bears, penguins, do not forget the poison that clogged the skies and melted your homes until the ice caps were no more...

Similar injunctions not to forget all sorts of historical horrors continued for over an hour.

Should I tell Laura about this? I asked when he was done.

Don't you dare, he rapped his claws on the table. *She'll think I'm trying to kill a bunch of people.*

Aren't you?

"No!" He yelled out loud. *We are just securing an army in the event that things go south.*

I didn't know what to say or do other than watch. Yes, I was scared, but he looked so happy, and I couldn't risk upsetting him and being alone.

—

Sunset approached. Laura got in touch with us to say that the polls were closing soon. We called a taxi and neared the City. Varuna told the megafauna of the Biomes to approach the City and stand by for further orders. We hovered around in our taxi for a while, making circles. The sun dipped below the horizon. It got dark. We waited for longer than we had expected.

Varuna emitted a threatening rattle. *Where is she?*

Finally, after what must have been an hour, Laura got in touch. *I am so, so sorry,* she said. *I missed the victory announcement. My sister had an emergency. I needed to save her. I had no choice. I'm still working on it, actually. I have to go. We'll talk later. I'm sorry again.*

She disconnected. Varuna stood still for a full minute, then slammed his fist so hard against the taxi's windshield that it cracked. His whistle gained volume. The words that came from his mind were a full-blown roar.

*That **FUCKING HUMAN BITCH** betrayed us again!*

40

The Reprogramming Stations sat on every floor, in the part of the residential sector that faced the tundra, though there were no windows to take in the view. When Laura received the call from the fourth floor station that her sister (or, as the voice on the phone called Michelle, her "brother") had been arrested for a second offense of wearing feminine dress in public and was up for tongue removal if an older guardian did not immediately report to the station and sign a release form, she had no choice but to drop her plan with Varuna and me.

Laura waited in the station lobby as the policeman at the front desk prepared some forms for her to sign. Through the doors nearest her, she could see the screens in the reprogramming rooms playing the films that those who had just committed their first offense needed to watch.

"We all must serve the algorithm," the film said over cartoon images of supposedly queer people committing various crimes—acts of vandalism, rape, murder. "Deviance throws the Arkology into chaos and puts us all at risk of social collapse."

Laura remembered the time she had needed to watch the film. A girlfriend of hers had tricked her into kissing her in fourth grade. The film was only half as terrifying to see outside the room's door; those inside had to feel the electroconvulsive shocks that supposedly provided the actual reprogramming to one's neural circuits. The fact that people could commit repeat offenses threw this into question, of course.

The policeman returned to the front desk from the backroom, where he had been detaining Michelle.

"Minors get one additional warning before tongue removal," he informed Laura in monotone. He placed a form in front of her. "By signing this, you state that you agree that your brother's next offense will result not only in removal of his tongue but of your and all other family members' tongues. We'll also need you to accompany him home."

Laura nodded and signed. She took Michelle's shoulder on the way out of the station and opened her mouth to speak, but Michelle interrupted.

"Don't say anything. I'm fine. I just forgot to take my earrings off before going to school. You can drop me off at Sammy's."

Then, after some nervously silent walking, once they got to the nearest tram stop, Michelle pinged her sister over Specter.

We're not going to Sammy's. We're going to the Melampus store. It's one more stop over.

Laura reacted by stepping back and bulging her eyes at Michelle, then remembered that she could be seen on the tram station cameras. *What?! Why?*

Sammy's dad works there, Michelle said, as though this were an answer. *There's something I want you to see in there. And before you say anything, my thoughts are totally private— just like yours. He's been letting us use the private models people bring into the store to exchange. He knows the invasion talk is bullshit.*

How did you know I'm wearing a private model? Laura asked.

Michelle scratched her nose, just below her own Specter. *If I squint hard enough, I can see just a tiny streak of dried paint.*

Laura shivered a little. She hoped nobody else knew what to look for like her sister did.

They boarded and unboarded the tram. The Melampus store sat between two housing tenements—the one abutting the chaparral, and the one abutting the desert. As such, it had alleyways on either side. Michelle led her sister down one of these alleys.

Another fun thing about Melampus stores, Michelle thought before opening a door in the store's rear, *is that they don't have any cameras. Probably because Terrarchist managers snort drugs in them and do other things that their more intelligent family members typically do on the Ark.*

Laura followed Michelle into the store. They were in the back rooms, behind the sales area. Michelle approached an office door with a nameplate that belonged to Sammy's father. She knocked, then leaned her head in and shouted. "Heads up, everyone! My sister's coming in! Don't worry. She's cool."

Sammy opened the door and welcomed them inside the office. Laura gasped. Six or seven other young teens Michelle's age sat on the floor. All over the ground were loose motherboards, batteries, and strips of metal that, Laura gathered, had been fashioned by the 3D printer in the office's corner. Sitting by Michelle were various pamphlets that had AGRIPPA labels on their covers. These, Laura knew, were some of those that Wanda had brought home from work earlier in her career, when she had the duty of building watering bots.

"Welcome to "gardening group."" Michelle said with air quotes. She and Sammy sat on the floor.

"You're...building something?" was all Laura could manage to stammer out in her confusion.

"Drones. Mist dispersal drones, based on the designs of watering bots at the Agrippa farms. Those plants I've been growing? All poisonous. We're creating a mechanism to spray their fumes out. I stole the Agrippa manuals from Mom's drawer, and we're hoping to have them done in time for the "invasion." Those cyborg animals, or Martian soldiers, or *whoever* tries to catch us won't know what hit them. Nobody's going to steal *our* brains."

Laura sat down on the floor next to her sister and examined the various parts of the drones-to-be. She looked into her sister's eyes. "Listen, Michelle. You know I'm on your side. Ever since I got to the Ark, I've been thinking about ways to reprogram the AI and—"

"Why just reprogram it?" Michelle interrupted. "The AI

does nothing good for us at all."

Laura sighed. "Michelle, we would die without the AI."

Michelle and multiple friends of hers groaned. "You don't know that. That's just what you've been told."

"The AI keeps us all safe from the Pathogen. We have records of people throughout the centuries trying to leave the bubble and dying. It's the truth."

Michelle rolled her eyes. "Oh, just fuck off, Laura. You sound like Mom."

Laura touched her sister's knee. "Michelle, I'm trying to keep you safe."

Michelle laughed with disdain. "Oh, really? Were you keeping me safe when you went to the Ark and left me at home with Mom and Dad? You wouldn't know. You're never around. It's been constant fighting since you left. Dad on his politics ego trip and Mom invading my privacy all the time. She doesn't let me leave the house unless I wipe my face off and change my clothes right in front of her. It's humiliating."

Laura beat her fist on the carpet in frustration. "Well, look what almost happened at the station! Maybe she had a point."

Michelle's face went pale. All of her friends exchanged uncomfortable looks. Laura realized how hurtful she had just been.

"I'm sorry. We're just—"

Michelle raised a hand and stood up. "No, stop. I don't want to talk to you anymore if you're just going to side with them. What the hell are you even doing now? Driving rich people around the Biomes for pocket change and milling around with the crowds on your daily commute, waiting to get your mind zapped? If you want to join them in staying deliberately ignorant about what's going on, go ahead, but I don't want to be a part of it." She pointed at the door.

Laura stood up, then moved toward her sister to hug her. "We're all just trying to keep you sa—"

Michelle backed away with a sneer of disgust. "Go!"

She shoved Laura out of the office and slammed the door in her face. Laura's heart stung. She felt more alone than ever.

41

Varuna's apoplectic screeching only got worse on hearing that the highest-flying birds in his network had spotted the Mayor back in his quarters.

Keep your voice down! I said to quiet his whistle. *They'll pick up our audio, and we'll have faked our deaths for nothing!*

Who cares? This has already all been for nothing! Varuna spat from the back of his throat. *We may as well just have the animals storm the City now.*

Just calm down. I put a paw on his back. *Let's land this taxi somewhere and figure things out.*

He streamed a slow exhale through his blowhole. *Let's go to the sea. I would like to conduct some research.*

Research?

At the grotto library. It's closest to the shore of the taiga. I'll drive.

He took the controls and jetted us off away from the City. Within minutes, we had zoomed over the steppes of the savannah, over the prairies of the grassland, and then crossed over into the thick conifers of the taiga forest.

What are you trying to research? I asked on the way there.

I want to know if there is any way to access the Servers without the Mayor letting us in directly.

Nemos might know that, I said. *Stewart always used to talk to her about his time as an architect for the Servers.*

270

Well, Nemos isn't available to talk, is she? His tone was bitter and sarcastic, and he made me feel too stupid to say anything else.

The trees of the taiga thinned out and gave way to a rocky beach. It took a moment for Varuna to locate a small patch of flat sand where we could land. As we emerged into the windy, cold, frothy night air, I recognized where we were.

"This is the beach where we first met all those years ago!" I wagged my tail with excitement.

"Huh?" Varuna spidered toward the water without looking at me.

"You played with me here." My tail drooped.

"Oh, right. Listen, I may need a little time to get down to the grotto. You just wait here and keep watch."

"Um...okay." I felt a little useless just sitting in the sand, but I saw nothing better to do. And he was too frightening when angry to talk with for long.

Varuna retracted his claws into his skin, dove into the waves, and leapt quickly toward the horizon.

Once I could no longer see him, a thought entered my mind. Nemos was incapacitated, yes, but her daughter, Emily, remained out in the savannah, as far as I knew. Deep worry for the no doubt lonely calf overtook me, and I decided to contact her.

Hello? She lay on her side beside a mud puddle. I worried that she was ill.

Emily! Are you all right?

Yes. Just depressed. I miss my mother. Do you know if she's still alive?

Yes. I think so. Varuna and Laura and I are all working hard to get her back to you as fast as we can.

After we spent a little time talking about her life—how hard it was for her to be tossed between different foster parents in the herd whenever Nemos was away on the Ark—I broached the question of Stewart. She confirmed that her mother had told her all about her conversations with the lost engineer.

Emily, did Nemos ever discuss alternative modes of entry into the Servers? Something that didn't involve the Mayor's physical presence?

She plunged into the reserves of her elephant memory for a second. *She never said anything about that,* she said. *But wait—there's a second set of Servers somewhere. Deep under the sea. Backup servers. To be accessed in the case of emergency. They keep a copy of everything programmed on the top floor. The underwater Servers are always in communication with the Servers in the City. You could, theoretically, reprogram things from there.*

I did a little pirouette on the beach in excitement. *How do we get down there?*

You would need the Ark, Emily said.

Oh. I flopped on the ground. *Not going to happen.*

Emily sighed. *I'm sorry. I wish I could be more help.*

It's okay. I huffed into the sand.

I wished her strength and disconnected.

The moon rose over the next hour. As I waited for Varuna, I tried to contact Laura a few times. She didn't answer. I wondered if her father might know of any secret passages or tunnels that could at least get us into the Mayor's quarters, if not the Servers. But it was unsafe to contact him directly, now that he was hooked up to the network.

Varuna emerged from the water. I trotted up to lick him, and he put a claw up to keep me away.

"Did it not go well?" My ears sagged.

"I couldn't find much," he said. "I did find out one thing that was quite interesting, however. You know that Pathogen that will kill all the humans if they step foot anywhere else on Earth? Apparently, it doesn't affect animals. I found a historical record from a couple centuries back. The humans flew a dolphin into the sea outside the bubble, and he survived."

"Ok?" I waited for him to explain the significance of this. It was a little surprising—Dante had never mentioned this to me—but I didn't see why it was relevant.

"Just an interesting detail," he said. He tilted his head so that his right eye looked toward the sky. "How was your wait up here? Nothing to report?"

I told him about my conversation with Emily. His eyes at first narrowed into slits, like he was angry at me for conducting any kind of research without him. Then, when I introduced the underwater Servers, his jaw hung open a little. Once I had concluded, he turned away from me and leaned against a small cliff that overlooked the sea. I shook my tail slightly with agitation. Water lapped up at my paw. I backed away in surprise: it was high tide.

"You know something, Prince?" He said at last. "I think we are thinking about this all the wrong way. Maybe we should just let things...run their course."

I didn't want to believe that this meant what I thought it meant. "What do you mean?"

"If things are as they appear, then in just a few days, all the humans will have disappeared into a black hole, and the animals will be running around the City. We'll have free reign over everything. The Ark will still be here, right?" He spread his fins open in expectation of a reply.

"I suppose..."

He spidered toward me. He took my face in his claws. "So, we can demolish the AI entirely, and then we can get out of here and roam the Earth the way we all used to!"

"But what about..." My heart quickened. "What about Laura? And Dante?"

"Oh, you poor thing." Varuna scratched behind my ears, a gesture I would normally love but that sent my spine tingling then. "Don't you see that they will never really care about you? They've both abandoned us. And they always will, every time you give them the chance to prove me wrong."

He fixed his eyes on mine, scanning my loyalty. "That's...that's not true," I stammered.

"Isn't it, though? Say a miracle happens, and we undo this whole hivemind plan, and we get Dante and Laura back here. They'll get married, have a family, do whatever humans do, and they'll be so busy fixing everything here that they'll forget about you completely. Good riddance to them, I say. Animals can only trust each other."

I made the slightest motion to move away. He gripped my neck tight and scratched me harder. "But what about what Dante said about the black hole?" I asked. What if it destroys the Earth, too?"

"That's a good point." He let go of me suddenly. He looked at the moonlit horizon and whirred his little spider legs in the water to create a playful splashing motion in the tide. "I guess we'll just have to destroy the AI before it happens. Martian ships will be here in a few days. Maybe we can get the animals to storm the ships, and then you and I can steal one and shoot a giant missile onto the top floor."

I cocked my head at this. It sounded absurd.

"OK, fine, that's a bit much," he said. "I'll be honest: I don't know how we'll do it, but it's our only choice, clearly."

I averted my eyes. "I'm not going to do it," I whispered.

He chirped with derisive laughter. "Fine. I have plenty of other animals on the island willing to help."

To my surprise, he scurried off toward the taxi.

"This is what you've wanted all along, isn't it?" I shouted while rising onto two legs and following him. "To get rid of humans. I've just been a means to an end for you."

He opened the taxi door. I couldn't believe it. He was going to leave me.

I whined, "Did you ever even care about me?"

He paused outside the taxi. "I'm not going to dignify such an insulting question with a response."

I couldn't help it. I howled.

He pivoted around and zoomed back toward me. "Look, Prince. This is it. You either join me and fight for the new world, or you're against me, and this is where I leave you."

"You would really do that? Just leave me?"

"I don't want to work with weak housepets."

I slid out of his claw as I sank back onto all fours. "Look where we are, Varuna." I gestured toward the moon's reflection on the water. "How can you talk to me like that here? The place where we met and played together?"

He turned around once more. "I lied about that."

"What?" The tide was still rising around my legs.

"It's bullshit. That was some other dolphin you met. The one time I ever made the mistake of caring about anybody." He tipped his beak down a little. I feel quite stupid now, looking back, but I didn't believe him at first. I reached forward to hug him. He pushed me away, so hard that I fell into the water. I looked up at him in horror.

"You were right!" He shrugged his fins. "What else do you want me to say? I've been using you this whole time. That dolphin told me about you, and I used the story to manipulate you."

"How could you...?"

He spidered back to the taxi. He climbed inside. Overwhelmed by betrayal, I whispered, hoping he wouldn't hear me, "You're a monster."

But he did hear me. He leaned out of the taxi and looked at my shaking, whimpering body in the waves. "I may be a monster. But what does that make you? A pathetic servant. That's all you'll ever be. Serving one monster after another. You have no identity of your own, so you just cling to whoever can give you a sense of purpose. You think that you're benevolent and self-sacrificing, but all you do is sap the emotions of those stronger than you. The world would be better off without you."

I rose and ran toward the taxi. "You don't believe that. I know you don't believe that!"

"Goodbye, Prince."

He slammed the door in my face and flew away. I flopped down in the water and let the dark tide drift me around. It was the most painful moment of my life yet.

42

The tram roared into the station. Laura walked up to the transparent plastic wall that stood on the edge of the platform. She glimpsed her reflection. The wall prevented passengers from killing themselves on the tracks. She had never made that connection before. Doors in the wall slid open. The tram doors blew open.

The air in the tram was stale and pungent with passengers' sweat. The seats were torn and dirty. The people were tired, angry, or both. They listened to whatever played on their Specters and did not speak or look at one another. Laura sat and attempted to contact Varuna. He did not answer. She attempted to contact me. I did not answer, for I did not want to burden her, swept up in the tide and adrift with desolation as I was.

She studied the faces and bodies of those around her, darting her eyes every half-second to avoid an uncomfortable moment of eye contact. Different skin colors, different sizes and shapes, different clothes. All of them, cramped and pinched together in the car. Laura had taken the tram to and from school every day in her youth, and she had taken it every day to and from work these last couple of weeks, but this was the first time in her life that she believed she was one of them. Not someone who could *help* them. Just...one of them. One of the scared, lonely, ordinary people moving from one room to another in this giant building in the center of this giant island in a bubble in a massive ocean on a massive planet that they would never, ever get to inhabit in a way that felt like they were at home.

Her thoughts moved too quickly to move in any direction, too quickly to transcribe in words. And in that sense, they were still, a cloud of buzzing that lost all boundaries with the shrill buzzing and rickety clatter of the tram car. Were Varuna and I in trouble? Was it even worth considering getting a spot on the ship to Mars that would leave first thing in the morning? Was there anything more she could do to protect those she cared about from whatever was coming very, very soon? *Did* she care about anyone? Was there anything she could do to protect *herself?* Or was she just trapped in one room or another until she gave her mind away? Did she, or anyone else in that car, ever even have their minds?

All of these questions and more rattled around in Laura's head on the way home, but once the tram had stopped at her tenement and she had exited, the fear of seeing her father when she entered her apartment gripped her most.

But he was not there. The kitchen and living room were empty. Perhaps her parents had gone to bed early, Laura thought. She opened the freezer and removed a microwave dinner.

She pushed the button to open the microwave, which hung above the counter between the cabinets, and as she brushed her fingers away, they caught on something that had been taped to the microwave's underside. A piece of paper. She craned her neck down to look. It was a letter, handwritten, clearly meant to be read in one of the few spots of the apartment that were invisible to cameras:

"Dear Laura, Wanda, and Michelle,

First, I need to say sorry to Laura. Sorry is not enough, I know. I failed to control my anger, and I hurt you. It is far from the first time that has happened, and I don't deserve another thousandth second chance. In an ideal world, I could enter treatment to get a handle on my drinking again, but the money is not there, and it may not be practical anyway to enter a long-term program when the world is, apparently, about to end. Since I'll no longer be making any money from Wilcox, I've taken on a sanitation job in The Dump—going back to my blue-collar roots. Maybe it will be a humbling experience. They need me on call 24/7, so I may not see you all for a while. I will wire you money whenever I can.

Love,
Dad/Peter"

The letter annoyed Laura, especially the bit about going to the first floor being a "humbling experience." Was that what it had always meant for Peter, born on the fifth floor, to go closer to Earth for Wanda, born on the third? Had she and Michelle only ever been there for Peter's personal growth? Yes, the letter felt sincere in its remorse, and for that, Laura was grateful, but she knew as soon as she finished it that the fantasy of an eternal synchrony between father and daughter was over, that if there was an absolution for Peter (and she did, even then, still want there to be), that it would not be hers to give. Forgiveness does not require absolution.

But she could not remain in her own feelings for long. A soft sound from her parents' bedroom, which had seemed like ambient noise since she arrived home, revealed itself to her. A quiet weeping. She tiptoed to the door, cracked ajar, the way one leaves a door when one is too consumed by her emotions to worry about keeping them private, and pushed it open.

Wanda moved her hand off her face to look at her oldest daughter. She lay under the covers. Her cheeks glistened with tears. She smiled at Laura. Laura smiled back. And then the wailing. And Laura rushed to the bed, climbed onto the covers, and held Wanda for as long as she needed to cry, which turned out to be a long time. Laura had prepared herself to fight with her mother all night, but it was impossible now. As the thought of what she had planned to do in the morning drifted into her mind—going to Mars, to rescue a boy, which felt so silly as her mother sobbed in her arms, though part of her knew that it wasn't, that she should be kind to herself for wanting to save someone—she had to confront the truth that she, too, wanted the same thing that her mother always had, for someone to stay and not to leave, and while she could fault her mother for a lot of things, she could never fault her for finding that idea beautiful.

—

The water of the taiga's ocean was ice cold. It felt good to release control. Endorphins of abandonment and freezing flooded my system. It's okay to let go, they said. It's okay to die.

My brain would not allow me to drown myself, and I lacked the energy for it, so I did the next best thing and waited for hypothermia to numb me out. My heart slowed. My breathing shallowed. The paws that had been treading water on reflex fumbled and gave out. Warmth of stasis. My head sunk under the surface...

I woke up on the sand once more. A wave had pushed me to shore. The sand was soft. It held me. I did not want to die. I let the air fill my lungs again. I panted. I whimpered, quiet, then louder, louder. I howled. I was howling. "Oh-wooooo!" I held my eyes to the moon.

For the love of the cosmos, I tried. *Help us.*

For the love of the cosmos.

For the love of the cosmos.

He did not answer. I wanted to die again. I wanted a drone to find me. I wanted a poachbot to come.

Another howl. "Oh-wooooo!" Reflex of emotion.

And then, from above, from the cliff, where the pine trees glowed beneath the moon, the unexpected answer.

"Oh-WOOOOOOOOOO!"

Shadows congregated in the wood. One emerged to the promontory to look down at me. A shape like mine but larger, bolder. The shadow retreated. It had dismissed me for nothing, I figured. I let the sand hold me again.

A scratching from behind me. I lifted my head and turned to see the shadow descending the crag. It gained form in the light of the stars and the moon as it reached the beach: A gray wolf.

He approached and sniffed me. I would normally have been frightened—I always stayed away from the wolves—but now I was resigned. He could do what he wanted. I flopped my head down.

My apathy surprised him; he gave a quick snort and backed away. His eyes scanned my body. Once more, he leaned his snout forward just a little and sniffed around. He was studying my cyborg suit.

What happened? His voice entered my mind.

I did not answer. Apart from the fact that I had no will to explain my circumstances, he wore a SpecterX, which meant that any conversations we had by thought were liable to be encoded in the Servers and accessed.

He did not give up. He extended a paw and scratched my leg. His short, straight fur made contact with my long, curly poodle's fur. I smelled a feebleness, a vulnerability. I looked up at his yellow-green eyes.

I want to help you, he said.

I believed him. I could not believe it, but I believed him. And so I sank into the language of pheromones and pine trees and the moon and let out a low growl that I expected hopelessly would be interpreted as a threat.

"Not safe here," my growl said. A simple message—all I could manage in my ancestors' tongue.

He pattered away. Again, I assumed he had left, until a quick bark came from the crag. He stood on the rocks and looked back at me, one paw raised, universal canine sign of expectation, and waiting, and an offer to be followed.

I heaved myself up. The water and sand logged in my fur did not even add as much weight to my body as my suit had, but I may as well have carried a thousand pounds. I fought with every leap up the rocks of the crags. It was not that steep, but it was steep enough to make me feel like I had accomplished one small thing by the time I reached the top.

I followed the wolf into the trees. An owl or two hooted. I did not care where he took me. I noticed that I did not care where he took me. I judged myself for not caring. I told myself I was weak. I told myself I was weak for telling myself I was weak. I told myself that I was weak for telling...

The spiral of shame halted once the trees thinned out to reveal a cabin. The wolf led me around to the back. It was a research station, I could see, but I had never been here. It was not the one Dante and I had visited. This one was run down. The wood was moldy. The doors hung open, and it smelled of frequent animal visitors.

I followed him through the back door. What stood in the living room stunned me. There, installed behind the television, was a Smellogen. It was much larger than the one in Dante's room. If his was a typewriter, this was an organ. It was older, less sophisticated, less efficient, but more beautiful.

It was here, I gathered, where Dominic had first trained the wolves to communicate in smells that could be translated into words.

The wolf went to the keyboard and used his nose to tap the keys. From the organ-styled pipes came pheromones that conveyed his earlier question.

WHAT HAPPENED?

I went up to the keys. The layout was different from Dante's, but similar. I pressed a few to experiment before gaining the confidence to answer.

I LOST MY LOVE.

He responded quickly. WHAT ARE YOU TALKING ABOUT? YOUR LOVE IS INSIDE YOU. YOU ARE A WOLF.

My tail wagged an instant. NO, I typed. I AM A DOG.

His tail wagged a few times as he replied. YES, I CAN SEE THAT. DOGS ARE WOLVES. YOU ARE A WOLF AND A DOG.

If I were talking to Varuna or a human, I would have stood up and shrugged my front legs. With him, I could only type. I GUESS.

He typed more urgently. YOU HAVE YOUR LOVE, BUT NOT YOUR STRENGTH. SOMEONE HAS TAKEN IT AWAY. HAVEN'T THEY?

I lowered my head and did not reply. I fixed my eyes on the floor and let my solitary thoughts run mad.

He doesn't know what he's talking about I never had

strength there was never anything to take away Varuna was right all along you're a useless puppy still pissing in Dante's bed still getting stung by tasers still getting Dante in trouble still entitled still spoiled still passive still unable to be with yourself—

His breath jerked me out of it. I looked up to see his eyes were a few inches from mine. I shook with fear—not of him but of myself. My thoughts were so strong that even those who did not have words for them could feel them. But it was okay, his eyes said.

He licked me. His warm rough tongue soothed me enough for me to let him rub his neck against mine. I let my heat touch his heat. I let us both fall on the floor. I let him let me sob. I let him let me be held by the shape of his body. I let him let me fall asleep.

I awoke to sunlight coming in through the windows. He was gone. The lifelong impulse to chase another entered my mind, then passed. Something had changed in me. Nothing huge, but enough to be felt. I was, at least a little, stronger.

—

Laura had woken up shortly before I did. Her mother, already awake, stroked her hair. The artificial window streamed LED sunlight through the room. Laura shifted. Her mother turned.

"I know you still want to go to Mars," Wanda said.

"It's okay," Laura said.

"You should go." Wanda squeezed Laura's hand. "I'm sure you have a good reason."

"I don't know." Laura sighed. "I would be going to save someone, and that's never a good idea, is it?"

Wanda laughed. "If I didn't save someone all those years ago, I wouldn't have you and Michelle."

Laura pursed her lips. She debated whether to tell Wanda about Michelle's latest project. Was it any of her business? "I thought *he* saved *us*," she said with an eye roll.

"He kept us on this floor," Wanda said. "But no. God...it was almost thirty years ago now. He had just come back from diplomatic tour on Mars—"

"Dad's been to Mars?!" Laura sat straight up.

"Oh, yes. He never told you? He spent two years there. Right after the new trade agreements went in place. Hated it, he told me. His brain was fried when we met. Huge drinking and drug culture in the army. His father was horrible to him, too, always making him think he'd never quite reached his full potential. Anyway, he showed up at the farm one day. Said he was looking for herbal remedies for addiction. I offered him some analgesics, but I told him we didn't have anything quite like that. So he looked up—God, it was so corny—he looked up from the table and right in my eyes and said, "Are you sure you don't have anything to fix me?""

Laura wanted to retch, but her mother was laughing so hard that she couldn't help but join her.

Wanda sighed and continued. "I fixed him for a while. But then he landed the job on the top floor, and the culture there got to him. You were there. You saw it. And I'll tell you the truth. I wanted to leave him. But the AI...did you know people used to be able to leave their marriages?...we can't do that *this* century. Then he got better, and it was ok again for a while. And now here I am again. And you know what? I still love him, as messed up as he is. Now don't get me wrong—" Wanda turned to face Laura, brows raised. "—the way he treated you the other night was inexcusable. And thankfully, the AI doesn't force children to live with their parents. So, *you* do whatever *you* have to do. But me...well...""

Wanda's face crumpled once again into tears. Laura lay a somewhat awkward hand on her shoulder. She wanted to console her, but she also wanted to console herself. She felt quite strongly what it was she had to do. But was it the right thing? To rescue Dante? To try to rescue the world? To keep doing the same thing she'd been doing, now that she saw with new eyes how much she had hurt herself?

Did she even have a choice?

"What is it?" Wanda asked, studying Laura's thinking eyes.

"I'm worried..." She couldn't finish the sentence for fear of hurting her mother. But Wanda did it for her.

"You're worried you're making the same mistakes I did."

Laura nodded, squeezing her eyes shut to contain more tears.

"You won't," Wanda said. "You're too stubborn. You've got too much of him in you, and it's not as bad as it seems right now. Besides, sometimes there are mistakes you have to make. You have too much to lose if you don't make them."

The fake sun had lost its early morning shades of pink. They could see each other in full light, every line on one another's face.

Laura checked the clock on the bedside table. 7 AM. The ship would leave in an hour.

"It's time for work," Wanda said. "Go."

Laura hugged her mother for another minute, to remember how she felt in case it was the last time they saw each other, then got up and exited the apartment.

She took the tram to the nearest elevator downstairs. The crowd surprised her. It was mostly men, much larger than her; some of them were older and wore military uniforms—veterans, she gathered, preparing to join a new cause. They filled up the elevator before she could board. She would need to wait for the next one.

She called me while she waited.

Hello? I responded, still lying on the floor of the abandoned research station.

What the hell, Prince? Are you ok? I tried to call you and Varuna three times last night.

I'm fine, I said, only half dishonest. I didn't want to burden her with my desolation, and I could see the crowd around her. *You're going to Mars, aren't you?*

Yes, she said. *It's the only path left for me. For us. We need answers. And I owe it to Dante. I spent too much time trying to fix him not to see it through. I can't live with myself if I don't.*

I restrained a moan.

Where's Varuna? She said. *He's mad at me, isn't he?*

Oh, no. No no. He's busy talking to animals. He's going to start something new, I think.

That's good. I feel bad leaving you.

Take me with you, I wanted to say. But there was no time.

Well, just make sure you can talk to us when you get there.

Laura froze. A new idea occurred to her. She checked the clock above the elevator. 7:15. She might have time, but only just.

I have to go, she said with an abruptness that pricked my heart. *You reminded me of something. I'm going to try to get an extra Specter, just in case.*

She disconnected. As I lay on the floor, pondering my life, she was running: back to the tram station, onto the tram, then off into the alleyway beside the Melampus store. She halted as she reached the back door. Michelle, leaving before the store opened to head to school, faced her.

"What are *you* doing here?" Michelle sneered.

Laura drooped her shoulders with contrition. "I need to get inside. I need...well...." She glanced at the camera mounted on the store's wall. "Just let me in. I'm going to Mars."

Michelle's eyes twinkled. "Well, well, well. You have a spine after all." She held the door open for Laura to run inside and grab what she needed from a box that sat in the corner of the backrooms. She stuffed the syringes—one for deactivation, one for activation—and the Specter into her pocket and left.

"Good luck," Michelle said as she locked the door behind Laura. Laura wanted to hug her, tell her sister she loved her, but Michelle did not look at her to give her the chance. It would look strange on camera, anyway.

Laura returned to the elevator and descended to the spaceport.

She was not the only woman in the crowd that fed up to the shuttle that awaited the conscripts, nor was she the youngest person, but she was the youngest woman. The raucous army types around her—muscles and tattoos, cropped haircuts and buttoned uniforms—made her feel like she was about to enter a more dangerous version of the Ark. She felt an urge to pivot on her heel and turn right back home. What the hell was she doing?

"All aboard!" An officer yelled from the airstairs. "Two minutes to takeoff."

No. She had come too far now. She had to go. If she didn't,

there would be nothing left for her here. She pinched her arm, ran up the stairs, nodded to the officer, and entered the shuttle.

43

Laura told me about what had happened with her father before she entered the hypersleep chamber for her trip to Mars. The ship's captain (who would himself go under for the trip) surprised the passengers with his announcement that the cutting-edge technology on their craft would allow them to travel to Mars in just four hours. Laura assured me that she would do her best to contact me upon reaching Mars, but she warned me that she would need to work to find Dante as soon as she arrived.

Her absence left a void as I let the sunlight flood into the abandoned station and wash over me. I considered my next move. Things still seemed very bleak. I hoped the human lovers would get their reunion, but it was still up to me, it seemed, to gain access to the Mayor's Quarters and find some piece of information that would convince Edie to stop working with Stella and Mars. I needed to get to the City and find Peter in the Dump, I decided. I had mixed feelings about talking to him after hearing about his slapping Laura, but he was the only person who might know about an access route up to the top floor that wouldn't get me spotted by cameras and killed.

If I retracted my armor, I looked like an ordinary dog. Perhaps, if I got close enough, I could find a way to sneak into the City and pass off as a stray pet wandering the Dump. I went outside and called a taxi. But when the taxi arrived and presented itself in front of me, a quartet of horned owls swooped down from a nearby tree and blocked the taxi's door.

Halt! They shouted as they flapped their wings. *We have our orders from the leader of the revolution to prevent any and all animals from using human transports until we have amassed the forces necessary to storm the City. The risk of being caught is too dangerous.*

I scratched behind my ear. I tried to dodge them and get inside the taxi, but they flapped their wings in my face and shrieked at me.

You all know who I am, right?

Of course we do! You are Prince, the great betrayer!

Is that what he told you guys? I considered shooting them, but they were innocent, misled creatures, and it would have disgusted me to do so. Moreover, if I even raised my arm, they clung to it and pecked at me.

After about a minute of this, the taxi gave up and returned to the City.

Have you been following me all night? I asked with despair.

We have, they said. *And if you look at how high the sun is getting, you'll see it's way past our bedtime. But don't worry, the thrushes and the warblers will take our positions. Wherever you go, you'll be watched! Of course, you're always welcome to make amends to the one you have wronged...*

They flew back to their tree. They closed their eyes to sleep, though one of them blinked an eye open every now and again. I looked up and around; the other trees were too thick for me to see into them, but if I listened closely, I could hear the small fluttering of wings. I sensed eyes all over. Varuna was keeping me prisoner.

Defeated, I went back inside the station, ready to open the refrigerator and binge on what was sure to be extremely expired dog food.

To my surprise, the kitchen was occupied. The pantry was open, and sticking out from behind the doors were four bushy wolves' tails. I froze as they heard me enter and backed away from the pantry to face me. I recognized my companion from the night before; he was the first to step toward me. He looked back at the others; they then circled around and smelled me. I smelled them in return, a little less sure of my instincts than they were. Their pheromones revealed a family relation. Two of the wolves, who had fur much lighter and whiter than my friend's, were his parents. The other, a she-wolf more similar in coloring, was his sister.

My tail was limp. I was scared. Wolves were feral, savage, hierarchical, and I could not compete with them. Or at least, that is what the books Dante had read to me about them led me to think. I waited as my friend trotted over to the Smellogen in the living area. The others followed, and I followed them cautiously.

WE THOUGHT YOU HAD GONE, my friend typed. I WENT TO GET HELP. YOU SEEMED LIKE YOU NEEDED A PACK. BUT THEN YOU WEREN'T HERE.

I HAD TO STEP OUTSIDE, I typed back, confused. The others all stared at me, but they did not look menacing. On the contrary, their tails wagged, and they panted softly.

The mother approached the keyboard. WHO ARE YOU? She asked. YOU LOOK LIKE A PET, BUT YOU ARE MADE OF METAL, AND MY SON FOUND YOU ALONE.

I ducked my head a little in fear as I answered. I AM FROM THE ARK.

They all exchanged nervous looks. The mother made a small yip to her son. The father growled. My friend barked at them. The sister whined. I couldn't quite pick out the precise meaning of their vocalizations, but they were clearly debating whether I was safe to be around. This went on for a while before I decided to interrupt and state what I needed.

I NEED TO GET TO THE CITY.

The wolves calmed down. They studied me. They wanted to hear more.

THE FATE OF THE WORLD DEPENDS ON IT.

They all closed their mouths and widened their eyes. GO ON, the father typed.

I explained as much as I could, simplifying things wherever possible. This must have taken an hour, and there were frequent questions, but by the end, they believed me. Once I had finished explaining my story, they conferred among themselves once more. My friend pleaded my case to his reluctant family. It hadn't been long, but I was already starting to understand their communications better.

Once they seemed to reach an agreement, my friend reapproached the keyboard. WE CAN TAKE YOU TO THE CITY, he said. WE KNOW ABOUT A DEN THAT CONNECTS TO THE SEWERS. IF THE DEFENSES ARE DOWN, YOU CAN FOLLOW THE SEWERS INTO THE DUMP.

I thanked them profusely. We all licked each other.

JUST ONE THING, my friend said once we had all exchanged saliva. TO FOOL THE BIRDS, YOU'LL NEED TO LOOK LIKE A WOLF. FOLLOW ME.

He led me to the bathroom behind the kitchen. He poked his nose at a drawer. I stood up, opened it, and found an electric trimmer. I looked in my friend's eyes and understood his suggestion. I trimmed off almost all my fur. Then, he poked his nose at another drawer, which contained a comb and some old hair gel. I combed my fur straight, then gelled it in place.

I looked in the mirror. My breath halted. I was a wolf—a wolf with white fur that made him look a thousand years old, but a wolf nonetheless.

We returned to the Smellogen. The family sniffed me, then jerked their heads in approval. I was in the pack.

44

A few hours later, Laura awoke to the beep of a timer and a blast of cold air as the door of her hyperbaric chamber opened. A Martian soldier's hand grabbed her arm and yanked her out. He wore an APWD, as did the dozen other soldiers who rapped their guns on the passengers' shoulders and ordered them into column formation. The ship had by then already latched onto the Martian elevator and descended into the spaceport; the shuttle's open bay doors looked out on the spaceport's vast interior, at one end of which sat a row of hangars filled with sleek red and black shuttles, which were unlike any the Martian military had previously bragged about.

"Listen up, everyone!" The Martian captain shouted by the ship's exit. His eyes were glassy, soulless, just like Dante's had been at the initial announcement of the extraterrestrial invasion. He pointed to the hangars behind him. "Behind me, you'll see, is a fleet of mint-new ships designed for rapid travel between Mars and Earth like the one you've just flown in on. We have reason to believe the aliens' attempt to conquer Earth will begin in about 24 hours. We need you all to help us finish building the network that will help these ships to communicate with one another and allow us to evacuate all the lovely Citizens like yourselves to Mars."

Bullshit, Laura thought to herself from where she stood in the second-to-last row. But all around her, people nodded and waved fists with pride.

"If you'll follow me..." The captain led the columns of Citizens marching down into the spaceport. They walked past the hangars on their left. On their right, giant windows looked out on the Martian terrain. Citizens oohed and aahed at the view of this unfamiliar world's constellated domes, stretching across the red desert sand in the distance. But what grabbed the attention most was the set of automated vehicles that were busy at work putting the finishing touches on a set of solar panels erected just outside the spaceport's dome.

"New power source for the control room you're all headed to," the captain shouted in response to the Citizens' gawking eyes. "Our artificial intelligence operations are housed there, but we needed to make a significant expansion. We're going down one floor."

They arrived at a large elevator on the spaceport's far end. The soldiers ushered the Citizens in row by row. On nearing the elevator, Laura spotted a map beside the doors. It was a diagram of the dome they were now in, labeled the "Intelligence and Security Operations Center." The spaceport was above ground, while below it were two floors that sank into the Martian underground: the first labeled "AI operations," and the second labeled "law enforcement and reprogramming." (Laura shivered a little; she could assume what "reprogramming" meant. It was, in fact, a tactic that the Terrarchists had learned from Mars.) Branching off this bottom floor were indications of various subway lines that fed through the tunnels connected to surrounding domes. Laura's eyes fixed on the line marked "Cognoscenti." If she could find a way to sneak down to the bottom floor and take the subway to the Dome of the Cognoscenti...

But it was too risky to sneak away from the columns; soldiers' eyes were all over. Not to mention the cameras all over. She would be spotted and killed the second she exited the train. She had no choice but to remain among the flanks of Citizens, board the elevator, and have faith that she would find an opportunity.

The elevator opened onto a dimly lit vestibule that contained a metal detector of some kind. Most Citizens went through without problems, but a few set the alarm off and were asked to stand on the side. Laura held her breath as she walked through...

BEEP!

"Step aside, please," the captain pointed to the group of five other Citizens on standby. Looking at them, Laura could see that, like her, they all still hadn't given up Dante's model of private Specters.

"The models of Specter you're wearing are flagged as mind invasion threats," the glass-eyed captain informed them once it was just them in the vestibule. He opened a couple of small boxes that sat by the detector: One with installation syringes, and one with gleaming SpecterX's. "While we do not have enough APWDs at this point to provide you all with foolproof protection, the Melampus corporation has been generous enough to provide us with their updated version of the SpecterX. These should keep you safe for now."

The captain went down the line and replaced each Citizen's Specter. Laura's fingers moved to her pocket and traced the outlines of the syringes and the extra private Specter she had brought from Earth. Her heartbeat swished in her eyes. She would have to act fast, if she would even have time at all.

The captain made his way to Laura's position in the line. His gray flat eyes bore into hers. Was it Stella's eyes behind his? Laura braced herself for a confrontation of some kind.

But no, it was, in fact, Zelda guiding the soldiers, and Zelda did not know what Laura looked like.

And so the captain injected a deactivation syringe into Laura's temple, removed her Specter from between her brows, put the new X in place, and injected the installation fluid.

It would take a minute for the new device's fibers to wrap around her brain. The captain waved his arm to allow her to exit the security vestibule, and she followed the other Citizens whose devices had just been replaced into a hallway. She glanced to make sure the captain was not behind her, then dodged into a restroom. She detached her mind from her racing heart as she removed her extra syringes, deactivated the newly installed X, and replaced it with her spare private model.

No more than ten seconds had passed before she reemerged into the hallway. She ran to catch up to the other Citizens before the captain entered the hallway with the last row of conscripts. (Fortunately for her, the stigma around spying on the surveillance cameras in restrooms was the same on Mars as it was on Earth.)

The Citizens all gathered at the end of the hallway. A shimmering chrome-white vault door greeted them. An officer let the Citizens in row-by-row, in groups of eight, then closed the door for a moment before reopening it. Just before the door opened, Laura noticed, each row of people shook, just slightly. It was the moment of their capture, the moment the images of their deepest fears seized them.

When it was time for Laura's row to enter, she faked a little spasm, just like the others. She worried that the officer would not allow her to enter the control room, but there was no independent sentience there to notice her absence from the network.

Laura, imitating those around, shuffled into the room in zombie-like fashion, but the sight inside nearly caused her to gasp: Not the ring of computers around the room's perimeter, each of which was manned by either a Citizen or a Martian subject (their civilian status clear from their lack of uniform), but the screen that covered the ceiling. Clusters of nodes danced all over. Minds were being brought into convoluted relationships. And in the middle of the nodes, a crude symbolic drawing: two lines below a sphere.

The THING.

Laura couldn't stand and gawk at the ceiling without drawing attention, so she shambled across the room with the other Citizens and took a seat at the nearest empty computer. She peeked to the side at her neighbors to check what she ought to be doing. As soon as each Citizen sat down, they would enter a set of login credentials (Laura made a point of memorizing them), open a terminal, and run commands to open a file directory. Laura recognized the directory immediately as the network Stella had built for her initial plan. The Citizens would then open the files of individual subjects, make some edits to the code that Laura couldn't figure out, and then export the file over to a separate directory, which Laura inferred would serve as the new hivemind built to communicate with the APWDs.

Laura made random typing motions for a while before gaining the confidence to sneak a peek at the ceiling. The nodes bounced around, either one at a time or in groups of eight. They grew larger or smaller depending on their number of connections, but two nodes sat at the center of all others, the largest of all: they were marked "S" and "Z"—Stella and Zelda. Their circles remained independent of one another. A third independent circle, not as large as theirs, and with only eight nodes that remained static, sat to the side with the label "E"—Edie.

Laura, careful to avoid the stares of Martian soldiers, did some digging around in the different directories. They were labeled by number rather than name, so it would take a long time for her to find any individual person or animal's file. She observed a few key patterns in every file's code: various denotations of species, occupation, age, and other demographic factors., as well as one or more "directives." She found some files that contained the directive to BUILD_NETWORK, for example, while in others the directive was to INVADE_CITY. Many of the directives had a timestamp variable, such that they would only become active later. From this information, difficult to parse though it was, Laura gathered that the captain was correct in saying that the invasion would begin within 24 hours.

Then, after several hours, Laura found a file that contained a unique directive: STAY_WITH_MOTHER. It was Dante's.

It was time to take another risk. She moved Dante's file into the trash.

Immediately, an alarm blared. Her hands froze.

Shit, shit, shit.

But nobody around her stopped what they were doing, even the soldiers. Then, after a minute, the alarm stopped. She inhaled deeply and resumed her fake typing. Perhaps it was nothing. Or, she'd gotten away with it. She imagined

Dante, waking up from his mental prison, and she imagined herself sending him positive psychic energy. But her thoughts kept going, and she began to feel afraid once more: What if he was the one who would be blamed for what she'd just done? Did she even do what she thought she'd done? How could she have been so impulsive? Her thoughts spiraled for a half hour.

Then, a bell rang.

"Dinner!" The captain yelled with robotic dreariness.

Everyone marched in single file to a door at the end of the room. Laura took her cue and followed. It led out to a subway station. They all waited for the train and boarded. Laura considered staying behind and making a run for it, but there was nowhere for her to run. She boarded the train and waited to see where they would emerge. She looked up at the map inside the train and pinched herself to stop from gasping when she discovered they were on the Cognoscenti line. But the Dome of the Cognoscenti was two stops down. After one stop, at the dot labeled "cafeteria," the crowd swarmed out of the train and brought her along with them.

Memories of books she had read about Mars came back as she exited with the others and followed the mass of Citizens and Martians down the station's hallways. Even more than the Arkology, the Martian society depended on strict, minute-by-minute regimentations of everyone's time. Everyone, except for the Cognoscenti, needed to eat, sleep, and even have sex at assigned hours.

She entered the cafeteria. Long lines of tables sat beside dispensary booths, where automated machines plopped out an unappetizing gray slop onto people's trays. She followed the line, took her slop, and sat down. It tasted like wet ashes. She forced it down. The workforce needed to stay alive for the Cognoscenti's plan to work, whatever it was, so she figured it couldn't kill her. But she had a very hard time keeping a straight face as she swallowed.

She glanced a couple of tables over, where diners who had already been present when her group entered were eating. There was just enough of a twinkle in their eyes, and just enough variation in their movements, for her to see that they had not been automated, not yet. But they did not look free. They had twigs for arms and legs, and they had the sunken eyes of those who spent their entire lives in mechanized sorrow.

Then, as everyone neared the end of their slop, a tinny, prerecorded melody of violins played over the speakers, and all the diners rose to face the double doors through which they had entered. The music was just bombastic enough for Laura to infer that something ceremonious was about to happen.

Sure enough, when the doors opened, a man who bore the black and red cloak of the Cognoscenti, draped over his fuchsia and scarlet military uniform, walked inside and trudged his way between the tables. Though Laura did not recognize him, it was Officer Sludge, the third-in-command Cognoscentum, who had no eyebrows and looked like he hadn't exposed himself to sunlight since birth. Six lesser soldiers followed him, their hands on their weapons.

Sludge stopped at a table near Laura's and pointed to two people. Two soldiers grabbed them and dragged them to follow. He did this two more times, selecting three more people.

Laura had an urge to run. Another memory hit her, this one from a documentary that her father had shown her about Mars when she was little.

"Every evening," the narrator had intoned over a scene very much like the one Laura now inhabited, "an officer of the Cognoscenti reports to the cafeteria and selects a group of Martian workers they find attractive. They then return to the officer's room, and they all spend a night of pleasure together."

"Pleasure!" Peter scoffed. "All kinds of depraved things happen in those rooms, I guarantee it. I would hate to be a woman on Mars."

Laura was about to give up and run when Sludge found his way to her table. Sure enough, he pointed at her. A female soldier took her arm and dragged her to join the other selected diners. Laura, careful to keep faking soullessness, noticed that Sludge had not just selected anyone: he had selected the six Citizens whose devices had been flagged in the security vestibule earlier that day.

Perhaps, Laura realized, this was not an ordinary operation of sexual servitude, but an attempt to rat out whoever it was that had deleted Dante's file.

Sludge snapped his fingers. The soldiers poked their guns at the Citizens' backs, and they all exited the cafeteria toward the subway.

45

While Laura navigated her surroundings on Mars, I followed my new wolf pack on our trek to the City. We left the station through the back door, and my friend—whose Ark-assigned name, I learned when he tapped it out on the Smellogen—was Rudy (Roses, Umami, Dandelions, Yucca)—stayed behind for a bit in case any birds spying on us would notice there were now five wolves leaving instead of four. He caught up with us a few minutes later.

We only walked through the forest a short time before arriving at the entrance to a cave beneath a cliff. The parents and sister ducked inside. I stopped before entering and let out a gruff bark. *Why are we stopping here?* I tried to ask.

Rudy rubbed his face with a paw. *Sleep*, he was saying. I had forgotten about the wolves' nocturnal cycles. As I learned later, Rudy had forced his family to stay up past sunrise just to come help me.

We burrowed into the den. I whined. *Emergency*, I said. Rudy snorted with understanding and went up to his family. Barked negotiations that I half-understood went on before the father talked to me on Specter.

We will get you to the City faster if we rest first. We have been up all night. We can run together after sundown and get you to the Dump by morning.

Sorry, Rudy said to me as his family retreated to begin their ritualistic pre-sleep circles. *But I got a little sleep with you, so*

I could go with you myself...although you'll be safer and harder to spot in a pack of five. The birds might not know your smell, but other animals will. You'll need all four of us to mask your scent. The drones are less active at night, too.

He was right. I wanted to find Peter as quickly as possible, but even if we had left then, we wouldn't have reached him until nighttime anyway. Speaking through my pheromones, I agreed to wait until sundown.

But if it helps you feel less nervous, Rudy continued, *I can stay up with you a little and keep you company. Maybe teach you some wolf.*

Surprising myself with an instinctive gesture of affection, I licked him.

Human readers tend not to enjoy reading the details of intercanine communication (it involves our anal glands), so I will leave out the details, but suffice it to say that I found myself understanding more of what Rudy taught me and doing so in less time than I had expected, as though the wolf tongue had remained in my subconscious all this time, waiting to be unearthed. Within a couple of hours, Rudy and I were able to have complete conversations with one another.

He told me about finding his family that morning to inform them about me. *They were surprised to see me. I've been wandering the wilderness on my own the last few weeks. I'm growing older now, thinking about starting a pack of my own. Haven't found a mate yet, but that's okay. You have to learn to be enough out here. You have to learn to trust yourself. Of course, that doesn't mean you can't have a pack to support you when times get tough. And times seemed tough for you.*

Rudy's message struck a nerve with me. *Someone once told me I needed to trust myself more,* I said.

He placed a paw on mine. *The one who took away your strength?*

Yes. But he gave me strength, too.

I understand.

He nuzzled me, and I broke down with whimpers. I told him all about Varuna, about the words he had said to me on leaving.

Sounds like a projection, Rudy said. *Only those who feel least free would call others servants.*

What would you know? I flopped my head on the ground. *You're a wolf. I'm just a pet.*

What? Just a pet? Rudy sat up, stunned. *Do you know how much respect the wolves have for dogs like you? For your compassion? For your peace of mind? It isn't just any canine that can learn to put up with humans. Your compassion is your greatest strength.*

It was an idea I had not considered before. I remembered what Nemos had said to me months earlier about supporting Dante's growth. *Don't treat love like a limited resource.* As Rudy and I cuddled ourselves to sleep once more, I envisioned a version of myself that didn't view compassion for others and compassion for myself as mutually exclusive things.

—

We awoke after sundown. And then, we ran through the taiga with only the light of the moon and the stars there to guide our way. And as I followed the pack, I found all my old prejudices about wolf life dissolving. Where I had thought there was rigid hierarchy, there was communal support and equality: Yes, it was the father who decided when we would leave, but it was Rudy who was fastest and led the pack, and it was the mother who kept her nose and ears out for threats, and it was the sister who talked me through the pack's movements and made sure I was okay to keep going. I didn't tell them that I would have been capable of outrunning them on my own with the aid of my mechasuit; I would have felt like a showoff, and I was having too much fun being a part of something greater than my individual eccentricities would have allowed me to be.

So which one of you is the alpha? I asked them all when we stopped at a creek for a salmon break.

The sister hung out her tongue with amusement. *Alpha? There is no alpha. We only do that hierarchy crap when we're in captivity. Where did you learn about wolves?*

Feeling a little shame, I thought back and remembered that all I had learned about wolves had been through words written by humans. I thought about how much support these new friends of mine could offer one another when they felt free, and I wondered if the things I had learned about myself and my species of origin had been projections by those who had never felt free. I thought about Varuna and all the projections he had thrown at me. I wondered if there was a world where both of us could feel free.

The stars were just starting to fade with approaching dawn when we reached our den of destination, a cave near the bank of the river on the taiga's perimeter. The lights of the City were a half-mile away. We went into the cave and skulked our way into the darkness. After a few minutes, the pack stopped. I sniffed around. Inside the rocks that lined the cave's back wall was an opening made of metal—the entrance to an aqueduct.

This aqueduct will take you to a floodwall at the edge of the City, Rudy said. *During the wet season, they retract the floodwall and use this channel to send additional water into the river, but it will be completely empty now. When you get to the floodwall, you'll see a ladder. Climb the ladder, and you'll be inside the sewage treatment facility that serves this sector of the Dump.*

I thanked and licked my companions one last time.

Don't forget, Rudy commanded me before I entered the metal tube, *your compassion is your greatest strength.*

—

The stench hit me as soon as I climbed the floodwall and found myself in the treatment center. All around me, pipes churned with the waste from floors above, sent to reservoirs where they would either be recycled for additional use in the City or channeled out to the Biomes.

But the rotten smell lingered long after I had left the treatment center and began to wander the residential alleyways. People were just waking up and leaving their one-room apartments for work. They sagged with hopelessness and looked at me with indifference. Garbage bags overflowed into the alleys, and children left alone screamed for their parents.

I knew that Laura's family lived in the sector of the fourth floor that faced the chaparral, so I decided it was a good assumption that Peter would have moved directly below his family's residence and worked my way over there. The trams were neglected and rarely in service in the Dump, so I had to go on foot. And on the way there, I witnessed the absolute horror of living on the ground floor. The people here were abandoned, left for dead, and this had only become truer in the runup to the "invasion." Starving, fighting, running in and out of derelict grocery stores and pharmacies, half rageful, half numb. And the heat at the bottom of the City was like the rainforest's, but the smell was worse. The people looked no different than they did on other floors, but for one reason or another, the AI had decided that their genes were disposable.

Perhaps the saddest sight was the Body Recycling Center, where the dead, human and animal, from all over the Arkology were sent to have their corpses broken down into constituent molecules that could then be repurposed elsewhere. Old widows and orphaned children laid their palms on the window and watched as their departed went down a mechanical chute and disappeared from view.

I was losing hope to find Peter by the time I reached the chaparral sector. Then, with both hope and disappointment, I remembered one place I might find him: the neighborhood bar.

And sure enough, at 8 o'clock in the morning, there he was, his nose in a pint of beer, with sunglasses and a cap on, unshaven, modestly disguised but still unrecognizable to anyone who wasn't looking for him by his smell. He was in the middle of a large crowd gathered by the bar to watch the television mounted on the wall. The sight on the screen was unsettling: INVASION TO BEGIN TODAY, read the City News chyron. Delivering an address was none other than Stella Melampus, standing together with Dante and the Martian president. The crowd was loud, but I could just catch some snippets of what Stella was saying:

"...APWD distribution sites in every sector on every floor..."

"...fully deactivated the AI's defense systems to allow

martian ships access..."

"...answer the door when visited by martian soldiers..."

I pattered up to Peter's side. He looked down at me with indifference. I pawed him and whined. He looked again, then knelt down and scratched me. I whispered at the lowest audible volume.

"Psst. Peter."

"Oh, my..." His eyes widened with recognition. He looked around at the crowd. "I take it we can't talk here."

I nodded.

Peter, putting on a show for the crowd and any cameras, stood up and projected his voice. "What an adorable stray dog! Does he belong to anyone?"

Nobody even bothered to look at us.

"Well, I'm on my way to work," Peter continued. "Come with me, boy, I'll give you some food at the factory."

I followed Peter out of the bar and down the alleys that provided access to the industrial ring. We entered the site of the landfill, where he had worked the last couple of days since leaving his family. He led me to a particularly noisy cell, where large tractors were depositing or picking up giant batches of trash. He knelt down and spoke right in my ear.

"It's noisy enough here that our voices won't get picked up by any cameras," he said. "It's good to see you. What brought you all this way?"

"Well, Laura told me what happened."

He backed away for a moment and slumped his shoulders. "Oh. Here to tell me what a fuckup I am, then? Don't worry, I know."

His eyes were dim but pleading, though not to me. I saw someone who had been monstrous but still had the humanity to know it. "No, Peter," I said. "I'm here to give you a chance at redemption."

He laughed. "Giving me one last way to fuck up, you mean? Look, I've had plenty of second chances. Whatever brought you here must be pretty important. Hell, based on what I know, which isn't much, today may be the single most important day in human history. Animal history, too, for that matter. No, listen, if you need help, you're best off asking someone else."

He turned to walk away. I grabbed the leg of his pants in my teeth and pulled him back. He looked back at me and raised his sunglasses to reveal tears in his eyes.

"There is no one else!" I said. "That's the truth!"

He knelt down again and wiped his face with his hand. "What exactly do you need?"

"Since we last met, I've had an interesting...surgery performed." I extended just enough of my metal fingers for him to get the gist.

"Oh...oh! Wait, you're one of them!" He backed away once more.

"No, stop! No! I got away. I'm not an...*invader.*" He studied my eyes and assessed my honesty. I continued, "Look, it's too long a story to tell you now, but I need to get to the top floor. I need to get into the Mayor's Quarters, specifically. You used to work in transportation up there, right? Well, I need you to lead me through the maintenance tunnels on the tram lines. The Mayor has a private tram station, yes? With your help, we can climb our way to the top before the invasion is too far along to stop, and I can find the information I need to expose what's really going on here."

Peter frowned, thought for a minute. "It won't work. There are AI security checkpoints on the ladders between floors. And I don't have government access anymore. Except, wait..."

He and I came to the same realization simultaneously. "Those checkpoints aren't going to be active now that the defense systems are deactivated!" I said. "Martian soldiers and animal aliens are going to be moving freely between the floors."

"In that case," Peter said. "We had better move now, before the first ships arrive."

I barked in agreement. He left the landfill, and I followed. We went back into residential, then into one of the out-of-service tram stations. We jumped off the platform and crossed the tracks to the nearest access point to the maintenance tunnels. Before we entered, he turned to me, shaking, and asked, "Do you think there's a world where my daughters forgive me? I don't mean a world where they want to be around me...I know that ship has sailed. But do you think that if I...if we...make a difference today...that they can at least stand to think of me as their father?"

"I can't speak for them," I said. "But before you worry about them, you have to believe that there's a world where you can forgive yourself."

He held back one more surge of tears. He nodded, sighed, scratched behind my ears. He stood up straight and turned toward the tunnels. With that, he was strong enough to go on.

46

Over on Mars, a little before I entered the aqueduct, Laura followed Sludge, his soldiers, and the other Citizens he had selected onto the subway train. Sludge wore a thin-lipped smile as they traveled one stop over to the Dome of the Cognoscenti station. They left the train and took the spiral staircase at the back of the station up to the gleaming lobby with its swimming pool and marble tile floors. He then led the group farther up the stairs toward a hallway of bedrooms on the second floor.

"I'm going to invite the subjects into my room one by one," he said to his six soldiers. "Each of you will be in charge of bringing one of them back to the control room once I am done." He pointed his finger to assign each soldier to a prisoner. The soldiers grabbed their assigned prisoners, and Sludge began to invite the pairs in one by one.

It was an agonizing wait. He saved Laura for last. She stood in the hallway with her soldier and pondered what she might do when she got inside. Every ten minutes, a prisoner would enter Sludge's room and exit ten minutes later. "Next," Sludge would yell behind the door, as the previous assigned soldier would then leave with their prisoner.

Laura caught a glimpse of her soldier's nametag: Abigail. Abigail wore a visor, so her face was not visible, but Laura sensed a strange nervousness in Abigail's shallow breathing.

307

"Last, but *certainly* not least!" Sludge hollered as the fifth prisoner left his room and left only Laura up for whatever kind of interrogation this was to be.

Abigail brought Laura inside. Sitting in front of Laura was the most disgusting naked body she'd ever seen.

"I knew it was you all along." Drool crept out of Sludge's lips. He pointed at this Specter. "I'm the one who's linked to you all in the control room, after all. I could see your point-of-view was missing."

He wrapped his sausage fingers around Laura's wrist.

"Why..." She nearly vomited. "Why did you make me wait?"

"I needed to use the others as foreplay," He licked his lips and leaned forward. His breath smelled like gasoline. "I don't know who you are, but I figured we both deserve to have some fun before I turn you over to the President for what you did to Dante."

His hands were like ice on Laura's neck. He brought her face close to his, and he puckered his slug lips for a kiss.

Laura, seized by intense terror, hoped he and Abigail would not see as she reached into her pocket. She had kept the emptied syringes.

In a flash, she swiped a syringe up to his neck and slashed it down along his carotid artery. His eyes bulged, and he grabbed her neck. She took the second syringe in her other hand and stabbed him in the back repeatedly. He let go and fell over, drowning in his blood. He dragged her down with him, but she kicked his head until his hand came loose.

Laura rose and looked at Abigail, who brandished her weapon, then, to Laura's surprise, lowered it, once it was clear that Sludge was dying.

"Well?" Laura raised her hands. "Aren't you going to shoot me?"

Abigail just stared at Sludge's disgusting, writhing body. He took his last gurgling gasps of air, fluttered his eyes, and died. She raised her visor. A woman of about forty revealed herself. "He deserved to die," she said.

Laura was in shock.

"We're both going to get killed for this," Abigail said. "But watching that happen was worth it."

"I don't understand," Laura said. "Aren't you a Martian, Abigail? Aren't you sworn to protect your superiors no matter your personal feelings? Don't you care about your survival?"

"Who cares?" Abigail shrugged. "Everyone I know has either gotten sick or disappeared. This man kidnapped my brother and me from our parents when we were children. We both served on his guard until about a year ago, and then my brother disappeared. He was on a research assignment, supposedly. Well, I barely hear from him for a year, and then I see him on the news, killing himself because of a so-called "mind invasion." But I know what happened. I know Mars killed him. Before he went off the map, he told me about all kinds of warped images getting pumped into his head." Abigail broke into tears.

"I understand," Laura said. She hugged Abigail and allowed her to cry for a minute.

"Call me Abby," Abby said. "But no, we don't have time for this. We need to get you out of here. I have spaceport access. I can get you on a ship back to Earth."

"No, wait," Laura said. "I came to Mars to save someone."

"Dante Melampus," Abby said with a sigh. "His disappearance from the network was what sent Sludge down to look for you. But you're too late. Dante doesn't have just one node—he has two; one linked to his mother, and one linked to…well, I just know the diagram has it labeled as "E," whoever that is, for when his mother is asleep. I've heard he's meant to be under 24/7 surveillance. He made a brief run for the spaceport once you deleted the node linked to his mother, but he was quickly spotted and brought back onto this "E's" circuit."

Laura sighed. E, of course, was Edie. "Is there any way I can see him? I know he won't recognize me, but…I can't have come all this way for nothing."

Abby frowned. "Well, after dealing with you, Sludge was scheduled to go to a meeting in the president's office. Dante will likely be there with his mother. If Sludge has his key card in his clothes, I can sneak you into the office. It should be empty for another ten minutes, since they're all out to dinner still. You'll have to find a place to hide. You'll probably get caught. But it's the only way I can think of to get you into contact with Dante."

Laura agreed. She rummaged through Sludge's clothes and found his card. Abby first led Laura to her own room, a little down the hall from Sludge's, and invited Laura to put on an extra Martian military uniform of hers. This would allow her to wander the Dome freely, Abby explained, and perhaps buy her some time if she was caught at the meeting. Abby then led Laura back downstairs to the door of the president's office.

"Good luck," Abby said on leaving. "I still don't know who you are, but I can tell this is very important to you. I wish you the best. If you get out before the meeting, you're welcome to hide in my room."

Once alone in Zelda's office, Laura got to work opening every drawer in her desk. She looked for any kind of incriminating evidence that she could somehow, some way, disseminate to the public before they all got APWDs and it was too late. But she found only two seemingly useless documents. The first was a copy of *The Diary of Olaf Melampus*, a fundamental text of ecotheocracy. Laura opened to the first page, and found a passage underlined:

"Last week, I was very worried about the latest developments in artificial intelligence. I worried that those who are programming machines to save the Earth do not realize that the machines might consider getting rid of humans to be the most efficient means of accomplishing that goal. I took an evening walk and considered how I might use my wealth to address this challenge. Then, it happened: A white hole in the sky, which sent all around it undulating, filled me with divine and transcendent knowledge of all I needed to do in my life. Let these words be a promise: I shall develop my own AI, purchase an island in the Pacific, and use the AI to terraform it into a self-sustaining biosphere that can house all the people and animals of Earth, into perpetuity."

While it was interesting that the Martian president had a copy of this book, which the original Martian founders had rebelled against in their mission to form their own colony, it did not (at least then) seem relevant to Laura's mission.

The second document Laura found was in a folder labeled "Stella—I.U.L." She opened it and found only a single sheet of paper with quickly handwritten notes:

"For emergency use, Stella's deepest fear: Her, all alone, in the Dump, abandoned by anyone who means anything to her. She washes the feet of Evelyn, who has returned from the dead to torment her."

Below this note was a photograph of a young woman about Laura's age. "Evelyn, when Stella met her," the caption read below.

It all intrigued Laura—especially the revelation that Zelda planned to imagine Stella's deepest fear back at her in the event of a betrayal (was this a way to resist influence altogether?)—but nothing was a smoking gun. She moved to leave the office and run upstairs to hide in Abby's room, but voices outside the door told her she had missed her chance to escape. She looked around for any doors to closets or bathrooms that she may have missed, but found nothing. Her only option was to hide behind the curtains on the window and eavesdrop.

Zelda, Stella, Dante, and Johnson entered the office together. Zelda carried a small box. Stella carried Iguazu on her shoulder, and Dante (under Edie's control) carried Edie in her tank. They all took seats around Zelda's desk. Zelda opened her box to remove and distribute four consoles—one each for herself, Stella, Johnson, and Edie.

"All right," she said. "The camera crew will be here in five. First, Edie, you're okay handling Dante's node?"

(There was a pause as the conspirators waited for Edie to think her agreement to them.)

"Great!" Zelda said. "I wanted to invite you all in here before the big show starts to give you a chance to see how the consoles we've designed work. As you'll see, they are very intuitive." She held up the screen of her device and showed the others how to swipe nodes up and down the chain of command: because this new network was based on Edie's contributions, it was possible to move them in groups of eight.

"Stella and I have ultimate co-pilot controls, but Johnson, you'll be in charge of the other Cognoscenti's nodes. Unless we need to redistribute for whatever reason, I'll be in charge of the animals for the initial takeover, except for those on Edie's chain. Then, once Stella gets to Earth and is able to control operations there on site, she'll assume control of the animals as well as the Citizens. Meanwhile, I'll control the Martian army. As for the subjects already here on Mars, I wanted an update from Sludge, since he was in charge of the subjects in the control room at the time the incident with Dante happened, but I can't reach him. He's disappeared from the network, which is quite worrying...But anyway, there was a brief disruption in the control room, but I quickly passed his nodes over to the next ranking officer, and everything is back under control. Any questions so far?"

Stella and Johnson shook their heads. Dante shook his on Edie's command a second later.

There was a knock on the door. Zelda rose and invited Officer Tracy, one of the lower-ranking Cognoscenti, to enter. She carried a camera with her.

"Come in, Tracy," Zelda said. "Stella, you'll deliver the address? Oh, and Edie, please get Dante to put your tank down. We don't need everyone wondering what an octopus has to do with any of this at the last second. Oh, and please, get the bird to fly out of the frame as well. And Johnson, you can leave and wait in the Cognoscenti conference room for the rest of us. Alert the other officers that our operation begins in a half hour."

Johnson nodded and left. Iguazu flew onto Officer Tracy's shoulder. Dante, meanwhile, carried his tank behind Zelda and placed it just a few feet in front of Laura's curtain. How hard it was for Laura not to reach out and touch him!

Stella, Dante, and Zelda gathered around the desk and faced Tracy's camera. Tracy held a hand up and counted down from five, and the camera turned on.

"Good morning, Citizens of Earth. I speak to you on a fateful day. As our two planets' intelligence services have warned us, the invasion of the City will commence today. This is not a time for panic. We have the resources to control and defeat this threat. Mayor Wilcox and Melampus are working together to set up APWD distribution sites in every sector on every floor. Stay tuned to the News to learn the location of your nearest site. In addition, the Mayor has fully deactivated the AI's defense systems to allow Martian soldiers access to the City. Over the next several hours, brand new ships from the Martian fleet capable of rapid travel will arrive to evacuate all Citizens off Earth and deliver them to the secured Red Planet. Please answer the door when visited by Martian soldiers..."

As Stella continued to speak, Laura peeked from her curtain and studied the eyelines of all the humans in the room. She was, she determined, outside the camera's frame, and if she could wait until the second Tracy looked off to the side...

She ducked a foot out from the bottom of the curtain and gently kicked Edie's tank.

Edie, jarred, extended an arm out onto the floor to locate the source of the disturbance. Her tentacle slithered up Laura's pantleg and onto her ankle.

Edie, it's me! Laura thought.

What...how...what are you doing here? Edie's mantle turned a shocked neon violet.

I came to Mars to save Dante, but it looks like I'll have to talk to you about that.

I'm not letting him go, Edie said. *He, and you, and all those idiot animals you had working for you have meddled with me for the last time. I'm going to Ophiuchus tonight. And the best part is, Dante and Nemos and Gunny and Soda and Iguazu are all my pawns now. And once I tell Stella you're here, you'll be my pawn as well. Unless she wants control of you herself.* Edie squeezed her tentacle around Laura's leg with a pulse of menace.

No, Edie, listen! You've been tricked, and I'm going to prove it to you!

That's what Dante said. I gave him a chance to prove it, and he failed. Or I guess that dog failed. I can't wait until Stella gets control of him. And that dolphin.

Stella was wrapping up her address. "...God bless Earth, and I will see you all here on Mars."

Laura's mind leapt to one more option. *Edie, listen, I know I can't convince you yet, but I'm very close. I found a copy of Olaf Melampus's diary in Zelda's desk. There was a passage about a white hole in there that she had underlined. Don't you think that's related?*

Edie relaxed her tentacle a little. *I guess that's a little strange. But what are you saying?*

I don't know. But I will find out. I promise you. All I need is for you to lend me an arm and synchronize with me. I will keep you updated on everything I find.

Fine, said Edie. *I suppose I can lend you a tentacle. But you'll have to act fast, as I'm sure you know.*

Edie's tentacle pulsed as she synced its electrical field with Laura's body.

Thank you, Edie, Laura said on their new, Specter-free channel.

Unfortunately for Laura, convincing Edie had taken just a little too long for her to escape the office unseen: By the time the synchronization was complete, Tracy had turned off the camera, and it was Stella who was walking over to pick up Edie's tank. She knelt down and saw Laura's foot poking out. She rose and yanked the curtain back.

Laura put her hands up in terror. Zelda and Tracy both raised their guns and aimed at her. They would have shot if not for Stella's shrieking laughter.

"Who is this, Stella?" Zelda asked.

"It's the girl in love with my son. Peter Delacroix's daughter. No, no, don't shoot. I want to handle her myself. Put some cuffs on her, and give me a hat and a gun. She's coming with me to Earth. She'll be useful as a hostage in case any of Peter's fans cause trouble."

"Good thinking," said Zelda. Tracy left the room and returned with handcuffs, which she placed around Laura's wrists, as well as an APWD, which she placed on Laura's head, and an extra gun, which she handed to Stella. Iguazu also returned to Stella's shoulder.

"I'm off to Earth, then," Stella said with a flirtatious wave. She dragged Laura along with her as she gave Zelda a cheek kiss. "Talk to you in a few hours!"

Over the next several minutes, Stella then dragged Laura down at gunpoint onto the subway, which they rode to the spaceport.

"Why don't you just kill me?" Laura asked on the way.

Stella smirked. "Perhaps I respect you. You must have fought your family pretty hard to come here. Took a lot of brains to get as far as you did. But I'll tell you the biggest reason. I need you as insurance. What you did with Dante's node scared me so much that I realized he would leave me in an instant if he could. But if I have control of you, I have control of him."

This cryptic comment got Laura thinking. Whatever the vessel on top of the THING was being used for, why would Stella worry about Dante being under her control if she, he, and Edie were all going to the same place?

Laura focused on her breathing to stay calm. "Are you going to control my mind, then?"

Stella stroked Laura's hair. "Of course. But that can wait a few hours. We have a lovely trip to Earth ahead of us. In fact, there's something I'll want to show you as we enter its atmosphere. I'll program the hypersleep chamber to wake us up just before landing."

The subway arrived at the Intelligence and Security Operations Center. Stella took Laura up to the spaceport. Laura, thinking on her feet, turned her head to look at the map of the Dome she had studied earlier. It could, she realized, be Dante's only hope of escape.

Edie, take note of this map. I know you don't think I'll prove Dante right, but if I do, and you decide to set his mind free, please transmit it to him.

Edie did not respond.

Stella and Laura then boarded one of the new rapid craft. Stella threw Laura and Iguazu into hypersleep chambers, then entered sleep herself.

Back in the Cognoscenti conference room, meanwhile, the military operation had begun. The Martian conspirators donned their cloaks and took out their consoles. A set of screens on the wall broadcast various video feeds synced to the Arkology's surveillance systems.

47

Peter and I had expected the cyborg animals to arrive around the same time as the first Martian ships, but this was not the case. The animals came first, Nemos and Gunny and Soda among them. Two of every species, outfitted with the adornments given to them on the Ark, spent about two hours converging on the City, then swept inside, starting with the ground floor and moving upwards.

Looking at it with hindsight, there was something beautiful about those first moments when animals could roam the City, even though they were not in their right minds. At the time, of course, it was terror for all Citizens. Reindeer and rams and ibexes had drills on their horns that allowed them to break through walls. Hawks and falcons and woodpeckers and toucans had lasers on their talons. Coyotes and foxes and lions and tigers broke into factories and, rising on two legs, hunted anyone who refused to wear a hat.

The sight of these "alien" android animals on televisions all over the City convinced anyone who had seen the warnings to go to their nearest distribution site and don an APWD at once. And then, once the first Martian ships arrived, those Citizens would be controlled through the very same network that was controlling the animals.

Peter and I were only aware of these events through various explosive sounds and screams that shook the walls of the maintenance tunnels through which we climbed. Getting up the first five or six floors had been easy, but once the animals accessed the City, we discovered that they, too, were using the tunnels to locate their prey. Fortunately, my mechanically heightened senses of smell and hearing allowed me to ferret out any threats, but our ascent slowed down as we took less direct routes.

—

Meanwhile, if Peter and I had had the chance to stop on the fourth floor and visit his family's apartment, he would have found his wife in a great deal of distress.

Having woken up to the alarms that went off all over the AI's public broadcast intercoms ("ALERT: EXISTENTIAL THREAT. CONSULT CITY NEWS FOR FURTHER INSTRUCTIONS") shortly after the early morning address delivered by Stella, Wanda had called Sammy's parents to get information on Michelle's whereabouts.

"We were just about to call!" They said. "We thought Sammy was with you!"

Wanda, now panicked, then opened her apartment's front door and found a letter folded in three had been placed inside the doorjamb. "READ IN PRIVATE," its writer had quickly scribbled on the fold facing Wanda. She recognized the penmanship as Michelle's. She went into the bathroom and hunched over the note:

"Mom, Dad,

If you are reading this, it means that the "invasion" has started, and I have taken things into my own hands. I do not believe that Mars is coming to help us. I believe that they are coming, somehow, to destroy us all. I do not know what you both think, since you are clearly now too scared to voice your real opinions, but that is what I think, and you are not going to change my opinion just as I am not going to change yours. I would, however, ask you not to do anything that Stella Melampus or the Martian army tell you to do. I have gone into the chaparral. I am with Sammy. I am safe. DO NOT FOLLOW ME.

Love,
Michelle"

It irked and saddened Wanda to know that her daughter found her to be such a wet noodle that she was willing to do something so stupidly dangerous. But it also emboldened her. She was already terrified to know that one daughter of hers might be gone. She had to find Michelle. She descended to the ground floor. The gate had been completely abandoned now given the imminent threat of animal alien invaders. She ventured out into the chaparral.

—

Once we had reached the eighth floor, a trio of sonic booms alerted us to the first arrival of Martian soldiers. Though we did not know it at first, there were, in fact, at least a few hundred Citizens, who, like Michelle, had decided to take things into their own hands. For them, however, this meant entering the tunnels like we had and attempting to hide out. We encountered one such group of Citizens as we turned a corner to access the ladder to floor nine. Bullets whizzing by my head were the frightening first notice of their presence. Clearly, military veterans with their own arms were among them.

"Alien!" They shouted, referring to me.

"No, stop!" I yelled. But they charged toward us. Peter and I pivoted and ran.

"I'm with Peter Delacroix!" I tried yelling. It worked; their footsteps halted.

"Prove it!" Someone yelled.

"It's true," Peter said. He went out to face the group with his hands up. "The dog is a refugee. He can't hurt you."

The group was willing to believe anything Peter said. I found their politically motivated credulousness a little distasteful, but these were, for better or worse, potential allies.

The group's leader invited me to speak and explain myself, which I did as quickly as I could. When I said that I was seeking to break into the Mayor's Quarters, they offered to escort us.

And good thing they did, too, for on the ninth floor, a squadron of Martian soldiers located us. They were fewer than we were, but their weapons were superior. The group shielded Peter and me as they engaged in fire with them. They told us to go ahead to the top floor without them. The group succeeded in defeating the Martian squadron, but all but two of them were themselves killed. Those two caught up to us on the top floor. Fortunately, they had raided the dead Martians' weapons, which meant that we had quite an arsenal for our meeting with Wilcox.

The four of us ran through the tunnels and reached the mayor's private station. We exited the station and found ourselves inside Wilcox's study. He was not there, but I imagined he was somewhere inside the penthouse. I told Peter and our two remaining assistants to guard the exits as I rifled through drawers in search of a smoking gun. Once I found it, I told my human allies, we would locate the Mayor, restrain him at gunpoint, and force Zelda and Stella to allow us on television. They couldn't bear to see the Mayor killed, I thought, because without his body, they would be unable to use his bioscan to access the innermost Servers and the Source.

If they were really planning to kill themselves in a black hole, of course (or fly off to Ophiuchus), this wouldn't matter—but something inside me suspected that this was not the full story, and that Stella in particular would not have built such a sophisticated hivemind only to destroy it or leave it behind.

48

A half hour before this, Laura's hyperbaric chamber had opened. She faced Stella, with Iguazu on her shoulder. Stella wasted no time in yanking her out by the wrists.

"As I said before we left," Stella began, "there is something I want to show you. Normally, ships will enter the atmosphere above the Arkology, and then descend directly to the space elevator. I figured, however, that I owe it to you to let you see the truth of this planet you've worked so hard to save before I take your consciousness away. So I programmed the ship to make a brief detour. We're flying 30,000 feet above the continent once known as North America. Take a look."

Stella took Laura to the window. Laura seemed to feel her soul hovering above her body at the sight of the continent below. It was not, as the City's schools had taught her, an ashen postnuclear wasteland, but a green, flourishing paradise. She could even see a herd of buffalo if she squinted.

"I...I..." Laura stammered. Her entire worldview, literally, was disintegrating.

"I figured this would impress you. Here's the truth, Laura. There is no need to re-terraform the Earth to make it habitable. The Earth has healed itself fine. No, the only thing stopping us from getting back out there is ourselves. The Pathogen is not, as they no doubt told you in school, a bacterium or a virus. It is an artificial superintelligence, evolved from the technologies we developed to save us from ourselves. Look, there it is now, telling us to get on our way." Stella pointed to the window on the opposite wall and led Laura over. A strange triangular object of some kind...a drone?...floated alongside their ship. It blinked menacing red lights. Laura was surprised to hear a thought that at least seemed to originate from the drone. *Leave for your own good.*

"That's enough, Ship," Stella proclaimed to their craft. She had heard the same voice. "You may take us to the Arkology."

The ship responded to Stella's command and accelerated. Laura wanted to speak but couldn't. She kept her face glued to the window as the land turned into ocean. Her scalp tingled as Stella stroked her hair.

"Believe it or not, Laura, I was like you once. Eager to change the system. Resentful of the wrongs that had been done to my family. Such a family as I had, anyway. My mother died in childbirth, and my father could barely stand to look at me as a result, let alone take care of me. As soon as I could walk, I ran all over the Dump, going to anyone I could find for food or love. No single person on the ground floor could give me the tools to get out of there, but in aggregate, I got enough of a picture of the world around me to decide my education was important. You think you had a hard childhood? I sold my body to strangers in return for programming textbooks. And when my father learned what I was doing, he decided to help."

Stella paused. Her voice had caught in her throat. Laura glanced over. She had never seen her show genuine emotion, but it was clear that she was on the verge.

"And then Evelyn knocked on our door. She was 22. I was 14. She had been a tenacious enough Dumpling to get into the college and earn her gatekeeper's certificate. She lived in a third-floor apartment and commuted down to the gates. As soon as I saw her in her gatekeeper's uniform, I had a crush on her. And she had one on me. I thought nothing of the age difference. I was so desperate for genuine affection. She told me about a mentorship program that the Melampus corporation was running in the Dump, and she applied to take me on as a mentee. For two years, I got to live with her and master my programming skills. She had windows in her apartment. Windows, you understand! I got to see the Biomes for the first time. And because she worked at the gates, she knew all about the animals, and she took me to work with her and pointed them all out to me. She had applied for the internship and lost, but she believed I could get it if I wanted it. But I didn't want it. Not then. Because, when I was 16, Operation Bubbleburst happened. Another thing you'll never hear mentioned in school anymore. Citizens aren't even allowed to speak of it, and the Arklings are too embarrassed to do so. Young and inspiring Dominic Melampus would get on TV with the CEO, his father, who would tell us all that he had designed an algorithm that would defeat the Pathogen once and for all. Dominic's father himself had gone onto the continent and survived. Attempts to do something like this had been made before, but it was the first time a human had touched land on the continent and lived to tell about it. So Melampus launched an operation that would take twenty lucky Citizens onto the continent to establish the first colony of the new Earth. And Evelyn and I both threw our names into the ring. Evelyn promised me that she would not go unless I got to go with her. And I promised the same. And then, the announcement came. Her name was read. Mine was not. I went over to the gates to talk to her, but she was gone. She had left without me. And the next day, I watched her face on television as the Pathogen ate her and the other colonists alive. The Pathogen had tolerated one human, but it did not allow anything more. And from then on, I knew, there was no escaping this system. I entered the lottery and won the internship. I consoled young Dominic as he took over the Ark in the wake of his father's death. And we looked in one another's eyes and saw how much we had in common. There was not enough space in the Arkology for us to trust humans. The animals were the only ones we could trust."

The ship lurched downward. Stella grabbed a handrail, and Laura did the same. Stella did not lower her gun from Laura's head as the ship latched onto the space elevator. She spoke once more as the ship descended into the spaceport and detached onto the tarmac.

"And it was about that time that the rot took over. Both in the City and on Mars. All hope for an expanded world had abandoned us."

She then, with her gun still raised, walked over to the dashboard and opened a safe underneath, inside which she had stored the APWD that Tracy had brought her. Stella held down a button on the hat's exterior for eight seconds: this registered the hat on the network. Laura shook as Stella approached. The ship taxied toward the nearest empty hangar.

"Well, it was nice chatting with you," Stella said," and I hope the moral load is off your shoulders. There is nothing more you could have done. I know what you and Dante think about people like me, about my generation, but greed and destruction are the only things that make us feel whole in the wake of our own parents' broken promises. Is there, in an ideal, pie-in-the-sky world, a way to reprogram the AI and distribute resources so that we keep Olaf's silly little island lurching on another hundred years? Yes, probably. But why bother? Why bother when we see so plainly the aliens within us? Goodbye, Laura."

Stella placed the hat on Laura's head. She took the console out of her coat, and swiped Laura's newly activated node to connect with hers.

Laura's brain spasmed. The ship disappeared from her field of vision and disintegrated into the familiar, yet newly petrifying in their visceral immediacy, stuff of nightmares: creatures with dragon wings and pig tails; werewolves with flies' eyes and mantis arms; snakes with dagger-toothed smiles and scissors for rattles; sasquatch-like beasts with oozing scabs, black and brown and blue and green.

But Laura was ready. She held on, in the corner of her soul, to the competing image that Zelda had described: Stella, all alone, in the Dump, abandoned by anyone who meant anything to her. She washed the feet of Evelyn, who had returned from the dead to torment her.

The images struggled for control with one another. Laura's face convulsed. She concentrated as hard as she could on Stella's fear. And then, finally, Stella let go. Her face was pale.

For a second, she even lowered her gun, and Laura could have made a move had she not slumped on the floor with exhaustion. But Stella had once more grabbed her and heaved her up by the time she returned to her senses.

"You fucking brat," Stella whispered with spitting venom. "Where did you...no, I don't care. I have more than enough minds at my disposal to make sure you don't cause me any trouble. I know just the place to put you."

Stella pulled Laura by the arm as they exited the ship and traversed the spaceport toward the nearest elevator. (Iguazu, meanwhile, under Edie's direction, flew off and joined Nemos, Gunny, and Soda.)

"Where are we going?" Laura asked.

She wanted to try to run, but they were surrounded by both zombified Citizens and animals who could attack her if she tried. As soon as the ship had opened Stella's chamber, she had pinged Zelda to alert her of her imminent arrival and ask her to switch over the nodes of all networked Citizens and animals to Stella's sphere of influence. This meant that all the rodents and reptiles scurrying around, as well as yes, larger animals like Nemos, who lumbered around the ground floor making sure all the Dumplings stayed in their homes and awaited Martian troops, were now under Stella's control.

"Shut up," said Stella. "You've gotten enough answers for today." They boarded the first of the two elevators they would need to take to reach Stella's intended destination: the Mayor's Quarters. Inside the Mayor's Quarters, Stella knew, was a bioscan-operated vault that the Mayor could use to store valuables and private documents that belonged to himself and other top Terrarchist officials. She planned to throw Laura into this vault and lock her inside until she figured out what to do with her next.

Unknown to Stella, however, I was standing outside that vault, the entrance to which was inside Wilcox's study, at that exact moment. I did not know for sure what was inside, but it seemed as good a place as any to store information regarding a black hole that would destroy all human and animal life. Making sure each of my three soldiers kept their guard up at either the main entrance, the tram station entrance, and the patio entrance, I went on a search for Wilcox. He was the only one who could let me into the vault.

Keeping my two guns raised and checking behind every corner before walking into a new room, I skulked out of the study through the dining room, kitchen, and living room before reaching the door of the master bedroom. I peeked inside, and there he was, sleeping, which Stella, before her ship had departed from Mars, had influenced him to do until her arrival. I went to the bed and heaved his sleeping body up into my claws.

Stella and Laura were now on the second elevator to the top floor. And unfortunately for me, Stella needed Teddy to let them into his penthouse, which meant that it was time for him to wake up. I nearly dropped him when his eyes opened to face mine. He did not fight. He simply looked at me and smiled.

Stella, remotely accessing Teddy's point-of-view from the elevator, erupted in manic laughter. Laura, meanwhile, had been attempting to contact Michelle, but Michelle wouldn't answer. She then turned to me.

Prince, where are you? I showed her my present situation. Laura gasped. *I think we're headed right toward you! And Prince, look how she's laughing. I think she knows you're there.*

I froze. Neither Peter nor our two newest friends had Specters, so I would need to yell out loud to warn them. If I did that, however, Stella-as-Teddy would hear me and know of their presence. I stuck to my original plan and continued carrying Teddy to the study, albeit with a bit more speed.

Stella, seeing that she was about to have a confrontation with me, redirected her mind to recruit reinforcements. She focused her attention on Monty, a mandrill monkey who was currently patrolling the top floor, making sure all the Terrarchists were locked inside their homes and ready for capture. Stella, too, knew about the private tram station, and she could see that this would be the only means of access into the penthouse so long as I had Teddy in my claws. So, as she and Laura exited the elevator, she commanded Monty to enter the nearest tramline and zip at high speed toward the Mayor's private station.

"We're not going inside just yet," Stella said with a sly smile to Laura. They stood in the top floor's outer gallery, facing the desert Biome, about a hundred feet from the penthouse's main entrance.

I, meanwhile, had reached the study and placed the mayor's hand on the bioscanner next to the vault door. Peter stood by the door to the tram station and watched with me as the bolts on the door slid back and unlocked. "Peter, hold Wilcox for me while I go inside," I said. I handed Wilcox over to Peter, who put his arm around Wilcox's neck and a gun to his head. Wilcox's body did not resist.

We held our breath in anticipation as I pulled the door open to reveal...

Nothing.

Well, not nothing. There was, I could see, a single sheet of paper lying face down at the very back of the vault. I had expected piles of money and jewels, along with shelves of file cabinets, but there was just one sheet of paper.

Stella continued to laugh. Laura showed me their position. *Prince, listen,* she said. *I don't know what Stella's planning, but if she ever tries to control your mind, there's a way to stop her. You can stop an influencer from controlling your mind if, in that moment that your worst fears are coming up, you throw their own worst fears right back at them. I tried it myself.* She shared with me some of the images that had saved her mind from Stella.

Thank you, Laura. But I may not need it. Then, with a little hubris, I said, loud enough for Stella-as-Wilcox to hear, "I wouldn't be laughing so much, Stella. I can see where you are" (this prompted Stella to glance with a smirk at Laura) "and we can shoot Teddy, and make sure nobody can ever get into the servers again."

Stella's eyes squinted for an instant—enough for me to see that this concerned her just slightly—then relaxed. She smiled larger than I had ever seen her smile.

I made my way into the vault. I picked up the piece of paper and showed it to Peter for him to read to me. I could at least recognize signatures that belonged to Teddy Wilcox, Stella Melampus, and several top Terrarchist officials.

"Plan of Succession Approval," he read the title. "I, Teddy Wilcox, declare that I have programmed the AI, in the event of my death, to hand over the title of Mayor, along with all associated bioscan access permissions, to Stella Melampus." He looked up at me.

"Shit," I muttered. Then, a second later...

Stella-as-Monty the mandrill opened the door to the study and fired one, two bullets from the gun on his arm: Peter Delacroix and Teddy Wilcox, the latter still in the former's arm, dropped dead to the floor.

I raised my paw and fired a shot, but Monty dodged. Then, from a few rooms over: "What was that?" Footsteps ran toward us. Our two friends were coming to the study. Monty's head perked up; he ran out of the study toward the approaching Citizens.

"Stay where you are!" I screamed. But it was too late. Out in the kitchen, I could hear, Monty had fired one, two more bullets into my other allies.

I watched as Stella, now Mayor, took Laura to the penthouse's front door and used her new bioscan access to enter. "I don't know what you thought you would find in there," she said so that I could hear her over Laura's feed, "but surely you didn't underestimate my intelligence so much as to think I would leave anything truly damning."

Panicked, I went into the dining room, gun raised. Monty stood there, his own weapon raised to match mine. I froze.

"Relax," Stella said, walking with Laura through the living room and kitchen, now close enough for me to hear her voice directly. "I'm not going to kill you or her, Prince."

She and Laura at last walked into the dining room. "The two of you mean too much to Dante for me to do that," Stella said. "Imagine how he would feel about me if I killed you. That would be a problem if his mind became untethered for any reason. No, all I need is for you to get into the vault."

"What?" I blinked.

"Get. Into. The. Vault." She and Monty approached me in tandem. I backed away, back into the study. Laura screamed at the sight of her father's body. She wrestled to get out of Stella's headlock. Stella fired a warning shot.

I slowed my retreat as we neared the open vault, looking for something, anything I could do, but Monty marched right up to me and poked me with his gun.

I crossed the threshold into the vault. Stella threw Laura in next to me. Monty pushed the door shut. Stella's shrieking laughter rang through the vault's metal walls. We were in pitch darkness.

"It's good to see you," Laura said, too shell-shocked to cry.

49

Having locked both Laura and me in the vault, and high on the drama of Martian ships releasing continuous sonic booms as they broke through the atmosphere and latched onto the space elevator, Stella decided the time for an impassioned speech was long overdue. Her muffled voice echoed around the vault's metal walls.

"I know you think I'm the villain here, and that I'm working for Mars, but it's not completely true. I do wonder if there's any way we could come to an arrangement so you all could stop getting in my way. It does look bad for you at the moment, but I know by now not to doubt that you may have other tricks up your sleeve."

"Work with you? That's gonna be a no for me," Laura said. "Unless you somehow *aren't* planning to destroy the entire solar system in a black hole."

Stella laughed. "A black hole? God, no. Not all disruptions of spacetime are the same, dear. No. First of all, the hivemind and the machine were all Mars's plan. Dominic and I participated by providing them with the data they needed to prove their plan would work, but the plan to create a wormhole that would allow the Cognoscenti to travel back in time to the moment when Olaf Melampus first conceived the Arkology, years before the Pathogen emerged, was all theirs."

Laura and I focused our shocked reactions on two different points. Whereas the notion that Dominic was complicit in what was unfolding stunned me most, Laura's mind went back to the words in Olaf's journal: "A white hole in the sky, which sent all around it undulating, filled me with divine and transcendent knowledge of all I needed to do in my life." *They think it was a portal,* she thought to me, though I didn't understand.

Stella continued. "Second of all, I am not going with them. No, I'm staying here on Earth. Do you know how nice it will be here once all the humans are gone? Sure, that wormhole might shake things up a little, but it's not going to destroy the whole solar system. Don't be so dramatic. No, here's what will happen. You, Laura, and all the other zombified humans will board ships to Mars, go into the tunnels, fire up the wormhole generator, and the Cognoscenti and Edie will all either get to go back a thousand years in a parallel universe or get vaporized in a singularity. I don't think anyone knows for certain which will happen, but I don't care, and they don't either. They are so addicted to control and power that they would rather plunge into the void and destroy all they have built than work to create a world where things worked differently. I, however, am giving this world over to those who had no role in fucking things up the way we all have: The animals. As I speak, the Arklings are making the finishing touches on the Specter to influence all Specters: the Ur-Specter, I like to call it."

Laura rolled her eyes. I, however, couldn't stop shaking in fear. Stella suddenly sounded a lot like Varuna.

"Once the Cognoscenti leave on their little trip, I'll sync all the animals to my Specter and send them off in ships around the globe to tend to all the mines that the Martians have stolen from us. They'll be immune to the Pathogen, and they'll be able to finish all the geoengineering projects we started and failed at. I'll keep turning them all into cyborgs, and they'll have the talents of their native species together with a technical intelligence that surpasses humanity's. And because they have all been here to see what we did to them, and because they can see so much more of what life offers than we can, they will build a new world that will live forever."

"What makes you think the animals will be happy this way?" I asked. "What gives you the right to control us and tell us what's good for us?"

"Oh, Prince. You're such a sad case. Neither human nor fully animal. Can't you see this is the only way out for Earth? Don't be like the Martians and long for the past. It isn't coming back. I'm here to take you all to the future. You remind me of Dominic, you know. He took one look at how scared you were after your first mirror test and tried to back out of our deal with Mars. Told me we were doing something wrong, that giving you human intelligence would get you to hate us. But let the animals hate us, I said. They'll thank us later. It was *his* deal he made with the Terrarchists, you know. First thing he did when he took over from his father. He hated humanity as much as I did. He hated the world and the family he was thrown into, just as I hated mine. He was..."

Stella paused. She exhaled, with sudden anguish.

"He was gay! And so am I! It was what drew us together. We pretended to be in love, but really we were two lonely people in desperate need of friends. I admit it, I didn't want a child. But he needed an heir. And I love Dante. I do. Everything I have done has been to protect him. I know he thinks I killed his father. But I didn't. He killed himself. He wanted to back out of the deal, and I wouldn't let him. There was no turning back. We had sold our souls to the Terrarchists who hated us for the purposes of destroying them, and if we turned back, they would win. So he killed himself. Really, he had Stewart kill him. An assisted suicide. God, he should have never hired that prick. Yes, his research into trauma across species was what yielded the IUL—the Images of Universal Loss, which you might know as the "aliens"—but he felt so bad for the animal subjects, and when he learned what he was doing it all for—that he wasn't, in fact, helping us design a technology that would resolve trauma, and that Mars was replicating his experiments on humans—he got so mad. And Dominic, who had of course fallen in love with the only other gay man he had gotten the chance to know in his entire life, began to listen. When it was clear he and Stewart had no way out, they made a pact. Stewart would hack a poachbot that would kill Dominic in a horrible "accident," and Stewart would kill himself shortly after. Nobody on the Ark knew what happened to Stewart—he told everyone he'd quit to go work on Mars, but Dominic's suicide note told me everything. Stewart's body is at the bottom of the sea somewhere. It makes me extremely sad. But they betrayed me, and they betrayed themselves, and life must go on."

I shook so hard that I had to hang my tongue out and pant. My and my master's entire lives felt like they were based on lies.

Laura, however, had kept her mental wheels spinning, and a specific channel to Mars open. "What about the other octopuses?" She asked. "Are they going back in time, too?"

"Of course not," Stella said. "They're a nuisance. Mars is going to load them all onto one ship and blow them up."

Tens of millions of miles away—about three light-minutes—Edie listened into everything through the arm she had lent Laura. The realization that both Dante and Laura had told her the truth all along turned her mantle blue. But she did not sulk for long. She had to act fast. She relinquished control of the arms she had linked to Nemos, Gunny, Iguazu, Soda, and Dante.

And three minutes later, the four animals found themselves confused and terrified and suddenly self-aware once more in the chaos of the spaceport. Seconds earlier, they were firing their guns and roaring and trumpeting and leaping on people and forcing them to board the Martian ships. At that moment, Stella was on her way outside of her penthouse and calling a taxi craft to the Ark, where she planned to seize the Ur-Specter and assert ultimate control.

It's done, Edie said to Laura as soon as she let control of the animals go.

By then, it was too late to stop what was underway. People with hats kept capturing people without hats and adding them to the network. Certain groups were already flying off on ships to Mars. The only solution was to disrupt the network entirely, and for that, we would need Stella's assistance in accessing the AI.

Laura explained the situation to Nemos, Gunny, Iguazu, and Soda as quickly as she could. *Stella's about to escape to the Ark and we need someone to stop her, now!*

Once he had come to his senses, Iguazu squawked to draw the others' attention to the craft Stella had called, which was leaving its hangar to fly out through the tunnel to the desert and ascend to the top floor. Nemos and Soda agreed to stay behind and act as though they were still under Edie's influence (though they would make a point of being less violent to any humans still trying to resist). Gunny and Iguazu, meanwhile, called a craft of their own to fly up to the penthouse and meet Stella.

Stella, walking down the patio, froze when she saw not one craft waiting for her, but two.

Gunny emerged from the sunroof of the one on the left. She raised her tiny arm and pointed it at Stella. *If you try to board that craft, you die.*

Stella raised her hands. Gunny had her target-locked. There was no way to escape.

What do you want?

I don't know, Gunny said with a cheeky chattering of her teeth. *I just showed up. Ask Laura.*

Stella repeated her question to Laura.

We want you to free Prince and me, said Laura, *then take us into the servers. You're going to deprogram the network.*

The patio door sliding open behind Stella was warning enough for Iguazu, keeping watch behind Gunny, to see Monty attempt to take Gunny down on Stella's command. Iguazu flew up in the air and shot Monty in the arm—enough to stun him.

"OK! Don't kill the monkey!" Stella yelled. "He has nothing to do with this. I'll get him out of here. I'm influencing him back down to the ninth floor."

Stella had Monty reenter the penthouse and go into Teddy's bathroom, where he could open the medicine cabinet and bandage his arm before continuing back to the tram station exit and resuming his terrorizing of Citizens on the lower floors.

I can't deprogram the network, Stella said, resuming her conversation with Laura. *Zelda has equal access to the Source. She will lock it down if she sees I'm messing with it. The only way I can stop her is with the Ur-Specter.*

While Laura suspected that this was true about Zelda, she had no desire to give Stella what she wanted.

Bullshit. One thing you can definitely do is to reactivate the AI's defenses. Just get it to recognize the Martian ships as a threat and take them down.

Fine, Stella said. With Iguazu flying behind her, laser-shooting talons at the ready if she made any funny moves, Stella reentered the penthouse to liberate Laura and me from our prisons. We made our way through the living room—Prince and I in back, Stella with Iguazu and Gunny's weapons pointed at her in front—where a door in the wall programmed to respond only to the Mayor's bioscan granted us access to a horizontal elevator that offered a shortcut to the inner Servers.

Stella had not just given up, of course. Inside that elevator, she brainstormed ways she could escape. Perhaps she could get the AI to recognize us as a threat as well. And we, too, kept our guard up with her.

But it didn't matter, as we soon learned. What greeted us when Stella opened the door to the innermost cell was nothing short of complete ruin: Screens shattered, towers ripped off the floor, motherboards smashed all over the ground. Every single console was rendered useless, but one in particular had drawn the most rage from those who had done this: The spot that was formerly occupied by the console linked to the Source, now a literal smoldering crater in the darkness. Loose sparks still fired from torn wires, and smoke still filled the room. This had all gone down very recently.

Not saying a word, we went through the door into the next outermost cell, and then the next. In every cell, complete cybernetic destruction. And in each of the walls between the cells, a giant, cleanly carved hole. The AI was no longer accessible from the top floor. Only one animal, I knew, had both the interest in doing this and the potential ability to accomplish it. As Laura and Stella traded dumbfounded looks of total shock amid the debris, words that I had been unsure I would ever hear again entered my mind.

For the love of the cosmos, help us.

I answered the call, and I granted full access to what I was seeing through my eyes at that time.

Varuna, however, chose only to transmit his words.

Well, look where you are! I imagine you'll want to know how that happened.

PART FIVE:

HOW THAT HAPPENED

50

I suppose this is the part of the book where you'll want to hear how I, Prince, the good dog, defeated Varuna, the big bad dolphin who yet again must have deceived me for me to continue talking to him. And I suppose that is the story I was planning to tell at this part of the book when I started writing it. It is, after all, an easier story, one that I know will make more sense to more people, but there is so much about this story, I can see now, that already makes so little sense if you weren't there, at that time, in our bodies, and love makes so little sense to begin with. On hearing his voice, my heart had no space to be angry at him for what he'd clearly done. The possibility of our reunion filled my heart completely, and the weight of that fullness sank me down into every word he thought to me. And you know what? I don't think he was trying to deceive me. Not right then. Not at that moment.

On seeing the defense drones around the top floor deactivate and fall to the Earth, Varuna explained, he had known there was nothing to stop him from calling a craft and ascending. He used his gun to smash the windows outside the main entry point to the Servers, then, once inside, used his laser to carve a hole into the wall of the outermost cell. In every cell, he pointed his beam and his gun at every tower and every screen and incinerated every part of the system that he could, then blasted his way into the next cell and repeated the process. He focused a particularly angry laser on the Source,

341

then left.

Why did you do it? I asked. *Why destroy it completely?*

There is no other way to stop this, he said. *The network Mars and Stella have built has too many nodes and too many points of control. As soon as we try to reprogram it, someone will see and shut it down. No, the only way to stop this is to shut the AI off completely.*

You just want all the humans to get exposed to the Pathogen and die, I said.

No, Prince. Believe it or not, I don't want that. Yes, there is a vengeful part of me that does, but...losing you opened my mind. I thought you would chase after me, get me to come back. But you didn't. And I know I have to change. I believe that humans can change, that the world can change, that I can change. Or, if I don't believe it, I at least want to believe it, very, very much, and you're the only being who has ever gotten me to believe it for half a second.

He sobbed. I believed him. And you know what? I still believe him. He could not have lied when he felt such anguish and such longing to win me back in that moment. He spoke with no second voice. And I know he could not have lied because he let me feel it, too, and it felt real. It was real.

I want to free Dante, he said. *He is good. I want to save all the good people. I don't know if we can, though. It's either let the Pathogen in, or let the wormhole destroy us all.*

It was at this point that I, Prince, the supposedly noble and virtuous, declined to be forthright with Varuna. I declined to tell him what Stella had just revealed to us about the wormhole and about her plan to hand the world to the animals. I told him we had captured her and were trying to get her to reactivate the defenses, but no more. And can you blame me? I was afraid to say anything that might get Varuna to reconsider his change of heart. More selfishly, perhaps, I was afraid to say anything that would threaten to put distance between us once more.

He heaved a deep breath through his back and regained composure. *We need to destroy the underwater Servers,* he said. *And for that, we need control of the Ark. And I can't do it alone. The entire Ark is under hivemind control now, and my army will be no match for the Martian fleet once they see our attack. I need help. I don't know where to get it from, but I needed to ask you. And more importantly, I needed you. Even if we fail, and we all sink into the void, I need to sink with you by my side.*

With that thought, he won my undying loyalty. Or at least it felt that way. *I will see what can be done.*

I interrupted Laura and Stella's arguing ("It's all your fault!" "My fault? It's your fault for working with that dolphin") to inform them that Varuna had spoken with me. They listened with fascination as I relayed the conversation.

"He's right," Stella was quick to say. "Turning off the AI is the only option left. By the time we get to the backup server, everyone will either be on Mars or on their way there, so there won't be any point in altering the defense systems."

Laura snapped at her. "You and I and everyone else will die from the Pathogen within minutes of shutting it down."

"Those exposed to it will," Stella said. "But anyone inside the Ark or on Mars will survive. If the people on Mars fight back once they regain their minds, they can defeat the Cognoscenti, and they will be safe on Mars while those of us on the Ark find the time to reprogram the AI."

Laura and I were not so dumb as to think Stella had miraculously forgotten about the Ur-Specter, and she was not so dumb as to think that we suddenly trusted her, but the plan she had just outlined really was our only hope.

"How do we get onto the Ark?" I asked.

"I don't know," Stella admitted. "I have control of the Arklings, but Zelda can take it from me if she senses anything is off, which she definitely will if I just have the crew fly the Ark up to the City. We would need to go there ourselves and blend in as Martians. Disguised in their uniforms, maybe, and arriving in a Martian ship. Once on board, you and the other cyborg animals can use your weapons to kill anyone who tries to stop us."

It didn't sound like the safest plan, but it was all we had. I alerted Varuna of the plan while Laura alerted Gunny and Iguazu, who agreed to work with Nemos and Soda to take down some Martian soldiers once we got to the spaceport and needed to steal some uniforms and a ship.

Meanwhile, as Nemos and Soda fed us information about what they saw on the ground, and as our group developed a plan of attack, Wanda had just found her younger daughter in the chaparral.

—

Wanda had needed to fight her fears as she followed Michelle past the City perimeter. She half-expected a fictional species of giant bird to swoop down and grab her as soon as she passed the gateway and ventured out into the open (or at least more open) air. But she didn't have time to look up; she was tracking several pairs of shoeprints in the dirt. Fortunately, the chaparral was in the winter phase of its seasonal cycle, which meant that climate control bots sprayed a cool rain that left the normally dry and cracked earth moist and impressionable.

She jogged for several minutes through the low scrub of yucca and mesquite, but when the vegetation became a little thicker and gave way to a copse of eucalyptus trees and date palms, the tracks went off into the grass, and she lost her daughter's trail. She was on the verge of tears when two voices rose loud enough to be heard inside a tall patch of senna bushes.

"No, you're not grinding it enough."

"I can't grind it anymore!"

The second voice, sharp and irritated, was unmistakably her daughter's.

"Michelle?" Wanda choked with emotion.

"Shit," she heard her daughter whisper. She pulled aside some senna branches to find Michelle and Sammy sitting together on a patch of grass.

"Oh, God, Michelle. Peter and I were so scared."

Wanda's eyes darted to the several materials that Michelle and Sammy had beside them: a few sacks that contained bunches of white flowers unlike any Wanda had seen on the Agrippa farms; a mortar and pestle that Wanda recognized as stolen from her kitchen cabinet; and most strikingly, a drone that had been disassembled with its cartridge removed. In Sammy's hand was a remote control.

"What are you doing here?" Wanda asked.

"We're trying to protect ourselves. Because the adults clearly aren't up to the job."

Wanda's shoulders slumped. Her daughter's disappointment in her stung. "What's in the bowl?" She pointed at the mortar, which held a white paste identical in color to the flowers.

"Wouldn't *you* like to know?" Michelle sneered.

Wanda sighed and got on her knees in the dirt. "Michelle, please. I'm on your side. What is it?"

Michelle looked down with some slight guilt, then looked at Sammy, who gave Michelle permission to answer with a nod. "Poison hemlock. We've been using your Agrippa manuals to build remote-controlled climate drones. We're trying to load the hemlock into the drone and get it to spray out like a mist. But I don't think it's going to work. This is the fourth time we've tried, and the paste keeps jamming inside the barrel."

Wanda picked up the mortar and studied the contents. "Sammy's right. You can grind this a lot more. Here." She grabbed the pestle, added some water, and dug her elbow deep into the work of grinding the paste as finely as possible. "Are you two alone?" She asked as the two girls exchanged surprised looks.

"Yes," they both said.

A shout from another young voice nearby alerted Wanda to their lie. "It's not working, Michelle!"

Wanda raised her eyebrows. Michelle groaned. "Okay, so we brought a few friends. And they have their own drones. They're trying this with nightshade and sumac."

"Just how many drones did you all get?" Wanda asked.

Michelle tugged at her hair. "Ten, maybe?"

Instead of shouting, Wanda surprised Michelle by grabbing her hand and smiling.

"Let me help you all," she said. "I can prove that your mother's useful for something."

It wasn't clear at all how ten mist-spraying drones could

stand up to the Martian army when the time came. But ten drones, they all figured, were better than none.

—

Over on Mars, Zelda and her Cognoscenti colleagues noted that Stella was no longer feeding them visual information. *All is well*, was the only thought they could prompt from her. *Just packing a few things before leaving for Mars.*

Ambassador Johnson had also pointed Zelda to some footage he had just received from the City News, which showed Gunny and Iguazu, whom they believed to still be under Edie's control, making their way into the craft they would use to meet Stella.

"Very strange," Zelda said. She pinged Edie, who at that moment was admitting her mistakes to Dante.

Let me make it up to you, Edie said to him before answering the call. *But first, get back in bed. Zelda's calling!*

Zelda transmitted the footage she was watching and communicated her thoughts with an exaggerated false warmth. *Edie, can you tell me why Gunny and Iguazu just boarded a taxi? I thought we had agreed to keep your subjects on the ground floor.*

Edie curled her tentacles nervously. *Oh, no need to worry there,* she answered with feigned confidence. She turned herself a bright, friendly pink. *I sent Gunny and Iguazu up a few floors to scare some of the last holdouts.*

Edie's lie did not convince Zelda. There were no sightings of Gunny and Iguazu anywhere inside the residential sector.

Any chance you know what Stella is up to right now? Zelda asked next.

No idea!

All right. Thank you, dear. Carry on. As soon as she disconnected, Zelda turned to two of her colleagues. *Something isn't right. Grab that octopus and take her to the interrogation room. Now.*

The two Cognoscenti goons ran down the hall and took the stairs to Dante's room. When they got there, however, they found an empty tank.

Edie was already snaking her way through the vents that would lead underground, where she planned to access the control room and give Dante as much information about the network as she could. She remembered to transmit the map of the Intelligence and Security Operations Center that Laura had shown her. *In case you make a run for the spaceport,* she said to Dante.

Dante rushed to pack a bag, but he wasn't fast enough. The Cognoscenti officers took one look at his pale face before yanking his arms behind his back and dragging him into the halls.

51

Nemos and Soda reported to Gunny and Iguazu that Martian soldiers were accessing the residential sector on foot. Once each ship descended the space elevator and arrived inside the spaceport, it would detach and fly to a free hangar; the soldiers would then disembark, enter the insulated tunnels that ran through the energy ring, and board the elevators that would take them to various floors—first ascending, then horizontally traversing the energy and agricultural sectors. Moreover, each group of soldiers seemed to be going to the floor above the one the previous group had visited, as Soda had ascertained through some sneaky surveillance on the perimeter of the energy ring, where she watched soldiers board and leave the elevators.

This meant that Gunny, Iguazu, and myself could potentially intercept a group of soldiers as it entered a residential ring. We used the Mayor's secret elevator to descend to the seventh floor, where a group of Martians was about to arrive. Stuck in an automated loop of the hivemind's script (and, fortunately, not currently being monitored by Zelda), they were not quick enough to respond as we raised our arms and fired. We then invited Laura and Stella to descend and meet us. They undressed themselves and two of the Martians and swapped clothes. We prevented Stella from taking any of the soldier's weapons. Laura needed to have full control over her.

Next, hoping their Martian uniforms could blend in and evade the eyes of any Cognoscenti watching the spaceport's cameras, Laura and Stella descended to the spaceport and, with the help of some subtle gestures from Soda, ran as fast as they could to the ship that the killed Martian soldiers had just vacated. In the meantime, Gunny, Iguazu, and I returned to the top floor, where we would exit onto the mayoral patio and meet the ship.

Laura took one look at the ship's controls and moaned with frustration: she had no idea how to operate it. Stella, however, had been in the cockpit of various Martian ships (making out with Zelda) long enough to have an idea.

"Let me do it," she said.

"Fine. But one funny move and I shoot."

This was a bluff of course, but Laura did not have to worry about acting on it. Stella wanted to get to the Ark as badly as we all did. With Laura's gun pointed at her, Stella raised the ship above ground and tilted it 90 degrees to a completely vertical angle; the two women's stomachs lurched and their calves shook a little as the ship's gravity mechanisms locked them into place.

"Hang onto something," Stella warned Laura. She guided the ship toward the space elevator, their only means of exiting the spaceport and flying freely around the Arkology.

"Commencing acceleration," the ship's computer announced. An audible click signaled the ship's attachment to the elevator. Within seconds, they blasted into the sky. Laura dug her nails into the back of Stella's pilot's chair. She felt herself thrown back.

They passed through the hatch on the roof of the City. Then, just an instant before they would have passed through the gate that led into the filtration chamber at the top of the bubble, Stella detached the ship and glided away from the elevator. She returned to a horizontal level and guided the ship to the patio outside the Mayor's quarters. Gunny, Iguazu, and I all boarded.

"Are we going to get a fight from the Arklings?" I asked Stella.

"No," she said. "They're all under my control."

"How do we know you're not commanding them all to kill us as soon as we get there so you can get the Ur-Specter?"

Stella rolled her eyes. "You'll have to trust me, I guess."

Laura and I exchanged looks. We didn't, of course.

I had an idea. "Varuna can help," I said.

For the love of the cosmos, help us. I connected with him. *Varuna, where are you currently?*

I took my craft back to shore. I'm on the temperate forest beach, about a mile from the Ark.

Can you use your sonar to get a bead on where all the Arklings are located? We're going to land on deck and take the wheelhouse, and we want to make sure Stella isn't leading us to an ambush.

You got it, he said. He whistled into the distance and mapped out the Ark's interior as best he could.

As Stella flew us over the forest toward the Ark, I looked through the ship's side windows and caught a glance of the space elevator rising from the City: ships full of captive Citizens were now leaving for Mars.

We would not get a chance to test our initial plan. In the time it took for us to take the ship and leave the City, Ambassador Johnson had noticed the disappearance of the soldiers we had killed from the network.

"Units from ship #84 offline," he told Zelda. "Ship itself won't respond to radio contact. Radar detects it has entered the Biomes and is on a trajectory toward the Ark."

Zelda considered her options. A ship would ultimately need to head to the Ark to fetch the Arklings, but there was no reason for contact to be lost with its pilots. And still, no word from Stella.

"Scroll through video of the ship's location in the spaceport in the minutes before its departure," she instructed Johnson.

She had no time to acknowledge her feelings of betrayal when he sent back the video of (as she could see upon squinting) Laura and Stella boarding the ship. Stella had gone rogue.

She then opened her console and put the network up on her display. She selected Stella's nodes and dragged them all under her own. She now had full influence over the Arklings.

Shoot that ship down, she commanded Naismith's body, which stood over the Ark's radar screen in the wheelhouse.

A stealth rocket, invisible to our ship's radar, whizzed out of the Ark's hull and raced toward us. Had Varuna not been playing recon, it would have killed us all instantly.

Rocket heading toward you! He screamed in my brain. *Dodge, NOW!*

"Rocket inbound!" I shouted. I rose on my hind legs and pushed the steering controls out of Stella's hands. Everyone tipped sideways as the ship lurched to the right. We avoided a direct hit, but the rocket still managed to graze our wing.

The ship jolted. We dove toward the beach in a tailspin.

"Brace for crash landing!" Stella yelled.

We all covered our heads. She fought to steady the ship before impact.

52

Once Edie got into the control room and logged in using the information Dante had received from Laura and transmitted to her, she could see the changes Zelda was making to the network. Not only had Zelda moved the Arklings from Stella's nodes to her own; she also moved Dante's, a change that Edie saw happen on screen before her eyes. Fortunately, Edie managed to switch him back from Zelda to herself with a quick swipe of her tentacle.

Dante, are you there? She asked him, unaware of his capture until he replied with a view of his surroundings. The two Cognoscenti marched him toward the interrogation room.

I blanked out for a few seconds. What's going—

She lost him. She looked back on screen to see his node was back under Zelda's. Edie quivered with fear. Zelda had seen the switch and responded, which meant that she was probably on to Edie and sending someone to catch her.

Edie switched Dante's node back to herself just long enough to convey her question. *Dante, Zelda won't let me maintain influence over you. Do you think there's a way to erase you from the network completely? It's drastic, but at least you'll keep your free will.*

Edie watched his node: Back to Zelda. Back to Edie.

You'll have to open the terminal and run a query on my name, he said. *Then delete the file.*

Edie followed Dante's instructions with frequent interruptions as she and Zelda continued to fight for control. Meanwhile, the two officers led Dante into a windowless room and restrained him in a chair with straps on its arms. Sweat pooled on his face. What would happen once he and Edie lost contact? She might be able to delete a few more nodes, but Zelda had surely sent someone to the control room to see what was going on by now. Edie wouldn't have time to make a significant dent in the hivemind. And any hopes of hacking into the servers looked foolish now.

Then, he remembered the map of the Intelligence and Security Operations Center that Laura had shown him through Edie: the control room had been on the floor below the spaceport. And one floor below that...

Edie, wait, before you delete me, I have a plan. Once you delete me, I need you to find Officers Hewett and Lopez. Move their nodes under yours, then get them to move as far away from the spaceport as you can. If Zelda fights you for them, just delete them, too. I'm going to try to steal a shuttle. Meet me at the spaceport in ten minutes. I hope we make it.

Good luck, Edie said. She deleted Dante's node, then moved the two spaceport guards'. It took Zelda a minute to realize what had happened with Dante, which in turn distracted her from seeing the switch with Hewett and Lopez. Edie, in fact, went beyond Dante's orders: For Dante to break into the spaceport, it wasn't enough to remove the guards from the network; she needed to remove them completely. She didn't want to cause violence, but there was only one clear solution:

She influenced the two guards to shoot themselves in the head.

A surge of energy rushed through her. How many nodes would she have time to delete? She reopened the terminal and went through the animals she had previously relinquished, making sure that Nemos, Soda, Gunny, and Iguazu would all have free reign over their own minds.

Unfortunately, this was as far as she got before footsteps crescendoed outside the door. She darted away from the computer and slithered back into the vent just in time to avoid Ambassador Johnson's attention.

Back in the interrogation room, the two Cognoscenti whipped Dante with their guns and told him to stay quiet as they communicated with Zelda and Johnson. Finally, they turned back to him with twisted smiles. "You and that octopus sure are clever," one said. The other opened a cupboard and removed an APWD.

"Unfortunately," he said, "we can get you back on the network just as quickly as you took yourself off."

Dante swallowed. What he was about to say would take courage, even if the desperate circumstances made it somewhat easier. "Before you put that hat on me..." He looked directly into the guards' eyes. "I have something I want to confess."

They chuckled. "Oh yeah?" "What's that?"

Dante whispered it first. "I'm trans."

The Cognoscenti blinked. "Excuse me?"

Dante raised his head and screamed into the microphones he knew were in the ceiling. "I'm trans! I was born with two X chromosomes!"

This did it: "GENDER DEVIANT DETECTED!" The shrill AI voice blared throughout the room. "GENDER DEVIANT DETECTED! REPORT TO REPROGRAMMING IMMEDIATELY."

The Cognoscenti froze, checking for instructions from Zelda.

"REPORT TO REPROGRAMMING WITHIN TEN MINUTES OR FACE INSTANT DEATH."

He's losing his mind, Zelda thought to them. *I'm on my way to the control room to link my Specter with the new hat, but I can't get there in time. We need him alive as a bargaining chip for Stella, so just take him to reprogramming, let the AI do its thing, and bring him to me when you're done. It shouldn't take more than a half hour. I have to get my army reorganized on Earth anyway. He's trying to buy time somehow. Just don't let him out of your hands.*

But them letting him out of their hands, for just a split second, was what Dante had counted on. They kept him cuffed on the journey down toward the reprogramming room, but as Dante knew, they would need to free his hands to allow him to interact with the console inside. Dante fixed his attention on the gun that sat in the officers' holsters, and in the split second between the moment the officer on his left undid his cuffs and the moment the officer on his right opened the door to push him inside, he grabbed the former's weapon and darted backward as fast as he could toward the elevator.

The officers chased him down the hall. The one who still had a gun shot for Dante's leg and missed. Dante fired a few bullets aimlessly as he threw himself into the elevator and slammed the button to close the door.

He emerged onto the spaceport and bolted past the two dead guards' bodies toward the nearest ship. He ran up the gangway and found Edie waiting for him by the ship's hatch door. As he wheeled open the hatch, she held up an installation syringe and a private Specter in her hand. She had stolen them from the guards' bags. He didn't have time to put it on yet, but he got the message: He would be able to talk to Laura and me.

"You're incredible, Edie. Hurry, get inside."

They shut the door, locked it, and made sense of the dashboard. The two Cognoscenti had made their way to the spaceport by now, but bullets were useless against the ship's exterior. The Martians could only watch as Dante initiated takeoff. The spaceport's wall slid down. The ship blasted down the runway and shot off into space.

53

Laura and I, unsure we would survive the landing, contacted our closest and most accessible loved ones by Specter in the final seconds before impact: Michelle in her case, Varuna in mine. *If I don't survive this crash,* we both more or less said, *I want you to know I love you.*

But we did survive, albeit with some bruises. The ship careened several hundred feet along the ground through the acacia trees, throwing our bodies against the left side as it sank into its damaged wing.

I'm echolocating you. Varuna said once it was clear we were alive. *I'll bring my craft there and meet you.*

Michelle, however, needed a few more answers. *What the hell were you doing in a stolen Martian ship?*

We were trying to get to the Ark, said Laura. *We need it to shut off the AI's deep sea backup servers.*

Wow! Michelle laughed. *Finally seeing things my way?*

Look, I stand by what I said about the AI's benefits, but it's either that or let Mars and Stella send us all into a literal black hole.

Sounds fascinating, but I have to go. Michelle transmitted her surroundings. Wanda and Sammy stood beside her with remote controls in their hands. Above them flew two drones. The drones flew out a good distance, then, with the push of a button on their operators' controls, spritzed out a visible mist.

"It's working!" Sammy shouted. "You're a genius, Ms. D."

"How exciting," said Wanda. "Let's bring them back in now."

Damn. You actually built them, Laura said.

That's right. Mom thinks we're just using them for self-defense, but little does she know we're going to send them out to the spaceport and poison the Martian pilots.

Michelle, that's a terrible idea. First of all, you can't poison the generals without poisoning the Citizens. Second of all, tha won't stop the hivemind. The program will just find new pilots. Getting everyone to Mars is all it cares about. And what about the ships that already left?

Michelle slumped. *Who are you to judge my plan? You just tried to steal a Martian ship.*

Yeah, and look how it turned out. Laura paused. *But I think I may have a better use for your drones...*

By now, we had exited the ship and taken stock of our situation.

"Shit! Shit!" Stella cursed on discovering she no longer had influence over the Arklings. We didn't have much time to stand around, though.

Second missile, inbound! Varuna shrieked into my brain. Zelda was trying to make sure she had finished the job.

"Everybody, run!" I howled. We all sprinted into the bush beneath the missile's sonic boom, then threw ourselves to the ground and shielded ourselves while the ship blew apart into a thousand pieces.

"There goes any hope of fixing it," Stella sighed.

Moments later, Varuna glided toward us in his craft.

"Looks like we're in a tough spot," he joked out loud. Then, to me privately: *What's the plan? Shall I send my cetacean army out again?*

No, don't, I said. *They can't take another defeat.*

What do we do then? Varuna growled in frustration.

"Hey, everyone!" Laura waved her arms with excitement and saved me from having to think of a response. "I think my sister can help us!"

Getting Michelle to give up her dream of singlehandedly orchestrating the defeat of the Martian army had been a tough sell, but the promise of helping us to enact a complete reset to the AI convinced her.

I'll do it, she agreed, *as long as you take me on the Ark with you once it's done. I want to see what all the fuss is about.*

Of course you're getting on the Ark. Anybody not on the Ark gets exposed to the Pathogen and dies.

Varuna agreed to get into his craft to go pick up Michelle and Wanda. During that time, Laura contacted Edie to make sure she could get the octopuses on the Ark to stay out of their way. Laura gasped when Edie presented her surroundings: Dante was piloting his stolen ship. He waved hello to her.

What the hell happened? Laura asked Edie. *I thought you were going to break into the control room.*

We tried, she said, *but we didn't get very far. We're lucky to be alive.*

What are you going to do now? Laura pinched her brow. *Does he know the plan has changed? If you can't get into the control room, we need to turn off the Martian servers another way.*

Here, he can talk to you himself.

Edie invited Dante onto the channel.

Laura! I can't believe we've survived long enough to think together again.

I missed your mind, Laura said.

I missed yours, too.

Edie conveyed disgust. *Either you two get your own channel, or let's talk business.*

Right, Dante said. *We're just floating in stealth mode for now, and I've got to build Edie a tank so she can survive the trip to Earth. I'm thinking I'll fill up the kitchen sink and add some table salt. What do you think, Edie?*

Works for me, she said.

Once that's done, I'm going to make a pass over the solar farm they built for the servers and see if I can launch a missile into the panels. What are you all up to?

Laura outlined the plan to use the Ark to turn off the Arkology's servers. She made sure that Edie knew to tell her octopus contacts to get all the cephalopods off the ship. *I have no idea what will happen in the end, she said. We can only hope that the number of people on Mars at that point will be able to overpower the Cognoscenti. And that Martian infrastructure is strong enough to house everyone in the time it takes for Varuna and Prince and the others to rebuild the AI.*

I think it is, Dante said. *They survived without an AI for hundreds of years. But damn. So many people are going to die, even in a best case scenario.*

Laura stayed silent for a moment. She sensed the immense grief she was going to feel later—for her father, for the world. *I'm getting my mom and sister to stay on the Ark with us, at least. We'll be safe there for a while.*

Varuna flew back into sight with Michelle and Wanda. They hugged Laura as they disembarked. To our surprise, Sammy and Michelle's other friends followed in separate crafts. They all had drones in their hands.

I've got to go, said Laura to Dante. *I'll let you know how my plan goes.*

Likewise, said Dante.

The two lovers disconnected to go on their separate missions.

I confess that, although I still found killing distasteful, I had come to believe in its necessity at that moment. And although I felt bad that we were killing the Arklings who were not even present in their own bodies at that moment, I remembered all the torture they had inflicted, not only through their experiments on animals but through their political campaigns and donations, and I couldn't help but feel some relief on the part of all the animals and all the queer people and the poor people and all the people who'd done anything at all to resist Terrarchist and technocratic hegemony. And yet, still, I know that killing is wrong. Forgive me, reader, if I still don't know what to do with all these feelings.

Anyway, seizing the Ark with the drones was not as difficult as we had feared. Because Zelda controlled the crew, and because she had never been on the Ark, we had the advantage of knowledge over her. Stella's precise familiarity with every square inch on the Ark was the deciding factor. Michelle and friends sent the drones in through the broken windows of the medical sector, then positioned them over a key access point in the Ark's ventilation system. Oleander, nightshade, and sumac drifted through the vents into the wheelhouse and flooded the room. The entire C-suite hacked and wheezed and choked and fell to the ground before Zelda even checked in to see what was happening. Then, Michelle and friends sent the drones throughout the rest of the ship and eliminated any holdout Arklings.

We waited a bit for the poison to dissipate and stream out of the Ark before boarding our crafts and flying out there. As Laura, Stella, Michelle, Wanda, Sammy, several other young teens, Iguazu, Gunny, Varuna, and I all found our way onto deck and entered the wheelhouse, we felt unstoppable.

—

Dante, however, had met with less success. He passed over the solar farm around the time that we were all streaming into the wheelhouse. He was able to lock a target on the solar farm and launch a missile, but a defense system he hadn't expected launched two countermissiles from the roof of the Dome of the Cognoscenti, intercepting his strike. Moreover, as Dante inferred immediately, anyone looking at radar would have seen the missile and been able to track its trajectory back to the location of Dante's ship.

Shit, he said to Edie. *We have to get out of here.*

He slammed the accelerator and kept going until he was out of Martian orbit and sure that nobody was following him.

I guess we just wait and see what our next option is, he said.

A sense of inevitable doom washed over him and Edie.

It's ok, Edie tried to reassure him. *At some point, all those Cognoscenti will be boarding that ship to go off into the wormhole. They won't be at their stations then, and maybe at that point, we can hit the solar farm.*

I hope you're right. Dante crossed his arms. *All we're going to need is a ton of luck. And perfect timing.*

54

I've almost reached the end of the story. Not the whole story, of course, but my story. The story of the dog and the dolphin. Are inadequate words better than no words at all? You had to be there, humans will often say. But this neglects to mention that even when you are there, the events can still surprise you, and you can see them transpire as though you take no part in them at all, even though they would never have happened without you there.

Everyone's adrenaline transmitters were on full blast in the wheelhouse. The smell of death was just starting to fill the room. I rose on two legs and dodged the bodies of people like Naismith and Rosen and Sherman to make my way to the radar screen. Fortunately for us, the last of Zelda's ships had just left the Arkology's airspace, and she would have to command it to fly back in order to launch a retaliatory missile. But she had no reason not to destroy the Ark, we knew, so we had to act fast and get ourselves underwater.

Laura poked her gun into Stella's back. "Get us into submarine mode."

"I can do that," she said, inputting commands on one of the terminals Sherman had left open, "but it's not enough. Nobody has entered the underwater server in hundreds of years. It's 10,000 feet below sea level. The Ark will implode after about 3,000 feet. To get there, someone needs to go in a separate vessel: the bathyscaphe. It's stored in the hull of the

361

ship. It only has room for two of us, and because it's so valuable, it needs to be released both from inside and from outside the ship. The protocol is for someone to put on scuba gear and swim down there, but we don't have time for that."

"I can do it," said Varuna, catching Stella's implication. "Laura and Prince, you board the craft."

"How can we trust what you're saying is true?" I asked Stella.

"We can check with Dante," Laura said.

"Dante?! I couldn't hold my tail back. You talked with Dante?"

"I did. I'm sure he would love to hear from you."

"Talk with him while you head downstairs," Stella snapped. "Zelda is on to us now for sure. We have no time to spare."

I agreed and sent Dante a message both expressing my excitement that he was safe and asking him to confirm the information Stella was giving us. We left Stella in the wheelhouse with Gunny, Iguazu, Wanda, and the kids while she fed us all instructions to release the bathyscaphe. Varuna dove off the side of the ship and shimmied down toward the hull. Laura and I took the elevator down to the lowest level, the engine room, and made our way through the deafening roar of the machines that had kept the Ark running. At the extreme stern side, we found a hatch in the floor. We opened it and descended into a small submarine that felt like a tin can. Laura and I sat in pilot's and co-pilot's chairs and studied the controls. The "release" button stood out in the dashboard's center.

By now, enough minutes had passed for me to receive Dante's reply. *Prince! It's so wonderful to hear you. Who's a good boy? I don't know if "safe" is quite the word to describe my current situation, but I'm alive and ready to act further when the time comes. You're right to remain suspicious of my mother, but everything she has told you there sounds true. Good luck, and let me know how it goes.*

I spent a few seconds fearing for Dante, but a knock jarred me back to the present moment: Varuna tapped his steel fist on the submarine's exterior.

I'm about to release the tethers. You all ready in there?

I wasn't sure what to answer, but Laura was on top of it. She had located the radar screen that, when fully zoomed out, gave a clear view of our position relative to the Arkology's underside, the mass of underwater earth that we would need to dodge on our way down to the island's nadir.

Ready, she said. The zips of cable unwinding gave her the cue to trigger the bathyscaphe's release.

We sank deeper, deeper, deeper. The vessel picked up speed as it angled downward. I kept an eye on the only porthole while Laura steered us toward the server. Whatever light filtered down to our initial depth disappeared. We dove further and further into total darkness. But I assured myself we were nearing victory. The ships on their way to Mars needed a few more hours before they reached their destination. Once we took care of this, I believed, we could figure something out with Dante to take out the final server on Mars.

10,000 feet under the sea: I couldn't see a thing, but I can only imagine the server as a giant metal vault in the middle of a jagged, slimy, upside-down cliff. A jerk and a clicking sound signaled our arrival: the escape trunk from our vessel had latched onto the server's entrance. We didn't know what we were about to see, so we decided it was safer for one of us to stay inside the bathyscaphe while the other went up and worked to shut things down.

Laura opened a channel with me and immersed me completely in her experience. She climbed the ladder into the escape trunk and ascended toward an extremely wet, algae-covered door. She wiped the muck aside to reveal a button. She pressed it, and the door slid open.

Inside, lit bright by nuclear-fueled generators that had run for hundreds of years, was a room with a single computer. She powered it on.

"WHAT WOULD YOU LIKE TO DO?" The screen asked in green block text on a black background.

Unsure what to type, she entered. "HELP."

A "LIST OF AVAILABLE COMMANDS" scrolled onto the screen. There were three.

DIRECTORY: ACCESS BACKUP COPIES OF ANY AND ALL DAMAGED SERVERS.

GOODNIGHT: SHUT ME DOWN. DO NOT DO EXCEPT IN THE EVENT THAT EARTH HAS BECOME EITHER COMPLETELY INHABITABLE, OR COMPLETELY UNINHABITABLE

RESET: RETURN ME TO INITIAL SETTINGS.

We had not expected a reset option. It seemed miraculous. Could we really keep the AI's filtration systems and main homeostatic functions intact while undoing all the extra nonsense that people had programmed in the last thousand years?

What do you think? Laura asked me.

Reset, I said. *And then we can work on launching an offensive against Mars.*

The solution to all our problems seemed to be at her fingertips. She placed her hands on the keyboard:

R-

E-

S-

E-

Blackout.

Laura? Laura?!

Our connection was gone. Then, a moment later, the images. We were being taken.

I responded immediately with the image of Stella's greatest fear.

But it didn't work. The images kept assaulting me. I was losing my grip. Then, it hit me. Stella wasn't sending these. Someone else was. I took a guess who—the only guess I could have taken, for he was the only other one whose deepest fear I knew. I imagined Varuna, armor and weapons gone, in a tank, being pointed at and laughed at by all the Arklings who had ever tortured him.

The images dissipated. I returned to the present to see Laura back in her pilot's chair. Dead-eyed, she took the controls and steered us away from the server. She was taking us back to the Ark.

"Did you do it?" I asked stupidly.

She shook her head and said nothing. She didn't look at me.

Then, the words.

For the love of the cosmos, help us.

I accepted his call.

You lied to me, he said. *Stella told you what she really wanted, and you hid it from me. You had a chance to prove your faith in me, and you didn't take it. You're just like the rest of them. You'll always be a human pet.*

Varuna was in the central hub of the manufacturing sector. On his face was the Ur-Specter. It was only slightly larger than the other nine-pointed stars, but it reflected all colors, and its points looked fractal somehow, like they each broke off into further, tiny stars.

What did Stella tell you? I asked.

She told me about this neat device, and that she was going to use it to give the world to the animals, but that you and Laura didn't seem to like that idea, and that if she couldn't have the ultimate control herself, then she'd be willing to hand it over to me. She and I have a lot in common, it turns out.

As I learned in my future research, Stella had seen her opportunity to turn Varuna against us and soon as the bathyscaphe departed.

By the way, she had said into his mind while he was still in the water, *my final invention should be just about ready by now.*

Invention? What invention?

Something that I think would be of great interest to you. Before you head up to the wheelhouse, you may want to stop by manufacturing.

As she then explained to him, the final stages of completing the Ur-Specter had been automated, simply a matter of compressing and copying all of the network's data onto a single chip.

Now that I am wearing this, Varuna said to me, *a near-lightspeed wave can radiate from my brain to the brains of everyone on Earth. Any model of Specter at all—APWD, SpecterX, private models, original models, succumbs to this wave's effects. In other words, Iguazu, Gunny, Laura's family, the kids, and then, every single animal in the Arkology—all of them will fall under my influence as soon as I turn my attention to them. Everyone except you, of course. You who know my greatest loss and my greatest fear. I can still love you, you know. I understand why you lied to me. But I pity you. Can't you see the inescapable truth? Can't you see where things are going, regardless of what you try to do?*

Where is that? I whined. Laura continued to pilot the bathyscaphe up toward the Ark. We had a few thousand more feet to go. I reached for the controls to see if I could dissuade her. She snatched my paw and shot daggers at me with her hollow eyes. There was no budging her, unless I wanted to exert violent force, and I cared about her too much to do that.

You know, Varuna said. *We, the animals, are going to conquer the Earth. And the humans are going to disappear. Isn't that right, Stella?* He invited her to join our channel. She was still in the wheelhouse, sitting under the unsuspecting Gunny's gaze. She suppressed a laugh as Wanda and Michelle asked panicked questions.

"Why is the bathyscaphe turning back?" "Why won't she answer us?" "Why won't Varuna answer us?"

That's right, Varuna, Stella said in my brain and his. *And let me just add how helpful Varuna has been. As soon as I looked into Iguazu's memories, and I saw how much he hated humanity, I knew I could keep him as my backup option. What misanthropic dolphin could resist the dream of becoming a cyborg and leading the animal kingdom into space? I look forward to working with him to make that vision a reality.*

Yeah, about that, Stella, Varuna opened his jaw into a little smile. *That's not going to work for me.*

Stella's eyes bulged. "...You promised," she whispered aloud.

Have fun in the wormhole. Varuna directed his attention to the space between her brows and winked. In an instant, she ceased to be a separate mind. She was still there on the channel, but she was flattened out; she offered no resistance, no apparent free will. She was coterminous with Varuna.

You and I can agree she had that one coming, Varuna joked with me.

I growled. *What happened to saying I was right? That humans can be good? That you wanted to save the good ones?*

He shrieked with dolphin laughter. *You really believed that? I just said that to be with you, to make you happy. I would have acted on it, of course, because I believed you were beautiful. I believed you were as loyal as you claimed to be. But you are not. You are a liar, just like those who raised you. I was right. I can trust no one. In the end, I can only trust myself, and my vision. I can't control you; you know too much about me. But I can control everyone else, and then, you'll have no choice but to be loyal to me. You'll be as loyal to me as I need you to be. Actually, wait, no—I can't even trust myself. There is no me, and there is no you. There is only the cosmos and its uncompromising, unforgiving progress toward nothing. I can see now that my only mistake was to distrust technology. The AI can be my friend, I see now. You were right about the humans, insofar as they were all pawns in the great game that is about to end. I am grateful to them for inventing the means of their own destruction.*

Varuna then began to expand the scope of his power. One at a time, he focused on the faces of everyone in the wheelhouse in quick succession. Gunny, Iguazu, Wanda, Michelle, Sammy, the other kids: Wink, wink, wink...all of them lost the light in their eyes and fell under his influence.

Meanwhile, the bathyscaphe neared the Ark. To my surprise, Laura declined to slow down. She zoomed us up past the Ark, toward the surface.

Where are you having her go? I asked Varuna.

You're going up to land. His attention flickered a little farther out, up into the sky, off toward the City, toward the space elevator, where the ship Zelda had ordered to return to take care of the Ark was now unlatching and flying toward the ocean. *I'm going to control the crew on that ship and have them take her away. Her and all the humans here on this Ark. And then that ship will join the others on Mars, and they will all go into their separate timeline or their vaporized nothingness or whatever they want to do. It will be wonderful. Not a single Homo sapiens on the planet.*

I felt powerless. *What if I go with them?* I asked.

This gave him pause, I could tell. He waited for a swell of emotion to wash over him and pass him by. *Fine. See if I care.*

For the love of the cosmos, Varuna.

He relaxed a little, then caught himself and clenched his claws. *What the hell is that supposed to mean?*

I whimpered. *You saw it once, I think. It means that love is worth the fight. You say the cosmos is marching toward nothing. You say there's no me and no you. But even in spite of all that, there's love. Even in your rage and your spite and your vengeance, there's love. The love of a future. Don't exclude me from that future. Don't exclude yourself.*

I can't control you, was all he said. *This is all out of my hands now. You'll either stay or you won't.*

The bathyscaphe, the Ark, and the Martian ship, all of them now vicariously piloted by Varuna, reached the beach of the chaparral at about the same time. I followed Laura out. The zombified crew escorted her onto the ship, then Stella, Michelle, Wanda, and the kids. They left Gunny and Iguazu behind.

Goodbye, Varuna, I said. I stepped onto the ship with the humans.

He screamed. As the shuttle launched and exited the Earth, he exerted the full fury of his expanding omniscience, and I got to see as he compelled the animals of the Arkology to take over the City. One by one, he focused on every animal, winked, and then had them call the AI-powered crafts that would bring them to the places once reserved for humans.

He was all of the animals, mechanized and non-mechanized alike. He was the reindeer and the rams and the ibexes using their antlers and their horns to smash the screens of the televisions in the electronics stores. He was the hawks and the falcons and the woodpeckers and the toucans using their beaks to crack and shatter the lenses of all the surveillance cameras in the walls and ceilings of every room. He was the coyotes and the foxes and the lions and the tigers raiding the meat freezers of all the restaurants on the top floor. He was the elephants and the polar bears and the hippos and the rhinos and the black bears smashing the dams that kept the rivers from flowing into the City. He was the salmon and the piranhas and the catfish and the bullfrogs rushing through the dam and swimming into the sewers and finding their way into the toilets of every home and breaking out into the abandoned bathrooms of every family. He was the hyenas in the bowling alley and the chipmunks on the playgrounds and the kangaroos playing with stethoscopes in the hospital and the horses galloping into the parks, and he was all of them shitting all over the place, shitting and pissing all over the place. He was the crocodiles and the seals going down the slides at the water park and the termites eating all of the papers in the courtroom. He was the penguins in the prisons and the rats in the grocery stores and the monkeys (if the world couldn't have apes then it could at least have monkeys, aye ayes and lemurs and mandrills and baboons) tearing up sheets in empty bedrooms and ripping up piles of money in the banks. He was all of them both mad and sad that they needed to exist in a world so alien to them but elated and ecstatic that at last they knew how to conquer it.

He was all of them, but he was not me.

As I watched the process unfold, an idea came to mind. It took him time to add other minds to his point-of-view. Not much time, but time nonetheless. The time it took to focus and wink. Every time he established influence over someone, as I discovered later, the wave needed not only to travel between his brain and theirs, but from theirs back to his.

I wasted no time and sent the images of Varuna's deepest fear off to Edie and Dante. I prayed that they would receive it in time to prevent him from controlling them. The Martian soldiers put us all to sleep for the journey. Before they came to me, I tried one last time to appeal to Varuna's heart.

I understand how hard it was to go through life after losing someone. But please, feel the truth: Everybody has lost someone. Doesn't that make you want to reach out and help? And to let others help you?

No. They don't know what it's like to be me.

And you don't know what it's like to be me. But I forgive you for not knowing, and for being scared of not knowing.

I haven't simply lost someone, Prince. I have lost many someones. The original dolphins all died before the first clone of my species was born. So I have lost myself. I lost myself before I was born. And so did you, I know, but you're too naive to see. But it doesn't matter now. Justice is coming. Justice is happening.

He, through the soldier that faced me, threw me into the hyperbaric chamber and sedated me. For a few hours, I was asleep on that ship and had no conscious thoughts. I had to wait and see where things stood when I woke up.

Meanwhile, the wave progressed throughout space. Martian captains that had been under Zelda's control fell to Varuna and disappeared from the network. The Cognoscenti all screamed at one another.

"Why is this happening?" Zelda punched the walls. "Which one of you is responsible?"

Varuna kept winking and winking, until finally, his focus got to Mars and found its way into the Cognoscenti's Dome. As all the officers in the room with Zelda lost the light in their eyes, and as, at last, Zelda did as well, their fears at losing control vanished. *It's all okay,* Varuna conveyed to their bodies. *You're going to get what you wanted. Now, let's all head into the tunnels.*

Varuna (his body) stood at the bow of the Ark and tilted his head to the sky to receive as much power from the cosmos as he could. The giant wave of righteous rage that emanated from the tiny device between his eyes circulated tens of millions of miles between two planets. All the animals who rushed into the City and destroyed as much as they could shared a single creature's broken heart with all the humans who filtered through the tunnels deep into the earth of Mars. As the Cognoscenti had planned, the vibrations that traveled back and forth between every individual human that formed a part of this composite amplified further and further the closer they stood in proximity with one another.

I awoke to frantic transmissions from Dante.

How can I help? How can I help? Wake up! Wake up!

A soldier lifted me out of the chamber and stood me next to Laura. I followed her as she followed Stella and her mother and sister and her sister's friends out of the ship and into the spaceport.

I don't know, I told him. *Look where I am. Things are following their course now. We couldn't take out the server on Earth or the one here. It's over.*

Dante wept. The two of us held one another across the distance between his ship's height and the surface of Mars. I felt sucked toward the THING. The charge of a flattened being that once could have been called humanity swept me closer and closer to a void whose existence could be anticipated more and more closely.

A tentacle brought Dante back to the present. *If I may,* Edie said to us both, having left her tank, *can I suggest that we keep fighting until the bitter end? That wormhole's not open until it's open.*

Dante inhaled, then wiped his tears. He looked all over the dashboard. Present moment. Present moment. What is there that remains in the present moment?

Then, he saw it: A panel on the dashboard's corner that read "escape pod." He lifted it and found controls to launch and navigate a capsule that was somewhere on the ship.

He rose. Where was it? Where was it? *Edie, come with me.* He picked the octopus up, plopped her into her tank, took the tank in his arms, then ducked into the hallways of the soldiers' quarters and ran.

My group of humans and I, initially alone because we were the last to arrive on Mars, neared the center, where we met a teeming mass of drooling automated bodies fighting their way through smaller and smaller entrances.

Dante shouted with excitement. There, at the far end of the ship, was the entrance into a vessel that could eject a single passenger.

What are you doing? I asked him. *You're not going to reach Earth in time to do anything. And it's not as though anything can be done.*

I'm not the one who's going, he said. *Edie's going. She's going to go to the bottom of the sea and reset the server there for us.*

If you say so, Edie said. Dante placed her tank in the pod and sealed her inside. He dashed back to the captain's chair and programmed the capsule on a trajectory toward Earth.

Did he see the genius of his plan? The tragic genius?

What are you thinking? I asked.

You will see. Love will win.

He ejected the lonely octopus into the depths of space back toward Earth.

I, meanwhile, found my way into the laboratory. The THING stood before us. Zelda and her Cognoscenti were all inside its bubble. A silent roar churned. The air above the THING undulated. SomeTHING threatened to emerge. Varuna arranged all the residents of that room into closer and closer proximity. Those at the edges needed to get as close to the center and to everyone else's bodies as they could.

Love will win, Dante said to me one more time. He locked the ship's trajectory onto the solar farm beside the server dome. *And Prince: I love you.*

He thrust his full weight into the accelerator and descended toward the surface. He reached terminal velocity. He felt blameless and weightless and faultless. All of his life's circumstances—the family into which he'd been born, the gender he been assigned and the gender that was actually his, the desire for distinction and power and nobility that had led him down this path and the forces that had taken away what he had hoped would lay at the path's end—none of it was his cross to bear, nor anyone else's, for none of us, in the end, is who we think we are, who we say we are, who we want to be. We are all heading toward death, toward whatever lies beyond that portal. In his final seconds, the panels of the solar farm grew larger and larger through the cockpit windshield, and the pixels of our present reality scrambled just slightly as the wormhole, in only its incipient shimmer, its last reversible form, came into being...almost.

I understood what was happening. *Don't do this!*

Dante was silent.

For the love of the cosmos, help us. I invited Varuna onto our channel. I screamed, both with howling and in my mind. *Look what you're doing! Look what you're doing!*

Opposite to that sense of disorder and doom that swirled in the underground tunnels was the blast of light that greeted Dante when the sparks flew up and turned into the fireball that enveloped his ship and his body. In his final instant, he saw what it was all for. He saw how silly it was that he and the rest of us had fallen into such an intricate and calcified story, the story of a man who lived a thousand years ago, a man nobody knew except through words on a page. But he also saw how wonderful it was, how wonderful it was that any one story, at any time, could become the entire world. If one man's story could, then maybe everyone's could, and the world where that could happen, he perceived in his ultimate dissolution, was the world for whose sake he had lived and died.

Varuna, meanwhile, saw me howl and thrash and gnash my teeth. "*You did this!*" I bellowed with both voice and mind. "***You did this!***"

A whistle of horror crescendoed out of the dolphin's throat, taking him by such surprise that he lost track of what he was doing. My grief was the only emotion so intense that it could match the intensity of his own. And when he saw it, he saw what he had denied for so long. He loved me. Not the pawn he had hoped for me to be, but me, Prince, the bereaved and terrified poodle.

And when he saw that he had caused such immense pain to the one creature left in the cosmos that had a claim on whatever love remained in his wretched body, his body turned against itself and all the pain it brought into being.

Varuna, gazing at the sky on the bow of the Ark, raised his right fin, aimed his cannon at the point on his jaw that sat in front of his brain, and made the choice to set us all free.

CODA:

FIVE YEARS LATER

55

The parks on the top floor of the City make for very nice writing locations. They sit in what were once the backyards of properties that belonged to Terrarchist leadership. I write in the one that overlooks the taiga. A cool breeze blows the fur back from my face as I remember once more all that happened here.

I imagine you'll want all the loose ends tied up. You'll want to hear about how, a few moments after Varuna released control, Stella and Zelda saw where they were, glanced with hate into one another's eyes, and, simultaneously, screamed one another's deepest fears for all the crowd to use against them.

"She's afraid to be alone!" Zelda said.

"She's afraid of the future!" Stella said.

You'll want to hear about how the Cognoscenti, seeing that their leader no longer could hold power over them and that the THING had lost its power, took control of their own respective clusters and turned them against one another, hoping to usurp Zelda and become the new Martian leader. You'll want to hear about the bloody battle that ensued as the separately controlled factions of Citizens and Martians took up arms and shot one another or simply engaged in hand-to-hand combat and chased one another throughout the tunnels. But I was not there for it. In the seconds between Varuna's suicide and the eruption of total chaos, Laura tapped her sister

377

and mother's shoulders, and she picked me up, for I was not really even in that room (I do not know where I was—I went where he had gone, and I went to a place before he or Dante had ever made me who I was; I went to a place of complete animal silence, complete loss of ego), and she led us all bolting out of that room and back into the spaceship on which he had arrived as fast as she could.

You'll want to hear about Edie, whose escape pod arrived on Earth within the hour. The animals all over the City were too stunned and confused once their minds were freed to look up and take note of her pod as it latched onto the space elevator and then, on her command, released and flew down into the sea. She ejected herself into the water and pumped herself down deeper and deeper as fast as she could. But as the pressure of all that water she was burrowing into built up, she felt herself losing energy, and she could tell that, though her species could make it several thousand feet deep underwater, she could not quite reach 10,000, and so she needed help. She found a nearby cuttlefish and flashed the colors of her mantle like lightning, and after some initial struggles to communicate across the dialects of their species, the cuttlefish understood Edie's mission and went a little deeper, until it found a squid who could go even deeper, and it transmitted the message to the squid, and the squid went deeper still and found a Dumbo octopus, who could handle the depth quite well, but he was quite small, and so he needed to find all the other members of his species, and they all banded together and congregated at the door to the servers and used the collective strength of their tiny arms to open the door, and he went inside and pressed the R-E-S-E-T letters on the keyboard and then hit enter.

You'll want to hear about what happened once the network was once and for all dead and gone, how the people then panicked, and the Martian generals turned their arms against the Cognoscenti and killed them, and the Martian people attacked the generals, and the Citizens attacked the Terrarchists. But I wasn't there.

You'll want to hear about how Stella escaped at some point, and she went to the spaceport and stole Zelda's ship.

You'll want to hear about how she activated the stealthing cloak and evaded the animals' detection as she flew to the shore where the bathyscaphe was stationed. You'll want to hear about how she was so desperate to find Varuna's body and bring it back to the surface so that she could retrieve the Ur-Specter that she forgot about the laws of physics. She dove the bathyscaphe a thousand feet below the surface to where Varuna's corpse, still sinking from the weight of his inundated lungs, hovered in the water, then tied a tether to her waist and tried to go out into the water to bring him back into the vessel, only to die instantly as the water pressure crushed her lungs. That's how the story goes, at least. Weeks later, we would find her and Varuna's corpses floating together on the beach, her holding his; the bathyscaphe had taken them both to the surface once it had run out of fuel and activated its emergency air tanks to restore buoyancy. It's a little hard to believe, but it's the only story we could come up with. And I wasn't there to see. Nobody was, besides her.

You'll want to hear about the outpouring of emotion in the Martian tunnels once we all saw how much we'd lost and how trapped we were. You'll want to hear about Laura's communications with Nemos and Gunny and Soda and Iguazu; they worked as informal diplomats on the humans' behalf and, after several weeks, convinced the animals, most of whom were quite happy to have access to those of the City's resources they hadn't destroyed on Varuna's behalf, to let us return if we promised to let them stay.

But I wasn't there. I wasn't there. For several weeks, my fur grew back, unkempt and matted, and grief seemed to remove my mind from my body. I remember no words from that time. I remember only smells, and I remember that Laura let me stay in the Dome of the Cognoscenti and sleep in Dante's room for a long time. Sometimes she would be the one to feed me, and sometimes it would be Michelle or Wanda.

You'll want to hear about how the rebuilding started, the rebuilding that continues to this day. You'll want to hear about how Laura became Mayor on a near-unanimous vote, and it was on her initiative that we found the console Stella had used to communicate with the AI directly, and we found that it still worked. You'll want to hear about how the AI still retained memories of its former self, and how it could answer our questions to help us to repair both the devastated parts of the City and the neglected parts of the Biomes, especially the tundra. It's quite morbid to admit, but having so many fewer people around did make it easier to restore the equilibrium of the Arkology's climate. If only so much tragedy had not been the cause, and if only those with power had been able to face their responsibility when it could have made the difference...

It has not been a miserable five years, that all said. The birth of Nemos's new calf woke me up a little out of my bereavement. I showed her all I knew about the Biomes and the Ark. I told her about Dante and the Melampus family's tragic story. And I told her about a vision, though I did not say from where it came, that Earthlings and Martians of all species could embark into the cosmos together. I sometimes go up to the top floor for dinners with Laura and her family and the other mechanized animals (except Nemos, who won't really fit inside the Mayor's quarters). Gunny and Iguazu are both able to return to their homes without fear of being ostracized, but they prefer to stay in the City and work on projects where they are needed. Soda is happier now that she can return to the tundra without worrying about its melting, but she, too, comes back to the City, often for classroom visits with children who want to see a polar bear. Rudy and his family don't come around much, but they are doing well. Edie passed away last year, after living her natural lifespan, but she had a wonderful life and will always be remembered for her heroic actions.

One thing that I *was* there for was the reconstitution of the Source. It's funny that it took us so long to consider that it might still be in the AI's memory somewhere, but I think our experience with the hivemind traumatized us all so much that we weren't even able to consider whether anything positive might have come from its existence. But little by little, misunderstandings among us survivors intensified, as it came time to allocate resources and assign jobs. A couple of years ago, it seemed like civil war might break out between the humans and the animals. "Give away your arms," was the first solution the AI proposed. Some of the other mechanized animals and I were all willing to redesign our suits and do this, but many of them, and many of the humans, were not. So, in hopes that we could return to that solution another day, we asked the AI again for another solution.

"LOVE EACH OTHER," was what it said.

"HOW?" We asked.

"KNOW WHAT YOU HAVE LOST."

It was then that I wondered whether the Source might be retrievable. Laura, after consulting with the public, decided she could ask the AI to rebuild the Source if she could also ask it to install a program that would prevent anyone from creating a hivemind ever again. The AI cooperated. After much discussion, we agreed that I should be the first one to explore the Source for the purposes of writing this book. I was both one of the greatest heroes and one of the greatest victims of the uprising, or so the story went, at least.

And now, after months and months of plumbing the silicon depths to know what I have lost, and after hopefully showing my readers what we have all lost, I have run out of time. The doctors tell me that the tumor in my brain has grown to such a size that, in just a few days, I will no longer be able to interface with the AI and continue transcribing my thoughts. I have asked to be put to sleep tomorrow. Everyone has agreed to honor my wishes. All that is left for me is to write my letter to the publisher and send this manuscript off for whoever wishes to read it.

Hold on. Someone's footsteps are approaching. I turn around. It's Laura. She holds a piece of paper. She looks so much older now, at least in her demeanor, even though she is still so young. That's what serving as Mayor after an apocalypse will do to you. Not to mention all the grief and trauma of her own. Hold on. Let me talk to her and see what she needs. I'll be back soon.

—

She was coming to give me my ballot registration credentials. Do you know about the ballot, you who read this in some unknown nearer or farther future? I have tried my best to make this book readable to you, distant stranger. Since the first chapters, I have done my best to explain the details of this world I inhabit in ways that anyone can understand, even details that nobody here right now would need to be reminded of. But there is only so much information I can give. And there is only so much one body can do.

Maybe you, reading this, are me. Wouldn't that be funny? I am on the ballot, after all. Laura explained my medical situation to the public and got the required number of signatures to put me there. She told me that, according to her polling, I am guaranteed to get a "yes" vote, but I am not so sure. I have heard that many are mad that someone still alive, albeit on death's threshold, could get onto the ballot, and I have to say I recognize their feelings. So many of those who we lost could not get onto the ballot, and what is so special about me? Yes, I have come to accept, as Laura keeps telling me again and again, that none of what happened is my fault. Egos are just constructs, after all. We are all just being pushed by greater cosmic forces impossible to comprehend. But by that same logic, none of the good that happened, none of the last-minute salvation that allowed at least a thousand humans and several thousand animals to remain living, were my doing, either. And so, I ask, why would I deserve to be brought back from the dead?

But I guess that is not a fair question. Dante will certainly be brought back, and he deserves to be, in my opinion. I will admit, though, that it unnerved me when Laura recovered the blueprints for his resurrection technology during her search of the Ark. Implanting memories from prior lives into clones? Clones printed by the same machines that gave us our synthetic meat? It was a little unsettling. And how would the dead feel on being brought back? Should we bring them back in their infant bodies, or in the bodies they had upon dying? In Dante's case, we decided that the best course of action was to plan for him to come back as his 18-year-old self, both because of all the work he had already gone through in expressing his gender and because nobody wanted the responsibility to raise a child, least of all a young Dante Melampus.

Assuming that I come back as well, I have asked to do so as a newborn puppy; I believe it would be a healing experience to go through my birth again in more controlled and less traumatic circumstances. I do look forward to seeing Dante again, even though I harbored a lot of resentment toward him in the first months after his death. Laura did as well, I know—more than me, even, maybe, since she did not get the chance to speak with him and hear him say goodbye. She scolded herself for falling in love with a man who, in retrospect, always seemed destined for tragedy. But in the end, we consoled each other with the knowledge that none of us would be here if not for him, and that he would have done more to leave us whole in his absence if he could have.

Who else will come back? It did not escape us how powerful the tools of resurrection could be. They promise both to heal and to bring up unforeseen consequences. For that reason, we all agreed to proceed cautiously, and to nominate for return only those whose deeds played a major role in resisting the hivemind and assuring our survival. The holdouts who stayed in the City until the last Martian troops killed them will come back. Edie asked not to; she was content with one life, she said in her final days, and she assured us she would find a way to come back without an instrument so crude as a cloning printer. Peter, meanwhile, may also have the votes to come back, though I know that both his daughters have mixed feelings about it. Laura talked to me about him a bit just now, as the two of us sat on a bench and looked down at the low-hanging clouds of fog the climate drones had decided to seed among the temperate forest's beech trees today. One of the very first changes we agreed to make to the Arkology's system of governance was to unify the Biomes and the City under the AI's global scripts. The second was to assure that all changes to the AI received majority democratic approval. And the third was to assure that every individual had control over what the AI could and could not see in their private residences, and especially in their Specters. Yes, further conflicts will come. But it's a start. At the very least, we all agree that we want to see the rest of the planet again, and that greed will never get us there.

"It's taken a very long time to be at peace with him," Laura said about her father. "And even longer to accept that being at peace with him may mean that I cannot hold a place in my life for him anymore, whether he comes back or not."

Too weak now to move my limbs without technical assistance, I instructed my Specter to send an electrical impulse down to my paw that would place it onto Laura's hand.

"Did you ever consider going public about his problems?" I asked. "Making sure everyone got the full moral picture?"

"No," she said. "He made a lot of people believe in a future. And I can't be responsible for him anymore. Besides, your book is going to do that." She winked.

A gust of wind shook us both.

"Really, though," she continued. "I imagine that you relate to my conflicting feelings. How you can feel justified in your anger toward someone, and you can feel that their path and yours must forever go separate ways, and yet you forgive them all the same, and you feel it isn't your place to deny them the chance to come back. Especially when a tool like the Source lets you experience their final moment with them, and you can see just how much they could see themselves as they vanished from view."

I did not answer for a while. I watched the clouds. I thought about fog, and about how the ocean is even bigger than it looks, how its vapors circulate all over.

Sometimes, when something triggers me and sends me back to that moment on Mars when I lost the two creatures I loved most, I can see him, a faint outline on the air.

"The difference," I at last said to Laura, "is that people will probably forgive Peter even after they know his whole story. I am not sure that is the case with him. And," I would have whined if the nerves in my vocal cords allowed me to cry, "I do still feel responsible. If only I had trusted him more. If only I had..."

Laura placed a hand on my snout and made me face her. "You can let him go," she said. "It's okay to let him go."

I sighed through my jowls. "I know that it's okay," I said. "But I don't want to. Sure, I could have never set foot in the City again and gone to live with the wolves. Nobody would have blamed me. But I looked around at this world we needed to build. This world that's starting to emerge, where we can all work together toward a common purpose. Like it or not, it's his world. It never would have happened if not for him. And it's not all bad. It's not all bad. No, I don't want to. Not yet."

She nodded. Because I could not cry, she cried a little for me. "Okay. That's okay, too."

She rose and kissed my fur. She left the slip of paper containing my ballot registration information on the bench. I watched her walk away. It will be the last time I see her in this lifetime, the one person who feels as deeply as I do the potential for absolute forgiveness that attends absolute loss.

Here I sit, now, commanding the AI to transcribe the final words of this book, deciding what to do for my ultimate decision. Though I have not made it yet, it approaches ever closer, and I know what it will be, and I will transcribe it here as though it occurs in the present.

To access my ballot, I mentally recite for the AI the passphrase Laura assigned me: *The star we both come from.*

The image of a ballot forms in my mind's eye, and I check every box next to every name. Dante's, Peter's, mine, everyone's.

At the bottom of the ballot is a box labeled "Write-in," followed by a blank space. Those whose names appear in this space on enough ballots will be eligible for the next election of returns. And I will confess, now that you have reached the end of this book, that this was one of my goals: to make his case, and to hope that you can give him one last chance at redemption.

The letters of his name materialize on the invisible ballot. And then and only then, once his name appears before me, do I feel him leaving my body and letting me let him go at last.

VARUNA.

I disconnect. I inhale the mist as it rises from the fog below. I think a thought to no one.

For the love of the cosmos, help us.

THE END

ABOUT THE AUTHOR

Graham L. Bishop (ze/zir/he/him) is a queer and neurodivergent writer and climate justice educator from San Diego, California. He holds a Ph.D. in Comparative Literature from Brown University and an MFA in Creative Writing from the University of Alabama.

If you enjoyed this book, Graham would love to hear your thoughts in an Amazon or Goodreads review. You can connect with Graham on Instagram at @animalcosmonaut, and you can receive updates on future projects by joining Graham's mailing list at grahamlbishop.com.